SHAKING THE SLEIGH

SINGLETREE BOOK 3

DELANCEY STEWART

Get early releases, sneak peeks and freebies from Delancey Stewart!

Join my mailing list at www.delanceystewart.com

And join Delancey's Fancies on Facebook for fun, frivolity and the latest news!

Don't miss new releases, book bundles and flash deals in my shop!

CONTENTS

THE GRINCH'S LAST CHANCE
APRIL

"**Y**ou should be grinning from ear to ear right now," my uncle told me, leaning across his mahogany desk and jabbing his finger into the brown paper blotter on its surface to make his point.

I was definitely not grinning. I'm pretty sure I was frowning. And I'd been doing a lot of that lately, probably, but I hadn't had a lot to smile about since my life had imploded three months before. I'd lost my job and my self respect in one dramatic moment totally worthy of the reality television show that had inspired it.

"You came to me desperate. With nothing. Begging, April. You begged." He raised his bushy gray eyebrows and sat back, letting that sink in.

Ouch. The truth hurt.

I shifted in the leather seat, my suit skirt threatening to burst at the seams, thanks to the stress eating I'd been doing since I'd ruined everything. But cookies still loved me. And cookies never looked at me like Uncle Rob was looking at me now. My uncle's office was intimidating, with its dark-paneled walls and Emmy awards and Golden Globes perched on the shelves around us. It hadn't been easy calling him. It had been downright humbling. He was the one who'd inspired me to get into television in the first place, and to come to him now was beyond embarrassing.

"I know, Uncle Rob. It's just ... I mean ... *Holiday Homes*?" I cringed even saying the name of the show I most despised.

Rob grinned. "Holidays. Homes. What's not to love?"

When I didn't jump up and clap my hands, his smile dropped. I tried, "There's really nothing else? Something un-Christmassy? Maybe *Fix it Up* or *Hating to Dating*? I'm good with people, Uncle Rob. Not houses."

"Look April, I'm gonna tell it like it is. You screwed up a good thing—with people—and there aren't a lot of ways to come back from that. You had a top gig producing *Run Away with the Bridegroom*, but maybe someone should've pointed out to you that you were not actually supposed to be the one doing the running away with the bridegroom."

My stomach twisted at the painful reminder of the most humiliating moment of my life. "We didn't run away ..." I began, realizing too late that bringing up the details of the scandal that had ended my high-profile position at my last show probably wouldn't help.

"No, but you probably should have. Far, far away. To get caught on camera making out with that sleazy jerk ..." My uncle's words were coming faster, and his eyes scathed the surface of my face before searching the room, probably seeking a less disappointing subject to observe. "Ape, you made a mistake. A big one. And you got caught. Though that little twist did give the ratings a pretty solid boost ..." He sighed and his eyes returned to mine.

"I'm really sorry, Uncle Rob."

"I know you are, darling, and that's why I'm willing to pull these strings and get you another chance. You're sorry, and you're a damned good producer when you're focused on your job and not on the assets of the cast." He leaned back in his chair and watched me, steepling his fingers in front of his mouth. His voice softened. "Did you love the guy?"

I swallowed hard and dropped his gaze. It would almost have been better if I *had* loved Antonio, the bachelor from my last show. But I didn't love him any more than he loved me, or any of the fifteen women he was supposed to be courting on television. I was a conquest, and if I was honest, he was a conquest for me, too. "No," I said firmly. "I don't think I do love."

"Well, that's the right attitude if you're sticking to television. A hell of a lot cleaner that way."

I'd tried love in college, but I just wasn't very good at it. I got bored, distracted. I knew I got that from my father, another trait I wished I could cut from my personality somehow, but had long since accepted. "Right," I said, hoping my agreement could put an end to the rehashing of all the ways I'd screwed up my last job.

Rob placed a contract in front of me. "So, four specials annually—takes a little of the pressure off, not having the weekly churn, right? Next one is the biggest one by far, the Christmas home tour."

I tried to keep my face neutral as I imagined the sheer quantity of holiday cheer I'd have to withstand to make this work. "But I just handle initial setup and pick targets, right? Take care of contracts ... you've got the location producer for the actual show?"

"Kind of. No picking homes. For this first one, Juliann will handle the details of actual production. She's done the Christmas show for years. You just get the homeowners finalized—like I said, most have been on board for months. Just get them to sign on final details and behave, and then throw the reins to Jules."

I relaxed a little bit. I could do this. I wouldn't have to decorate, or set up any fake snowmen. Maybe I wouldn't even have to enter any artificial-snow-encrusted, pine-tree smelling, twinkling houses. That part was Juliann's gig. I would just be getting things ready for Juliann, who could waltz in wearing striped tights and a felt elf costume, for all I cared. I, myself, would be far away by Christmas, enjoying a tropical drink on a hot beach somewhere, pretending it was any other day.

Uncle Rob's phone rang on his desk and he raised a finger to me as he picked it up—the universal symbol for 'you're not as important as this potential telemarketer.' "Rob here."

Uncle Rob's eyes found mine as he listened, and his eyebrows shot up comically as I watched. "Oh," he said, little lines appearing around his mouth. "Two casts, huh?" He paused, his lips pressing into a firm line. "Traction?" He rubbed a hand over his forehead. "Well I'm glad you're okay, Jules."

My attention riveted to the phone in his hand. Jules? Was that Juliann? What was that about casts and traction? My stomach tightened and I sat up straighter.

"Well you don't need to worry about anything here. You just focus on healing," Uncle Rob said. "The network will send along a fruit basket."

"A fruit basket?" I yelped, and then slapped a hand over my mouth as Uncle Rob's eyes narrowed at me.

"Bye now." Uncle Rob chuckled as he put down the phone. He looked up at me. "All that stuff I just said? Scratch it. You're it. Juliann's out."

"What?" I heard myself ask, my voice higher than usual.

"Broke both legs skiing at Whistler, poor thing. She's gonna be out for months."

"Oh no," I said, picturing how difficult two broken legs would make the wearing of an elf costume. Then something else occurred to me. "Wait, you said, 'I'm it'? For the Christmas show?"

"The whole shebang. Trial by fire. Go get Jingle-y, April. They need you on location this week. Little town in Maryland, evidently they really go all out for Christmas. Need everything wrapped up by the middle of the month to get the footage all set for the hosts to do their review show on the 23rd."

The turnaround was crazy. I knew the Christmas show operated on the tightest timeframe of the *Homes* episodes, since I'd heard Uncle Rob talk about it before. From what he said, the home footage was edited almost daily as they gathered it. The hosts stayed in Los Angeles and filmed their segments, reviewing the décor just before airing on Christmas Eve.

"You can do this, right April? It's not gonna be too much for you?" My uncle had begun to look skeptical. The last thing I needed was for him to second guess my last chance. I needed this to be a home run if I wanted to stay in television and not end up back in my college job at Tacos Loco, where the manager said I had been the best taco assembler he'd ever had. I hoped my tombstone might bear something more illustrious than "Master of beef and cheese in a crunchy shell."

"I can do it," I said, stress pulling my shoulders tight as visions of reindeer and candy canes drifted through my head. and I wondered if I really could.

🍬

"Singletree," I repeated for the third time to my best friend, raising my voice and shouting into the rental car's overhead microphone.

"What kind of name is that for a town?"

"I don't know, Lynn, but the name of the place was not really the point of this story." I let out a slow breath as I guided the car down a curving two-lane road lined with huge trees dropping leaves that ranged in color from dark green to blazing gold. It was like every postcard I'd ever seen of what fall was supposed to look like. A far cry from the screaming freeways and swaying palm trees in Los Angeles. "I think the bigger picture here is that I'm in Maryland. To produce the Christmas show." I hissed the word Christmas as if it burned my tongue.

"I know how you feel about the holidays, April. But maybe this will help you get past all that." Lynn was an eternal optimist. We'd been friends since kindergarten, and Lynn had always been the bright shiny yin to my skeptical darker yang. "Maybe a season in Littletree is exactly what you need."

"Singletree."

"You said the name of the town wasn't the main point, remember? The point is that your hatred for all things red and green needs to die. You're missing out."

I sighed again as I maneuvered through yet another traffic circle that felt like it had me literally driving spirals into the heart of nowhere. I looked down at the phone to check the directions, but the screen had switched to my call, and I had no idea if I was going the right way. "Damn," I said. "Lynn, I need to go, I think I chose the wrong exit from the last circle of death."

"Circle of death?"

"They have all these crazy traffic circles here. I have no idea how I'm supposed to do those ... just give me an eight-lane freeway any day!"

"Adventure, Apes. Remember, it's an adventure."

"I miss Los Angeles. And it's not an adventure, it's a Christmas show."

"There's a reason why most people like Christmas."

"Right. Well."

"Love you," Lynn's sweet voice said. "Go now so you don't get lost and end up in Doubletree instead of Singletree."

"Love you too." I ended the call and swiped my phone's screen back to my directions. Miraculously, I was still going the right way. Nothing outside the little car's windows looked anything like Los Angeles. The roads were narrow and winding, the vegetation was thick and green, and dense gray moisture hung in low clouds that hugged the sprawling fields around me. I wondered for a moment if I'd driven into some picturesque no-man's land, where there were no towns, no people ... only this never-ending farmland draped in fog. I shivered. Fifteen twisting green miles later, I saw signs for Singletree and breathed a sigh of relief.

Singletree wasn't big, and despite my trepidation, it was hard not to be just a teensy bit charmed as I made my way to the center of town. I drove slowly down the main street feeling like I'd been transported to another world—one that existed in some earlier, simpler time. There was a town square surrounded by quaint shops with storefronts lovingly maintained and painted in yellow, white, and light blue, and buildings of brick and stone that looked like they'd stood for hundreds of years. They probably had. The central area was a grassy square that stretched several blocks between the buildings, featuring manicured lawns and neatly trimmed bushes, low-hanging trees and a central gazebo. There was one huge tree in the middle of the square, and I shook my head as I drove by the impressive group of people gathered beneath it with ladders and strings of holiday lights ready to drape the tree, which I guessed was pretty normal even though it was technically still November. They'd probably barely had time to put away the gravy boats after their Thanksgiving feasts, and they were already here, tossing around shiny bulbs. I sighed in dismay.

I drove slowly down the long street that stretched behind the central square, turning in when I saw the sign for the Candlelight Inn, the hotel where Juliann had booked the crew. Despite Juliann's absence from the day-to-day production of the episode of *Holiday Homes* she was supposed to handle, she'd done most of the legwork and had passed her extensive notes and plans on to me. From here it should be simple—check in to this hotel (which looked like it could have been constructed of gingerbread and spun sugar, thanks to some seriously overeager Victorian styling), and begin visiting the homes Jules had identified to finalize contracts. Jules had assured me there would be no issues because *Holiday Homes* was a well-known franchise at this point, and homeowners practically bent over backwards to have their homes featured. It increased their resale value, and if they were looking to sell after the episode aired, it usually resulted in multiple offers and sometimes in a bidding war. And if they weren't looking to sell, I knew that having their homes identified as "special" gave folks something to feel good about, and something to lord over their neighbors if their personalities leaned that way. As for the decorating, the homes that were selected generally went over and above for the holidays.

"You're just there to keep things running smoothly, that's

all," Jules had assured me from her hospital room when we'd spoken on the phone.

I parked and took a deep breath, and stepped out of the car.

"Hello there," a young man in a dark red uniform greeted me as I approached the front entrance of the hotel with my roller bag. "Welcome to the Candlelight Inn."

"Thank you," I said, distracted momentarily by the intricate scrolling woodwork that seemed to garnish every free surface of the building. The Inn looked a lot like a castle, except that it was a soft yellow color. The turrets and wide-open front porch were like nothing I had ever seen up close.

The attendant took my bag from me and escorted me up the stairs to the front door, pulling it open with a flourish and a smile.

I thanked him and gaped at the army of workers busily wrapping railings in evergreen boughs and erecting an enormous tree in the middle of the front lobby. The interior was probably normally dim compared to the daylight outside, but this had been solved by the hundreds of strands of holiday lights a woman was holding at the far side of the space. Two other workers were arguing loudly about how best to erect the small cottage they were working on—a cottage that was made to look like gingerbread but could hold life-sized actual humans. My stomach turned as the sheer Christmasness of it all engulfed me. I stepped around the ladders and tools, tinsel, and a standing army of nutcrackers, and approached the desk.

"Welcome!" The woman at the desk called. "Forgive our

mess, won't you? We're a little behind in getting our holiday decorations up this year, and I don't know if you heard, but *Holiday Homes* is being filmed in Singletree," the woman paused, leaning over the front desk and looking around conspiratorially, "and we want to impress those folks."

"Okay, well," I said. "I'm just checking in." I slid my ID and credit card over the smooth polished wood and managed a smile for the rosy-cheeked woman. "April Hall." The woman who accepted my cards with a wide cheerful smile was wearing a sweater that was woven to make her look like a Christmas present. It had actual ribbon stitched against a ridiculously busy pattern of snowmen and skiers. The bow sat on her shoulder and the ends of it kept popping into her face, where she had to repeatedly push them away. I wondered how many times a day she had to push that ribbon out of her face.

The woman punched a few keys on the computer behind the desk, and made a few noises of concern. She raised a finger to me and then ducked beneath the desk, shuffling around in a drawer. "Just a second, so sorry," she squeaked, popping up again and punching a few more keys as she batted the shiny green ribbon from her mouth. "Would your reservation be under a different name, maybe?"

The cross-country flight and confusing drive began to weigh on me, and I leaned an elbow on the desk. "Oh, right. Yes, look up Juliann Stevens. I took her spot."

"Aha, here she is! Oh, but ..." the woman's eyes widened and she glanced quickly from the screen to me and back down again. "Ms. Stevens was part of the show," she said, her voice breathy. "Does that mean you're ...?"

I cringed. I would have liked to maintain my anonymity, at least at the hotel where I would be coming to escape all the Christmas craziness every night, but I didn't see how that would be possible, given that the whole crew was also staying here. "Yes, I'm the producer of *Holiday Homes*," I confirmed, my voice ragged with exhaustion.

"Ah!" The woman chirped. "Wonderful! I'll be right back!" She disappeared into a room behind the check-in area and I slumped farther over the counter, wishing for nothing more than a quiet room and maybe a warm bath. "Here it is!"

I couldn't see the woman's face because she returned carrying an enormous basket wrapped in cellophane. It was hard to tell what was inside, but I could see a variety of items decorated with crabs and the Maryland state flag, and plenty of Christmas mugs and candy canes and glittery ornaments. The entire thing was tied with a huge ribbon that shone in metallic and glittery red and green and seemed to be vomiting silver glitter. "A little something from the Inn," the woman said, hoisting the basket to the counter and into my face. Tiny showers of sparkly glitter cascaded to the counter.

"Oh," I said, leaning to the side to see around the massive basket. "That's so ... well, wow. That's lovely. Thank you."

"We're tickled to have you," the woman told her, her face pink with excitement under the close-cropped gray curls, which were now dusted with red and green sparkles. "I'm Annabelle Adams. I own the inn, and don't you hesitate to come to me for just anything at all, okay?"

"Thanks so much." I considered asking for a dust buster and lint roller to combat the glitter I was now certain would be attached to me for the remainder of my stay in Singletree.

"Now, let's see. Miss Hall. I've got you in our Dickens Suite. That's on the top floor."

"That sounds lovely," I said, accepting my card and ID back and tucking them into my pocket.

"It's our most festive room during the holidays," Annabelle said with a nod.

My spirits sank further. Evidently producing the Christmas episode meant everyone I met would automatically assume I was just as Christmas-crazy as the people who decked out every inch of their houses on the show. "Great," I said with no inflection at all.

"Here's your key, and you call me if you need anything. We've got a cocktail hour every night here in the lobby at five, and there are usually guests in the library after that playing board games and sitting by the fire."

"Great," I said again, nearly desperate now to just sit down somewhere quiet. The bustle of the workers around the lobby was almost comical. People were dashing to and fro, carrying bells and faux candles. Just as I turned from the desk, a looming presence appeared behind me and I stifled a scream as a life-sized St. Nicholas doll stopped inches from my face and then moved in a jolting progression farther across the lobby.

"Isn't he amazing?" Annabelle asked.

"Erm. Yes," I said, watching the enormous old- fashioned

Santa make his way to a far corner, carried by a worker about half the statue's size.

A few minutes later, I was unlocking the door to the Dickens Suite and stepping inside. The young man from the front door was behind me with my suitcase and the oversized Christmas basket in his arms. A festive trail of green and red glitter spilled down the hallway and through my door as he moved past me to put things down, thanks to the exuberant bow on the basket.

The suite was lovely, if you could overlook the wreaths and glittering globes and the huge tree standing in one corner wafting pine scent throughout the space. The tree was festooned with ribbons and balls, gleaming in the light, and I knew that anyone else stepping into this charming room would feel their spirits lift and would probably experience some kind of warm nostalgia relating to the holiday season. But the sight of the tree and the stockings hanging from the mantle caused a hard knot to form in my gut and settle there as my own memories soured any enthusiasm I might have scraped together for my new job.

"I'll just put this down here," he said, setting the basket on a table. He left the suitcase by the door, accepted the tip I extended and wished me goodnight, and finally, I was alone. I looked around, a dark feeling of something like sorrow filling me as the tree twinkled merrily in its corner.

"Nope," I said, realizing I'd never be able to function in a room decorated to within an inch of its life. I moved quickly through the suite of rooms, removing every holiday item I could easily detach from where it had been stuck, hung or placed, and deposited as much of it as I could in the dry-cleaning bag hanging in the closet. I couldn't think with all the sparkle and cheer around me. The stockings came down, the reindeer was removed, and the festive hand towels in the bathroom were switched out for the plain white ones I found in the top of the closet. I wrestled the glittery bow from the basket, hoping to banish it to the trash can so it couldn't infect one more item with clingy glitter, but I mostly managed to explode the stuff all over the room and myself in the effort.

When I was finished undecorating, only the tree glittered mockingly from its corner, and I almost believed I could feel my mind clearing, despite the glitter I'd probably never get washed from my hands.

TAKE YOUR CODE AND SHOVE IT

CALLAN

I pulled my car up to the big iron gates at the address I'd been given over the phone, taking a moment to marvel at the sheer size of the house beyond the gate. It was big, and it was isolated, that was for sure—I'd driven down a long lane with fields on each side, and turned onto that from a quiet country road. I couldn't see another house from where I sat. No people. No cars. No neighbors.

Good. This was exactly what I told the real estate agent I wanted. And now it was mine.

As I sat staring at the tall iron gates of my new home, another car pulled down the long lane and stopped behind my own. A tall woman with dark hair slicked into a knot, wearing a huge scarf and big sunglasses got out and approached my window. "Callan Whitewood?" She leaned down, grinning, one hand holding the scarf down to keep it beneath her chin.

"That's me," I said, trying to sound cheerful or friendly or at least not psychopathic while I tried to figure out the purpose of wearing a scarf so big it tried repeatedly to take over your head.

"Jessica Betts," she said, sticking a hand through the window and narrowly missing my face with her long nails.

I shook her hand, forcing a smile. "Nice to meet you," I said. "Thanks for your help with all this." She had been helpful, I reminded myself. So I could be friendly for five minutes even though I was pretty sure the blackness inside me contained less friendliness than that.

"Well, we don't usually sell houses sight-unseen over the phone, but I guess we can always make an exception for soccer stars."

"Or people willing to pay cash," I guessed. I'd signed everything in my agent's office back in San Diego, essentially sleepwalking through the process and dropping my signature wherever I'd been directed. I just wanted to move on, get started with this next phase of my life—the phase that didn't include being featured as the media's favorite pity-inducing ex-soccer star.

She smiled wider. "Right. There was that. The seller was thrilled."

"I'm sure." I'd pulled the trigger based on location, isolation, and the fact that Singletree, Maryland didn't seem like the kind of town that followed pro soccer. Driving down from DC after arriving from San Diego, I'd figured it was more of a crab or oyster fishing kind of town, maybe a hunting town, a good American football or NASCAR town. Based on my questions to various real estate agents I'd spoken with and the input of my brother, it was not a soccer town. And hopefully that meant anonymity.

"It's funny," Jessica said, looking at me with a little tilt of the head. "We just had another celebrity buy a place here recently. Maybe southern Maryland is going to be the next hot celebrity escape."

I really hoped not. I had heard that Juliet Manchester grew up somewhere near here, and that Ryan McDonnell had recently bought a home nearby. But I definitely didn't make my decision based on them. More on my brother and my own desire to be isolated and far away from San Diego and the career I had loved. The one I'd been great at. The one I couldn't have anymore. I doubted they even aired the South Bay Sharks games out here in the middle of nowhere.

"I bet you'd like to go in, lay eyes on the place for real." Jessica's excitement wasn't contagious, but she was right. I wanted to go in.

"Sure."

"Well step out here and I'll show you how to put in the gate code. Normally you'll just drive right up, but since we're both here ..." She stepped back from the car and I swung the door open and then used my hands to help get my left leg out and onto solid ground. My left ankle didn't do much of what I wanted anymore, which was part of the reason I was here in Singletree.

I stood up, ignoring the pain ricocheting through my left leg and limped to where Jessica stood. She was clearly trying not to look surprised by my unsteady gait.

"Just type in the code here," she said, her fingers going through four numbers. "And the gate swings open."

I nodded. "I'll probably just get some kind of swipe access installed."

"Right," she agreed. "But for now, you've got the code. Five, six, seventy-two."

"Right. Five, seven—"

"No, hon. Five, six, seven, two."

"Got it." I did. not. care.

"Do you?"

"Five, six, seven ..." I trailed off. Failing. I was winning at failing lately.

"Want me to write it down?"

"Sure." I limped back to my car.

"Okey dokey," Jessica trilled, heading back to her own car to follow me into the circular drive in front of the huge house.

We parked near a fountain that stood quiet and dry like a sentinel, and I gazed up at my new home. It was stately—I guessed that was the right word. It looked like something one of the founding fathers would have lived in—white and colonial, with columns and a sprawling front porch. The place had wings, more rooms than I could ever possibly use filling the enormous space inside the place. But in my mind, all that mattered was that it was isolated, it was far away from San Diego, and it was mine. Jessica unlocked the massive front door, and we stepped into the huge old house.

"This was originally a plantation house, as I mentioned on the phone," Jessica said, gazing around with clear approval. "And it's been restored and updated, but so many of these wonderful architectural details are original. Once you get it all done up for the holidays, it's going to look just amazing."

"Great." I was ready for her to hand me the keys and get lost. I didn't have much with me to move in, but I did have a bottle of scotch, a camping chair and a sleeping bag, and between those three items I figured my next forty-eight hours were pretty much accounted for. As far as decorating for the holidays, I had no plans for that, so I ignored this last comment.

"I'll just give you the quick tour," she said, heading for a doorway off the entrance hall.

"Ah, actually," I said quickly, my tone halting Jessica's step and causing her to turn, one hand on the giant sunglasses she wore atop her head and another on the ridiculous scarf. "I'm pretty beat from the drive. I think I can manage."

"Oh, of course." Her face fell for a second but she shook her head with a laugh and recovered quickly. "Well then, here you are, Mr. Whitewood." She handed me a large silver key. "And may I be the first to welcome you officially to Singletree."

I repressed a strong urge to roll my eyes. To her, maybe becoming a resident of Singletree was something to be celebrated, but for me it was just the final nail in the coffin of the life I'd had. The one I'd very much enjoyed having. Before. "Thanks, I really appreciate all your help."

"If you need anything," she said, turning and heading back to the front door.

"Yep. Got it."

"I'll check in on you in a couple days." She patted my arm and stepped onto the porch. "And if you need any help decorating—"

"Won't be necessary," I said, interrupting her. She was really hung up on this holiday thing.

"Well, you know there is the thing I told you about, the contract—"

"I've got it," I assured her, ignoring every word and practically pushing her out the door.

"All right then, talk to you soon!" She skipped down the steps to her car, and a few minutes later, I stood alone on the porch of my new home.

After unloading my few things from the car, I turned slowly and went back inside. The empty space of the old house seeming to echo and expand around me, making me feel small and insignificant as I stood in the cool silence. I took a deep breath, and for the first time in a long time, I exhaled and felt myself relax.

I spent two nights in the new house, sleeping on the floor in the living room in my sleeping bag, a whiskey-fueled hangover dogging me through the days, and dark dreams full of doubts chasing me through the nights. I didn't even go upstairs. For one thing, my ankle hurt too damned much to climb the stairs just for the heck of it, and for another, I figured that when you've seen one house, you've seen them all. Just because this one belonged to me now didn't make it special.

The movers showed up on the third day, their huge long truck lumbering down the lane in front of the house, making the road look even narrower than it actually was. I pressed the button next to the door to let them through the gate, greeted them at the front door, and then limped into the far bathroom to take a much-needed shower. My plan was to hang out on the back porch until they were done, staying out of the way and avoiding conversation—and potential recognition—as much as possible. I'd called my brother that morning to let him know I'd arrived, though I should have done it the moment I'd taken ownership. I shouldn't have put it off, but even dealing with Cormac seemed like more than I could handle.

I had just positioned myself back in the folding camp chair, my gaze aimed out at the sweep of the Potomac that wound around the bottom edge of my property several acres below, when I heard a female voice drifting through the open window. I swiveled and squinted inside, but didn't see any female movers hustling furniture about. Just when I decided I'd been mistaken, I heard it again, a soft melodious voice that definitely couldn't belong to one of the movers I'd just let in.

Wandering the house, dodging moving couches and rolled-up rugs, wasn't what I felt like doing, especially with my ankle protesting every move I made, but my curiosity got the best of me. Was I hearing things now? Maybe I'd been alone a little too long in this strange old house. I went in and prowled the downstairs rooms and then climbed the stairs slowly, cursing the shooting pain that accompanied each step I took with my left foot. The staircase was grand and wide, the oak-planked risers creaking under my weight as I gripped the curving bannister. I imagined myself tripping and falling down the expansive steps, and I could picture the media coverage of that one. *Former Soccer Star Callan Whitewood Suffers Another Debilitating Injury!* Because I hadn't been hounded enough after the first one.

After exploring the upstairs rooms—all gleaming and bright, mostly empty of furniture—I was beginning to doubt myself, and to believe I was most likely losing my mind. I glanced out the second-story window at the moving truck in the drive, and spotted a small silver Honda next to my car. Someone was definitely here, but this stupid house was so big I couldn't find her.

I was just about to head back down the stairs when a woman appeared in the hallway where she definitely had not been before. She had inky dark hair that flowed over her shoulders, and bright blue eyes that glittered in the half-light of the upstairs hallway. She was pretty, I realized, but that didn't begin to explain what she was doing wandering around my house with a clipboard and appearing in empty hallways. "Hello," she said. "You must be Mr. Whitewood. I'm April Hall."

"Uh, hi," I said, hating the way the confusion made me sound uncertain. This was my house, dammit. Who was this woman? "Where exactly did you come from?"

The woman gave me a puzzled look, her nose wrinkling

in a way that I was sure most found adorable, but that I perceived as her simply not answering my question. "Just now?" she asked.

"Yes. Just now."

"Because I came to Singletree from California, but I didn't think that was what you meant." She laughed lightly and then spun around. "There's a secret hallway back here." She pulled open a panel that had been standing slightly ajar. "It was probably a servants' passage. A lot of these old houses have these little nooks and crannies. Part of the charm. If that's your thing." She shrugged and looked at me expectantly, maybe waiting for me to chime in about whether or not old houses and secret passages were 'my thing.'

Annoyance flooded me as my ankle throbbed. I didn't like a stranger knowing more about my house than I did, and I didn't like being surprised in my own home. I was also oddly annoyed at the tiny flicker of interest I had felt leap to life in my chest when I'd gotten a good look at this intruder. It was hard to hold onto my annoyance when part of me—the old part of me that was good at flirting with attractive women— was prodding me to keep her talking. I shoved that part down and remembered that I was done with women, done with being good-natured and friendly, done with people in general.

"Can I ask what you're doing in my house, Miss Hall?"

"Oh, of course." She had the grace to blush, certainly realizing that she was essentially trespassing. "I'm with *Holiday Homes*, and you're on my list, and well, the gate and the door were open, and there was so much hub-bub down there with all the men moving things around ..." she babbled, looking nervous.

"And so you're here because," I began for her, gripping the banister at the top of the stairs as my ankle throbbed.

"I was looking for you, actually." The bright eyes found my own and then dropped to my hands, taking in the white-knuckled grip on the bannister and darkening briefly before meeting my gaze again. "Is there somewhere we could sit?"

For a split second, I wondered if she knew. That look—it had held a touch of pity, and while I'd come to Singletree to get away from lots of things, pity was first on that list. I straightened, forced myself to put weight on both feet evenly and released my grip on the bannister. "No, actually. There's nowhere we can sit. Maybe you noticed I don't have any furniture just yet?"

"I did," April said, "and I'm so sorry to just barge in. I just wanted—"

"I'm going to stop you right there," I said, feeling my anger dissipate into exhaustion. "Maybe you know who I am, maybe you don't. I don't really care. I moved here because I only know one person in town. There's no one here who needs me for anything, no one who expects anything from me. There's no one here who I have to worry about disappointing because they'd hoped for anything at all." The words sounded bitter coming out and I almost regretted them as I watched April's pretty face tighten, her chin lift slightly. "I don't need whatever you're selling. I'm not in the market for candles, makeup, or Boy Scout popcorn, I don't want to save the turtles or the unicorn habitat, and I'm not looking to sponsor a puppy, a wombat, or a child." I waved an arm at the stairway, indicating that April should go down.

She stood still for a long moment, evaluating me with that sharp gaze. "Okay then," she said. "Good speech, by the way. I liked the part about the unicorns and wombats." Then she stepped past me, toward the stairs, but spun around to face me after descending only two risers, and came back up.

I sighed. The woman's eyes sparkled as red spots appeared high on her cheeks, and—was that glitter glinting just below her left eye?

"I'll be totally honest. I have no clue who you are—I mean, if you're someone I should know, well, I don't, sorry. So you don't have to worry about me asking you for a selfie or anything like that. And I don't really need anything from you," April said, her words coming fast. "I just need your house."

Surprise flooded me and I couldn't help a bark of laughter that rolled out of me at her honesty and her pitch for my new home. "It's not for sale."

"No, no." April ran a hand through that mass of dark hair and it fell back around her neck and shoulders, glossy and thick. "Look, I'm sorry for barging in. I'm the producer of the show *Holiday Homes*. I was sent out here to solidify locations in Singletree to feature on the Christmas show, and your house is at the top of our list. Someone should have spoken to you already, and my executive producer says the contract was signed long ago, but maybe since you're just moving in ..."

Frustration made my head pound. A contract? A television show? She had to be kidding. "No thanks."

"Mr. Whitewood, you bought the oldest and most historic house in town—the place was a plantation manor in the seventeen hundreds, and it's a critical part of the area's history. There's only one other house here with the same merits, history, and charm, and the woman who owns it ran our producers off her land with a shotgun in one hand and a joint in the other when they made their initial site visits. Your house is it, and featuring it on the show is a way to honor that incredible legacy, and if everyone I've talked to in town so far is right, the show won't be complete without it. The real estate agent my predecessor worked with promised us she'd spoken to you about it and that you signed the show contract, agreeing to be featured."

I scanned my foggy memory. Jessica *had* said something about decorating, or holidays ... I hadn't paid much attention once I'd had the keys. Still, no one could barge in and force me to hang tinsel in my own house. I shook my head, "I didn't sign a contract that I recall, and I'm pretty sure I just told you no thanks." I moved around April, hoping that if I started walking down the stairs, she might follow, and it would put an end to this ridiculous conversation. I came here to get out of a spotlight, not to shine one directly inside my home.

April followed me down the stairs. "Look," she tried again, but I didn't stop limping toward the exit. "It's just that, I mean ... I'm kind of in a bad situation." Her voice softened, and I could hear that she wasn't trying to sell anything now. She sounded legitimately sad, and I hated the way my blood warmed in some misplaced protective instinct. I faced her, against my better judgment. "It's kind of my last chance, this show ... and well, if I can't feature your house, I'm pretty sure I'll lose my job." The bright eyes glistened as she stopped on the bottom stair, turning and looking back at me, her pretty lips pressed together.

I chuckled as I realized she was definitely still selling me —this was just another tactic. She was good, I thought. I almost believed her, not that it would have changed my mind. I was about to say something that would probably have been less than friendly when her face seemed to crumple, but then she quickly regained composure, pushing a hand through that incredible hair once more.

"I'm so sorry. That—that last part—that shouldn't make a difference. That's my problem, and clearly, I just need to do a better job explaining things, and—"

"No," I said, wondering now how much of her explanation was an act and how much was real. "Look, it has nothing to do with you. And I'm sure it's a great show and everything, okay? It's just that I'm really trying to keep my life private right now," I said. "To keep a low profile. You understand? I'll talk to a lawyer if I need to. I was kind of on autopilot when I signed all the paperwork, so whatever I signed—well, I'll just get it undone. I'm sorry for the confusion."

We stood on the bottom step of the grand sweeping staircase, and the movers came in and out the big front door ahead of us, carrying furniture and boxes. The sounds of scraping and shifting floated through the air along with the damp fecund smell of moist leaves littering the ground outside. April stared at me for a long moment, her eyes piercing the shield I'd been working impossibly hard to maintain as I felt a little piece of my wall shatter and fall, and then she nodded quickly. "I get it. I do."

She stepped down the final step and looked back up at me, her bright eyes glowing again. "But you should know I don't give up easily."

"The gate out front isn't usually standing wide open, you know."

She peered out the front door at the iron gate standing open at the entrance of my driveway. "I think I can scale it. I'm pretty athletic." She winked at me and then strode to the open door, turning. "See you again soon!"

That simple statement should have irritated me—I hated it when people wouldn't take no for an answer—and it did bother me, a little bit. But it also struck me like a promise, and despite the many promises broken in my life lately, I couldn't help feeling a little flicker of hope that April might keep hers. Even if I had no intention of being on her show, I wouldn't mind seeing her again.

THERE IS SUCH A THING AS TOO MUCH CHEER

APRIL

I returned to the Inn that Christmas ate, only slightly demoralized by my less-than-successful attempt to confirm the most important home on the list. At least I'd had no issues with the other two homeowners I'd visited. They'd been friendly and almost too excited about the whole thing. I was shuffling papers into my bag as I entered the inn, wishing I'd paid more attention to my mother's organizing tips, when Annabelle at the front desk called out for me.

"Oh, Miss Hall!"

The front desk was an explosion of cheer now that the lobby décor was finished, and Annabelle wore an elf hat and a little white collar with peppermints fastened to the points that draped around her shoulders and chest. I approached, unable to stop my mouth from dropping open as I got a good look at my hostess. Annabelle's ears were usually hidden by the soft short gray curls that framed her face, but today they were visible. And they were pointed, like an elf's. Only upon closer inspection could I see the lines around the prosthetic additions to the woman's natural ears.

"Aren't they marvelous?" Annabelle raised a hand to touch the pointy tip of one ear.

I smiled to keep myself from laughing at the ridiculousness of it all. "They are something," I agreed.

"I have something special for you," Annabelle said, reaching beneath the counter and producing a huge gingerbread house on a foil-covered tray, dotted with gumdrops and candy canes and absolutely screaming of Christmas cheer.

"That's ... for me?" I stared at the thing, which was easily as large as my overnight bag.

"The third graders had a field trip to the corner cafe today and they all worked together to make this in honor of the show coming to Singletree." Annabelle said, her smile wide and open. "Everyone's just so excited about it."

"Not everyone," I said, before I could stop myself.

Annabelle's smile faded and she shook her head a touch, as if trying to imagine who in the world wouldn't be excited about my insane holiday spectacle of a show. Her eyebrows pulled together.

"Is something wrong, dear?" Annabelle set the house on the reception counter.

I hadn't actually meant to confide in Annabelle, and a little spike of fear edged through me, accelerating my heartbeat. I needed to walk a fine line producing this show. I couldn't break any rules, couldn't even slip a toe into the rule-breaking pool. I needed to pretend that pool wasn't even there, not even spare a glance at any rule-breaking skinny dippers who might be cavorting over there, trying to coax me toward the swim-up bar. So I wondered, was confiding in an innkeeper about a difficult host breaking a rule? "It's not a big deal. Just ran into a little reluctance today over at Singletree Manor."

Annabelle drew in a sharp breath. "Oh. Him." Her expression soured.

"Do you know Mr. Whitewood?" I suddenly realized I might be able to enlist some help if I could find someone in town who Callan Whitewood might listen to.

"No," the older woman shook her head. "I just can't believe this town let someone like that buy our grandest home. That place holds half the history of Singletree. The town was practically born there. The man who built Singletree Manor—Mr. Joseph Calvin—planted the tree in the town square that gave our town its name."

I called up a quick mental image of the town square I'd driven past yesterday, and remembered the large tree around which the rest of the square seemed to be arranged. Then my mind fastened to the other thing Annabelle had just said. "What do you mean, 'someone like that'?"

Annabelle leaned over the counter, her voice dropping to a whisper. "A playboy. A sports star." She scowled, looking like someone had just eaten one of the cookies she'd set out for Santa.

I felt my eyebrows climb. Callan Whitewood was a sports star? He'd practically tripped going down the stairs, and though I'd never point it out, the man had a very pronounced limp and a terrible attitude. What sport could he have played? Maybe he played horseshoes or some other sport most people didn't follow. Like shuffleboard. Or sheep rolling. I'd heard that was a thing in the tiny island country of Durnland. "Is that right?"

"Word is he's retired now, but he made plenty of noise and trouble when he was a big important soccer star."

Soccer. I thought back to the solid presence of the man I'd met—he wasn't especially tall, but he did look strong. I had tried to focus on the work of convincing him to let me use his house for the show, but that hadn't stopped me from noticing the soft dark hair tousled on his head or the soulful chocolate brown eyes. Now that I thought about it, I felt like maybe I had seen him before. My mind ticked and whirred, and suddenly I could picture a billboard standing over the 405 Freeway, one I passed most days on my way to work. When I brought it up in my mind, I realized it was Callan Whitewood's moody gaze and bare muscled chest under which I had driven every single day. It had been a year or two ago, and another player had replaced him there recently, but I remembered those eyes. "Huh," I said, understanding clicking into place as I recalled him saying something about knowing who he was. "Kind of full of himself, maybe."

"Most likely," Annabelle agreed with the sentiment I hadn't meant to speak out loud. "Those types always are. His brother is nice enough, though."

"You know his brother?" I found it hard to fathom there could be another man from the same gene pool that had produced someone as handsome as Callan Whitewood.

"He lives here too. He's a quiet type though, family man. He's the reason that playboy came to town, though, so my opinion of Mr. Cormac Whitewood has dropped a bit."

I nodded. Maybe I'd just been given a new way to approach this problem. "Thanks, Annabelle." I turned and headed for the stairs, purposely forgetting the gingerbread monstrosity.

"Don't worry about the gingerbread house," Annabelle called after her. "Andrew can bring it up to your room for you,"

"Great," I called over my shoulder, hoping Annabelle didn't hear the flat note of sarcasm in my voice. I climbed the stairs and entered my room, preparing for a quick round of Google stalking on the Whitewood brothers.

I was just settling in with my laptop on the table before me and a hot cup of hotel-room coffee in my hand when my phone rang. I checked the screen and my stomach dropped upon seeing Uncle Rob's name on the screen. I set down my coffee, took a deep breath, and pressed the speakerphone button. "Uncle Rob!"

"Hey April, just checking in. How's Appletree?"

"It's Singletree, actually, and things are going well." My voice held a bright note that sounded false and foreign to my own ears. I hoped Uncle Rob wouldn't notice.

"Right. Singletree." I heard the clack of a keyboard and realized Rob was distracted. Which was normal. "So you've got all the homes on board? The production team arrives in a couple more days to get started staging and filming."

"I'm working my way down Juliann's list," I said, planning to check in with the last two homeowners in the next day or two and make sure they were on board.

"And we're all set with the feature spot? That big plantation Jules was so excited about?"

I leaned back in my chair, pulling my long hair into one hand and dropping it over my shoulder. "That house has recently been sold," I said. "I visited with the new owner, but he'd barely moved in. He didn't think he'd signed the contract, and I'm not sure he's very interested in—"

"I'll stop you there. We're not inviting the guy to prom, April. He doesn't have to be interested. Someone signed the contract and we're paying this guy—handsomely, by the way—for the use of his house for a couple hours. Get him in line. Without the plantation, there's a lawsuit ahead of us and no show in Silvertree."

"Singletree."

"No show. That house is the anchor. There's a whole hour of *House or Spouse* reruns queued up in case this goes off the rails." His voice was dark, and I felt the threat percolate in my stomach. No show meant no job. No job meant I would likely be done working in television. For good.

"I'll get him," I promised, Callan Whitewood's dark eyes flashing through my mind. I would get him. I had to. I just had no idea how.

4

HANGING WITH ELVES

CALLAN

When the front gate buzzed, I cursed my ankle and the size of this house. It took me a full five minutes to get from the master bedroom upstairs down to the front door to answer the buzzer and open the gate. Luckily, I figured, I probably wouldn't have many visitors since I didn't know anyone in town. I could share the gate code with Cormac. If I could remember it. Seven-six something? I wasn't sure, but since I hadn't left the house since getting to town, it hadn't mattered.

I pulled the front door open and watched Cormac guide his truck around the fountain in the center of my driveway.

"This," Cormac said, hopping down from the silver truck and waving a hand to indicate the house and yard, "is pretty fantastic."

I tried for a smile as I stood on the front porch and waited for my brother to open the back doors of the cab. As soon as he had, a curly blond head appeared and big wide blue eyes took me in as Cormac swung the little girl down and set her on the driveway. My other niece hopped out behind her, and held her book in the air by way of greeting. "Uncle Callan!"

Madison and Taylor were beautiful little girls—probably because Cormac's wife had been beautiful—and I had always enjoyed spoiling them. Now Maddie trundled toward me at top speed on chubby legs, her wide three-year old smile melting some of the ice inside me as I stepped down the wide stairs to catch her, scooping her into my arms.

"Hey Maddie," I said, hugging the little girl tight and then opening an arm and bending down to hug Taylor, too. "Hey gorgeous."

At three and six, the girls were beginning to become their own people, and I loved noticing all the ways they changed between visits. They were a big part of the reason I'd chosen Singletree—the girls, and my brother, Cormac.

"Come on in, guys." I gave my brother a nod over Taylor's head, and we all went into the big house, where most of my things still sat in boxes. The place had a musty smell I hadn't noticed before.

"Love what you've done with the place," Cormac joked. "Planning to actually move in, or is this just a stop on your way to something better?"

The words stung. Cormac was the older brother, but I had had always felt the bite of his jealousy as my soccer career had developed and then exploded. Dad had been a huge sports fan, and my natural athleticism had pulled an unequal amount of his focus, probably leaving Cormac feeling abandoned at times.

"I'm staying," I said, leading the little group to the back porch, where I had actually arranged furniture and put down an outdoor rug. "Come hang out." I waved at a chair for my brother and put Maddie down on the porch next to her sister, who had already climbed into a chair and opened her book in her lap. It was unseasonably warm for late November, and the porch caught a light breeze coming up off the river.

"Maddie," Cormac said, catching the little girl's attention as she climbed down the big steps to explore the wide grassy expanse behind the house. "Stay up here where I can see you. Don't go down to the water."

Maddie nodded and then turned to stare at the Potomac sliding quietly by at the bottom of the long rolling hill. "Big water," she remarked, and then began turning circles on the grass just beyond the porch, her arms extended outward and her head tilted back at the bright blue sky.

"The girls look good," I said. I examined my brother's face, taking in the dark circles beneath his eyes, the drawn cheeks. "You look less good. You okay?"

Cormac sighed and gave me a half smile before turning his gaze to the water. "I still miss her. Every day." He whispered it, as if he didn't want Taylor to hear, but then cleared his throat and spoke more loudly. "We're managing. It's hard."

"I'm so sorry, Mac. Linda was a great catch. I miss her too."

I watched my older brother swallow hard at the mention of his late wife, his eyes dropping shut for a long moment and then clearing. Linda had died suddenly just over a year before, of an aneurysm. It was shocking and horrible, and Cormac had been devastated. From what I could tell, he hadn't recovered.

Cormac cleared his throat and turned his attention to me. "What's your plan here, Callan? What are you going to do? This is a small town—not a big market for former sports stars."

"Happy enough to leave all that behind," I said, though it was more what I wished than what was true. "Beyond just getting this house set up, staying out of the spotlight, I don't really have plans."

"How'd the team take the news?"

"The Sharks have plenty going on without me. Just brought on two hotshots recently. Some guy they're calling the 'fire' and another guy who talks more like a computer geek than a pro striker. But he is pretty good, I guess. Max Winchell." I didn't like the way the names of my replacements felt coming out of my mouth. The Sharks had been my team for a good run, and walking away had been difficult. Especially because walking was difficult. I didn't really walk away. I limped away. All the more reason to leave.

"You're gonna get bored."

I shrugged. My life had been the opposite of boring for so long, I didn't know if my brother was right, or if it would be good to have a break. "Want a drink?"

Cormac nodded and I rose and went to the kitchen door at the far end of the porch, returning with a beer for each of us and juice boxes for the girls. We took seats in the big wooden chairs that overlooked the lawn.

"At least you've gotten out to go shopping."

"They deliver groceries now, Mac." I told him. "Welcome to the Internet age."

"Surprised that's legal in this county. This place has the craziest laws ..." he shook his head and took a swig of his beer. "It's the smallest county in Maryland, and half the stores and restaurants here straddle county lines. Did you know there's a distillery here that's only legal because half of it is in the adjacent county?"

I frowned at my brother. Who cared? "And?"

"It's just nuts here. You'll see. You can only drink at the bar there if you stand on one side of it. The other side is in the wrong county."

"That's ridiculous."

He nodded. "It is." Cormac gave me a long look over the top of his bottle, and was about to speak again when Taylor stole his words. "You walk funny now, Uncle Callan. Does your foot hurt?"

There it was. I nodded and struggled to keep my expression neutral, pleasant. "Yep. That's why I can't play soccer anymore." I kept my tone light, and hoped it didn't betray any of the bitterness I'd been working so hard to contain.

"You're going to physical therapy?" It was more statement than question, and I heard the judgment in my brother's voice.

"Not sure what the point would be." I had tried physical

therapy right after I'd gotten the cast off. It was painful and pointless.

Cormac barked out a laugh. "My six-year old notices your limp. Maybe you can't play anymore, but you can at least rehab so you might have a chance at walking normally again."

"Kids are more observant than other people," I said, knowing that even a baby would notice my limp. It wasn't going away, though. No amount of physical therapy could mend what was broken in there—or in my heart. I'd never been anything but an athlete, and that was over. I didn't care about the limp. If anything, the pain and my slow gait felt right—an outward expression of how twisted and broken I was on the inside.

"Gonna just stay in your big house and feel sorry for yourself, huh?" Cormac's tone was bitter, and even though his words cut and I felt my little-brother instinct kick into high gear, ready for a fight, I also guessed my brother might be talking about himself. He was broken too. I restrained myself and changed the subject, feeling mildly proud that I hadn't taken the bait.

"How's work, Mac?"

Cormac had moved to Singletree a few years back to start an accounting firm. Linda had been charmed by the little town, and they'd agreed it would be a good place to raise their family.

Cormac frowned and took a long drink of his beer. "Work is fine. Harder now without having help for the girls. A lot of late nights to keep up."

I nodded. My brother's sadness had fallen heavy over the

back porch, coating everything in a blanket of grief. A glance at my older niece told me she could feel it too, and my heart twisted in my chest at the thought of these bright little girls being anything but light and full of fun. "You could bring the girls here," I said before I'd really had a chance to think about it.

"You want to babysit?" Cormac was already shaking his head.

I sat up straighter, suddenly feeling like it was the right thing, maybe the first right thing I'd found in a while. "When you need it. Maybe after school, give you some time to work?"

Taylor was following this conversation with clear interest, her book forgotten in her lap. "It'd be better than daycare," she said, a high note of hope in her voice. Her dark wide eyes met mine and my heart twisted again at the plea I saw there.

Cormac stared out at where Maddie rolled in the grass, pulling together little piles of leaves that had fallen from the ancient oaks bordering the yard. Her pink coat was covered with dry grass and dirt, but she was smiling to herself as she played. "I don't know," he said quietly.

"Give it a try?" I asked.

"They're already set up at daycare," Cormac said. "That's no small task, by the way. There's doctor's notes and immu-nizations and multiple changes of clothes and ziplocks full of everything you can think of, and you basically sign your life away just to get a spot at these places ..."

"So don't give up their spots. We'll keep paying for them, just in case."

"Easy for you to say, super star. I'm not in the business of paying for a service I'm not using. Things are tight, Callan. Kids cost money."

"I'll cover it." I said, selling myself on the idea as I convinced my brother. "I could use the company." I was surprised to hear myself say those words. I'd spent the better part of a year trying to convince myself I didn't need anyone.

"I'll think about it."

"He needs us, Dad," Taylor said, and I couldn't help the shock that flooded through me at her words. I turned to look at her. Was I so transparent a six-year old could see the wounds inside me? "Look at this place," she continued. "He doesn't have up a single Christmas decoration up and it's almost December."

Oh, thank god. We laughed—me with relief that my need for human company hadn't been quite as obvious as I'd feared. I thought of the woman who'd dropped in the day before to talk about Christmas decorations. The woman with the silky dark hair and the wry smile. If she and Taylor got together, the house would be done up and featured on television before I even got a word in.

"Do you even have a tree, Uncle Callan?" Taylor asked. Maddie had wandered back up to the porch and now she stood next to her sister's chair.

"Yeah, where's your Christmas twee?" she asked, her eyes going even wider as she looked around her, hoping to spot a glowing pine somewhere nearby.

"If you guys help, maybe we can get one set up this week," I said, glancing sideways at my brother, hoping to see him going along with the plan.

"Fine," Cormac said in a near-whisper. "Just a couple hours when Taylor gets done with Kindergarten. You'll have to pick them up. I'll come get them by six."

The happy smile that lit up Taylor's face felt like a win—the first one I'd had in a long time—and I leaned back in my chair, feeling a little less directionless than I had before.

5

UNDERWEAR AD OF DREAMS

APRIL

Googling the Whitewood brothers had been only partially productive, and I spent over an hour on the phone with Lynn, crawling through our findings.

Cormac Whitewood was basically a unicorn. The guy had no digital footprint at all—no humiliating Facebook or Insta selfies, no Twitter rants I could find, and nothing written about him publicly besides a very nice piece in the local paper about the accounting firm he opened, and a very sad short piece about the death of his wife. Nothing I could really use, though I did write down the address of the firm's main office and its phone number.

Callan Whitewood, on the other hand—not a unicorn. Not even a donkey painted white with a toilet paper roll taped to his head. The guy was an open book—a very famous, very social, painfully handsome—open book.

His face was everywhere. He'd done sponsorships for water, beer, underwear, some kind of Japanese foot powder, and shower gel, his smoldering gaze (and his almost impossibly toned abs) staring out from photo after photo of him holding (or wearing) the products.

There were action shots of him playing for the South Bay Sharks, his shorts stretching to contain the powerful muscles of his thighs as he ran, kicked, and celebrated in the game shots. There were other photos too, along with tabloid stories about women and illegitimate children, marriage rumors and celebrity hookups. I knew most of that stuff probably wasn't true, and while it was interesting to see him on a red carpet in a tux (oh Lordie, he looked good in a tux), the photos I kept coming back to were the shots of Callan Whitewood in action, because in the soccer shots he was actually smiling. Not a sexy little smirk designed to make girls like me clench my thighs together, and not a cultivated lift of one side of his mouth meant to show off his dimple as he stood next to Katy Perry at some event. The soccer shots caught him full-on grinning with glee like a ten-year old getting to do his favorite thing in the world. And while Callan Whitewood wearing a practiced smirk was sexy, Callan Whitewood actually smiling lit up parts of me I didn't think could be activated by a photo alone. The guy was gorgeous.

Ogling a sports star was not my usual MO, but I told myself this particular brand of online stalking served a specific purpose—saving my own ass. I needed to get this guy on my side, even if my side was the somewhat unfamiliar side where all things Christmassy grew and bloomed in glittery red-and-white striped craziness. So when I came across more than one photo with the same woman, a tall blonde I didn't think fell into the category of model or movie star, I stared a little longer. And when I found stories about Callan White-wood's ongoing relationship with a San Diego nurse, I read every line. The relationship was real, it seemed, and had lasted for several years. I wondered what had happened to the nurse, or if maybe she was still in the picture, so to speak. She wasn't in any of the photos I had found of Callan since his injury, however. And those were hard to look at.

Callan had broken all three bones in his ankle when another player had crashed into him, sending them both tumbling in a championship game. The other guy had gotten up, but Callan had stayed down, and his career had ended there on the pitch that day. The description of the injury turned my stomach, and the few photos I found of Callan afterwards showed none of the joy I'd seen on his face in the game shots. His eyes were hooded and his jaw was tight in all of them, a look of intense hostility and pain replacing the open grin that had drawn me in.

"Gah, poor guy," I said, shutting the laptop and turning my attention to the phone I'd been holding to my ear as I surfed for something I could use.

"Did you read the article about the breakup in *People*?" Lynn was an excellent partner when there was online stalking to be done.

"I saw it, but I'm starting to feel like I'm invading the guy's privacy," I said, standing to walk to the window in my suite. I had a view of the open square where the huge tree now stood decorated but unlit. The tree-lighting ceremony was scheduled for sometime at the end of the week, according to the flyer that had been placed under my door that morning, which I had immediately scrunched up and thrown away. "I feel a little bit bad for him."

"Well, he's feeling bad while rolling around on a bed made of money. The guy did well, Apes. But this girlfriend sounds like a B."

"Money isn't everything," I said, though I wouldn't really know. I'd never had enough of it to feel secure, and even offering standard platitudes about it made me feel like a phony. "He doesn't seem happy, you know?"

Lynn sighed. "Most people aren't happy. Speaking of which, how are you holding up in Sparkle Tree?"

"You know that's not the name of the town."

"It will be when you're done with it."

"I don't know. Uncle Rob is putting on the pressure, and the grumpy soccer star is making my life harder than it needs to be. It's a flipping decorating show, for crap's sake. It shouldn't be this hard."

"You've seen my apartment. Decorating is no small task." Lynn had moved into her apartment at least three years earlier, and still hadn't managed to decide where to hang any of her framed pictures, which all leaned against the wall in the bedroom gathering dust.

"This is true," I said.

"Well, what's your plan? How will you get the grump on your side?"

"Not sure. I mean, the guy signed a contract," I said. "But

given that he has more money than most small countries, I think he's probably got a team of hot shot lawyers who can get him out of that, or at least tie it up long enough that I'll miss my deadline and lose my job."

"You'll have to win him with charm."

I blew out a harsh breath and slid onto the small couch, remembering too late that I'd ended up covered with glitter the last time I sat on it. And I was wearing black pants. I stood back up, moving to the mirror over the table to get a look at my backside, which was now subtly sparkly. "Perfect," I sighed. "Yeah, charm is not my strong suit these days. The closer we get to Christmas, the less charming I feel. And it's officially December tomorrow."

"So ...?"

"I'm going to go talk to his brother tomorrow morning. He's an accountant. Contracts must mean something to him."

"Sure, because ... are you getting accountants confused with lawyers?"

"Grasping at straws either way."

"Okay then. Good luck!"

"Thanks. Talk to you later."

When I'd ended the call, I punched the address of Cormac Whitewood's firm into my phone. It was across the square, down a little side street. I could walk.

After hotel-room coffee and a protein bar in my room the next morning, I shoved my phone into my bag and left, wiping furiously at the butt of my pants as I took the stairs to the first floor, hoping some of the glitter that seemed to coat every item I owned might let go, though everything I'd ever learned about glitter told me it was hopeless.

Cormac Whitewood was in, which was easy enough to discover when I arrived at the office—just one small room inside the storefront under the awning. There was a tiny reception area, but no one occupied it, and when the bell on the door chimed, Cormac called, "come on back."

"Hi," I said, poking my head into the small windowless room. Talk about a need for decorating, sheesh—the place looked like a cell.

"Hi," Cormac said, standing up from the desk and running a hand through a thick mop of dark hair. He looked a little bit like his brother, same penetrating eyes and thick hair, but Cormac was taller and fairer, and the atmosphere around him didn't seem quite as intense as it did around Callan. Still, he didn't seem like a jovial guy. "Can I help you with something?"

I pasted on a bright smile and stuck out my hand, which Cormac shook. "I'm April Hall," I said. "I was hoping I could chat with you for a quick second about something I need a little help with. I wasn't sure where else to go."

"Have a seat," Cormac said. "My curiosity is piqued. I don't get the sense this is a bookkeeping issue."

I laughed, the sound false in my own ears. "No, it's not. It's actually about your brother ..."

Cormac stood back up quickly, and pointed at the door. "If you're a reporter or a fan, you're going to have to get your information somewhere else. The poor guy came here for some peace and quiet, can't you just let him have it? He's been through enough." His face was dark, stormy.

"No, no, sorry. I'm not a fan. Or a reporter." I stood. "Could I just talk to you for a quick minute? And then I promise I'll go if you want me to."

Cormac lifted an eyebrow and sat back down, crossing his arms. "Go ahead."

"Okay, well. Here's the thing." I took a deep breath and tried to still my spinning mind. I wasn't a reporter, but I was pretty darned close if you looked at it from the perspective of someone who didn't want any publicity in their lives. "So I'm out here for work," I began. "I'm from California."

"Long way from home," Cormac said, something in his face softening slightly. "Me too," he said, but didn't offer anything else.

"This place is quaint, isn't it?" I said, leaning forward. When Cormac didn't say anything else, I sat up a bit, continuing. "So the thing is, I got sent out here to do preproduction for this show that's on DecorTV called *Holiday Homes*."

I had been worried that uttering the word TV would end this whole conversation in a matter of seconds, but Cormac's lips had parted just slightly and he'd uncrossed his arms. "I know that show, actually. My wife—" he cleared his throat and looked down before seeming to regain himself. "My wife used to love that show."

"Oh, yeah?" I grinned. Maybe I'd find an ally here after all. "I hope I'll do a good job this year for her, then." Maybe this was exactly what I needed.

He cleared his throat again and his smile thinned. "She won't care. She died a while ago."

Oh god. Oh shit, why had I forgotten about the article I'd read? "I'm so sorry." I swallowed hard, trying to get the foot I'd just swallowed out of my windpipe.

"Not on you," he said lightly, but the bitterness in his voice was toxic.

I didn't know exactly how to continue, but barreled ahead. "Well, so you know it's all about the houses, then. And I came into this whole thing late—all the contracts on the selected homes had been signed, and the participants all agreed to decorate their homes for Christmas by the first week in December so the camera team can get the shots they need to send back to the hosts in Los Angeles."

Cormac was nodding, watching me.

"And, well, whoever used to own Singletree Manor signed our contract. And then they sold the house, and the contract, to your brother. And he signed it."

Cormac's face cleared as understanding dawned. "And now he's refusing to participate."

I sighed, nodding. "I asked him nicely," I said, feeling a little bit lame.

"Yeah, that won't work with him."

Clearly. "What will work? If I can't get him to agree to feature Singletree Manor on the show, I'll lose my job. And my whole career, actually. This is kind of my last chance." There. Now I'd told all my dirty secrets to a complete stranger. I really couldn't sink much lower.

"You know you have some glitter in your hair?" Cormac

said, taking me completely off guard. "Kind of caught in the front part there." He moved his hand above the left side of his face to show me where, and I batted at my bangs, wishing I'd never laid eyes on that enormous basket of glittery Christmas terror—or had just left it alone on the table.

"Thanks," I said, trying to pull my bangs down so I could see any clinging glitter. Finally, I gave up and pushed them back. The universe was determined to force me to be festive, even if it was completely against my will.

"Yeah, so, Callan ..." Cormac trailed off. "He's probably not going to be willing to open up the house to a bunch of cameras at this point."

"I got that."

"And you can bring him lawyers all day long, trying to enforce that contract, but his agent will probably help him out of that."

"Right."

"And I don't know if there's money involved, but that won't win him over either."

"Great. So far you're not really making me feel good about this."

Cormac sighed and leaned back, his golden eyes scanning my face for a long minute as I perched on the edge of my seat. I didn't know how he could stay in this small close room. I was beginning to feel like the walls were caving. I waved a hand in front of my face, trying to move some air around.

"This office is the worst, huh?" Cormac laughed.

I shrugged. "I mean, it's ..."

"Terrible. I just needed an office address, really. I work across from home half the time."

I smiled, realizing Cormac was just a nice guy who'd lost his wife and was doing the best he could. I needed to leave him alone. I sighed and stood up, picking up my purse. "Well, I'm sorry I bothered you," I said, feeling like we must be finished. "Thanks for your time."

"Hang on a second," Cormac said, his voice low and thoughtful. I sat back down. "You seem like a nice person," he said, narrowing his eyes at me.

"Um. Thanks." Where was this going to go?

"So I'll give you a tip. The thing my brother needs most is a reason to get up every day. He thinks he's lost everything. And in a way, he kind of has. The guy might be good looking and richer than God, but he's miserable because everything he ever believed his life was about is gone."

My heart squeezed a little for the handsome stranger I'd met in his big empty house, and I thought of the last article I'd read, a feature with Callan's ex-girlfriend, describing that she'd had to leave him because he'd become a miserable hermit since his injury. "I don't think a Christmas home show is going to be able to touch that ..."

"No," Cormac said. "But you might."

"Ah, I'm not following." Was this guy trying to set me up? He didn't even know me.

"I'm just saying none of the usual tactics are going to work. So your only hope at getting my brother to agree to feature Singletree Manor on your show is if you win him over some other way. And the guy has a shortage of human interaction and kindness in his life. Though if my daughters have anything to say about it ..." he trailed off.

I wrinkled my nose at him, confused. Now he was dragging his daughters into it? Where was this going exactly, and how much work would I have to put in to get this to actually happen?

"Sorry," Cormac laughed. "I never thought I'd see the day, but my brother volunteered to babysit my kids. That's how I know he's desperate for some kind of interaction, though I imagine he's going to get tired of chatting about Santa Claus and Dora the Explorer in another day or two."

"Okkkaay," I said slowly. I had no idea how to use that information. "Well, thanks."

"Just go back over. Be nice. Get to know the guy."

I really didn't have time for any of that, and getting to know the stars of my shows hadn't worked out super well in the past. "Sure."

"And if you mention the need to decorate for Christmas, I think you might find a couple little girls on your side on that one."

"You're sending me over to recruit your daughters to my cause?"

Cormac smiled at me. "They could probably use some interaction, too," he said. "Like I said, you seem like a nice person. My gut says so, and my gut is never wrong about that kind of thing."

I frowned at him, and understood that he must have loved his wife very much to end up looking so sad and tired. The Whitewood brothers both seemed like they needed someone to be kind to them—it wasn't just Callan who needed a friend. "Well," I said. "I guess I've got nothing to lose."

"Good luck, April," Cormac said. "I hope to see you again."

I shook his hand and left the cramped office, heading for my room. I needed to do some paperwork back at the hotel, but this afternoon, I was going back out to Singletree Manor.

6

CHRISTOPHER MOVES IN
CALLAN

Waking up to the sun streaming over the back lawn as it rolled down to the shores of the Potomac should have been enjoyable—uplifting maybe. Especially since I had always been a morning person. Only now, mornings were close to torturous.

My morning process before my injury went something like this:

1. Open eyes.

2. Feel like the luckiest guy in the world.

3. Roll out of bed and put feet on the floor.

4. Head out into my awesome life to do all kinds of awesome shit that probably included playing soccer, posing for pictures for some new endorsement deal, and being invited to rub shoulders with other pretty awesome people (which, honestly, wasn't my favorite part, but it was still pretty ... awesome.)

My morning process since the injury was more like this, and it was pretty solid:

1. Open eyes.

2. Feel like the luckiest guy in the world.

3. Roll out of bed and put feet on the floor.

4. Be nearly felled by crippling pain shooting up left leg and by the subsequent memory that everything I ever wanted in life had disappeared in the course of five minutes on the field.

5. Lay back down and curse the world.

6. Close eyes.

7. Plan to build in-bed bar so morning drinking was more feasible.

And when you had an established morning routine that was working so well for you, the weather could do little to alter it.

Only today, I actually needed to get up. The girls were coming over after school, and I needed to get a few things ready and clean up the house.

I repeated steps one through four of the usual routine, and forced myself to hobble to the bathroom instead of climbing back into bed a second time. I flipped on the hot water in the shower and leaned over the sink, resting a hand on either side and staring down into the bowl. I took a deep breath and pulled together the courage to look myself in the face.

There. There was the bastard who'd taken everything for granted and actually believed he'd deserved it. God it was hard to look at myself. I scoured my face in the mirror, letting my eyes linger on the dark circles that had developed beneath the sockets, the scruff covering my chin and neck, the slightly haunted look I couldn't seem to shake.

"Get it together, Whitewood," I muttered, and then stripped off my boxers and stepped into the blazing heat of the shower.

The ankle hurt worst in the mornings, and once I'd warmed up a little bit and moved around, it seemed to loosen. While the pain was always a dull throb, it became tolerable once I forced myself to move. The pain in my chest and head was harder to anticipate. I was actually feeling a little better there since the move, though there'd been a point early on, right after Becky had left, when I'd believed it might be worse than the ankle.

I knew now the pain had more to do with my love of the game than it did Becky. She had been a constant in my life over the past couple years, and I'd come to think of her as permanent—but once she'd left I almost felt relieved after the initial shock had worn off. Becky had been in it for the wrong reasons, and I realized now, so had I. Without her by my side pushing me to go to the next big event, to take the next high-profile sponsorship, I was able to think more clearly, not that events and sponsorships were exactly falling in my lap these days. With the distance, I realized Becky had been in it for what I could do for her, *but not for me.*

That had been clear enough when she'd left, telling me she did enough nursing in her day job.

Good riddance.

I shut off the water and cleaned up, shaving and actually

combing my hair and putting a little bit of pomade in it to hopefully keep it all going the right direction. Not that the little girls would care, but I felt pressure to put myself together for them, to try to be whole. Or at least to appear that way.

I cleaned up the house, ignoring the pain as I managed to unpack the last few boxes and put together the playroom I'd set up since they'd last been over. It was a surprise for them, and I hoped they'd love it.

When the clock ticked near to three-thirty, I picked up my keys and wallet and ventured out to my car. I was actually going to leave the property for the first time. I'd installed a booster and a convertible car seat in the back of the car at Cormac's request, and he had even come by to ensure they were installed properly. I was ready.

The school wasn't far from home, and I picked Taylor up with no problems, her enormous smile upon seeing me confirming that yes, this was a great idea. We went to Maddie's daycare next, and I earned another giant grin and a little-girl hug that pretty much validated all my reasons for forcing myself out of bed and into the shower this morning.

When they were both strapped in, I turned around and addressed them both. "I thought we might need to make a stop on the way home."

"Ice cream?" Taylor piped up hopefully.

"Ice cweam?" Maddie repeated her sister, her big eyes wide.

My heart might have melted a tiny bit at their hopeful faces.

"That wasn't the plan, but we can probably fit that in, too. I was thinking that I probably need a Christmas tree, since I've got two helpers to decorate it with me."

"Yes!" the girls chimed. Their enthusiasm was infectious, and I let their joy seep in around the edges of my own misery, loosening my chest just a bit.

They picked out one of the bigger trees and the man at the lot helped tie it to the top of the car. The girls instructed me to drive slowly so "Christopher" wouldn't be injured.

"Is naming the tree standard practice at your house?" I asked them as I guided the car slowly back down the lane toward my house.

The girls were quiet for a long minute, and I found Taylor's eyes in the rear-view mirror. She looked thoughtful, and then said, "Mommy used to do it."

And there was the familiar pain of loss. I hated that these little girls were familiar with that pain, and wished I could take it away from them, but I also knew that the memories they had of Linda were some of the things they needed to hold onto as they grew. I'd lost my parents not long before Linda had died—Mom and Dad going in quick succession, and I knew that pain a bit. But these girls were so young. "Well, your mommy was a very smart lady. If she said we need to name our Christmas tree, then that's what we'll do." I rolled the window down and reached up to pat the roof of the car. "You doing okay up there, Christopher?"

"The twee doesn't talk," Maddie said, her voice full of the derision three-year olds can muster so easily when addressing silly adults.

I pulled up to the gate at the house to discover two things at once. One, there was a little silver Honda parked outside the gate containing a certain television producer I had wondered if I might be seeing again. And two, I couldn't for the life of me remember the code to open the gate. I parked and switched off the engine.

"You guys wait here a sec, okay? My security system is very high tech and it's gonna take just a minute to get it opened up."

The girls nodded as I got out of the car. I cast a glance at April, who was getting out of her car, too, and despite the fact that we had a fundamental disagreement between us, I couldn't help but smile at her. "You're back."

"I told you I would be," she said.

"I'm not going to change my mind about the cameras and the decorating and stuff." I tried to sound stern, but the two eager little sets of ears in the back of my car didn't need to hear me badmouth their favorite holiday.

"Looks like you might be willing to give just a little," April said, eying Christopher tied up on top of the car.

"That's for my nieces." I approached the keypad on the gate and stared at it. Six, five ...? Seven? I thought there might be a two in there somewhere. I punched in four different codes as April watched with a tilted head and sparkling eyes, but the gate didn't open.

"No joy?" she asked.

"I'm just practicing," I told her, trying one more useless combination as I felt an embarrassed flush crawl up my neck. I was an adult. I owned the biggest house in town and I couldn't even manage to open up the front gate without help. I grunted in frustration as I tried another code.

"Anyone you could call?" April had stepped closer and was staring at the keypad like the numbers might just pop out at her any second.

I blew out a frustrated breath and pulled my phone from my pocket, dialing Jessica Betts at her office. Voicemail. Perfect.

April watched all this with interest, and I felt myself flush hotter with embarrassment. Not that I cared what she thought of me, but being locked out of my own yard was not the coolest thing I'd done lately.

"Told you I think I can scale it," she said, eyeing the gate with a measuring gaze.

"No. No way I'm going to have you getting hurt on my property. Your network is already talking about suing me—can you imagine what would happen if you got injured on the job at my house? Not a chance."

While I was explaining how there was no way in hell I'd allow her to climb the gate, April climbed the gate. She now sat atop the massive steel doors, one leg on either side.

"When I get down, is there some way to open these from inside?"

"Be careful," I scolded. "I swear, if you get hurt—"

April cut me off by jumping down from the gate with an agile ease I both admired and envied. "I'm fine, see?" She asked me from the other side of the gate. "Do I need a key? Is there an alarm on the main house?"

I shook my head and passed her the key through the gate. "I'm pretending this isn't humiliating."

She grinned. "Is it working?"

I felt my face flush hotter. "Not even a little bit."

April's face smoothed, and she tilted her head, lifting a finger to her plump pink lips. "Do you think maybe you'll feel like you owe me anything if I let you in?"

Ha. Clever girl. "Tell you what, I'll repay you by not calling the cops to tell them you're trespassing."

She crossed her arms and frowned, jutting out a hip and tapping her toe on the gravel. "That isn't very nice."

April was an attractive woman. But when she pulled her false pout, I was surprised to feel an overwhelming urge to scoop her up and toss her over my shoulder to wipe that little frown right off her face. I took a deep breath, a little over-whelmed at my own reaction to her. "Just open the front door and push the button on the gate. We'll figure out the rest inside. These little girls should get out of the car, okay?"

She peered past me to the girls glued to the windows of the car over my shoulder and smiled. She gave them the "thumbs up" sign and jogged up to the front door of the house, her striped nautical sweater and fitted boyfriend jeans making her look like something from a J.Crew catalog, especially with the huge colonial house looming behind her. She was more than pretty, I realized. It was too bad she was the enemy at the moment.

April stopped on the porch and then disappeared inside the front door, and a moment later, the gate swung open. She jogged back out and handed me the keys, which I took before spinning on my heel to go back to the car. Distance. I needed distance from her before I did or said something I'd regret.

"You're welcome," she called. "Mind if I come in?"

I shrugged and got into the car, forcing myself to concentrate on driving and parking just in front of the house. As I got out, it annoyed me to realize I was happy to see her pulling up behind us. I released Maddie from her car seat, setting her next to the car as her sister climbed out.

"Since you're here," I told April, "and you're so into demonstrating your athletic abilities, you can help wrestle this monster tree into the house."

"Ahem." Taylor's small voice came up from my left side.

"Sorry," I corrected, dropping a hand on her thin shoulder. "I meant Christopher. You can help us show Christopher his new home."

April's eyebrows shot up and her face held a question, but she didn't ask. "Fair enough."

7

April was strong, considering she was a pretty small woman, and she hoisted the front end of the tree off the car and up the front steps of the house like she did this kind of thing every day.

"You got a stand for it?" she asked, once we'd laid Christopher on the floor in the middle of the front room where he was going to live.

"Yup, in the car, give me a sec." I limped toward the door,

but April sped past me, shooting a look over her shoulder as she trotted to the front door.

"I'm on it."

Great, I thought. She feels sorry for the gimpy guy. I didn't know exactly why I cared what she thought. No, scratch that. I knew why. April was hot. She was energetic and bubbly, and there was something strong about her that I was more attracted to than I wanted to admit. And I didn't want her pity.

I swallowed my pride as she returned with the tree stand, and together we lifted Christopher and got him set up in the front window of the room that was probably once called the parlor. Despite the tree's massive size, it didn't quite reach the ceiling of the room. Which was a bonus, since I didn't think the little girls would be thrilled to watch their uncle saw the top of Christopher's head off, and I sure as shit wasn't cutting a hole in the ceiling of my new house.

"He's glorious," Taylor breathed, looking up, and I had to stifle a grin at her use of such a big descriptor.

"Gloww-ee-us," Madison echoed at her side.

"Just wait until he's got lights and decorations," April said, grinning at the little girls.

I pointed to the back of the room where I'd hauled out the Christmas decorations Becky had boxed up last year when we'd shared a townhouse in San Diego. I had no idea what was in there—decorating had been her domain.

The little girls scrambled to the boxes, and soon the room was a scattered minefield of shining balls and whimsical nutcracker ornaments. April helped string the lights on, though as soon as she was standing on the ladder I'd found in the shed outside, wrapping the strands around the tree's top, her face took on a lost expression. When the lights were done, I stepped to her side.

"So you popped by to help me decorate the tree?" She hadn't actually explained why she'd stopped by. "You haven't even mentioned the show. Aren't you supposed to be trying to sell me?" I kept my voice low. If the girls got wind of the show, I'd never hear the end of it.

April gazed at me for a long minute, something troubled in her eyes I couldn't identify. "I haven't decorated a Christmas tree since I was seven," she said.

Oookay ... we were changing the subject. Maybe this was where the lost look was coming from. I raised an eyebrow at her. "Doesn't your family celebrate Christmas?"

The sad look in her eyes hardened into something else, something fiery and fierce that actually sent a little thrum of desire bolting through me. "Not anymore."

"Because ..." I knew I was prying, but for the moment I'd gotten distracted. Her hair floated around her shoulders, little specks of red sparkle dust caught in the front strands, and it was such a contrast to her flushed skin and glowing eyes, the combination was perfect. For a long minute, I didn't feel the pain of my ankle or the gaping hole where my reason for living had been ripped out of my chest. I only felt a compelling desire to know more about April.

"Long story," she said, breaking the sizzling eye contact that had developed between us.

"Come on, you guys," Taylor called, and I looked over to

see that the bottom few branches had been covered with ornaments, while most of Christopher was sadly bare. I didn't have enough ornaments for a tree this size, and the girls couldn't reach much higher than they'd already decorated.

"On it," I said, moving toward the tree to help disperse some of the lower-level ornament crowd.

April joined me, moving slowly around the other side, and I wondered what it was about Christmas that had her so much in her own head. "I like this one," she said, holding up a ballerina ornament that had been Becky's, and I sensed some determination from her to focus on pretending to enjoy herself, even though the strange heaviness remained in the air. I still had no idea why she'd really appeared at my gate today, but I wasn't going to lie to myself either. At least not about this. I enjoyed the company—hers and that of my nieces. I'd been lonelier than I wanted to admit, and distraction from the things that felt so wrong in my life was welcome.

"A balle-weeena," Maddie cooed, stepping close to April to see the ornament she held.

"We take ballet," Taylor told April. "We are in The Nutcracker this year."

"Both of you?" April knelt down and addressed the girls on their level, looking appropriately impressed.

Maddie nodded. "I'm a bon-bon and flow-oo."

"And I'm a flower too," Taylor said. "And we're both in the party scene."

I had no real idea what they were talking about, since I'd

never seen The Nutcracker, but April seemed to understand these code words.

"That's amazing," she said. "I'd love to see it. I wonder if I'll still be in town."

"It's in two weeks," Taylor said, but then she looked confused. "Wait. What's today?"

"December first," April said. "So two weeks would be the fifteenth."

Taylor stared out the window for a long minute, her hands moving in front of her. I realized she was counting. "That's when it is. The fifteenth."

I didn't really think through what happened next—my body and mouth moved before the rest of me caught up. But a moment later I was standing at April's side, saying, "We'll both be there."

April shot me a confused look, and I smiled at her, shrugging. Neither one of us seemed clear on exactly what the hell I was doing. At least I hadn't actually suggested we go together. Like on a date. Not in those exact words.

The girls went back to hanging ornaments on every available pine needle, and April stepped away, gesturing for me to follow her into the foyer. "Was that an invitation, or just an observation that we might both be in one place at the same time?" She was direct. I liked it.

"What do you want the answer to be?"

She shook her head and blew out a frustrated breath. "Nope. I'm not playing. Look, the only answer I need from you is about the show. Whether or not I go to the ballet has nothing to do with it."

Of course not. "Right."

"So are you in or out?"

"For the ballet?" I was messing with her and I probably shouldn't have been. Not when the contract for the stupid show was still with my lawyer and I was still determined not to let cameras back into my life. But she was so adorable I couldn't help it.

"For the show," she bit out.

"Contract's with my lawyers," I told her. "They'll let me know if I can get out of it."

"You can't." Her eyes were blazing again, and her cheeks were reddening.

"Why not just find another home to replace this one?" I asked.

"This is the biggest house in Singletree, and it's the reason the show came here in the first place," she said, her voice rising. "And if I don't get your house on the show and get this thing sealed with a shiny glittery bow in the next couple days, I'm out of a job. No," she said, jabbing a finger in the air. "Make that a career."

"Boxes are empty." Taylor stood behind April, the look on her face making it clear that she knew she'd interrupted something.

April took a deep breath and turned around to face her.

Taylor went on. "You need more stuff, Uncle Callan. Christopher is still half naked."

She was right. The ornaments we'd had were townhouse-tree sized. Definitely not adequate for a manor-house tree. "I guess we need to go shopping," I said. I looked at April and grinned. I couldn't tell if she found me charming or just completely aggravating, but she hadn't left yet and I was enjoying her company either way. "You in? Quick round of ornament shopping? You can get back to harassing me about other stuff after."

She let out a long breath before answering. "I don't know how you'll get back inside your house without me, so I guess I'd better come with you."

I had the weirdest urge to do a victory fist pump, but I suppressed it and smiled instead, turning to get my car keys.

TARGET OR THE NORTH POLE
APRIL

was supposed to be confirming the other houses on the tour, making sure all the administrative details were buttoned up and locked down. And instead, I was decorating a tree named Christopher with the two cutest tiny girls I'd ever met and a former soccer star who had eyes capable of dropping a thousand pairs of panties in a single glance. I tried to tell myself I was just doing my job, warming Callan up so he'd say yes to having the show filmed inside his house. There was nothing more to it.

But when his gaze slid to mine, his strong hands on the wheel as he drove and something playful in the depths of those deep eyes, I had to suppress a shudder. If I let it, my body could convince my brain to do things—assuming Callan wanted to do things too—and that was exactly what had led me to this last stop on the road before career ruin.

It wouldn't happen again. No matter how soft his voice was when he spoke to his nieces. No matter how strong and sexy he looked when he hoisted Maddie to his shoulders and let her ride up there through the parking lot, her little hands steering him by the ears as he tried to hide his limp.

"This is my favorite store," Taylor said, her voice full of awe as we stepped inside Target. We'd been relieved to find that Singletree, though a small town, had a whole stretch of big box stores just outside the town proper—including a Target.

"It looks like an elf exploded in here," I said under my breath. Avoiding these types of stores around the holidays was a long-observed part of my anti-holiday efforts. They were always a complete immersion into holiday hell. You couldn't swing a dead reindeer without hitting something sparkly, glowing, or painted with cheerful sayings. I shuddered.

"Ex-pwo-dered?" Maddie asked, her eyes like saucers as she took in the enormous tree set up at the front of the store.

"Exploded," Taylor corrected. "But if an elf exploded, it'd be a pretty small mess. And there'd be guts." She looked up at me for acknowledgment of her logic.

I stifled another shudder that had nothing to do with elf guts or Callan and my misplaced attraction to him, and everything to do with the memories that came slamming back whenever I was forced into an over-decorated holiday location.

Callan was watching me with one side of his mouth quirked up. "You okay?"

"Yeah. Fine. Why?"

"You look like you might throw up," he said.

I shook out my shoulders and forced myself to take a couple deep breaths. I hadn't been around this much holiday crap in years. I had a sudden vision of the last time my own home had been decked out in stockings and garlands, and found that I did actually feel a little sick. "I'll be okay," I said. I swallowed hard and focused on the girls, on their glowing faces and the way they were bouncing on their feet and clenching their little hands as they looked around. "What do we need?" I asked.

Callan crossed his arms, coming to a stop in the ornament section at the back of the store. "More tree stuff, right?"

"Yes, yes!" the girls cried, clapping.

"And stuff for the house?"

"Yes!"

"I don't think I can get lights up on the outside of the house," he said thoughtfully, his dark eyes scanning the shelves of lights. "It's just too high. I'm not exactly in shape to be climbing on ladders." His eyes slid to me, and I noticed him glance away when my eyes met his, his cheeks reddening.

He was embarrassed, I realized, and I wanted to say something that would make him feel better. "No one would get up on a ladder at that house," I said. "You can hire that done, though."

Our eyes met, and words were exchanged between us without anything spoken. He knew I was trying to downplay his injury.

"Yeah. I'll do that, I guess. Or maybe we don't need lights outside—"

"Of course you do!" Taylor said sternly. "That's how Santa finds your house."

Callan nodded, his face softening again as he looked at his niece. "Right. Then I'll just hire someone."

"Good," Taylor said, looking relieved.

A moment later, Callan and I stood alone as the little girls ran down the aisle, making appreciative squeals as they explored all the decorating possibilities.

An hour and several hundred dollars later, we were back in the car, decorations stuffed into every available spare inch of space around us. I sat up front, a huge stuffed snowman on my lap. I was forced to put my arms around it to keep it from sliding over to the driver's side on turns. If Lynn could see this—April Hall hugging a snowman—she'd never believe it. Lynn had been tolerant of my anti-holiday stance. Luckily, Lynn was Jewish, and I had nothing at all against Hanukkah. Lynn's simple menorah and few blue decorations were always a welcome relief from the madness, which seemed to begin in early September these days.

"I think you're going the wrong way, Uncle Callan," Taylor said as Callan turned off the two-lane thoroughfare and toward the town square.

"I'll do the driving, thank you very much," Callan said, his voice carrying a jovial note. Then he turned to me and whispered, "did I make a wrong turn? I haven't gotten out and about much yet."

I laughed. "I just got here myself. I'm not exactly your best bet for finding your way through these circles of death." We turned slowly through yet another traffic circle, Callan turning the car out of one of the exits, seemingly at random, and the main square of town came into view.

"Circle of death?" Callan asked, his mouth turned up in a smile as he glanced at me. This smile was the closest I'd seen yet to those full-blown grins he'd worn in the pictures I'd seen of him playing soccer.

"We don't have these in Los Angeles," I said.

"San Diego either," he said.

We drove slowly down the narrow streets leading into the center of town, where the sidewalks were busy with shoppers and strollers, and the parking around the square was stuffed to the gills. I avoided looking at the enormous tree in the center of the square now that it was decorated, but the girls had no such aversion.

"It's enormous," Taylor said, her vocabulary on full display again.

"Norm-usss," Maddie echoed.

"Uncle Callan," Taylor said, her voice shifting into a pleading tone even before she'd told him what she was hoping for. "Could we stop here a minute? Look at the tree?"

Callan's head turned, first to look at his niece, and then to scan for parking. "Not for long," he said. "That okay, April?"

"Yeah," I said, equal parts eager to get out from under the snowman and dreading the idea of being forced to stand beneath the humongous tree as the girls oohed and aaahed up at it.

Callan pulled into a spot, his brow wrinkling as he looked at me before turning off the engine. "It's just a tree," he said, too quietly for the girls to hear.

I smiled, relaxing a little bit when it appeared he wasn't going to push me for an explanation. "Okay. Yeah."

We stepped out of the car, and I shoved Frosty back into the passenger side. I unbuckled Maddie from the back and helped the little girl up onto the sidewalk. I was sliding my bag securely onto my shoulder when a warm little hand slipped into mine, surprising me. I gripped Maddie's small hand with my own, something in my chest tightening at the gesture.

"We'll do one lap of the tree," Callan said, walking ahead of us, holding Taylor's hand. "But then ..." Callan trailed off, and his limping gait slowed.

I let my eyes drift toward the monstrosity, but before we could get there, they landed on something else. Two vans, parked at the edge of the square near my hotel, and a camera crew pulling gear from the back of one to set up on the side-walk. The side of the van had the logo of my network embla-zoned across the side.

Crap. The crew was here. And I still had to get Callan's house locked up plus two more. And here I was, acting like a tourist, chaperoning snowmen and small children around to look at Christmas décor. How had they managed to fly across the country and still get vans that screamed the network name? Uncle Rob was good.

"What the hell?" Callan breathed, his eyes fixed on the cameras as we moved slowly forward again, toward the tree and the crew.

"Oh, them? It's just—"

"Hey!" One of the cameramen had caught sight of us, and

I was sure he was going to call me out, ask why I was wandering around and Christmas shopping when I was supposed to be working.

"Oh, hi—" I started.

"Aren't you Callan Whitewood?" The guy went on, ignoring me altogether. "The Sharks, right? Retired?"

Callan was rigid, standing on the sidewalk gripping his niece's hand like he was made from stone. I couldn't see his face, but his shoulders were high and tense. "Yeah," he said.

"Man," the cameraman went on, shaking his head. "That injury, man. Wow. When I saw it happen, I was like, there's no way he's coming back from that. I was like—"

"Yeah," Callan said again, terse and loud, cutting the guy off and practically dragging Taylor around the man.

"Okay, well. Good to meet you, man," the guy called to Callan's back as Maddie and I followed him.

On the other side of the tree, out of view of from the crew, Taylor looked up at her uncle. "You're hurting my hand."

I stepped up next to him, and Callan's face, which had reddened and gone expressionless, came back to life as he snapped his gaze to his niece. "Sorry." He let go of her hand, and mopped his face with that same hand.

"You okay?" I asked him, as his bottomless eyes slid up to study my face.

"They with you? Those cameras? Your show?" His words began flat, but by the third question, he was practically spitting them out.

I nodded. "Yeah." Why did he look so angry? Was it that

horrible to be recognized? "I guess the cameraman is a fan, huh?"

He scoffed. "You don't have fans when you don't play anymore. Only drama seekers who want to tell people you're still messed up. I'm sure that guy watched me limp away, all excited to tell his buddies how he's sure I'll never play again."

I pulled one side of my lip between my teeth. "Or maybe he was just excited to meet someone he admired."

Those deep eyes shot me a look full of venom and anger, and he didn't answer. After a second, he began moving again, practically dragging Taylor toward the car as Maddie and I followed.

When we got near the crew again, another of the guys called out to me. "Hey, we shooting the first house tomorrow?"

So they did know who I was. "Supposed to be December third, so two more days," I said. "I'm finishing up getting things sorted."

The guy gave me a thumbs up and waved at the girls who were looking at the equipment on the sidewalk with confused interest.

"There's your one lap around the tree," Callan told them, already dragging Taylor back to the car. "Now home."

We all climbed back into the car, but the mood had shifted. I could feel the anger rolling off Callan in thick waves, and though I wanted to do something to alleviate it, I wanted to understand it, too. Was he angry he'd been recognized? Or that he couldn't be the star he used to be?

When he'd found his way back to the big gates in front of his house, Callan turned to me. "Probably better let you go get your show sorted." There was no softness in the words, no friendliness.

"You need me to go inside and open the gate?" I asked, placing Frosty on the ground next to the car.

"I wrote down the code while we were inside," he said, lifting his hand to show me four numbers on his wrist. He punched them into the keypad and the gates swung open.

"She has to help," Taylor said, crossing her arms and looking up at her uncle.

"No, Taylor," Callan said, his voice softening. "She's not here to help. She's here to get what she wants."

Surprise heated my cheeks, and made my shirt feel suddenly uncomfortably warm. "No," I said quickly. "I—"

"Didn't you come back over here today to convince me to let that camera crew into my house?"

"Well yes, but—"

"Cameras? Then we need to decorate extra good!" Taylor said.

"Yeah," Maddie said, her little arms wrapped around Frosty in a fierce hug.

I was watching Callan's face, but it gave nothing away except a hot anger bubbling beneath the surface. I wasn't sure what to do. "I can help if you want," I offered.

"You've done enough."

"Ah, okay, well ..." I dug out my car keys and then knelt to say goodbye to the girls. "Good luck decorating," I said. "I can't wait to see it when it's done."

"Come back tomorrow," Maddie suggested.

I looked back at Callan, let my eyes climb back up to

Callan's face, and he shook his head slightly, telling me that I wouldn't be welcome back tomorrow. Or next month. Or ever. I let a sigh escape me as I stood. "Okay, well, look. The contract is legally binding. You don't have to be here—it's only about the house. You don't even have to decorate—I can hire people to handle that."

"Clearly, I'm decorating," he said bitterly.

"So maybe think about just letting the guys film the house?"

He said nothing, just stood there with his eyes clouded and his perfect chiseled jaw set.

"I'll come by tomorrow?"

He shook his head. "Give me your phone."

I complied, though it seemed a strange request.

Callan took it, jabbing at the screen for a minute or two. "Now you don't need to keep showing up. You can call. Like a civilized person."

I would have laughed at that, but there was no humor in Callan's face, so I just tucked my phone back into my bag and tried for a smile. "Okay, I'll do that."

The big gates had swung shut again, and another car was coming up the narrow lane now, sending a small plume of dust up behind it.

"Daddy!" Maddie said, jumping up and down. "Daddy can help."

The car rolled to a halt and Cormac Whitewood stepped out of it. "Why are you all standing out here?" he asked, looking between us. "Hello again, Miss Hall."

"You two have met?" Callan asked, suspicion coloring his words.

"Only briefly," Cormac said, seeming to sense the tension in the air. "In town."

"Hello Cormac," I said, feeling very out of place.

"Would opening the gate help move this situation along at all?" Cormac asked, nodding toward the keypad.

"I was just going," I said. "Just need to get my car." I nodded toward where my little car sat in front of the plantation house.

"Get back in the car, girls," Callan said in a not-too-friendly voice.

"Frosty!" Taylor said, seeing that we were all getting back in, but the snowman remained on the driveway.

"I can handle Frosty," Cormac said, placing the snowman in the passenger side of his own car.

We drove past the gates and stopped again in front of the house. I got out of Callan's car, which had turned very silent and very cold.

"Goodbye," Callan said pointedly, angling his head at my car.

"Bye," I said, lifting a hand to Cormac and the girls. And then I was driving away, wondering if I'd made progress on getting Callan's house nailed down or on something else. Or if maybe I was right back where I started.

Nowhere.

8

FROSTY IS A SMUG BASTARD

CALLAN

It took five trips to carry all the assorted ornaments, decorations, and lights from my car into the house. And once it was all inside, deposited in a non-decorous heap in the center of the parlor beneath the enormous tree, I saw the mess for what it was—an effort to cover ugly and empty with glitter and gauche.

"Shit," I whispered, staring down at it all, rubbing a hand over the back of my neck where the hair was beginning to curl around my collar. I needed a haircut. Hell, I needed a lot more than that.

"I see my girls were very convincing," Cormac said, coming to stand at my side as the little girls began to paw through the bags, pulling out their favorite things. Frosty stood silent just inside the front door, watching the scene with expressionless coal eyes and a one-sided smile. I thought he looked awfully smug for a guy standing naked inside another man's house.

"They were," I agreed. "But they had help." I spit these last words out, earning me a squinty gaze from my brother.

"You didn't have to go along with it," Cormac said, kneeling to help Maddie extricate four stockings from a bag. He handed them to the little girl and turned back to me. "What's your real issue? Something to do with April," he guessed.

I felt tired suddenly, and the ache that shot up my leg with every movement had become a singing pain that wouldn't stop, a constant reminder of what I had once been, and who I would never be again. "She wheedled her way in here. She's got this television crew in town, and I'm supposed to just roll over and do what she wants, let them all in here to film."

I gritted my teeth against both the pain and the memory of the last time the media had dug into my life—a meaty photo-filled spread in one of the popular tabloids had done an exclusive interview with my ex soon after the breakup. She'd given them some of her own photos—photos that showed me angry and broken down, grieving for the loss of my career. The words had been no better, Becky calling me pathetic and sad, painting me as a has-been who couldn't see past my own former fame. That particular piece had resulted in the speedy conclusion of the last two endorsement deals I'd had—ones I'd thought I might hang on to despite the injury. They didn't want to work with a guy teetering on the brink of depression and alcoholism, and their contract revisions had signaled the true and final end of the life I'd once lived. Becky had left just before the piece had published.

Cormac looked skeptical. "She's just doing her job, right?"

"Her job is to convince people who don't want anyone around to put themselves in a spotlight." I picked up a string of silver bells and stared at it like a slab of raw meat, with disgust. "Pretty shitty, if you ask me."

"Watch it," Cormac said, angling his head at the girls who were practically rolling around in all the shiny new decorations.

"Why are you defending her?" I asked, my voice rising as the fatigue and frustration inside me began to simmer and pop. "She's just one more person who's in it for herself, ready to use anyone she can to claw her way up."

"I don't think—"

But I wasn't done. Not even close. "She manipulated me and I let her. And she used your daughters to do it!" I was shouting now, and both girls had stopped what they were doing to watch me rant. "I don't understand why people can't just leave me the fuck alone. All I want is to sit here in my new house and have some fucking peace."

"Girls," Cormac ordered, pointing to the door that would lead to the back of the house. "To the porch. Taylor, watch your sister."

The girls' eyes had rounded and their mouths had dropped slightly open. Taylor took Maddie's hand and led her from the room as the sound of Maddie's shock turning to upset tears floated back to remind me that cursing in front of little girls was unacceptable behavior. The hard ball of anger inside me loosened a bit, unrolling into a knot of shame. Those little girls were probably the only people in my life willing to take me exactly as I was now. They were the last people I wanted to hurt or scare.

"You need to watch yourself," Cormac said in a low steady voice, stepping closer to me. "If you're in the midst of some kind of nervous breakdown, I need to know it. I'm not going to have my girls—your nieces—around you if you're raging around, drinking and cursing in front of them. They've been through enough." He punctuated this last statement with a hard poke to my chest and then stepped back, crossing his arms over his chest and moving to the front window. His voice broke as he added, "We all have."

"Cormac," I said, as I realized the level of ugliness I'd just modeled for my little nieces. "Listen, I'm sorry, I just—" I took a step toward my brother, but stopped, my feet suddenly as leaden as my heart.

"You just can't seem to see that self-pity isn't a solid plan for the rest of your life," Cormac finished for me.

Anger pricked my neck and I lifted my head to respond, but I didn't have the energy to form the words. Besides, Cormac wasn't wrong.

"Look," Cormac came back to where he stood, his voice softer. "I know you had to give up a lot. I know it was hard, heartbreaking, to end your career like that. But your life isn't over. And I can't have the girls around you if you're going to continue acting like it is. They love you, and they're excited to spend time with you. But I have to think about what's best for them. I want them to see understand that, yeah, horrible things happen. But then we take a step, and another, and we keep moving forward. There is no other choice."

Shame washed away the anger I had been feeling as I considered Cormac's words. Those girls had their mother ripped from their lives. And they were still able to smile and laugh and dance. If they could move forward like that, couldn't I? "You're right," I said, my voice barely above a whisper. "I'm sorry. I won't blow up in front of them again."

"Good." Cormac let the argument fall away—he'd always been good at forgiveness. He bent down to pick up the enormous bag with exterior lights in it. "You planning to put these up yourself?"

I shook my head. "Definitely not. I was thinking of hiring someone."

"Oh yeah? What'll you pay me?"

"You don't need to do that," I said. "I'll find someone."

"I'm here. You got a ladder that'll reach that high?" He peered out the window again at the soaring eaves of the huge house in the fading light.

"There's another one out in the shed," I said, looking at the low ladder April had used earlier. "They came with the house."

A little later, as Cormac strung lights across the soaring front of the enormous house, which turned out to have convenient hooks all along the roofline from some other holiday-inspired owner, I stood below, holding the ladder and handing things up as needed. We'd turned on the bright garden lights that shone up at the front of the house and all the lights in the front rooms, and between the lingering daylight and the glow from the lights, Cormac had insisted it was light enough to see what he was doing. Taylor and

Maddie circled beneath their father, watching the progress and commenting on it at intervals. They also gave me some advice.

"You should have let April help," Taylor said. "You didn't have to make her leave." Her lip poked out dramatically as she stared up at me.

"Ape-will," Maddie agreed, mimicking the pout.

"Plus," his older niece said, tilting her head and putting a finger to her lip in a thoughtful pose. "Maybe you should take her out on a date or something."

"What?" I said, not that I hadn't considered a few non-work related things I could do with April myself. I thought I had been pretty restrained when April had been with us, but clearly my nieces had picked up on something. Or maybe it was just that in their minds, any unmarried man and woman might be a good fit for one another.

"She's pretty and you don't have a girlfriend."

"Ape-will is pretty," Maddie agreed, taking my hand and melting my heart at the same time.

"She is," I said slowly, not wanting to promise anything to two little girls who seemed very invested in this stranger.

Cormac was climbing down the ladder to get the next box of lights. "They do have a point," he said. "You might get to know her a bit. She seems like a nice girl."

"Whatever she is, it's about the last thing I need," I said. "Besides, she's only here for a little while."

Cormac lifted a shoulder, but held my gaze. "What have you got to lose?"

"I'd have to agree to do that stupid show." I'd expected the words to be bitter coming out, but as I said them, I didn't find the vehement opposition I'd felt earlier. Maybe giving April what she wanted—helping her out—would be good for me too. And the girls weren't wrong. April was pretty.

Actually, April was more than pretty. She was smoking hot. I didn't want to admit, even to myself, how many fantasies I'd already had about wrapping that thick dark hair around my hand and pressing her against a wall so I could do dirty, dirty things to her.

"You have a weird look on your face," Taylor told me, bringing my mind away from April's body and back to the present. "Were you thinking about elves? Maddie gets a weird look when she thinks about elves. Or kangaroos."

Maddie nodded that this was true.

"I was thinking about kangaroos," I said. "You caught me."

"Me too," Maddie said, and let out a giggle. And she did have kind of a weird look on her face, I decided.

"When your dad is finished with my lights, I think I should make him finish decorating the tree while we have some hot chocolate. We can stir it with those candy canes we bought. You in?"

The girls clapped and hopped up and down while Cormac grunted from his perch atop the ladder.

"You're doing a good job up there, bro," I called up, winking back down at my grinning nieces.

"Shut it," Cormac called back.

I watched the girls dance and cheer excitedly, running

back and forth in front of my big house while my brother finished stringing lights. Maybe life wasn't as empty as I'd imagined it to be, after all.

Maybe I could learn something from these little girls. Maybe I could be resilient too.

9

TIPSY IN SANTA'S SHACK
APRIL

$\mathcal{I}$ returned to the inn, shaking my head at the overabundance of red, green, glitter, and candy-cane striping that festooned every available surface. I wondered briefly if this was some version of that old show, *Candid Camera*, and if someone was giving me some kind of immersion therapy by subjecting me unrelentingly to the very thing I dreaded most in the world.

"Cup of cheer?" Annabelle asked, appearing in front of me with one of her elf ears askew and her rosy cheeks rounded in a welcoming smile.

"Sorry, what?"

"You look like you could use some peppermint tea." Annabelle's eyes scanned my face, and her smile dropped, turning into a pensive line. "Or maybe something stronger?"

I let out a bitter laugh. "Is there a bar in this place?" I looked around. I'd run through the lobby so quickly every time I'd been in here I hadn't noticed. Plus, it was hard to see around all the little houses of the Christmas village that had been erected around the space.

"Kind of," Annabelle said, winking at me. "I'm off in ten minutes. Meet me back there." She angled her head to the back of the lobby.

I looked around, but wasn't sure where exactly I was being told to go. "Where?"

"Santa's house. Far corner."

Aha. The huge gingerbread-style house in the far corner of the expansive lobby, which was fronted with drifts of snow and cording to keep the excited kids in an organized line once Santa showed up. "Santa won't mind?"

"Nah, you'll see."

I went up to my room to deposit my bag and my disappointment, trying hard not to think of the hard anger I'd seen in Callan Whitewood's eyes when he'd basically banished me from his property. Not only was I not going to finish the job I was sent to do, but I'd somehow alienated the one person I'd felt a connection with recently. I didn't have a ton of friends back home besides Lynn, and having someone to laugh with this afternoon had been surprisingly nice. It had awoken something inside me I hadn't realized was sleeping. And now that my desire for companionship had been roused, my loneliness was that much more tangible.

That was the only reason I headed back down to the lobby, picking my way between snowmen and elves to Santa's cottage. There was a Dutch door leading into the little house, and I opened it carefully and sat at the small round table inside. I didn't take the armchair, choosing instead to sit on a low stool. The chair was obviously intended for Santa. And while I'd never actually met the guy, and didn't really appreciate much about his holiday or traditions, I also didn't want to incur any bad holiday juju by sitting in his chair. I had enough bad holiday karma as it was.

"Hello," Annabelle called, tiptoeing into the little cottage holding two glasses and a bucket of ice. She put the ice bucket on the table and deposited a glass in front of me. Then she extracted a silver flask from somewhere inside her voluminous skirt, and set it on the table. Finally, she added two small bottles of tonic water, which had also been stored somewhere inside her elf costume.

"There's a lot of storage in your skirt," I commented.

"Elves are very resourceful," Annabelle said, sitting in Santa's chair without apparent remorse.

Annabelle was probably at least fifteen years older than me, and her clear enthusiasm for all things holiday-related didn't make her an obvious choice for a friend, but her open smile and willingness to spend her free time with a guest made me willing to get to know her a bit. Even if the pointy ears might make serious conversation a bit difficult.

"I brought the tonic because the HalfCat Moonshine is a bit stiff."

I cleared my throat in surprise. "Moonshine?"

"Center County's best. And still illegal if you stand in just the right spot inside the distillery."

"What are you talking about?" I felt my brow wrinkle in confusion as Annabelle poured moonshine and tonic water over ice in each glass. I had never had moonshine—or even really considered that people might still drink it. I swallowed hard, thinking it was pretty appropriate to be on the brink of getting tipsy in Santa's house. It seemed just the right level of disrespectful to match my distaste for the holiday.

"The HalfCat Distillery straddles county lines. And Center County has some really outdated liquor laws, but I guess because it's such a tiny little county, nestled between St. Mary's and Charles, they didn't ever get around to updating them. So while it's legal to make liquor in the part of the distillery that sits in Center County, you can't drink it there. Only on the Charles County side. You should go visit the Straddler Bar. It's a hoot."

I picked up my glass, dubiously eyeing the clear liquid inside. "Sounds like it. I've never had moonshine," I confessed.

"Goes down like butter." Annabelle touched her glass to mine and took a long swallow. "Perfect way to end the day." Annabelle smiled as she leaned back into Santa's chair, her elf hat pushing forward over the grey curls as she did so. Her cheeks flushed a bit and she looked utterly content.

I was a little jealous of Annabelle's apparent satisfaction with her life, her world. Her ridiculous striped tights. I sipped the drink, forcing myself to swallow down the cough that threatened as the fire slid down my throat. "It's good," I said, the moonshine stealing my voice and leaving me with a throaty whisper.

Annabelle winked and took another sip of her own. "So how is the show coming along?"

"It's not," I said, and took a longer sip. I set down my glass. "I mean, it is, really. Tomorrow I think I'll be firming up details on the last three houses on my list, and now that the crew is here we'll start filming. First one in two days."

"Whose house?" Annabelle asked. "Can I ask?" Her blue eyes glowed with excitement—or moonshine—and her enthusiasm was obvious.

"Um, I don't know if I remember all the names. Tanner, I think. Do you know them?" I was already feeling a little buzz in my head from the moonshine. I took another sip.

"Of course, the Tanners. Lovely family. Lottie runs the little bakery cafe on the corner over on the square. Her daughter Paige is the local family doctor. She has a younger daughter too, Amberlynn, and an older one, Adeline, but Addie doesn't live here anymore. Little town wasn't big enough for her, I guess." Annabelle shook her head as if she couldn't understand how Singletree might be too small for anyone. "You'll probably have to film around the rodents over there, though."

Concern straightened my spine. "Rodents?" I pictured a run-down house, infested with mice or rats. That wouldn't work. How had this house gotten past Juliann? The rodents must be new. I needed to get over to the Tanners' first thing.

"They might be marsupials, actually. I'm not sure."

"Annabelle, what are you talking about?" I took another bracing swig of the moonshine.

"Chinchillas. Very cute, but extremely naughty. She used to keep them in a cage, but over time they got out, and now they pretty much have the run of the house." Annabelle informed me of this in a very matter-of-fact way, followed by a little hiccup.

"I see." I felt my eyes widening as I finished off my drink. "I guess I don't know much about ... chinchillas. Are they, like, pretty big?" I was picturing kangaroos, I knew that, but that was the only marsupial I could think of. And those got big. I'd seen a YouTube video where one was at someone's backdoor, scratching with knife-like talons at the screen and standing there with a chest muscled like a prize fighter's.

"No, silly," Annabelle laughed at my marsupial ignorance. "They're little. Like roly poly little fur balls. About yay big." She held her hands out, showing me something approximately the size of a softball.

"That's not tiny," I said.

"Maybe Lottie will dress them up for the show!" Annabelle appeared delighted by this idea, and my stomach soured as I pictured rats wearing Santa hats and carrying candy canes in long yellow teeth.

Annabelle may have sensed my need to change the subject, because she got her giggles under control and her smile faded into a more serious expression. "And how are things going with the playboy?"

Callan. I leaned back, forgetting for a moment that my stool didn't have a comfortable cushioned back like Annabelle's. I nearly fell over backwards, but righted myself just before my balance was too far off and leaned forward instead, dropping my elbows onto the table top next to my drink. "That's not going too well, actually. I don't think he's going to be willing to let the crew film his house." I squeezed my eyes shut, remembering Callan's rigid posture as the cameraman had spoken to him. "He seems really ... angry." I pictured his face again. "No, wait. Not angry exactly. Hurt, maybe. He seems like he's been hurt, I guess."

"Didn't he have some kind of injury? Isn't that why he doesn't play for the Minnows anymore?" Annabelle's voice hid a shade of the dislike she'd already expressed for Singletree's newest celebrity addition.

"Yeah," I said. "And I think it was the Sharks, by the way. They play in San Diego."

Annabelle's face brightened and she sat up, her voice turning low, reverent. "Isn't that the team that has the Fuerte Fire?" Clearly, Annabelle admired Fernando Fuerte, who I knew had joined the team around the time Callan was injured. He was easy to admire. But he didn't have that same soulful gaze that Callan Whitewood did.

"Right. I think so."

"Hmmm," Annabelle said, and I figured there might have been some billboards out here too.

"His brother said something kind of interesting to me too," I said, finding that talking about Callan was actually something I wanted to do and realizing almost at the same time that my interest in him might be slightly more than professional.

"What did he say?"

I considered my words, feeling almost like maybe I was sharing something too personal to Callan. But then I remembered his anger at me and went ahead. "He said that the thing his brother needs most is a reason to get up every day. That he's lost everything and that everything he ever believed his life was about has been taken from him."

"Well, I'd be hurt too, I guess," Annabelle said, her face softening a little. "How did Callan react when you went over there?"

I thought about my afternoon, about Callan's quick assertion to his nieces that we'd be attending the Nutcracker together and the careful flirting I was pretty sure had come after that. But then it had all turned. Confusion swept through my mind. "At first he was pretty cold," I said. "But then he kind of warmed up. His nieces were over—he's watching them, I guess—and we all decorated the Christmas tree he'd gotten for them, and things were pretty nice."

"Woah, really?" Annabelle said, dropping her empty glass hard on the table top. "Is that a normal part of your job—decorating and hanging out?"

I shook my head slowly. "Not really. I mean, the decorating part, kind of. I need to do whatever I can to get the houses set up for shooting. In Callan's case, that's pretty much everything. He's barely moved in, let alone decorated."

Annabelle lifted an eyebrow, making her elf hat tilt slightly to one side. One of her ears had become slightly detached and was askew, giving her the look of a deranged elf. "But you looked all gooey and cute when you were talking about the tree and the little girls." She pointed a finger at me. "You like him."

A little trickle of fear rolled through me as I downed the second glass of moonshine Annabelle had poured while I was talking. Did I? I certainly liked the way he looked. And maybe part of me felt a little pull to be what Cormac had suggested—to be a reason for Callan to move forward. But the last thing I needed was to become personally involved in another show I was working on. That was how I'd ended up here in the first place, swamped in a holiday I detested.

"I'm just trying to do my job," I said weakly.

"You're not a very good liar," Annabelle told me, pouring a bit more moonshine and then slamming it like a shot. She hiccupped and her other ear began to droop.

"Think we should lay off the moonshine?" I asked, feeling a bit tipsy myself. "Do you have to drive home?"

Annabelle began to giggle, swaying slightly side to side. "I'm just across the square. Apartment."

That wasn't the answer I had expected. I thought Annabelle must be someone's mother, must go home to a big house completely coated in Christmas, and a husband wearing a horrible sweater. But now that I looked, I noticed Annabelle's hands were free of jewelry, save for the reindeer ring on the middle finger of her right hand.

"Shall I walk you?" I asked, suddenly realizing I was becoming too involved with everyone here. I needed to get in, do my damned job, and get out. I wondered if the holiday cheer that infected this place like the black plague might be influencing me somehow. I'd thought I was immune, but the sound of jingle bells was insipid, worming in and striking when you least expected it. One time, years ago, I had found myself singing along to *White Christmas* when I was a little drunk and had sworn it would never happen again. I needed to harden my shields. No ex-soccer stars. No feeling sorry for lonely innkeepers. I had a job to do.

I walked Annabelle across the square outside, stopping to pick up the woman's ears as they toppled off and landed on the sidewalk along the way. I was unsurprised to find a sled leaned up against the corner outside Annabelle's door, decorated and painted. I had plenty of time to read it while Annabelle searched her purse for her keys. It read "Jingle all the Way." I smiled at the sentiment and at the innkeeper's single-minded obsession with the holidays, but then noticed another sentence painted in much smaller letters below. I squatted down to get a better look. It read, "Because no one likes a half-assed jingler."

I burst out laughing, and Annabelle shot me a confused look. When I pointed at her sign, Annabelle laughed along with me.

She'd found her keys and her door stood open. "Come in?"

I gave her arm a pat. "Another time," I said, feeling a little sad at the darkness that was beyond the door, no one to welcome Annabelle home—not even a chinchilla, I guessed. "Thanks for tonight."

Annabelle flashed a bright, half-drunk smile and went in. And I walked back to the inn, my mind simultaneously telling me to keep my distance and trying to figure out how to help the two loneliest people I'd met in a while as the moonshine buzzed through my veins, making me feel warm.

"Oh, hello!" A woman called before I had even managed to take three steps up the front path of the house where I'd just parked. This, according to my list, was the Tanners' house. It was an older Victorian style home, kind of like the inn, and it featured a wraparound front porch. The woman calling and waving to me from the railing had evidently been sitting on the porch, enjoying an afternoon cocktail with another, older, woman, who remained seated.

"Who is it, Lottie? Want me to shoot 'em?" the other woman said loudly, adding a cackle to the end of the question.

"Shush, Helen," Lottie said, turning to her friend. "We don't shoot guests."

"That's your first problem," the older woman said loudly. "Don't decide until you see who it is."

I approached the woman at the railing somewhat cautiously, hoping her friend didn't decide to go all vigilante and take matters into her own hands. Upon closer inspection, I doubted the old woman was actually packing. She had to be at least eighty, and she seemed too busy sipping a cocktail to be really prepared to shoot anyone.

"Hi there," I said to the friendlier of the pair. "I'm April Hall, from *Holiday Homes*?"

The woman on the porch squealed and clapped her hands. "Oh thank heavens," she said. "I thought maybe I'd been dropped from the list. I'm Lottie Tanner. Come in, come in!" She sang this last part and waved me up onto the wide porch, which was draped in garlands and smelled like a pine forest had been decimated and then made into a tea. Lottie

Tanner, on the other hand, wore a simple red sweater and a pair of dark jeans with black boots. Her hair was cut in a wedge style, longer around her face, which was plump and pretty and friendly.

The older woman, who wore a sweat suit I was pretty sure I'd seen Lizzo wearing in a recent interview, scowled at me.

"Don't mind Helen," Lottie said, waving a hand at her friend. "She's suspicious by nature. Plus she's older than Santa and it makes her grumpy."

"You're no spring chicken, Lotts," Helen said, lifting her drink.

"Well," Lottie said, waving away Helen's observation. "What can I do for you, April? Manhattan?"

It was barely noon, and I didn't think drinking quite this early was a good way to salvage what was left of my job here. I needed to nail down two other homes this afternoon and potentially replace Callan's house if he wouldn't come around. "No thanks. I just need to ensure that everything is ready for the crew to come tomorrow."

"Not to worry! Everything is all ready. All my little chinchees are so excited." Right. The chinchillas. Lottie looked past my shoulder. "You're coming too, right, Helen?"

I cringed a bit. I was pretty sure I didn't need the addition of a grumpy gun-toting grandmother to my list of problems.

Before Helen could answer, Lottie leaned in, "She's Juliet Manchester's grandmother. Did you know Juliet was from this area?"

"No," I said, surprise coloring my voice. I didn't know that. "Wow." I was definitely a fan of Juliet's.

"And did you know Ryan McDonnell bought a house here? He's marrying Helen's other granddaughter, Tess." Lottie nodded proudly now that she'd listed the celebrity-related attributes of her hometown.

"And now you've got Callan Whitewood to add to the list," I said before I could stop myself. "His home is supposed to be on the show too." Why did I constantly find myself making excuses to talk about him? Plus, I realized too late, Callan seemed to prize his privacy. But Annabelle had already known he was in town. He couldn't hide from his neighbors for long, right?

"Whitewood?" Helen asked loudly. "The Sharks player? The underwear model with the broken leg?"

I didn't think that was the way Callan would really want to be described, but it was clear the old woman knew who I was talking about. I was about to tell her she was right, but she went on.

"That fella was my only reason for watching soccer for a while. No one wore a pair of white shorts quite the way he managed them. I liked to watch him warm up, if you know what I mean, stretching that fabric this way and that over that tight round—"

"Behave!" Lottie barked, putting a hand toward Helen in the way you might quiet a dog. Lottie wiped her hands on her pants, taking a deep breath and focusing on April again. "Well, I'm sure Mr. Whitewood is every bit as excited about having his home featured on your show as I am."

If only that were true. "Right." I pulled the folder from my bag. "Is there somewhere we can go over the contract and the schedule for tomorrow?" I angled my head toward the front door, hoping maybe the rest of the conversation might go forward without the benefit of Helen's none-too-helpful insights. Now I found myself thinking about what Callan would look like stretching in a pair of white shorts, and some very unwanted tingling sensations were breaking out in parts of my body that should definitely not be involved with work. These tingly parts were the ones that had cost me the last job, and I couldn't lose this one.

"Shall I show you the rest of the house, first? So you can be sure we're appropriately festive?"

I glanced through the front window, which was frosted with spray snow, to the living room inside. Every surface had something Christmassy atop it, and through the pungent pine garland scent, I was catching wafts of cinnamon and vanilla. "I'm sure it's all great," I said, hoping to avoid being immersed in holiday hell.

"You have to see the gingerbread village Paige helped me make," Lottie said, pulling open the front door for me. "That's my daughter," she went on as we followed a hallway toward another room where a decorated tree stood in the corner and a large table held a very realistic gingerbread village. A small round pom pom sat next to the gingerbread village looking soft and plush and somewhat out of place. And then it moved. I let out a little squeal of surprise as the pom pom turned to cast a guilty glance at us.

I realized this was a chinchilla. It was eating part of one of the gingerbread buildings, but Lottie swatted at it and it scurried away, leaping from the table and underneath the couch.

"She's a doctor," Lottie said.

"That ...? The ... Um, the chinchilla is a doctor?"

Lottie burst out laughing at that. "What? A doctor? No, dear, don't be ridiculous. That chinchilla is simply an adorable nuisance. That one is Apollo. My daughter is a doctor," she clarified.

"Wow," I said, turning back to the gingerbread. "Is this ...?" I bent over the little model, with its big tree in a central square and buildings all around. One looked very much like the inn. "Is this Singletree?"

Lottie clapped her hands in delight. "It is!"

Despite the turning of my stomach at the thick smell of Christmas all around me, I managed a smile. "It's amazing, Lottie. Really very nice." I turned back toward the front door, deciding that sitting with Helen was preferable to lingering in the thick holiday miasma that filled the Tanner house, not to mention the chance of chinchilla bite. Did chinchillas bite? I wasn't willing to risk it.

The scents were inspiring memories that flung themselves through my mind one after another, all of them posing as cheery and bright until the final closing of the front door of my childhood home flashed back to me, dropping a stone in the center of my chest. I swallowed hard.

"Are you all right, April?" Lottie's hand found my arm, and I was being guided back to the porch. "You look white as a snowman," she commented, settling me next to Helen.

"It's white as a ghost, dammit," Helen muttered. "Why does everyone in this town insist on over-Christmasing every little thing? Did you see the town sign? Someone graffitied it and crossed out 'Single' so now the place is called 'Christmas Tree,' for fuck's sake."

I realized maybe I had a holiday-hating ally in the abrasive old woman at my side. "Too much," I managed to say, despite feeling particularly unwell all of a sudden.

Lottie had gone in to get some water and bustled back out now, shushing her friend and putting a plate of gingerbread men and a glass of water in front of me before sitting down.

"Even if you don't like Christmas, though," Helen said, snatching a cookie from the plate, "You'll like these. Lotts is the best baker in town."

"Thanks, Helen." The women exchanged a fond look, and I felt even more unwell. Something about the close bond these women clearly shared—had probably shared for years—made me feel lonely. I knew I wasn't doing very well at my job, but now I realized maybe I'd been doing a pretty piss poor job at life in general. What did I have to show for myself?

I took a cookie and bit into it, chewing and washing down the soft ginger-flavored cookie with water.

"And?" Lottie was watching me.

"These are amazing," I said honestly, feeling a bit of life coming back to me. If all else failed, maybe I could just live on my mother's couch and eat cookies. These just about made up for everything else. "You made these?" I asked, looking at Lottie with renewed admiration.

"I have a bakery in town," Lottie said, waving away the compliment. "It's what I do. Baking's the only thing I've ever been much good at."

"Well these are fantastic," I said. I washed down the last bite of the cookie and opened the folder I'd dropped on the table. "Okay, so this is pretty straightforward." I reviewed the existing contract with Lottie and went through the details so she'd know what to expect during filming. "Mostly, you just follow directions as they go through the house. You've indicated which rooms are off limits here," I pointed to the form, "so it should all be smooth. It'll take several hours, and then you'll be done. And actually, you really don't need to be here unless you want to be, except to let us inside."

"You can hang out at my house," Helen offered.

"Not if you're just going to play video games while I watch," Lottie sniffed, clearly having experienced this type of hospitality before. "Plus, I want to be here."

"Suit yourself," Helen said, taking another cookie and biting into it with obvious relish.

"Okay, then we'll see you tomorrow," I said. "Any chance maybe the chinchilla could be like, in a cage, during filming?"

"Who, Apollo?" Lottie looked surprised. "Well, maybe. I can usually lure him with food. But Adonis and Poseidon and Pat are not so easily captured, I'm afraid."

"Pat," I repeated somewhat moronically, my head spinning.

"She's not godlike at all," Helen explained.

I took another cookie and searched for appropriate words, but found none. After a few seconds, I nodded, hoping that would indicate that we were finished here, and got to my feet.

"Perfect," Lottie said as we stood. "Here, take these with

you." She produced a baggie full of gingerbread cookies from just inside the front door and handed them to me.

I accepted them, getting into my car with a wave, and had one in my hand as I drove away.

If all else failed, at least I had cookies.

10

SECRETS IN THE SHACK

CALLAN

I got up to begin my day and found myself feeling strangely lighter than I had in the past months. I wasn't sure if it was the oddly homey feeling my house had now, all decorated for the holidays, or if it was the after-effects of the time I'd spent with my nieces the day before.

Or if it was something else.

My mind had circled around thoughts of April Hall as I had finished decorating the house after Cormac and the girls left. It had been strange, actually. I'd pictured her in the house as I'd finished hanging the garland on the mantle-piece, imagined us sitting together in front of the fire, thought of us looking at the twinkling tree on a cold night. It was like decorating the house had passed me through some kind of temporal warp into a Hallmark holiday movie. And while there were bits of my own holiday movie that were definitely too explicit for the Hallmark channel, I also found myself thinking how nice it would be just to have someone—maybe

April—here, in this big house with me. Which was weird, because the whole point of buying a big house in the middle of nowhere was to be alone.

I knew it was probably ridiculous—I didn't really think April and I were destined to settle down and live happily ever after or anything like that. It was more likely that I'd been so wrapped up in myself and my injury and my failed career for so long, that now that I was finally establishing a new life, my mind was ready to populate it with other things. And April had popped up just in time to take a spot in my imaginings. Despite my fascination with her thick dark hair and the way her hips curved and swayed when she moved, I was pretty sure any woman who'd appeared just when she had would have given me a welcome mental distraction from my own misery. It wasn't April specifically.

Still, I thought, as I made coffee and took it out to the back porch, I probably owed her an apology.

But what about the ridiculous show? The last thing I wanted was to be on television at this point—even if it was just my house that would have to appear. It was always possible that this would turn into something unintended, that the media would take an interest in what had happened to the miserable has-been who'd once filled their newsfeeds and come to pick over what was left of me. I'd finally ducked low enough to avoid the cameras and reporters who'd hounded me for the last year, finally dropped off the radar to the point that they'd moved on to newer spectacles, fresher fare. But if I was suddenly profiled as the newest resident of Singletree, if the show mentioned me at all, there would surely be speculation about everything from my mental state to my grisly injury. And I'd had more than enough of that.

I knew I couldn't really apologize to April without giving her a firm answer about the show. I didn't really want to cost her a job.

Maybe there was a way ...

That afternoon, I drove over to the inn, where I knew April was staying. I spotted the camera guys sitting in the lobby, which looked like someone had fired off a holiday cannon, covering every surface with snow, glitter, reindeer, elves, or poinsettias. I lifted a hand in response to the wave one of them gave me, and felt relief flow through me when I realized they were not going to come talk to me despite having recognized me again.

I limped up to the desk, smiling at the woman behind it. Her name tag said "Annabelle."

"Hi there, Annabelle," I said.

She wore a red apron with striped ruffles, and a green shirt beneath it. She also had a Santa hat on her head and round wire-rimmed glasses. Mrs. Claus, I figured.

"Hello," she said. "Can I help you?"

I wasn't sure if she knew who I was or not. Her bright blue eyes were narrowed slightly at me, as if she didn't quite trust me, but her tone was friendly enough. "Yes, please. I was hoping you might be willing to call a guest for me? See if I might speak to her for a moment?"

"There's a lobby phone right over there. Past the nutcrackers and just next to the reindeer."

"Oh, right," I said. "Only, I don't know her room number."

"Well, I can't tell you that," the woman said.

"But maybe you could call up and see if she'd be willing to give it to me? Or to call me, maybe? She has my phone number."

Annabelle's brows lowered. "If you have her number, why not just call her?"

"I don't have her number. She has mine." This was becoming tedious. I shifted my weight as my ankle throbbed, reminding me that standing up for long periods wasn't a great idea.

"Hmmm," Annabelle said, pressing a candy-cane striped fingernail to the side of her chin as she seemed to think. "All right. I'll call her for you. But April isn't here right now."

Surprise spiked in my mind and I frowned at her. "How do you know I'm here for April?"

Annabelle's face flushed and she looked surprised too, but then she made an exasperated noise and leaned forward. "Let's just drop all the pretending. I know who you are, and I know you're giving April a hard time about her show. It's a very small town, Mr. Whitewood, something you may have noticed. And we tend to try to treat each other in a friendly manner around here."

"Is that why you're scolding me? This is Singletree's brand of friendly?"

"Oh. No," Annabelle said, recovering herself and looking around guiltily. "No, sorry. That wasn't nice. It's just that ... well, I like April."

"I like April too."

A third voice popped up over my shoulder. "You guys

talking about me?" I turned to find April standing directly behind me, her pale cheeks flushed from being out in the cold, and her gorgeous hair falling around her shoulders.

It was my turn to blush. What had I come here for again? I was having a hard time remembering now, after being chastised by a stranger and then declaring loudly that I 'liked' April as she stood behind me. "Hi, uh ..." I stammered. "Can I talk to you?" I glanced at Annabelle who was watching me with a curious expression.

April hesitated only for the briefest of moments, then said, "Yeah, sure. Hi Annabelle." She smiled at the woman behind the desk, and then moved across the lobby toward a little cottage. "We can talk in here."

I followed her, wondering if there wasn't maybe a conference room or somewhere we could have actual privacy instead of a fake gingerbread house in the corner. "Isn't this Santa's house?"

"He's not here right now," she said. "Mrs. Claus won't mind." She ducked inside and sat in a huge wing-back chair, leaving me a low stool at the table.

"Okay, well," I sat on the little stool, feeling awkward. "Listen, I just wanted to apologize to you."

Her face remained impassive, cold. "Okay. Thanks." She shifted her weight like she was about to stand up, and I found myself wishing vehemently that she'd stay.

"So, I'm sorry, April. I was rude and harsh, and—"

"No, you were right. I was trying to make you do something you clearly don't want to do, and I wasn't taking no for an answer." She leaned back in the chair again. "I should have just walked away."

"You still didn't deserve me being rude. You were just trying to do your job."

She shrugged. "Doesn't matter."

I wasn't sure why her attitude had changed so dramatically, but I realized I didn't like this beaten-down version of the fiery determined girl who'd barged into my house that first day. I wanted to bring her back. "Why not?"

"I've got all the other houses lined up. It'll just have to be enough. I didn't want to do this show in the first place." She sighed and put her elbows on the little table between us. "It was just that I had to leave my previous show, and my uncle runs the network. This was the only thing he'd give me, and it's my last chance. But I'm starting to realize that maybe television production isn't my passion anyway. Maybe I don't care."

"You seemed pretty passionate that first day when you popped into my house uninvited," I said, trying to get a rise out of her, bring back some of the fire in her eyes.

She squinted for a second, like she was thinking about that. "Yeah, well, I was worried about getting fired."

"So are you going to get fired?"

"Probably." She stood up. "Not your problem though."

As she crossed the tiny room in front of me, I reached out and grabbed her hand without thinking. But as soon as I held her warm skin between my fingers, my mind raced, and my heart accelerated. I didn't want April Hall to walk away from me, and I didn't want her to lose her job because of me. "Listen," I said, as she turned and looked down at to where I still held her hand. "Maybe it'd be okay. The filming thing."

"What?" Her eyes found my face and I reluctantly dropped her hand. "What about your privacy, and your peace, and your general desire to be surly and miserable and alone in your big old house?"

"Ouch." I stood to face her in the close space, the size of the cottage forcing us to stand just inches apart. "I deserved that, I guess." I imagined I could feel the warmth radiating off her body, and I could definitely smell her—vanilla and citrus and cinnamon. Wild thoughts ran through my head, and I imagined myself lifting a hand to bury in all that thick hair, pushing her back against the wall and kissing her hard. I tried to clear my mind but was finding it very difficult as April stared up at me through dark thick lashes.

"Are you serious?" Her voice was almost a whisper, and her eyes were locked on mine, pulling me in. "About the show?"

I meant to say yes. I meant to agree to let them film my house and then go back to my car and go home. But my mind was working through other scenarios, and I couldn't seem to control it. And my mouth and my mind were running their own plays, ignoring the advice of my better judgment. "Have dinner with me," my mouth said while my better judgment stood on the sidelines yelling, "no, you moron! What the hell are you doing?" It was weird how my better judgment sounded a lot like the Sharks' old coach.

"What?" April looked as surprised as I felt at the words that had just come from my mouth.

I was already in it. So I went ahead. Hesitation never won me a thing. Not on the pitch. Maybe not here. "Have dinner with me. We'll talk about it."

Her chest was rising and falling, and she stood there without saying anything for a long minute, her eyes wide. "Okay," she finally said. "Dinner. We'll talk about it." She ducked out the door then, breaking the spell that had held us inches from one another, staring into each other's eyes, breathing the same air. And as I followed her from Santa's house and back into the over-decorated lobby, something I hadn't felt in a long time took root in my chest and glowed there.

I realized the feeling was hope.

7

I walked just behind April as we left the hotel, descending the front steps and arriving on the sidewalk as a chilly wind blew through the small town of Singletree. And once there, we stopped and looked at each other.

"Where do people eat here?" I asked her. I hadn't left my house often and had definitely not been out exploring the culinary options in my new town.

April shook her head slowly, her eyes never leaving my face. "I have no idea."

"There must be something. Come on." We wandered up to the town square, where an enormous sleigh now sat on the grassy area near the central tree, the reins attached to a single feeble-looking reindeer. As we walked by, I got a better look at the thing, and while the sleigh was enormous, gleaming beneath a sheen of enamel red paint, the deer had absolutely seen better days. Its fur was coming off in patches, and one side of its head was pressed in a bit, making the eye on that side point in the wrong direction.

"What happened here?" April wondered aloud. "Poor little guy. Looks like he's seen better days. Where are all the other reindeer? Aren't there supposed to be like six or seven? Dasher, Dancer, Rudolph?"

I nodded. "This must be Thrasher."

April stopped walking. "I'm not a holiday expert, but I'm pretty sure there's no reindeer named Thrasher."

"Well, you don't hear about him much," I told her. "He's the hard hard-partying reindeer. Tends to overdo it and alienate the others, who are way more puritanical. You know Blitzen? He's in that twelve-step program now, and Prancer is a tee-totaler."

April's eyes widened as she held in a laugh, her cheeks turning pink. "Oh really?" She said, letting out a little guffaw. "Tell me more. I had no idea you were such a wealth of esoteric Christmas lore."

"Esoteric Christmas lore is my specialty," I quipped, nearly desperate to keep April smiling and laughing. This. This was the girl who'd bounced into my house that first day. My brain hummed as I realized how much I wanted to keep her.

We crossed behind the sleigh, both of us heading for the glowing restaurant across the way, which appeared to be the only option on the square. We stepped inside together, leaving the cold chill of the street behind as the warm atmosphere of the restaurant engulfed us.

"Welcome to Sam's Shack," the girl at the podium said.

"Normally I try to limit visits to restaurants called 'shacks' to a minimum," I said quietly into April's ear. "But since this is the only option."

April turned and smiled up at me, her bright eyes glittering in the soft light, and my stomach dropped as my breath caught in my throat. I lifted a hand and it was halfway to her face before I recovered himself. God, I wanted to touch her. She was so beautiful.

"This way," the hostess said, bringing me back to my senses. We followed her, weaving through the crowded seating area to a table in the very back. Little glass balls were suspended from the ceiling next to empty crab catching cages —crab pots, I thought they were called. The whole place smelled of seafood and something spicy. "This is all we have," the hostess said, apologetically. It probably wasn't a prime table, isolated as it was from the center of the dining room. But it was quieter, and a little bit more private, and I thought it was perfect.

"This is great," I said, and I stepped around to take April's coat and hold out her chair for her. She shot a look over her shoulder, like these actions were confusing or unnecessary, but the smile never left her face. I hung both our coats on a hook near the table, and returned, seating myself across from her.

"So," she said, after we'd we'd glanced at the menus.

"So," I agreed, feeling nervous jitters skate through me. I

hadn't been nervous around a woman since high school, but something about April, about the fact that really, this wasn't a date—no matter how much I suddenly wished it were—had me off balance.

"You've got me in your shack. Now what?" she asked.

A low laugh rolled through me. "Did you notice that half the things on the menu come in buckets?"

"I did notice that," she said.

I glanced around, not wanting to offend anyone in my new hometown any more than I might already have done. "This is a strange little place."

"Well, it's home now," April told me. "Guess you'd better develop a taste for Old Bay seasoning." She gazed around us, and I did the same, noticing for the first time that Old Bay was featured prominently in the décor of the little restaurant, with big spice box replicas swinging from the ceiling and old-fashioned prints with Old Bay ads in them on the walls.

"Have I ever had Old Bay before?" I wondered aloud.

She shrugged. "I don't know if I have." She pulled her phone from her bag and tapped the screen a few times. "It's a blend. Paprika, chili powder, celery salt, mustard ..."

"That's a lot of things," I said.

"That's only like half of what's in there."

"Howdy folks, I'm Jeff," said a voice from beside the table, interrupting the discussion of Maryland's favorite spice blend. "Can I bring you a punch bowl or a bucket of Old Bay fries to get started?" Jeff wore an apron with a crab on it that read *Get Crabs at the Shack* in bold letters. He had longish blond hair and bounced a bit as he spoke, as if he'd paused mid-run to help us.

We exchanged an amused look. "A punch bowl?" April asked, picking up her menu again, probably to see if she could figure out what that was.

"One punch bowl, coming right up." Jeff said.

"Better make it two," I told Jeff, wondering what we'd just ordered. "And the bucket sounds perfect."

"Bowls and bucket coming right up!" Jeff practically sang, and wandered away to the next table.

"Oh god, what did we just order?" April asked, still scanning the menu.

"I guess we'll find out."

And we did. A punch bowl, according to the menu, was intended to be shared among two or more people, and had every alcohol known to man (including the local distillery's famous moonshine) in it. The drinks were literal punch bowls, maybe a little smaller than what you'd find on the central table at a garden party, and Jeff set one in front of each of us, along with a very long straw.

"Okay then," April said, shooting me a smile before she wrapped her pretty pink lips around the end of her long straw. My mind drifted as I watched, and I had a sudden urge to get April alone, to kiss her until that pretty pink gloss was gone. I sipped my own drink, trying to maintain control of my racing mind.

The fries did come in a bucket, and they were liberally doused in Old Bay, which I decided I liked. "Kind of spicy, kind of salty," I said, narrowing my gaze at the long spice-covered fry I held. April wrinkled her nose after her first bite.

"Check Old Bay off the list of things I need to try in life," she said.

"You don't like it?"

"It's too confused for a spice," she said, still making that adorable face.

"It's a blend," I suggested.

"I'm a simple girl, I guess." April said this innocently enough, but suddenly everything she said and did struck me as intensely suggestive. I was thankful when Jeff came back to take our crab cake order, breaking the odd sexual tension that I thought might be only in my mind.

"This might actually kill me," April said, after taking a long sip of her punch.

"Do you want something else?" I asked, as April she stared into the huge drink.

"I don't back down from a challenge," she told me, her voice taking on an indignant tone.

"That right?" I asked, liking the fire in her eyes and remembering her determination the first day she'd come to my house.

She paused, tilting her head to one side and looking at me through narrowed eyes. "It is," she said. "So are we going to talk about the contract or not?"

The contract. The show. Right. That was why we'd come to dinner. "Yeah. We should." I already knew I was going to say yes. But I didn't want to give April a reason to say good night. Sitting here, across from this beautiful woman, was the first time in months that I'd felt like myself and not some shell of the guy I once was.

"Okay," she said.

"After dinner," I suggested.

April sighed and crossed her arms, but a tiny smile lifted one side of her mouth. "Which way are you leaning, Callan? Can you at least give me a hint?"

"Right now?" I said, taking a chance. "Toward you." My mind raced. The alcohol and the rampant attraction pulling me toward April had me feeling a little bit unhinged. I didn't have much to lose, and I was speaking almost before I'd decided to do so.

April's brows lifted in surprise, but she recovered quickly. "Okay, sports star, listen. This charming act might have worked for you in the past, but I've got a job to do. A bowl of moonshine and some fries coated in crap are not enough to make me forget that you are singlehandedly standing in the way of me getting it done."

"Best place I've stood in a while." I couldn't help it. April Hall was beautiful, but April Hall getting worked up and determined? She was fucking gorgeous.

She rolled her eyes, but a little pink blush was climbing her neck, and I wondered suddenly if that gorgeous shade of pink covered her smooth perfect chest. I could see the hollow at the base of her throat, thanks to the V-neck sweater she wore, and the faintly beating pulse there made me want to touch it, trace it with my tongue, maybe. I forced my mind back to the table, to my drink, to April's face. Other parts of my body continued considering what her skin might feel like.

"Look," I said, keeping my voice low. "I'm sorry. I honestly didn't plan to drag you out to dinner and waste your time if you need to get back and focus on work. I know you're not here on vacation, and I don't mean to distract you. It's only that ..." I ducked my head for a second, gathering my nerve. I took a big swallow of my punch. "It's just, I haven't really been myself in a long time. And I don't know why, but when I'm around you, I feel more like myself than I have in a while." Maybe ever, I added mentally.

April had that look on her face again, the narrowed eyes, head-tilted expression that she seemed to use when she was trying to figure something out. She pressed her lips firmly together, opened them as if to respond, and then pressed them together again. Finally, after what felt like years to me, she responded. "I have no idea what to say to that."

Great. I dropped her eyes, staring into my enormous bowl. Making myself vulnerable with women wasn't something I'd done a lot of before, and now I understood why. It would have been less humiliating to strip naked in the middle of this shack than to have April reject me after I'd basically just told her I was interested in her.

But she hadn't finished speaking, it seemed.

"I'm not really accustomed to things like this," she said, and I lifted my eyes in time to see her motioning between us, or maybe at the table in general.

"To things like Sam's Shack? Or bowls full of moonshine?" I hoped humor might distract her from the fact I'd basically just laid as much of myself bare as I was able to and she'd ignored me.

She cleared her throat and the beautiful pink blush climbed higher on her cheeks. "No, I mean ... to having honest conversations about whatever might be going on."

I realized she was talking about us. About whatever might be going on with us. Which meant there might actually be something going on. But I'd already thrown myself out there and didn't have the strength to do it again. Not so boldly, at least. "Oh," I said, as if I'd just understood her meaning. "Right. Well, so there's this show you produce, see? And I won't let you film in my house. So we're talking about that, and you're going to try to convince me."

She slumped back in her chair slightly, as if realizing I was not going to be straightforward at this point. "Right."

"So when are you going to start?" I asked, grinning at her.

"Start what?"

"Trying to convince me."

"Callan, I've been trying since I met you. You're evidently the most impossible and stubborn man to ever slurp punch from a bowl inside a shack."

I laughed at that. "Maybe I am." I ate a few fries, watching her, and decided to try one more time. "You done trying to convince me, then?" God, I hoped she wasn't done.

"I already know money won't work, and legal threats don't work either," she said. "Common decency doesn't seem to be your thing, since you don't care if I lose my job ..." she trailed off, and then, out of nowhere, a huge hiccup flew from her lips. Her hand went to her mouth and her eyes widened in surprise. "'Scuse me!" The blush deepened.

Oh, this was good. She was completely and adorable adorably embarrassed.

My head had begun to swim a bit as I found the bottom of my punchbowl, and I looked across the table, realizing April's drink was already gone. Jeff arrived just then, sweeping in with two more drinks and two plates of crab cakes on a platter, which he set down next to the table.

"Oh god, no more punch," April said in a half moan, followed by another loud hiccup.

"Courtesy of the women at the end of the bar," Jeff told us, and I peered down to see two older women giggling to one another and waving. One of them wore a very trendy track suit with a few gold chains around her neck, and the other was dressed in a simple sweater.

"Who are they?" I asked.

"That's Helen and Lottie," April said, waving a hand. "Lottie's house is on the show. Helen is just trying to see what will happen if I drink another one of these, I think."

"Huh," I said. "Well, you don't have to drink it."

April hiccupped again. "I told you, I don't back down from a challenge." She hiccupped again and then began eating, just as the Shack's sound system cranked into a higher volume, blasting "Jingle Bell Rock" throughout the small space.

"Oh god," April moaned, covering her face with her hands. "I hate Christmas music."

I stared at her. "What? No one hates Christmas music."

"They do. People totally do. I do."

"You're in charge of a Christmas-themed show. Your job is to make sure houses are decorated to within an inch of their lives with all things red and green and glittery and magical. You can't hate Christmas music."

"I hate everything about Christmas," she moaned, finally moving her hands and giving me a look so miserable and sad I had no choice but to believe her words.

"I've never met anyone who hates the holidays," I said, thinking back and coming up blank. "April, why?"

She shook her head. "Don't ask."

I thought back to the strange look April had gotten when we decorated the tree, and her comments in Target. She didn't just hate the holidays—something about Christmas must have really affected her. I wanted to know, but I didn't want the evening to end, and I wasn't going to push. "You don't have to tell me."

"Good. I don't talk about it."

"Okay." Now my curiosity was piqued. We ate and drank, the blaring Christmas music making it tough to talk anyway. April plowed through both her food and her drink, and though I had been worried that another drink might put her over the edge, the food seemed to have sobered April up a little. I felt better too, as I paid and helped her into her coat.

11

THRASHER, THE HARD-PARTYING REINDEER

APRIL

The night was brisk and bright as I pulled my coat closer around me. We stepped out onto the square, which was more crowded than I would have expected. Something about the milling crowd of townsfolk combined with two punchbowls full of God only knew what had me leaning into Callan's side slightly as we walked, and he put his arm around me, keeping me there. Warmth grew between us, a cocoon of comfort even in the cold night air, and I stayed there, tucked against his side as we drew closer to the huge tree and the shiny red sleigh in the middle of the square.

I knew I should step away. I should thank him for dinner and head back to the inn, back to my quiet room. At least then I would be in control. This situation—this warmth and nearness to Callan's firm hard body, the feeling I had that somehow we were closer in other ways too—this was a recipe for disaster. I'd been here before, kind of, though I hadn't had this same sense of security at any point with the bachelor on my last show. With him it had been illicit excitement. The thrill of something taboo. This was not that. I didn't know quite what this was, only that I didn't have the strength to separate myself from it, at least not after two punchbowls full of moonshine.

"Thanks for dinner," I said.

"Sure," Callan said, tightening his arm around my waist just a little.

"Maybe we could just sit a minute?" I asked, nearly tripping as we approached the wonky reindeer once again.

Callan's arm tightened around me more, keeping me upright, and we both looked around the square for somewhere to sit. There were people on all the benches, and no low walls or other obvious seating.

An idea flew into my head—an idea that probably wouldn't rank high on the good idea meter. I moved toward the sleigh, and despite Callan's quiet protests, I climbed into the back, making myself comfortable on the low cushioned bench.

"Come on," I coaxed, stifling a hiccup. I wasn't drunk, not exactly. But I was fuzzy enough that the little voice that would have told me what a terrible idea this was had been significantly muted.

"April," Callan hissed from the ground outside. "Come out."

I peeked back up over the side, loving the way he looked standing there staring up at me, his forehead furrowed, his dark eyes glittering in the dim light. "Come in," I suggested.

Something in my voice must have changed his mind, because his face cleared and a moment later, he was clambering up the steps and climbing in next to me. Luckily, the bench was so low that our heads weren't visible over the tall sides of the bright red sleigh, and we were hidden from the world inside it.

Inside the sleigh it was darker and quieter than it had been on the square, and it felt a little bit like we'd entered another world, a private space that was only ours.

We sat side by side, not saying anything, until I scooted close, right up next to Callan. Our thighs were touching and Callan put his arm over my shoulders, and I was suddenly conscious of every inch of him, every firm hard inch of his body.

"This is nice," I said in a soft voice, leaning into him and willing my mind to stay quiet, to let me enjoy the moment, even if it was happening in a sleigh.

"It is," he answered softly.

My mind was turning in slow motion, like the wheels in my head were moving through a landscape filled with cotton candy—or maybe the gears had gotten jammed up thanks to all the glitter they'd been exposed to recently. I knew the way my hand had fallen on Callan's leg wasn't quite innocent, and I knew the buzzing anticipation I felt humming through my blood was definitely not innocent.

When I turned my face up to look at him, my body reacted, unused and abandoned parts of me humming back to life at the connection I felt to those sad dark eyes. I ached to run my fingers along the hard planes of his chest, to trace that angular jaw. He was exotic and familiar, having been a part of my life for a long time in a way, standing guard over me on that billboard and playing in some of my fantasies, even before I'd known the actual man. Now here he was, and I could feel an opportunity arising between us, I just didn't know what it was an opportunity for, exactly.

My gut was pressing me toward him, telling me to act on the fuzzy warm feelings I was developing for this lonely pained man. It was telling me that life and work were two separate things, and that I could keep them apart, compartmentalize if necessary. My head, on the other hand, was telling me completely different things, tossing out warnings and reminders of the last time I'd gotten too close to someone on a show. But those alarms were muted by my time in the shack with a bowl in front of me, and by the way I sat pressed up against Callan, our bodies forming a bubble of warmth in the cold night air.

I took a deep breath. "So," I said. "This is the part where I'm going to try to convince you."

Callan raised an eyebrow, his chin angling down toward me. "Oh yeah?"

I turned my face up to his and met his eyes with my own. "Yeah." I stretched up, and as gently as a whisper, pressed my lips to his. It was a brief touch, a test maybe. But it was also an invitation, and Callan accepted. His arms went around me, and he leaned down, taking my mouth with his own as the removed din of the square and the faint Christmas music in the distance faded, and a soft, welcome pleasure filled my mind.

Callan's mouth was hot and insistent, and his tongue traced the seam of my lips until I parted them, and then pressed forward, teasing my own, and made me press myself nearer still. My body was lighting up, parts of me that had been in hibernation, draped in a blanket of self-doubt, stress, and worry, pushed off the covers and sat up, looking around eagerly at this new situation.

A little moan escaped my lips, and Callan immediately pulled me closer, his arms tightening. His hand slipped beneath my coat, sliding up my back beneath my sweater, his firm warm palm hard against my back, and my mind reeled. I wanted him to touch me, to trace the lines of me, to kiss me like this and never stop. I didn't care if there were consequences, I only cared that Callan Whitewood made me feel something I'd never felt before—not only when he kissed me, but just by being next to me.

I slid a leg over his lap so I was facing him, my hot center pressed against the erection I felt straining at the seam of his jeans, and I moved slowly, increasing the friction and feeling my breath coming faster. Callan's hands were both on my back now, and my body was beginning to flare up as if it had been waiting for something, for this exact moment. With anticipation banishing all my doubts, I pressed my breasts against Callan's hard chest, kissing him deeper, and light exploded against my closed eyelids.

Which was strange. I was close, but I wasn't that close. I wondered for a split second if I was having a cardiac event or something. My heart was definitely racing. Was it just the kiss? The amazing connection?

Then I realized with horror that it was an actual light.

A spotlight, to be precise.

Callan reacted immediately, pulling me down to the bottom of the deep sleigh interior just as a voice boomed somewhere nearby over a microphone. "Welcome Singletree! Thanks for coming out to our annual tree lighting ceremony!" A blast of "Deck the Halls" followed this announcement as we exchanged a horrified look and my stomach twisted, churning over crab cakes and punchbowls and dread. "Please help me welcome Singletree's most honored resident ..." there was a long pause and a drum roll as the sounds of a crowd roared into the once-quiet space of the sleigh. "Santa Claus!"

I sincerely hoped Santa didn't need his sleigh tonight. Callan and I climbed up to the edge of the door opening and peered out, and I was horrified to see the entire town gathered around the tree and the sleigh, and a huge man in a Santa suit striding directly toward us. "Incoming," Callan whispered as we both shrank back down to the floor of the sleigh, side by side.

"Welcome to Singletree, Santa," the announcer called out as a loud "ho ho ho" blared through the speakers. "If you'll just take your spot in the sleigh, you can light up our tree!"

"Oh god," I moaned from my huddle at the foot of the sleigh's interior. "God, I hate Christmas," I added.

This was it. My heart was in my throat as I realized I had done it again—made the exact same mistake all over again, this time in shades of red and green and coated with glitter instead of on a tropical island. But it was like I was acting in my very own version of *Groundhog Day*, doomed to keep losing my job, doomed to keep making the same mistakes. My life was a disaster. I held my breath and waited for the moment to unspool, for my life to implode.

The entire sleigh rocked then with the weight of a very large man climbing the steps to get in. A moment later, Santa's face appeared, looking down at us, as we did our best to sink into the floorboards of the sleigh. "Ho ho ho!" Santa called out, grinning at us. "What have we here?" He asked this last part under his breath, and winked at us, and then turned his head up to face the crowd.

The guy had to be at least six-foot three, and he stood on the floorboards of the sleigh, his head and chest just popping out from the top. Which meant, if he kept our presence on the down low, we could stay there, hiding, and no one would be the wiser. I really hoped Santa was a decent guy.

The crowd was roaring around us, and I huddled in Callan's arms. Part of me knew I should distance myself, move away from him and come up with whatever excuse I was going to give the huge man in the red suit when he asked. But my mind was blank, and there was comfort in those firm strong arms. I pressed my head into Callan's shoulder and clung to him.

"It'll be okay," he murmured as I huddled, my life flashing through my mind on endless repeat, mistake after mistake. "And April?"

I pulled my head back to look at him, comforted by the assurance in his eyes, the way his mouth pulled into the tiniest of smiles.

"You can use my house."

Yes. I nearly jumped up and did a little victory dance, but then realized it might not matter. I'd just gotten what I wanted. Kind of. Callan's house would be in the show, so that was good. But in the meantime, I was on the brink of being discovered in the arms of the homeowner about to have his house featured on the show. Flashbacks to *Run Away with Bridegroom* were flying through my mind, the cameras filming from a hidden alcove around the side of the building as the bridegroom and I had kissed one another on what I'd thought was a secluded beach under the moonlight.

Now here I was again, in the arms of an important part of my new show, about to be exposed by Santa Claus himself. If my hatred of Christmas hadn't yet been firmly cemented, that would definitely do it.

"Rudolph and I are so happy to see so many folks out tonight to celebrate the lighting of the tree! This town was built around this amazing tree, and we are honored to decorate it annually to pay tribute to this holy season of generosity and cheer."

"How can you hate a holy season of generosity and cheer?" Callan whispered, evidently figuring Santa already knew we were here so there was no point in staying silent.

"Shut. Up." I hissed. If anyone else discovered us here, the gossip would spread like moonshine on fire in this small town. And I'd lose my job again. And this time there'd be no second chances. Uncle Rob would probably disown me. Not that he owned me exactly, but the point was clear either way.

"We gather here every year to think about how we can

join together as a town to make each other better, hold one another up. Look around you, at your friends and neighbors. Is anyone struggling this year? Is anyone facing a challenge you could help them handle? This is the best time of year, because it encourages us to step away from the churn of our daily lives and help to bolster those around us."

Callan's arms were still around me, and while I hated the thought of being discovered, I knew I'd be lying if I didn't admit that hiding here, huddled together, with his strong hard hands on my back, wasn't the worst thing in the world. And kissing him? Feeling those firm soft lips pressing and moving on mine all insistent and demanding? Well, parts of me were still high-fiving one another. But the pleasant buzz created by the kiss and the friction of our bodies pressed together—and two enormous bowls full of boozy punch— was wearing off and giving way to anxiety and fear. And to the familiar heaviness in my chest that got heavier every year around this time.

"He says that reindeer is Rudolph," Callan whispered as Santa went on talking about taking care of each other. "I didn't see a red nose."

"Maybe Rudolph's had a hard year," I suggested. "Got in a fight or two with those other asshole reindeer who wouldn't let him play games and whatever."

"No," Callan said. "They're all good now. It's cool."

"Yeah, now that he did the job they couldn't handle. But don't you think there's probably some resentment there? He's like Santa's favorite now, that's gotta get old. Those dudes hate him."

"Never really thought about that," Callan said, pulling away slightly so he could look me in the eye. "I bet you're right."

"Often am."

"So those jealous fuckers broke his shiny nose." He looked pretty mad at the other reindeer right then, and I loved the way he looked ready to throw down on Rudy's behalf.

"I mean, we don't know that," I reminded him.

"And this is also a time of year when some folks really need to work to stay off the naughty list," Santa said loudly, glancing down at us before looking back up at the crowd. "And for those folks who just can't repress that naughty streak, I'd suggest they just try to hang tight and keep quiet, and hope Santa can find it in his big jelly-full heart to chuckle and look the other way." He looked down again, widening his eyes to make his point before looking back out at the people around the tree.

Callan and I stopped debating the scraggly reindeer and sealed our lips shut, watching Santa finish up.

"Without further ho, ho, ho," he shouted. "Light up that tree!" As he sang out this last part, a warm glow filled the bottom of the sleigh. We couldn't see the tree from where we hid, but I could hear the appreciative murmur of the crowd and I could see the shifting colors of the lights reflected against the sleigh's interior. The crowd broke into applause and Santa dropped onto the bench seat and then ducked down to talk to us.

"So, hey," he said, grinning through the big white beard. "I'm Wiley Blanchard."

"Callan Whitewood," Callan said, offering the man a hand.

"April Hall," I whispered, wishing he'd just go away.

"Blanchard," Callan said in a hoarse whisper. "Your family owns the distillery, right?"

"Yep," Wiley said, the hat flopping forward as he nodded. "Have for about a hundred years. You two should come see us. There's a great bar there. It's a good place to ... well, to do whatever you guys are doing here, I think."

"We're not doing anything," I said quickly.

"Right. Well." Santa/Wiley winked. "Nice to meet you guys." He pulled a card from his pocket and handed it down to Callan. I glanced at it, reading the words "HalfCat Distillery" printed over an image of a cat in some kind of wheeled contraption. Before I could ask about the cat, Santa was gone, climbing down from the sleigh and heading back out into the town square.

"I guess we sit tight for a bit," Callan said. At this point, we were both leaned against the side of the sleigh's interior, our legs stretched out before us. Callan's arm was still around my shoulder and I leaned into his side. Though this new intimacy was strange and my uncle surely wouldn't have liked it, I felt like Callan and I had been through something together now, survived, and I made no move to distance myself. Plus, Callan was warm and the air was taking on a more definite chill.

"I knew about the tree lighting," I said. "I just forgot it was tonight."

"Well, a person who abhors the holidays probably wouldn't make a special note about a tree lighting."

"You're the one who wasn't planning to decorate your house for Christmas at all," I pointed out, poking him in the side and hoping to shift the focus from myself.

Callan laughed, but the sound wasn't altogether cheerful. "Yeah, well."

"I've got my reasons, but why do *you* hate the holidays?"

He looked down at me then, the humor gone from his face. "I don't. Not exactly. But I asked you first."

I sighed and then twisted to rise up on my knees and peer out at the square. I felt like maybe I wanted to tell someone. Him, specifically. "I'll tell you," I said, sinking back down. "But not here. It's too cold and it's not a quick story. And then you'll tell me."

"Fine, but I might need another drink for that."

"No worries," I said. There was moonshine back at the hotel. I sank back down and together we waited until the noise in the square had died down and most of the townsfolk had wandered away, back to warmer spots. "Come on. The coast is clear."

We slipped out of the sleigh, Callan stumbling a bit coming as he came down the ladder. I noticed his face darken as he recovered, but I took his arm and smiled up at him. "Let's go to the inn," I suggested.

"More time in Santa's cottage?" Callan asked. "If I didn't know better, I'd say you actually have kind of an obsession for Santa-related things."

"Definitely not true," I said as we turned down the side street toward the inn. "It's more of a lack of other options in this nutty town. And I was thinking we could go upstairs." I paused and glanced up at him, realizing that suggesting he come to my room could be a little forward. "Privacy," I explained, hoping Annabelle and everyone else might be too distracted with the tree lighting to notice me dragging Callan Whitewood up to my room.

"Okay," Callan said, and we mounted the stairs and went into the inn, me leading the way to the elevator. I usually took the stairs up to my room, but Callan's limp had gotten worse over the course of the night and I was worried about him a little bit.

My heart was in my throat as I pushed open the door to my room and stepped inside, turning on the lights and then holding the door for Callan to follow. I hadn't intended to have company when I left the room earlier, so I did a quick visual scan to make sure there were no unmentionables lying out in plain sight.

There were none.

What was out in plain sight, however—and what had definitely not been there earlier—was an elf costume laid over the edge of the bed, complete with pointy shoes, striped tights and pointy ears like the ones Annabelle had been wearing the night before.

There was a card folded atop the costume, and I picked it

up and read quickly: *Thanks for walking me home. Thought you liked my outfit, so I got you one to match. A-*

"Nice," Callan noted, and I turned to find him looking down at the ridiculous outfit over my shoulder.

"They keep giving me things," I said, my tone more exasperated than intended. I gestured to the once-useful table that now held the enormous gingerbread house.

Callan glanced around the room, his eyes lingering on the sad stripped tree and the ribbon dangling from the mantlepiece, left over from my undecorating the first night. "Kind of seems like they forgot to finish decorating," he said.

I gestured him to a chair to sit down by the gas fire and switched it on. "No, I moved everything I could. There was so much red and green and glittery gaudiness in here I couldn't even think."

"The woman whose job it is to make other people decorate their homes takes the time to UN-decorate her hotel room."

I moved to the desk, where the enormous gift basket sat. I'd pulled cookies and chocolate out over the last day or two, and remembered seeing a little bottle with the HalfCat label in there somewhere. "I enjoy irony," I said flatly, finding the bottle. "Aha!" I held it up.

Callan had sat in one of the chairs by the little round table, and as I looked at him there, I had a rush of doubt. I'd brought a man to my room. Not just a man, but the most important part of the show I was supposed to be producing for my uncle. My job—my life, really—depended on me not screwing things up, and I was in the midst of repeating my most recent horrible mistake. Still, when my eyes met Callan's, it was hard to feel like it was wrong.

Callan smiled and pointed at the bottle in my hand. "The HalfCat again. I guess that's a thing."

I peered at the picture on the label. It was the same drawing from the business card Wiley had given us, but now I had time to really look at it. It was a drawing of a fluffy cat sitting a chair of sorts—a wheelchair, really. The cat had only its front legs, and the back of its body sat in the little chair. The absence of back legs didn't seem to bother the cat—at least not the cartoon one—if the silly grin on its face was any indication. "Poor cat," I said quietly. "What a weird mascot to choose."

"Maybe it's a real cat."

I looked up and met Callan's eyes. "No, it can't be."

"We should probably visit the distillery and find out."

My impulse was to agree immediately. To make plans for tomorrow and the next day, and next month with this man whose dark eyes made me feel warm and tingly inside, whose gaze made me feel understood and really seen all at once. But I'd jumped into things too quickly before, and technically, this was a work arrangement, no matter how much I might have liked for it to be something more. "Yeah, maybe."

If my sudden reluctance bothered Callan, he didn't show it. Instead he rose and pulled two glasses from the top of the dresser under the television and returned to the table. As I poured out a couple fingers each of the HalfCat, he watched me with a careful smile on his face. God, those lips were sexy. My body was tingling again at his proximity.

"So who goes first?" he asked. "You, I think."

I sat across from him, picking up my glass and staring into the brown liquid. "Fine." I swallowed the contents of the glass, intending to roll smoothly into the fastest version of the story I could. Instead, my throat ignited and I erupted in a sputtering coughing fit caused by the fire I'd just thrown down my gullet.

Callan looked alarmed, but when he stood up to try to help, I waved him off, doubled over and gasping in my chair. When I could manage, I coughed out, "Water. Please."

He complied and when I'd finally managed to get a few sips and ease the coughing fit a bit, I smiled at him, my watery eyes meeting his. "I'm okay." This was not the same stuff Annabelle had given me the other night. This had a touch of cinnamon or something. Probably some carcinogenic Christmas-related spices. Like nutmeg and arsenic.

"The cat's not messing around," he said. He sipped his own drink, his eyebrows rising in appreciation.

I had regained my breath, and with the additional bracing warmth of the alcohol sliding through me, I told Callan the story I had only told a couple times before. To my mother. To Lynn. And now to Callan.

"I was seven," I began, wishing suddenly for more bourbon but knowing I'd be on the floor if I drank anything else. "And it was Christmas Eve." I closed my eyes briefly, the painful image of my childhood home flickering to life in my mind like some well-worn photograph behind glass. "I lived with my parents, and we always went really big decorating for the holidays, so my house was completely decked out. I would have loved this town back then," I said, shaking my head lightly, thinking about it as what felt like an ancient sadness washed through me. "We'd had dinner, and I'd gotten to open one gift—that was our tradition. I remember exactly what it was because I thought it was such a big deal at the time."

"What was it?" Callan asked, his voice low and quiet.

I smiled and shrugged. I remembered everything about opening that gift, because it was the last Christmas present I'd ever opened before the holiday had soured for me. I remembered the green paper, the little white bow, the proud smile on my mother's pretty face and the way Mom had glanced at Dad, whose expression stayed neutral, even as I had squealed in delight. Grief shot through me and I took a steadying breath. "Just a stupid necklace. But it was the first jewelry I'd ever gotten. It was a heart with my birthstone in it. Not a big deal really, but it was to me. It was gold and I thought it was so fancy, and I wanted to wear it immediately, but my mom thought I should wait until I had an occasion, so she tucked it back under the tree. I still remember how it caught the lights and sparkled. Since my birthday is in April, the birthstone was a diamond. I'm sure it wasn't a real diamond—my parents struggled for money. But it was the prettiest thing I'd ever seen, either way."

"Sounds beautiful," Callan said, his voice low and reverent, and his dark eyes on my face as I spoke.

My heart stuttered as I remembered the rest, steadying myself to get it out without tears. "I couldn't sleep after my parents tucked me in, and I wanted to get up and get my necklace. Just to look at it a bit more. So I got up." I closed my eyes hard and then opened them, avoiding Callan's gaze. "And my dad was in there, pulling on his coat. The tree was right by the front door. He had a duffle bag with him, and I was really confused, so I asked him where he was going."

Callan nodded.

"He told me that he'd been helping Santa for years. That he went out on Christmas Eve to help distribute gifts, and not to worry."

"I'm guessing he wasn't helping Santa?" Callan asked, a hand gripping the armrest on the chair as if bracing himself for the end of the story.

All the shame and guilt I'd felt my whole life crashed down on me and my voice broke. "Of course not, but I was seven. I didn't understand until the next day, when he wasn't home, that he'd been in the middle of leaving us when I caught him. And even then, I was sure he'd come back. It seemed so impossible, in the midst of all that sparkle and glitter and happiness to have lost my dad. For him to have chosen to leave us. My mom cried for the next six months. I had to put away all the decorations myself, and drag the tree outside when it turned brown and the pine needles all fell off. Mom didn't get out of bed for weeks. And when Christmas rolled around the next year, I only asked once if we were going to get a tree. Mom shook her head, and that was it. We just never acknowledged the holiday again."

"You grew up without Christmas?" His voice was pained, tight, like he was angry and hurt on my behalf.

"I mean," I said, staring at my hands. "It was all around us, right? Like it is here. So it was hard to ignore. But all the stuff I saw didn't make me happy—it just made me angry. Sad, and lonesome and a little bit jealous." Admitting this out loud didn't lessen the feelings, but somehow I felt a little bit lighter having shared them.

"Because everyone else still thought Christmas was a happy thing."

"For them, it was."

"Was your mom okay?" Callan asked.

"Eventually she got out of bed and went on with her life, kind of. She didn't ever remarry. She took up smoking."

Callan dropped my gaze. "Did you ever see your dad again?"

I sighed. "He came back once on my birthday, but my mother sent him away, and then she stayed in bed for a couple more months. My grandmother had to come take care of things." I raised my eyes to meet Callan's, surprised to see that his eyes were shining with compassion and sympathy. "He sent a card on my birthday after that. I have thought about calling him, but I'm still so mad. And my mom would kill me."

Callan nodded.

"And that's the story," I said, my shoulders sagging, as if I'd just gotten to the end of a long journey and could finally relax. "Your turn."

He looked at me for a long moment, and then got to his feet slowly. He moved to where I sat, standing in front of me and then dropping down to his knees so our eyes were level. He took both my hands in his, and our gazes met and tangled up together, caught in the warm intimacy between us. "My story doesn't mean anything," he said. "Not like that. I'm just grumpy and mad about the way my life has changed."

"About soccer?" I asked, feeling like his story was important, that maybe hearing it would help me understand him better, might even help him in the telling.

"About everything." He rubbed his thumbs over the tops of my hands, our eyes locked. And then he chuckled and dropped his eyes, staring at our locked hands. "But I'm tired of being grumpy and mad."

I watched him, noticed the way the dark hair fell across his forehead, the smooth skin that pulled across prominent cheekbones and disappeared in a scruff at his jaw. Something skittered and jumped inside me when I thought about the billboard I'd seen over the freeway a couple years ago—he'd been an icon then, and now here he was in front of me. A man. A man with rich deep eyes and a voice that had dropped to console me, wrapping me in reassurance that my childhood hurt was legitimate, that maybe I wasn't as alone as I always felt.

He looked back up at me then, and moved slowly toward me, as if he was afraid I might change my mind or run away. But I leaned in to meet him, and I pulled my hands from his so that I could slide them around his neck as his lips brushed mine once again. Together, we rose, standing slowly with our breaths mingled and mouths pressed together, until our bodies touched all along the lengths of us, until the warmth I felt in his kiss sparked and ran like fire down my spine.

And then Callan's hands were at my hips, setting me away from him. "I should go."

Disappointment hardened into a little rock inside me. "Oh, well ..." It had been a long night, but I found myself wanting to prolong it, to keep this version of Callan Whitewood here, with me.

"I'll see you tomorrow, okay? We can firm up the details for the show. I promise to be cooperative, even without the benefit of the HalfCat." He smiled and my body warmed again, even as he moved toward the door.

"Yeah. Okay."

"Goodnight, April. I had a really nice time with you." His dark eyes glittered in the low light of my room, and a shiver moved through me.

I smiled uncertainly at him. "Me too." And then I was alone in my room, wondering what exactly had just happened.

CHINCHILLAS. IN HATS.

CALLAN

There was a time, when I'd been a "soccer star," that restraint with women was not an expectation. I'd been young—practically famous in my own small world right after college—and girls threw themselves at me on the regular. But with time, age, and experience, and thanks to having had my own heart broken, I found I was less likely to dive into any relationship—even one that was purely physical—without giving it some thought.

And so when I left April's hotel room, my better judgment congratulating me heartily while my balls griped and moaned about my piss-poor decision making, I knew it had been the right thing.

For one thing, April wasn't a soccer groupie. She hadn't come to me based on my looks or my position or my money. She *had* come looking for something from me, as I'd pointed out in my furious rant to Cormac that day after I'd run her off. But now that I'd had time to think about that, I realized it wasn't the same thing. She'd arrived in Singletree to do a job, had been told my house was under contract with her show, and had been promptly dismissed by a selfish and grumpy guy with a limp. I couldn't blame her for being less than accepting of it, and I was frankly glad she hadn't been.

Because the time I'd spent with April Hall had made me feel things I hadn't felt since those early days with the Sharks. Then, it had been the excitement of a promising career, the enticement of money and women, and the general feeling that I deserved a bright and bountiful future. Whether I had deserved it or not was debatable, I knew now. But that future had evaporated five years later thanks to the injury that had ended my career, and taken with it my belief that I had a shiny bright future ahead of me. But now? In these last few days spent with my nieces, my brother, and April, I felt some glimmer of that expectation rising in me again.

I'd had to give up everything I thought I wanted, and in the vacuum created by acceptance, something else had crept in. Something I couldn't quite put my finger on, could only perceive in glimpses, but something that felt similar to that promise of the future.

Whatever it was, I knew April had something to do with it, and now that I'd agreed to have my home featured on her show, I wanted it to be exactly right.

"Yep, that's perfect," I said, agreeing with the home decorator I'd hired in a rush (and at significant expense) to bring in enough furniture to fill my big house and make sure it all actually went together, something I could never have done on my own. Finding someone willing to come immediately and able to access existing stock in a variety of warehouses and showrooms throughout the mid-Atlantic in the short time frame I specified had not been easy. It had taken hours on the phone and it had been pricey. She'd brought a lot of pieces with her that very afternoon, but much more would be coming over the next week as she was able to get it delivered or go pick it up around the region.

On the heels of furniture being staged, a second decorator was hurrying around with a small team of high school girls who clearly worked for her, directing the hanging of mistletoe and erecting of second, third, and fourth Christmas trees around the house.

As the crews moved through his space, eventually I settled myself on the back porch with a beer, my ankle aching fiercely and my body reminding me that even staying on my feet for four hours was more exercise than I was used to at this point. I put my foot up and leaned back into the wicker chair, letting the chilly air wrap around me as I gazed down at the river flowing by below. After a bit, I picked up my phone and pulled up the number April had given me the night before. I took a deep breath and sent a text.

Callan: How is the filming going?

April: Good, I think. Very ... Christmassy.

Callan: I'm sorry. And the chinchillas?

April: One is wearing a hat. The others r not cooperating as well. One ate most of the gingerbread village overnight.

Callan: Oh no!

April: It's like an apocalyptic village now. More my style.

Callan: Would you be up for dinner later? Here?

I gazed over my shoulder, wondering if the decorating madness would be done by dinner. Cormac had opted to keep the girls in daycare today, based on my description of the excitement involved with decorating, so I was on my own.

April: That would be great.

Callan: What time?

April: Seven?

Callan: Perfect. See you then.

I set the phone down on the low table at my side and let my mind wander as I watched the peaceful water drift along. Something warm was blooming inside me, and I forced myself to just let it happen. I wasn't going to overthink it.

What I did end up overthinking, however, was dinner. I knew April was fine with eating things in buckets, and that she wasn't a fan of Old Bay seasoning. Beyond that, I wasn't sure what she liked, so I decided that an assortment of options might work best. And while I was a decent cook, my skills were limited to grilling steaks, microwaving vegetables and making eggs and pancakes. Breakfast for dinner was a totally viable option, in my opinion, but I thought maybe you had to be further along in a relationship before you could play fast and loose with the definition of "dinner." April was not coming over expecting waffles. So I needed other options.

The decorating vans were just pulling out as the deliveries for dinner began arriving. Singletree might have been small, but it did have its fair share of restaurants once you ventured beyond the tiny town square. I had discovered a whole street full of restaurants just beyond the Target on the other side of the peninsula, and most were willing to deliver —for a price, of course.

A low-country boil was first—shrimp and sausage, corn and potatoes. I'd asked them to hold the Old Bay, which had earned me a snort, but as I opened the containers, I found they'd followed my directions. Next, I opened some Thai food —most people liked Pad Thai, I figured. When April pulled up the lane just after seven, I had a veritable smorgasbord laid out on my new dining room table, and the steaks were resting in the kitchen.

I buzzed open the gate and stood in the open door, the nearly frigid air rushing around me on the porch as she pulled up and stepped from the car.

"Hey!" she called up, bundled in a big coat that fell to her knees. She wore boots and gloves, and her cheeks were glowing pink in the lights shining off my very-decorated house. "Wow, look at this place. You've really outdone yourself!"

"I think the decorator I hired outdid myself," I corrected, waving her through the door. "It's gotten cold all of a sudden,"

I said, and then cringed at the way I'd defaulted to talking about the weather like a ninety-year old man.

I wasn't sure exactly how to greet April. I'd always been polished and suave, but now I felt muddled. I wanted to take her in my arms. Actually, I wanted to pick her up and carry her upstairs and keep here there for days. But that was certainly not the polite thing to do. Instead, I went in for a hug, just as April began removing her coat, so I ended up grabbing her arms instead of her body, and it was almost like I was trying to stop her from taking off her coat. I went in to kiss her cheek at the same time, almost as a second thought, and as she reacted to the arm grab, she ducked her head, and we ended up banging foreheads and then each stepping back in surprise.

"Oh. Um. Sorry," I said, crossing my arms over my chest in embarrassment.

"No, that was me. I'm eternally uncoordinated." The pink that had risen in her cheeks in the cold was turning a deeper red. "Nice to see you," she said, finally managing to take off her coat and handing it to me. I hung it in the hall closet as April gazed around, her eyes wide.

"Wow, you've really made a lot of progress here. Did your big moving truck just arrive?"

I cocked my head at her, so focused on her face I wasn't understanding her words. It took a minute. "Oh, the furniture, you mean. No, I never had a lot to begin with. Most of what I had in San Diego I just left. This is all new. It was easier than trying to divide things after ..." I trailed off, not wanting to taint this evening with memories of my ex. "I hired someone to find things and decorate so the place won't be totally empty when you come to film. I needed a lot. It's not done."

"It looks great, though," April said, wandering into the living room where an area rug had been laid over much of the hardwood, covered with a plush leather sofa, two chairs, a low coffee table and a bookcase in the corner. Stockings hung from the mantle over the fire, and an array of angels stood on the mantel around a photo of me and Cormac next to a woman and two tiny girls. "That's the girls' mother?"

"Yeah, Linda," I said.

"Can I ask how she died?"

"Aneurysm," I said. "It happened really fast."

"Poor Cormac," April said, her voice sad and small.

"I know. It was really hard. He's doing okay, though." We exchanged a glance, and I felt a little tug in my chest at the shine in April's eyes, the sad set of her mouth as she thought about my brother's situation. "You hungry?" I asked, hoping to make her smile again.

"Starving," she said as she turned to follow me. I led her to the dining room, and then excused myself to get the steak. When I returned, she stood exactly where I'd left her, staring around with her mouth slightly open. "Did you invite some other people too?"

I set the steaks down. "Um. No, just you."

"But, I mean ... well, this is a lot."

"I wasn't sure what you liked." I felt sheepish suddenly. Had I made an error here? Was she overwhelmed? Did she think it was some kind of ridiculous show of wealth, maybe? "I just wanted to make sure ..." I trailed off.

April's open mouth stretched wide into a grin. "This is all for me?" She fastened me with a questioning gaze, the broad smile growing even wider. "Seriously?"

I nodded, still off balance.

"Oh my god, this is amazing!" She picked up a plate, and began taking bits from every dish on the table. "How did you know I love a buffet?"

Relief and pride surged through me. "You do?"

She shot the grin at me again and my blood warmed. God, she was pretty. "Yeah. I'm horrible with menus. I can never decide, or I end up ordering things I don't mean to— like the other night at the Shack." She gave me an earnest look and lowered her voice. "It's a real problem."

"Well, I'm glad I guessed right then."

"This is amazing."

We took our food back into the living room by the fire, which glowed with gas flames that danced blue and orange. There was a small Christmas tree in the corner—nothing compared to the monstrous Christopher, who stood in the parlor—but a lovely little tree, glittering with lights and spreading pine scent through the space.

We ate in silence for a few minutes, and I poured a bottle of red wine and then set it on the table between us.

"Thank you," April said, after a few bites.

"You're welcome." I was battling a feeling welling up inside me—a kind of comfortable acceptance, a familiarity. It was too soon to feel that way, I knew, but there it was.

She tilted her head to one side. "Well, good, but I didn't even tell you what I was thanking you for." A light laugh accompanied this, and my stomach tightened a bit. Everything she did appealed to me—it had to be chemical.

"Sorry, my bad," I said. "Proceed."

"I want to thank you for a couple things," she said, setting down her plate and picking up her wine glass. "One, for giving me a chance and agreeing to do the show. It really means a lot to me. I know it's silly. It's just some decorations ... but you really went all out, and it will probably save my job. So thank you."

I felt a rush of stupid happiness, just seeing her happy. I raised my glass and inclined my head.

"And also, for being so welcoming. It's nice to feel like I have a friend here. I don't really acknowledge the holidays, like I told you, but it's kind of a lonely time of year, you know? So it's nice to have some company—someone to hang out with."

"I get it," I said. I thought about my own Christmas the previous year. My parents were gone, and Cormac had just lost Linda and didn't want company. I had stayed in the small apartment I'd rented for myself when everything had blown up with my relationship, and I'd spent Christmas Eve and day —and all the way through New Year's, if you wanted the truth —in a whiskey-fueled haze, feeling sorry for myself and trying to forget the world even existed. "It's nice having you here."

She nodded, and our eyes locked for a long minute, sparks flinging through the space between us and the tight-

ening in my stomach turning to a full-blown storm of anticipation.

We ate slowly, talking and laughing as we exchanged
stories about living in California, places we'd each been
before coming here. We cleared the plates after dinner, put
away the plentiful leftovers and then sat by the fire again, this
time together on the couch.

"So filming happens ... when?" I asked.

"Your house?" April asked, and I nodded. "Yours will be
last. We did one today, and we'll do two more this week. And
then that film has to go back for review and we'll start again
on the 13th. Your house is scheduled for the 16th."

"Okay," I said, glad to hear April would be in town for a
couple of weeks. "And then what will you do? For the actual
holidays, I mean?"

"Well, there's a lot of post-production editing to do back at
the studio, and I'll need to talk to the hosts to give them some
insights about each home. So I'll probably be in Los Angeles."

Disappointment washed through me. I hated the thought
of her leaving. "You don't work on Christmas though, right?"

"The show airs Christmas Eve, but I'll be done just before
that," she said. "I guess I'll hang out with my mom for Christmas. I'd imagined myself on a beach somewhere, but I don't
think that will actually happen."

I nodded, feeling a wild urge to ask her to come back
here, to spend Christmas with me—or just not to leave at all.
But I kept my lips sealed shut. Our lives were on opposite
coasts, and whatever the warm encouragement I felt in the
space between us might be, it wasn't likely to be the kind of

thing that warranted cross-country flights and late-night long-distance phone calls and texts. It was just what it was right now, and that would be enough.

Or that's what I kept telling myself. Because the only thing I was sure of was that there was something between us.

April put her glass down and stared into the fire for a long moment, her eyes hazy and half-lidded as she pulled her knees into her chest and wrapped her arms around them.

"Long day?" I suggested, knowing that she would excuse herself at any moment, and wishing I could make her stay.

She glanced at me with a warm smile. "It was, but it's not that. I was just thinking how nice it is here, now that you've got actual furniture and everything. You've got a really nice home for yourself. And with your family close by ..." she trailed off, wistful maybe.

"Yeah, I guess so," I said, looking around. The house didn't feel like mine exactly, though I knew it was. It felt a little bit like I'd moved into someone else's home—I hadn't had time yet to settle into this new furniture, to get used to the art on the walls, to connect to any of it. "It might as well be a hotel right now," I said.

A little smile flickered across April's lips, and I raised an eyebrow at the wicked light in her eyes as my insides jumped and tightened.

Seeing the question in my gaze, she laughed, and then in a low sultry voice, she said, "I was just thinking we'd been spending a lot of time together in hotels, then."

I felt everything south of my waist tighten up as I wondered if that was an offhanded remark or something more suggestive, more playful. I knew what I wanted it to be. My fingers ached to slide into the dark mantle of hair hanging over April's shoulder, and I'd been thinking of kissing her again all night. "I like being in hotels with you," I said. It was honest, no matter how she took it.

The rosy hue climbed higher up her cheeks, and she turned her head to me fully, her pink lips open just a little bit.

I leaned toward her, tentative, and she closed the space between us. Her lips met mine, and when I slid my arms around her, pulling her body into mine and letting one hand finally weave through the silky dark hair I loved, it felt like coming home. I sighed, and let instinct take over, my mind stilling and my body coming to life in her arms. Kissing April wasn't like playing soccer, but it was the first time since leaving the pitch that I felt like my body had a purpose.

It had been a while since I had taken the time to just make out with someone, and every second I spent on the couch with April was perfect. Her body stretched out on the leather beneath me, soft and warm and curvy, and all that amazing hair spread around her in a dark shiny halo. I lay to the side of her, one arm beneath her and the other hand free to explore her incredible body, to feel the soft heat of the skin at her waist, to trace the curve of her thigh over the tight fabric of her leggings, to feel her mouth opening to mine, over and over, accepting and welcoming, insistent and pleading.

April's hands were exploring too, sliding up the planes of

my back, my fingers working through the fabric on my chest, seeking, and smoothing beneath my shirt, around the waist of my jeans. When her hands pressed lower, grasping the curve of my ass over my jeans, I felt myself harden to the point of near pain, my clear interest in moving past second base with April pressing insistently into her hip.

"So, um," she said, pulling her head back to look at me. "Have you decorated any of the bedrooms? I might want to check. You know, for the show."

A little zing of excitement flew up my spine, and I eyed her with amusement. "For the show. Sure, yes. I understand." I made my face serious and stepped off the sofa, extending a hand to her.

April stood, a little unsteadily at first, and then she followed me up the stairs, her hand in mine.

Lighted garlands draped the banisters, and a ball of mistletoe hung at the top of the stairs, so I stopped her there and took her in my arms again, kissing her gently. "I think it's bad luck not to kiss under mistletoe."

She nodded, still holding me tightly, but then stepped back. "That's a stupid superstition though, right?"

I glanced overhead at the little ball of greenery wrapped in white ribbon. "I don't know, it's working out pretty well for me right now."

"But, I mean ... bad luck? For who? What if the person who walks under it has no one to kiss? Is it bad luck for them?"

I bit one side of my lip and shrugged, not caring too much about mistletoe at that moment.

"This is what's so annoying about holiday traditions like this," April went on. "Things that are supposed to be cute or charming or whatever just end up being anxiety inducing."

"Well you don't have to worry. You're kissing me."

"What if I wasn't? What about your brother? You're so ready to condemn him to bad luck just because he's single."

"Hey, this isn't my tradition," I pointed out. April's voice was light and her eyes were shining and soft, so I knew she was still kidding, but maybe she kind of had a point. "Maybe it works if you just kiss anyone," I suggested. "Even yourself. Like, your hand."

"Okay then," April said, nodding with satisfaction. "That makes sense. They need to explain these things better."

"I'll be honest," I said. "I'd much rather just kiss you."

April's pretty lips pulled wide and a little dimple appeared on each side of them, and I couldn't resist bending my head to kiss her again. And then I led her to the bedroom, which was actually decorated for the holidays. The new furniture hadn't all arrived for this room yet, but I waved April in toward a very large sleigh bed against the far wall.

Looking around, April's lips curved up again. "Nice bed," she said.

"Thanks. They just set it up."

"Um, so ..."

I pulled her toward the bed, a feat easily accomplished since there was no other furniture in the room at all. There was, however a wreath on the door and a small tree glowing in the corner. "The rest will come sometime this week," I said. "But I think this puts the focus nicely on the main attraction."

"It's a sleigh," April pointed out, running one hand over the curve of the footboard.

"I guess that's kind of our thing," I said, hoping I wasn't going too far. We weren't exactly a couple. Could we really have a "thing?"

April turned and climbed onto the thick ash grey coverlet, crawling to the center of the huge bed. I watched, my eyes nearly popping from my head as she moved, her ass on perfect display as she crawled away from me across the expanse of my bed. My jeans felt about three sizes too small in one particular area. I had an offhanded thought about the Grinch's heart—hadn't it been a few sizes too small? But thoughts of the Grinch were quickly overshadowed by April turning to me and crooking a finger for me to follow.

We hadn't turned on the overhead light—the glow from the tree lit the room in a warm bath of golden light and it was enough to see by. I moved to where April sat in the center of the bed, and knelt in front of her, taking her face between my palms and kissing her gently.

She responded immediately, leaning into me, her arms pulling me near and the heat between us pushing away the chillier air of the bedroom, which didn't benefit from the glow of the warm fire downstairs.

As I slid my hands up April's soft skin beneath the big sweater she wore, I asked, "Are you cold? I can turn up the heat."

April looked at me and grinned. "Yep. We better turn up the heat." She dropped her hands to the hem of her sweater and pulled it off over her head. I watched in fascination as all that dark hair fell back around her shoulders, framing the lacy red bra she wore perfectly. My hands went to the lacy straps and I lightly traced them down to the gloriously full cups.

"Holiday underwear?"

She pressed her lips together and tilted her head at me. "Me? No. Just happens to be red."

"I like it," I said, pressing her backward and showing her exactly how much I liked it by exploring every inch of the lacy garment before removing it from her body. April's hands pulled at my shirt, and I sat up to unbutton it and remove it, flinging it to one side as April found my belt and began working the buckle. A moment later, we were each undressed, pulling back the coverlet to burrow together beneath it against the cold.

I forgot the chill the moment April's naked body was pressed up against my own, and we kissed and caressed, generating plenty of warmth between us. "If you have no furniture in here, where do you keep the condoms?" April asked, her voice almost raspy.

"What makes you think we're going to have sex?" I asked, feigning surprise as one hand continued its steady circular rub between April's legs.

Between breathy gasps and little moans, April almost missed the joke, but she managed to open her eyes long enough to shoot me an evil look. "There's an appropriate time for jokes."

"We've passed that time, haven't we?"

"We have."

"Be right back." I slid from between the sheets and walked into the attached bathroom, conscious of April's eyes following me there. I'd once won an award for best pro soccer ass, so I had no self-consciousness about her watching my butt, even though it had been a while since I'd had a decent workout. Those were the kind of assets people were just born with. I returned, three condoms in hand, much more conscious of her eyes on the front of my body. I hadn't won any awards for that particular physical asset, but I felt like I probably would if any were available. I slid back in beside her.

"You look good, Callan," April practically hummed it, and the compliment sent a pleased rush of warmth through me.

"So do you," I said, meaning it. I pulled her close and kissed her again, nearly losing it when her hand slipped low, grasping me between the legs. "Shit," I moaned without meaning to.

"Is this okay?" She asked, stroking me firmly.

"More than okay. That's ... ah ..." Shit. I was losing the ability to speak.

"Do you want me to put on the condom?" April asked, and I opened one eye to look at her. Part of me suspected I was just having a very elaborate dream, because a gorgeous girl like April holding my cock and asking if I'd like her to put the condom on was definitely something I'd have happen in a fantasy.

I smiled. "Okay."

She slid over my thighs, straddling me, and I struggled for control at the sight of her above me, her breasts standing up pert and beautiful, the heat of her center radiating enough that I could feel it on the base of my cock. She was still stroking me with her hand, and when she plucked the condom from the bed and ripped it open, I almost groaned at the loss of her touch. But it was back a moment later, steadily rolling the condom down the length of me.

She leaned forward then and kissed me hard, removing her mouth to say one more thing that practically had me spurting. "I'm big on consent," she said. "So do I have your consent to fuck you now?"

Somehow, I managed to indicate assent, and then April was there, on top of me, around me, everywhere I looked or smelled or felt. Her hair tickled my cheek. Her breasts pressed into my chest as she slid slowly down my length. Her wet heat inched down my cock as her thighs covered mine and her hands held my shoulders.

"God, you're perfect," I said, forcing myself to keep my eyes open so I could replay this later. She arched up again, her breasts jutting out and her cheeks flaming as she began to work up and down in a steady rhythm.

April gave me a steady, "Mmmmmhhhmmm," as she continued moving against me.

Though I wasn't opposed to the hard work of taking the lead during sex, I was definitely enjoying my reclined position, my view, and the fact that April seemed to be enjoying herself completely—there had been many times in the past where worry over a partner's enjoyment had made it almost impossible for me to enjoy sex. April was a refreshing change —in so many ways.

Watching April above me, letting her bring us both to climax through the steady rhythmic motion of her hips, was the most erotic thing I could imagine, and reality was far better than anything I would have imagined myself.

When I felt her clench over me, when her eyes had popped open and her mouth had made a sexy little "oh" of surprise, that was it. My hands sank into her hips, and my own pelvis ratcheted up as I ground out the words that were racing through my mind. "God, you're so sexy. You're perfect." My balls tightened up against my body as April cried out and threw her head back, and the sight of those amazing breasts, coupled with the squeezing of her muscles, stole the last bit of my control, and I released with a groan, pumping the last of myself into her.

It was perfect.

She melted down on top of me, her head to one side of mine as her body covered me, and I pulled the covers back up over us and then nestled one hand into her thick soft hair.

"You're amazing," I told her.

"You were there too," she said, her voice sleepy.

"You did all the work," I pointed out, grinning.

"Hmmm." April might have had a witty comeback, but it didn't get out before she slipped into a drowsy sleep. She roused when I slipped out of bed to clean up, and I was half afraid she'd pull back on her clothes and say goodbye. Instead, she shuffled out of the bathroom, still naked and bleary eyed, and slid back into my bed. "Is this okay?" she asked. "I'm so sleepy."

I looked at her, tucked into my big new bed, and thought

it was far more than okay. "Yeah," I said, sliding over to brush the hair back from her face and kiss her cheek. "What time do you need to be up?"

"Seven," she mumbled.

I set the alarm, turned off the tree, and nestled against April's soft warmth, pulling her into me and wondering if it would be possible to stay awake all night, just to enjoy having her there.

13

IT ALWAYS COMES BACK TO PIGS
APRIL

aking up in Callan's bed was ... different. I was used to sleeping in a hotel, so waking up in a somewhat strange bed was nothing new, but waking up surrounded by strong muscled arms and the mingled scent of pine and something that was distinctly manly—that was definitely new. As I lay in the circle of masculine arms, pressing back lazily against his chest and feeling a distinctly steely length against one side of my butt, I let myself relive the previous night, which had been amazing.

Callan was funny and sweet, not at all like the grumpy jerk I'd met when I'd first come to his house. Or like the miserable guy who had all but shooed me off his property after shopping for Christmas decorations. It felt like he had let his guard down with me, like this was the real Callan under all the bravado and self-pity. And this guy? Well, I liked him. A lot.

But that was a bit of a problem too, and no matter how I

tried to push away thoughts about what my uncle might say if he found out I'd just had sex with the key homeowner on my latest show, those thoughts were there. And I knew my uncle would be disappointed, to say the least. And that I'd be out of a job, and possibly a career. And maybe my apartment, since I wouldn't be able to pay rent ... really, my whole life was at stake.

Still, this didn't feel like an illicit island dalliance, as my last mistake had been. And Callan didn't feel like an ego-driven conquest. I hadn't planned to fall into this enormous wooden sleigh bed with Callan Whitewood—it had just happened. And honestly? I thought it had happened in a much more normal and healthy way than many of my previous relationships had come into being. I liked Callan. And he seemed to like me. Wasn't that how things should begin?

"Hey," Callan's sleepy voice came from behind me as his arms tightened around my waist, pulling me firmly against the rock-hard erection between us.

"Hey," I returned, wiggling against him.

"It's almost seven," he said, his voice half-whispered in my ear, tickling me and sending a shiver through me. "Do you need to get to work or can you hang out a bit?"

I wanted to hang out. I thought I might like to hang out all day, and maybe spend some time investigating the iron rod Callan had in his bed, but I really didn't have time for that. "I actually need to go," I said, rolling over and putting a hand over my mouth as I faced Callan.

"What are you doing?" he laughed, pulling my hand away.

"Dragon breath," I said, trying to put it back and turning my head so I didn't breathe in his face.

His eyebrows went up but he didn't release me, pulling me closer to his warm chest instead. "I have a theory," he said. "That if two people both have morning breath, neither of them will notice the other's."

I shook my head, afraid to open my mouth at this close range.

Callan planted a tiny kiss on my sealed mouth, and my eyes rounded in worry. I turned my head, "at least let me go gargle or something."

"Your breath is fine." Callan's eyes widened now. "Oh, is this one of those things like how you're never supposed to turn down a mint? Is it me?" He covered his own mouth with a hand.

Through my hand, I assured him it wasn't him.

"Now I'm paranoid," he said, and ducked under the covers. "But maybe down here it won't matter." He slid down beneath the covers, along the length of my body. I started to protest, but within seconds had lost the ability to do it with much force.

"I do need to get going," I moaned.

"I'll be fast."

I made a noise that sounded somewhere between 'okay' and just 'ohhhh,' and Callan was as good as his word. Minutes later, I was sliding from the bed to stand on shaking legs. "I don't know how you did that," I said, my skin still heated from his touch.

Callan lay with his arms behind his head, a satisfied grin on his face. "I'll show you tonight if you come back," he said.

I wondered if it would be better to try to put a little distance here, not to dive in too quickly. But every cell in my body wanted to spend as much time as I could with Callan, and before I could talk myself out of it, I said, "Okay. What do you have in mind?"

Callan's face broke into an incredible grin, his dark eyes gleaming and his perfect teeth on full display, just like in that underwear ad. "Well, I have the girls until about five-thirty," he said. "But I thought maybe after that we could go visit the HalfCat."

"The distillery?" I tried to weigh the pros and cons quickly. Pros included being with Callan, spending more time with Callan, getting to touch Callan ... cons included potentially being seen with someone I was not supposed to be seeing socially, potentially losing my job, potentially ruining my life.

"Yeah, the distillery. You up for it?"

I had never been good at pro and con lists. "Sure!"

"So just come over whenever you're done. If you get here in time to see the girls, I know they'd be excited to see you."

I wrinkled my nose, thinking about the way I'd left last time I'd seen them. Callan had been angry at me. Maybe it'd be better if I didn't get between him and his nieces, if we kept our relationship separate. "You sure?"

"Definitely."

A warm happiness spread slowly through my chest, and I took a quick shower in Callan's bathroom, thinking about how nice it was here in Singletree—with Callan, and the girls ...

"What are you humming?" Callan asked from outside the fogged glass door.

Had I been humming? "I don't know," I said. "I was humming? I didn't even realize it."

"Yeah, and I think it was 'Winter Wonderland.'"

"Impossible. I never hum Christmas music. I have a strict policy." I realized he might be right. I did have the song running through my mind, now that I thought about it. What was happening to me?

"Okay, if you say so."

A few minutes later, Callan was sending me out the door with a cup of coffee and a piece of toast. "I just have time to run to the hotel to change and get to the house we're filming today. I'll see you later!"

"Have a good day, dear," Callan said in a sing-song voice. He stood at the door until I had pulled away and could no longer see him at the front of his big house.

The day went smoothly for filming the second house. The homeowner, a cute older woman just outside town, had a farmhouse and no unusual house pets—at least none that the crew and I had to contend with as we were shooting the very festively decorated house.

Filene Easter didn't favor the plastic elves, snowmen and flashing lights that so many holiday fans seemed to insist increased their cheer, and I was glad for it. In fact, in the little farmhouse, decorated with pinecones and simple trees, hand-knitted stockings and the beautiful homemade wreaths Mrs. Easter said she made herself, I saw a glimmer of a holiday décor I could possibly get behind. That is, if I was If I were going to change my mind about the holiday, that was. And I was not. Not after all this time.

To me, Christmas was a painful reminder of everything that had gone wrong in my life from an early age. It was better ignored. Other people could have it.

"I want you to have this," Mrs. Easter said as we packed up to leave her house that afternoon. The old woman handed me one of the prettiest wreaths, woven in a dark brown wood with just a touch of red foliage tucked in here and there. There was a slim gold filament peeking out in a few spots, but otherwise no sign of glitter or glitz. Just a beautiful hand-made wreath.

"No," I said, staring openmouthed between Mrs. Easter and the gift. "This must take so much time to make. I couldn't ..."

"Please, dear. I had months to make it, knowing you were coming. I'd love for you to have it, to have a little something to remember us here in Christmas Tree."

"You mean Singletree."

The woman's mouth dropped a bit in surprise and I felt guilty for a moment. If this little old lady wanted to believe her town was called Christmas Tree, maybe I shouldn't have corrected her. "You haven't heard, then?"

I shook my head. "Heard what?"

"Some little ruffian, probably hopped up on goofballs and moonshine and a bit too much holiday spirit, spray- painted the town sign to say Christmas Tree instead of Singletree. The town council voted to change the name of the town officially in the month of December."

"Won't that be confusing for the post office?"

The woman gave me a disappointed look and said, "It's only a month, dear."

"Sure, you're right. Thank you so much, Mrs. Easter," I said.

I handed her the check from the network and found myself eager to wrap up and get over to Callan's. I just had time to dash through the inn and get a shower.

Mrs. Easter stood in her front yard as I drove away, looking sweet and happy, holding the check in one hand and waving with the other.

I sighed. I was staying in a town called Christmas Tree for a month. Because of course I was. This was how a universe that split up my family on Christmas operated, wasn't it?

Only ...

Only I didn't feel that same deep gutting sadness this year. I didn't feel broken and heavy and empty inside. I wasn't dreading seeing my mother and trying to pretend we weren't both reliving that Christmas morning so many years ago when we'd argued about where Dad was when it was time to open gifts. I had been sure he was just out with Santa, still delivering gifts on the other side of the world where it was still dark. And Mom had suggested that the whore's name was probably not Santa, but that if he did come home, she'd definitely kick him in a place where it was still dark. And then there had been a lot of crying.

This year, my mind wasn't hanging on that memory, circling it like a masochistic shark after its own tail. This year, any time I thought about that morning, the memory came, but it was foggier, misty. And when I thought about all things Christmas, my stomach didn't clench painfully. Instead, a pleasant tingle went through my body and I pictured Callan Whitewood—his house, his face, his touch, and just ... him. And it made me smile.

Back at the inn, I had a hard time finding parking in the lot, thanks to boxes stacked in half the spots. Something was going on. There were people in and out of the lobby, the steps crammed with boxes and flustered bellboys trying to shuffle them around. Annabelle stood at the top of the steps, her hands on her hips and a scowl on her face. I was in a rush to get a quick shower, but my friend looked upset.

"What's all this?" I asked.

"This," Annabelle said, "is all the decorations I ordered." She didn't sound happy about it, which was weird because if anyone loved decorations, it was Annabelle.

I gave her a frank look. "There's more? Annabelle, I don't think you can decorate a single thing more. The place is crammed with Christmas already!"

This earned me an eye roll. "I know. That's why I'm mad."

"But you said you ordered these?"

Annabelle turned to me, breathing out a sigh that told me she was gathering her patience for the explanation. "I ordered ahead. These are the decorations for the next thirty years."

Shock nearly made me drop my wreath. "Thirty years? Why would you order that far ahead?"

"The shop I order from was closing this year. I bought out their inventory."

I glanced around. It was a lot. Like really a lot. "Wait, then why are you mad?"

"They told me they'd ship it out of a storage facility over the next thirty years. A couple boxes a year. It would be like a fun Christmas surprise each time a box came. I planned it. It made sense." I had the distinct impression my friend had defended this choice more than once already today. "But evidently the guy who ran the store moved to Tahiti and sold the contract to someone else who either didn't understand or didn't care."

Aha. "Okay. So you just need a new storage facility."

"We don't have those in Christmas Tree." It seemed she'd gotten the memo about the name change already.

"There must be one around here somewhere."

"I'd have to pay for it. The storage was part of the deal." She sighed. "I can fit some of this in the basement, but ..."

My mind went to Callan's house—the empty rooms, the scattered outbuildings out back. I was willing to bet he might have room. I was less sure about his willingness to store thirty years of Christmas décor. "I might be able to help. Can you give me until tomorrow?"

Annabelle shrugged. "I don't think this is going anywhere."

I gave her a quick hug and dashed inside, dodging the boxes that were literally stacked everywhere.

An hour later, I was pulling up to Callan's gate and then to his front door, only to be greeted by Taylor and Maddie, who were jumping around like excited kangaroos. "Hey girls," I called, getting out of the car.

"Ape-will!" Maddie called, stopping her jumping to charge down the steps and hurl herself at my legs. When I'd recovered my balance, I had to snuff out the urge to cry just because a little girl was hugging me, and I accepted a less aggressive hug from Taylor, who looked up with big round eyes and said shyly, "Hi."

"Are you guys impressed with the decorations? Didn't your uncle do a good job?" We climbed the steps together to go inside. The door was standing open and Callan was just inside, watching us come in with dark gleaming eyes. For a heartbeat, I forgot about everything else in the world, caught up in those devilish eyes and reminded of how it had felt to be as close to him as it was possible to be.

"Hey," he mouthed, kissing my cheek as the girls went on excitedly about the decorations. They each wanted to show me their favorites, so the next ten minutes were spent dashing from room to room, being tugged along by eager little hands as the girls changed their minds multiple times about which decorations they liked best. Finally, we all sat down around the newly installed kitchen table and had a snack.

"So," Callan said, his cheeks slightly pink under the scruff of his beard and his eyes dropping when they met mine.

He was shy all of a sudden? The warm ball of happiness in my stomach expanded and seeped into my limbs. I felt languid and warm, safe and ... happy. "So," I said back, catching his gaze and holding it. Unspoken words flung between us, unobserved by the little girls absorbed in chocolate milk and goldfish crackers. Words about what we'd done the night before, about waking up together. Words about the holidays and time spent together, and especially about sleighs.

"So Cormac will be here in a bit, and then I thought we'd head over to the Straddler."

"I can do the straddles!" Taylor was suddenly on the floor, halfway under the table, demonstrating a very impressive straddle.

"Wow," I said appreciatively.

"Me too!" Not to be outdone, Maddie joined her sister on the floor, but once she was down there, she became distracted by my shoes and forgot to show off. "These has high heels," she commented, petting my boots.

"They do," I agreed. "The Straddler?" I asked Callan.

"Girls, get up please. Finish eating before your dad gets here." The girls clambered back up and Callan gave his attention back to me. "The bar at the distillery. I guess it straddles county lines."

"Oh right, yeah, someone said something about that."

"You up for it?"

"Definitely," I said. I was up for anything that kept me within a foot of the solid warm wall of muscle that was Callan Whitewood. "Hey," I said slowly. "Can I ask you a question?"

He lifted a shoulder and gave me his attention. I forced my warm ball of happiness to stop overheating at the gleam in those wicked eyes of his and concentrated on helping Annabelle. "So, in all those little buildings out back there, do you have any that might be used for storage?"

He raised an eyebrow. "Yeah, a couple of them are empty. One smells like pigs though—used to be some kind of pig coop."

"I don't think pigs are kept in a coop," I said.

"Yeah, Uncle Callan," Maddie agreed, vehemently.

"Pig house?" Callan tried.

"Nope," Taylor said.

"Well, whatever it was, it smells piggy and gross," Callan went on.

"Pen," I suggested.

"Right!" Taylor agreed, grinning at me as she lined her goldfish up on her plate. Just as she put the last one into line, a pudgy hand shot out and grabbed one, and the straggling goldfish had disappeared into Maddie's mouth before Taylor could say a word.

"Maddie," Callan scolded, but it was too late. Taylor was already becoming hysterical.

"She ate my fish! He was in line and she ..." whatever else Taylor was saying was impossible to decipher amid the tears and high-pitched warbling that accompanied it.

"Here," Callan said, taking a goldfish from Maddie's plate and replacing it in Taylor's line. "Okay?"

Taylor stopped shrieking and eyed the new goldfish skeptically. "Okay," she sniffled, but she set this fish just a little apart from all the others. Clearly, he was the stepchild of this goldfish family and would have to earn his place.

Now Maddie was shrieking about "go-fish stea-wers" and pointing her finger at her uncle.

I watched Cormac walk into this scene, looking tired and worn out from his day even before the goldfish apocalypse had swept him into the fray. "What's all this?" he asked.

"There's no problem," Callan assured him, dumping about fifty more goldfish into the center of the table. "See? Plenty for everyone."

Cormac walked over to the table, patting each girl on the head and taking a handful of goldfish. "Hey April."

The shrieking died down as a goldfish land grab ensued, each girl piling fistfuls of fish onto her own plate.

"Some of these are for grownups," Callan said, picking one up and eating it to demonstrate.

Maddie narrowed her eyes at him, but then seemed to come around to a more generous mindset, scooping up three fish and offering them to me. "Dere's no Cwis-mas ones." This was said in apologetic tones, as if Maddie thought I might refuse the fish if they weren't properly decorated for the holidays.

I realized that the little girls probably thought I was very focused on decorating and celebrating the holiday, and for a brief moment, I enjoyed seeing myself through their eyes. What would a carefree holiday-infused April be like?

"What were you asking me?" Callan asked, interrupting my daydream. "About the pig house?"

"Pig house?" Cormac said, pulling up a chair and eating more goldfish. "You getting pigs, Cal?"

"I hate pigs," Callan said. "You know this. Remember when we were kids and Auntie Maggie's pig tried to kill me?"

Cormac shook his head, giving his brother a disappointed look. Then he turned to me. "Callan got the athletic genes." He lifted a hand and mock whispered beside it, "but he's never been too smart."

"Nice," Callan said, laughing.

"Anyway, we had an aunt who loved animals. She had peacocks, pigs, a goat, a couple sheep, some horses and a cow—all as pets out on her property. She had taken us to visit them all the day before, and Callan got up early the next day to go back out and see them. He decided to snuggle with Hamhock, the pig. In the sucker's pen."

"How big was this pig?" I asked.

Both girls were listening intently, their mouths working goldfish while their eyes stayed on their dad, fascinated.

"Huge," Callan supplied.

"It was at least a couple hundred pounds," Cormac agreed. "And it either wanted to get closer to Callan, or was trying to kill him, because it rolled over and trapped his leg."

"Oh no!" I cried, picturing a tiny Callan caught under a huge horrible pig.

"He started wailing, and every animal in the place joined him, so there was an early morning cacophony that brought our aunt out in her nightshirt, running through the yard."

"She saved you," I said, feeling oddly relieved.

"She had to roll the pig off me. Pigs are mean suckers," Callan said.

"Maybe they just don't like snuggles," Taylor suggested.

"Or don't go in his house," Maddie said, her tone scolding. "Unless you awe invited."

"That's just good manners," Cormac agreed.

"Anyway," Callan said, evidently done with the romp through the pig pen of days yore. "The pig shack?" He looked at me pointedly.

"Oh, right. Well, Annabelle has a bunch of boxes to store and nowhere to put them at the inn. Any chance she could store some stuff here?"

Callan lifted a shoulder. "Sure. I don't see myself investing in pork futures anytime soon."

"Pork futures?" Taylor echoed, confused.

"Too-mah-wo pigs," Maddie said, as if this made perfect sense. Sure, tomorrow pigs.

"Okay, girls. We'd better get home," Cormac said, sounding tired. "You guys have big plans?" He looked between me and Callan as he helped the girls down from their chairs.

"Distillery," Callan said, and Cormac nodded.

"Have a good time," Cormac said, looking a little wistful. I would have invited him to come along, but I knew he couldn't, not with two little girls to look after.

14

CATS ARE CHRISTMASSY TOO - EVEN HALF CATS

CALLAN

As I escorted April out the door and into the truck, I felt a new and foreign satisfaction working its way through me. I watched her snap her seatbelt into place and something inside me snapped along with it. The house felt like a home now, between the furniture arriving daily and the somewhat ambitious decorating, but mostly because of my nieces and Cormac ... and because of April. This place—Singletree, or Christmas Tree, or whatever they were calling it today—felt more like home than San Diego really ever had.

Sure, there I'd had a stellar career, one I'd loved very much. But that was all I was there, all I had. Without soccer, I was being forced to figure out what else I was. And while I realized I'd need to discover some kind of purpose before long—I was still young and if I couldn't be a soccer player, I needed to decide what I was going to be when I grew up—at least a few things were falling into place.

"We going to go or just sit here admiring your twinkle lights?" April's voice broke me from my contemplation, which I hadn't realized had been going on an inappropriately long time while I sat behind the wheel.

"Yeah, sorry. I was just thinking ..."

"About ...?"

I smiled at her. We hadn't known each other long, but in some ways, she had been the catalyst that had made me start moving again toward a healthier place. "About this place, the people I've met since moving here."

"A little quirky, huh?" April clearly thought I was talking about some of the townspeople. I smiled, feeling my chest warm as I included them in my thoughts of happiness at my new home.

"Yep," I smiled back. It was much too early to admit to April that I'd mostly been thinking of her, wishing there was some way to keep her here. "I like it though," I said, starting the car.

"It's a lot," April said. "The house we did today was pretty normal though—a cute little farmhouse just outside town."

I glanced at her, encouraging her to continue. I loved listening to her talk. Her voice was low and sonorous, dancing with her expressions, ranging up and down as she spoke.

"The woman who lived there—Mrs. Easter—was so sweet. She's all by herself, but she seemed really content in this cute little house, and she made all the decorations herself." April's voice trailed off a bit and she gazed out the window ahead of them. "She gave me a wreath."

"Really?" I smiled over at her. "Did you burn it?"

April shot me a look, her lips pressed firmly together and her eyes narrowed. "No. It's in my room. It's really pretty."

"A Christmas wreath, April?"

"Yes."

"I think your little Scroogey heart is starting to thaw," I teased.

I felt April's eyes on me then as she said, "Yeah, I think it is, actually."

I guided the car into the distillery parking lot beneath the huge HalfCat sign, which had the image of the hand-drawn cat in his little wheeled contraption on it. We both gazed at the odd picture for a moment as we stood next to the car.

"Shall we?" I asked, offering April my arm. The wind whipped up around us a bit, sending the chilly air rustling through April's loose hair and prying at our collars and scarves with frosty fingers as we walked to the front door.

We stepped inside, and were immediately confronted with a choice. A huge sign read "Distillery" and had an arrow pointing to the left. Beneath it read "Bar" and the arrow pointed to the right.

"Which way?" April wondered aloud as she unbuttoned her coat.

"Let's check out the distillery first," I suggested, and we headed to the left.

We followed a narrow hallway filled with black and white photos of men rolling barrels, of strange-looking metal kettles and tanks, and of trucks poised outside the brick building, filled with kegs. There were a few newer shots in color, one of them featuring a tall lanky man with a familiar face.

"Hey guys," the face from the photo was the same one that greeted us now from the entrance door of the distillery. "You're the stowaways, right? From the sleigh!"

"Hey Santa," I laughed. "Blanchard, right?

"Yeah. I go by Wiley mostly, though." The man had a broad likable face with an easy grin that made me feel immediately at ease. Wiley Blanchard wasn't a big man—not like many of the athletes I knew—but he was tall, and the wiry muscle exposed by the flannel shirt rolled up his forearms told me he could probably hold his own when he needed to.

"I'm Callan, and this is April."

"Thanks for keeping things quiet in the sleigh that night," April said, shaking Wiley's hand.

"Of course. I know how it is," he said, the grin fading a bit to a smile that looked like it was probably his usual expression. "Hiding from the parents, were you?"

April laughed. "Something like that."

Wiley stood next to a tall counter made from whiskey barrels, and he leaned down now, resting on his forearms. "All right. Well, what can I do for you tonight? The bar's just through there," he pointed back the way we'd come. "But if you'd like a quick tour of the distillery first, we can do that too."

"We don't want to intrude," April said. "We can come back during regular tour hours." She was gazing up at a sign over Wiley's head that confirmed tours stopped after four p.m.

He waved a hand at us, straightening back up. "Nah, that's for tourists. Come on. I'll show you around."

He walked us through a broad barn-style door and into the heart of the distillery, where several huge copper tanks stood with soaring copper columns and complicated tubing and connections running here and there to various other metal containers and machines. Against a far wall, sectioned off from the machinery by a glass wall, were two long rows of barrels.

"White oak," Wiley said, pointing to the barrels. "Best wood for aging whiskey and bourbon. And these beauties," he said, walking over and laying a hand on one of the huge copper stills, "are the heart of the operation."

"Why copper?" I asked.

"Most bourbon stills are either made from or lined with copper," Wiley said. "Makes for a better flavor. If you want the science," he said, pausing and lifting an eyebrow in question.

"Yeah," I encouraged.

"Copper reacts with the compounds that contain sulfur— the stuff that gives the liquor bad flavors we don't want. The distillation sends those bad flavors and odors up this long column," Wiley pointed up at the tall copper column. "And the alcohol comes out these tubes down into this container here." He patted a smaller silver container with a glass dial on the front. "That's the long and short of it. Most folks care most what it tastes like though, not how we make it."

"We care about both," April said, wrapping her hand through my elbow and pressing herself to my side. A little thrill went through me, both at the contact, and at April's use of the word "we," something I wouldn't have expected to make me so happy.

"Well, the exact distilling method is the secret sauce, so to speak," Wiley said, lowering his voice. "And my brother Wade would not be pleased if I gave away all the goods, so that's about all the 'how' I've got for you."

"Some of the whiskey here has been aging for decades," Wiley told us, walking us through a door and into the barrel room. He pointed down to the darkest end of the racks. "A couple of those have been down there since before Prohibition. Grandpa had them back in the woods and he just rolled them in here and said they needed more time. We're a little afraid to tap them."

"You've never tasted what's in there?" I asked.

"I didn't say that," Wiley said, grinning at us. "But it's a good story, eh?" he chuckled. "A lot of our whiskey is twelve to fifteen years in barrels. Bourbon not as long."

April was walking the length of the racks, craning her head up to get a look at the soaring stacks. I watched her wander down the row.

"You guys local?" Wiley asked me.

I nodded. "Well, I am. She's here for work."

Wiley made a clucking noise of understanding. "Long distance then, huh?"

"Well, we're not really a couple." At Wiley's confused look, I added. "It's new."

"Gotcha." Wiley clapped me on the back and April turned, coming back to join us.

"So what's the 'half cat' all about?" she asked.

"You'll see," Wiley said, leading us back to the hallway through which we had entered. "So this hallway here is in Charles County, and the part that goes to the bar is in St. Mary's. Part of the distillery sits in Center, and part in Charles, and half the bar is in Center, while the other half is in St. Mary's. They drew the lines after the building was established."

"That's crazy," April laughed.

"What's crazy is that all three counties have different liquor laws," Wiley said, walking us into the bar. "So technically," he said, taking the shots the woman behind the bar had just set up at his subtle nod and handing them to us. "You cannot drink that here by the bar, ma'am." He pointed to a line on the floor, about three feet away from the bar itself. "You can stand over there and drink."

"What?" April was holding her shot, laughing.

"Right here," the bartender said, pointing at a sign over the bar that read:

"Um. These don't even make sense." I laughed. "If the bar is in Center County, how do you ring up orders?"

The bartender pointed to the end of the bar, which curved significantly and held a register. "That's in St. Mary's."

"This is hilarious," April said, stepping back up to the bar with her drink. She looked at me and grinned, holding up the little glass. "Ready to taste?"

"Ma'am, sorry, but can I ask you to sit down first?" Wiley pointed to a bar stool.

"Oh, you're serious?" April glanced around as if she expected a cop to appear at any moment.

"We're always on the bloody edge of getting shut down," he explained. "Depends on which county's turn it is to patrol around here. They split it up since we straddle the lines."

I chuckled. My new home was the best kind of weird.

Just as April was sliding onto a barstool, a scraping noise came from the other side of the almost-empty room, and a cat appeared. It paused, the scraping noise stopping, and looked at us with large evaluating eyes. Its fur was a silver grey, and it stood up in all directions.

"Come on Fluffy, it's okay," Wiley said in a coaxing voice. He glanced up at us. "His full name is a bit of a mouthful."

"His full name?" April asked, taking a sip.

"Mr. FluffyNuts," the bartender supplied helpfully.

April laughed, spitting the whiskey she'd just sipped. I laughed too, but hadn't taken a sip yet.

The cat chose that moment to emerge completely from behind the counter, his front paws pulling behind him a little cart with big wheels, which carried the back half of his body.

"Mr. FluffyNuts was a rescue," Wiley said. "About seven years ago, my uncle found him on the side of the road. His back legs were mangled by a car, so Uncle Beau and my brother Wade made him a cart."

"Oh my god." April's face was turning slightly red, and I suspected she was doing her best not to laugh any more.

"Half cat," I said.

Wiley lifted a shoulder in a half-shrug. "A little more than half, I guess. But you got it." He winked at them. "Though if you want the truth, the place has been called that for a hundred years, cat or no cat." April and I exchanged a confused look. "Enjoy the whiskey, y'all. That first taste is on the house. Try the bourbon, too." Wiley disappeared back down the hallway, and the bartender moved to the other end of the bar to help the few other people who sat against its edge. Mr. FluffyNuts wheeled himself off to follow Wiley, and April grinned at me.

"What?" I asked, feigning innocence about the ridiculousness of everything we'd just witnessed.

"Craziest town ever," April whispered, poking me in the chest to make her point.

I shrugged.

"And YOU live here," she added, poking me again.

I caught her hand and held it to my chest. "Yeah," I said thoughtfully, keeping her slim warm hand trapped in my own. "Yeah, I do."

April tilted her head to the side and one half of her mouth lifted in a smile. "How do you feel about that?"

"I think I like it here," I said honestly, thinking about the warm contentment that had been spreading through me all night.

She pulled her bottom lip between her teeth and seemed to be thinking about this statement. "Yeah," she said. "I think I can see why."

"I mean," I said, still holding her hand but dropping it to my leg, pressing it there, wanting to keep her close. "It's got an interesting mix of people, the only family I really have is here ... and I have to start my life all over again somewhere. Might as well be here, right?" As I said these words, they solidified in my mind into a certainty I'd only just acknowledged.

"Do you really?" April asked, putting her glass on the bar so she could put her other hand atop mine, on my leg. "Do you really have to start all over, or do you just think that because you can't see anything else?"

"Well," I said slowly. "My entire life was based on being a pro soccer player. Now that I can't do that, I need a reset." I didn't want to talk about what had happened. I wanted to focus on her, on today, tomorrow.

"But it wasn't," she said. "Your life was based on being a great athlete, on knowing how to get to the top of a game, on how to market yourself."

"As a soccer player."

"You're an expert at soccer."

"Um," I shook my head, confused. Where was she heading with this? "Right. I guess."

"So use that expertise in another way."

"Oh, like as a soccer consultant. Right. I think I saw a help wanted posting for one of those on the way in." I laughed, but the sound only revealed the depth of frustration I felt. I'd thought through all this. I needed a new direction.

"You might need to be a little more creative," April said. "Take it from someone who's lost a lot of jobs."

"How many?"

"Counting the last one?"

I narrowed my eyes at her. "Yes."

"I've lost three jobs so far."

"Like, fired lost?" I cocked my head to the side. There were a lot of definitions of 'losing' a job.

"Well, I don't think anyone's ever said, 'you're fired,'" she clarified. "But I can tell you it wouldn't have been well received if I'd come back to work after the talk."

"The talk?"

"The 'we think it'd be better if you worked somewhere else' talk," April explained. She pulled her hands away from where they'd been held on my leg and crossed her arms around her waist. "I was a horrible waitress," she explained. "So that made total sense. And then there was the barista job."

"Not mocha-tastic?" I joked, hoping to make her smile.

She frowned. "That was awful. And so was my barista game."

"What happened?"

"Someone ordered a decaf, sugar-free, nonfat latte."

"And?"

"I pointed out that they might as well drink water."

"They didn't like that?" I guessed.

"Neither did my manager," April said, her shoulders dropping.

"You're good at what you do now," I pointed out, placing a hand on her knee, trying to reassure her.

April just sighed. She looked at me, and for a moment I thought she was going to tell me something else, something to refute my statement. But she didn't. She picked up her glass and finished the whiskey.

I followed suit. "So," I said, sensing that changing the subject was the way to go. "What now?"

"Should we try the bourbon?"

"Well, I need to drive us back," I said. "Do you want to try it?"

April shook her head. "Not by myself."

We each slipped off our stools, and I looked around. That round had been free, Wiley hadn't charged us for the taste, and now we were about to leave without buying anything. I wanted to support a local business, so I signaled the bartender to come over. "Is there any such thing as a to-go glass?" I asked doubtfully.

"Only in Center County," she said.

I looked down, realizing I was standing in St. Mary's. I met the bartender again a few feet down the bar. "I'd like two glasses of bourbon to go."

"Done," the bartender said, placing them on the bar in plastic cups with lids.

"And I'll buy a round for everyone at the bar," I added.

The bartender's eyebrows shot up, but she accepted the stack of bills I handed her without a word. I couldn't help but glow under April's surprised gaze too. I didn't want to throw my money around, but if I could impress her a bit, that wasn't a bad thing. And there were like seven people in the bar.

April smiled and lifted the to-go cups off the bar.

"Ready?" I asked.

April nodded. "Yeah."

15

TAKING THE CAT ON THE ROAD
APRIL

aybe a more responsible person would have just gone back to her hotel room, I thought as I rode next to Callan in his truck, holding "to-go" cups filled with bourbon. He did ask if he should drop me off. But I'd looked over at him, caught that hopeful gleam in his mischievous eyes and seen the corner of his mouth twitch up. And I'd said no. "My place?" He'd asked then, and I had nodded, knowing I had already crossed some lines. Knowing that if something went wrong between us, I could end up adding this to the long list of jobs I'd lost.

But Callan had gotten under my skin. How could any sane woman see him—all that muscled perfection topped with dark hair and those eyes that drove me mad—and not make some bad decisions? He was the guy from the underwear billboard, for heaven's sake, right here smiling at me. And he had that wounded vulnerability, that little glimmer of the lost boy looking to be found. And I found myself wanting very much to find him. Even if I should be working on finding myself instead.

The town glowed around us as we navigated the narrow streets, heading back to Callan's house. Now that the tree was lit in the square, it cast a golden glow for blocks, throwing light into the close damp winter air and making it impossible to forget that Christmas was near. I imagined that Singletree—er, um, Christmas Tree, that was—must be a great place to be a little kid. Every day felt a little bit like something special with all the decorations and twinkle lights and general excitement for the holiday in the air.

As we pulled down the lane to Callan's, his own house glowed almost as brightly as the town square. "Man, look at that," he said, his voice warm.

"It's beautiful," I said, and I found that I meant it. The old plantation house was lit within and without. The windows glowed in a welcoming tint and the pillars out front were wrapped in twinkling lights that looked like glitter. A family of snowmen had been added since yesterday, and there were stacks of decorative presents on the sprawling front porch.

"You're starting to be won over," Callan said, pulling through the gate after pressing the remote button he'd had installed and parking the car. "Admit it." He turned and looked at me, his mouth lifted in that half grin again. But it was his voice, velvety and low, that had me thinking I'd admit anything he wanted me to.

"I am," I said, my eyes never leaving his. I was being won over, and I wondered quietly how badly this would end.

"Come on," he said, and he slid out of the car and came around to open my door for me. His limp was more pronounced than it had been earlier.

"Are you okay?" I asked, handing him the drinks.

"It's just the cold. It's a little worse when I'm stiff." He looked away from me as he said this, and I realized he didn't want to talk about his injury, so I let it drop. But my heart twisted a bit as we climbed the stairs, wishing I could do something to help him.

Inside, Callan put on music—not carols, though, I drew an absolute line at voluntary Christmas carol listening—and we sat on the rug in front of the gas fire, bourbon in our hands.

"I had fun with you," Callan said, taking a sip.

I felt my cheeks flame, though I wasn't sure if it was the bourbon or Callan's words. "Me too," I said after a minute.

"And I was glad you weren't ready to go home yet."

Home, I thought. Callan meant the inn, but my mind was wandering back to my quiet dark apartment, cold and empty. Was it strange that I had recently started thinking I might get a tree when I got back? "Yeah," I said quietly. Then I raised my eyes to meet his. I would have to go home at some point, of course. And then this would end. This—whatever this was. I might as well enjoy it until then. I'd gotten in a little too deep to back out gracefully now, and there wasn't a cell in my body that actually wanted to anyway.

"So," Callan said, clearly trying to draw me out. I knew I had been quiet since leaving the distillery. "You're off now for a bit, right? You said the next week is when the LA office reviews the film you got this week? So where does that leave you?"

I smiled. I had wondered that myself. "Well, tomorrow I'll need to write up a few things to go with the package we're sending back for review. The camera crew actually goes back —or one of them does—with the files, and does a bit of editing. So they'll review what we've got next week, give me any new directions, and then we'll wrap the last two houses."

"So you have the next week off, basically?"

"Yeah, I guess so," I said. "Technically I'm on call, but yeah."

"Maybe we can spend a little of it together?" Callan said, the hope in his voice making my heart leap. I wanted that— more than anything—but having time with him, without the distraction of work would make it all more real.

I nodded, my mind whirling.

"Not quite the enthusiasm I'd hoped for," Callan said, setting his bourbon on the table. "What's going on up there?" He lifted a hand to touch my temple and smoothed the hair away from my face. "Have I been reading things wrong?"

I sighed and then forced my eyes to Callan's, which were deep and smoldering as ever. "No, you haven't," I assured him, though such honest talk about feelings was hard for me. My family was all about shoving things down and ignoring them—the good, the bad, the ribbon- festooned and glittery. "I guess I'm just feeling like I've gotten kind of involved in something here, with you, and maybe thinking it wasn't very smart since I'm going to have to leave soon."

"Not for a couple weeks still," Callan pointed out, his brow lowering as a little wrinkle appeared between his eyes.

"True," I agreed. "But still."

Callan nodded. "So you're thinking it might be better not to get any deeper."

That was exactly what I was thinking. But with Callan's hand weaving its way through my hair, massaging the round of my skull, and those deep glittering eyes on mine in the firelight, it was hard to remember why.

"We don't gain anything in the world without risk," Callan said softly. "And sometimes," he added, stretching out his leg and wincing as he straightened his ankle, "sometimes we lose everything. But even the few moments when we have it all—those are worth the fall."

I knew he was talking about soccer, but he was talking about us too. Would it be worth the risk? Hadn't I already taken the risk without really ever deciding? "I just don't see where it will go," I whispered, knowing my defenses were weak, and that I was only fighting because I felt like I was supposed to resist.

But it was already much too late for that.

The electric cord that bound us together pulled and tightened between us, crackling and popping with tension, and when Callan leaned his head in, my body responded, leaving my mind a step behind. My lips met his, and I felt something inside me give as our tongues met. My rigidity turned to softness, my hesitation to relaxed acceptance. This was happening. And as our tongues tangled, seeking and teasing, I felt heat rushing through my core, pooling low in my belly.

I sighed, breaking the kiss for long enough to lean back into the plush rug, pulling Callan Whitewood down over me. And I gave myself over to sensation and emotion, leaving my rational mind standing in the dark distance, shouting things I couldn't quite make out in the rush of making love with the man in my arms.

BATHROOM BUSINESS

CALLAN

$\mathcal{E}$ventually, we worked our way upstairs, but not before I'd explored every inch of her soft golden skin in the light of the fire, kissing and licking, rewarded by her soft moans and gasps. We'd wound up wrapped in each other's limbs, her seated on my lap, her legs and arms holding me tightly as we'd exploded together in a burst of shimmering sparks.

April was like an unpredictable firecracker—the kind they didn't sell in California. Once lit, she burned slow and uncertain, but when she went off, it was thrilling and more exciting than anything I'd ever seen or felt. I liked the slow burn, the anticipation of the reward. With my ex, I'd never had that feeling. She responded to me exactly as she'd thought she should, like she read a book or just took her cues from movies showing men and women making love. I didn't like to think she'd been faking it all along, but she'd had none of the surprised gasps, the almost pained little moans April let out that set my skin blazing.

Maybe it had never been real.

Maybe nothing in my life had.

Soccer had been though, I thought wistfully as I held a hot cup of coffee between my palms the next morning and stood in front of the big windows looking out over the back porch. My ankle twinged, reminding me how real it had been. When I closed my eyes, I could still hear the crowd screaming at a low roar as I took the field, could hear Trace Johnson's bellow from the other end of the pitch whenever I scored. I could still feel my teammates clapping me on the back, the impact of them throwing their bodies at me in celebration. I missed it. All of it.

"Silver bell for your thoughts?" April picked up one of the decorations on the little wall shelf behind me and offered it to me with a smile. She wore a pair of my flannel pajama bottoms and a hoodie I'd pulled from the closet for her with the Sharks logo on the front. It was a strange combination of past and present, and it made my heart ache for some reason.

"Sorry," I said, turning and bringing my mind back to the present. "I was just thinking how the weather has changed." A cold wind was whipping down the hill behind the house, pulling tiny whitecaps from the surface of the Potomac and sending naked branches arching and swaying overhead. Winter had arrived.

"I'm not buying it," April said, the corners of her mouth lifting as she looked up at me. "But I'll take it." She bumped her shoulder gently into my side, careful not to spill the coffee we each held, and I wrapped an arm around her shoulders.

"I'm glad you stayed," I said, my voice growing rougher as my mind flashed through images of April by the fire, and later, in my bed.

"Me too," she said, and it felt like an admission. April was struggling, I knew. I sensed she had some inner monologue going on, telling her that getting involved with me was a bad idea. I couldn't promise her it wasn't, but I wished I could silence that little voice, for now at least. I wanted to revel in this thing we'd found. I didn't want to worry about the future. But maybe that was unfair. A guy who'd had no future for the past year probably worried a little less about that kind of thing than a girl in the midst of saving her career.

"Annabelle's going to wonder what happened to me," April said. "I should let her know I'm okay."

"Probably should," I agreed.

April went back to the front room to find her phone, and returned a few minutes later, setting it on the table nearby after sending a text.

"What's your plan for the weekend?" I asked her, angling my head back toward the kitchen where a timer was signaling that the cinnamon rolls we'd put in the oven were done.

"I don't know, really," she said. "Get my notes finalized and sent off to Los Angeles for Monday. But not much else, I guess. How about you?"

I gave her a grin over my shoulder as I went to get the

rolls. "I don't do a ton of planning ahead these days," I said. "Probably see my nieces, hang out with Cormac. Do something festive. You in?"

April looked startled, her eyebrows shooting up into her messy gorgeous hair. "Um."

"Just say yes," I suggested, sliding a spatula under a gooey roll and putting it onto a plate.

"I don't want to intrude. I'm sure your brother wonders why I'm here all the time."

I pressed my lips into a wry line, thinking about what my brother had probably already deduced. "I'm pretty sure Cormac has figured out why you're here."

"Great." April crossed her arms and leaned a hip into the counter.

"Say yes," I prodded, carrying both plates to the small round table.

When April didn't answer, I put the plates down and then turned back to her, spinning her by the shoulders and sliding my arms around her waist. "Don't overthink," I suggested. "I don't know what this is either. What I do know is that since you forced your way in here, scaling my gate and breaking into my house, I've been happier than I think I've been in years."

April's brow wrinkled adorably at that. "Really?" Her voice was a hesitant whisper.

"Really." I bent my head and kissed her then. I might have no idea what we were doing, but I was going to let it play out. I had nothing to lose, after all, and this felt good and right.

Nothing in my life had felt good in such a long time, I didn't care what it meant or how long it lasted. I was just going to close my eyes and hold on.

April's body relaxed in my arms and she pressed herself to me, her softness meeting my muscle and creating a reassuring warmth between us that told me I'd convinced her. At least for now. "Okay," she said quietly.

🍬

'Festive' that day ended up meaning spending most of the day in bed with intermittent runs to the kitchen for food. I did actually answer my phone when Cormac called though, and invited him and the girls for dinner. "April will be here too," I said, smiling at April, who was texting with someone on her own phone at my side. I thought it was her friend Lynn, but it might have been Annabelle. Either way, I'd glanced over, seen the words "underwear," "sexy," and "five times" and figured I was better off minding my own business.

"There," I said, putting my phone onto the nightstand and then rolling to position my head on April's soft stomach so I could look up at her. "I did something productive."

"I'm staying for dinner?" April asked, raising a brow at me over her phone.

"Didn't I already convince you to stay and stop overthinking?" I pressed my hand to the side of her thigh, sliding it slowly up her side to her hip. "Maybe you need more convincing?" My body was languid and loose, and for once, my ankle wasn't screaming at me. It turned out that all I needed to feel better was to have sex with April five or six times a day.

April put her own phone aside and let her hands fall into my hair. The gentle tug and rustle of her fingers made my eyes slip shut in pleasure. "I feel kind of useless and lazy though," she said. "We've been in bed all day."

"Most people would kill for the luxury," I said. I was thinking of the luxury not just of being in bed, but of having April there with me, having her soft moans in my ear, her pliant body in my arms.

"But most people," April said, "people like me, for instance, have jobs to do."

For some reason, April's words stung a little bit, but I did my best not to react. I left my head where it was and tried to focus on the movement of her fingers on my scalp, on the warm satisfaction tingling through my body. There were plenty of days ahead where I could go on feeling worthless. I didn't want to do that today. I gathered my motivation and sat up. "We have a job to do," I said, turning my head to smile at her.

"We do?" Her brows lowered over blue eyes and she frowned.

"We're making dinner for Cormac and the girls. We have an hour and a half."

April's face took on a comical look of horror. "Is that all? But I have to shower! And I don't have any clothes!"

I frowned. "Showering is not a problem. I have showers here."

"How novel," April quipped sarcastically. "A house with a shower."

"But you'll have to wear your clothes from yesterday," I said. "Unless you really favor soccer jerseys and shorts." My eyes wandered to the window beyond the bed. Shorts and a jersey didn't seem like the right thing for the current cold weather. "Or warmups."

April sighed. "I'll be okay. If your brother already thinks we're sleeping together, I don't need to advertise it by showing up at dinner in your clothes." She slid her hand into mine atop the comforter. "But after dinner, I need to go back to the hotel."

The thought of saying goodbye to April tonight had my heart protesting already, but I wasn't completely sure whether it was because I wanted her to stay or because I just didn't want to be alone. Having her here had been such a good change from my previous lonely existence. But if I wasn't appreciating April for April—but only as a warm body keeping me company—well, I owed it to her to find out.

She stepped from the bed and shot me a glance over her shoulder as she headed for the bathroom. "See you downstairs."

The door closed and the shower began to run, and after a few minutes, I pushed myself out of the warm cocoon of the bed, and pressed my feet into the cold hardwood floor. My ankle protested immediately, shooting a pang of agony up my leg. I had thought staying off my feet all day would have helped, but evidently not. It was only painless when I was actually in the middle of sex. I sighed, pulled on some jeans and a long-sleeved T-shirt, and went down to the kitchen to see about dinner.

I wasn't a fantastic chef, but I had always enjoyed being in the kitchen. I liked baking better than cooking—there were rules, after all, and if you followed those, everything worked out pretty well. Cooking was more like the Wild West, and the lack of clearly defined boundaries made me feel a little unsettled, like anything could happen. Maybe it was all the years on the soccer pitch, but I liked knowing where the lines were, knowing how to win.

Before long, I had music blasting through the kitchen, the walls of windows glowing with the light from overhead and the warmth from the oven and stove. I moved around, ignoring my ankle and enjoying the stark landscape outside the glass contrasted to the warm coziness within. I could hear April's feet above on the floorboards, and the knowledge that she was here created another kind of warmth inside me. As I made spaghetti sauce, my mind turned through images of the day like a nostalgic teenager might flip through photos on her phone. April, her hair cascading over us both as she sat astride me, leaning down for a kiss. April beneath me, those blue eyes glittering as she laughed. Less formed flashes of her skin, her scent, her sounds wafted through my mind, accompanied by the smell of the pumpkin pie I was making for dessert.

It wasn't just having someone here, I decided, trying to replace April mentally with Becky and feeling a cold frigidity settle inside me at the imagining. It was April. Even thinking of her name sent a little zip of pleasure through my chest.

Something about her in particular made me want her to stay.

The woman in my mind appeared in the kitchen as I sat on a tall stool, stirring the sauce and singing along with "Rudolph the Red Nosed Reindeer," which had just begun playing on Pandora. "Oh god, Rudolph? Really?" she moaned.

"If we're going to Christmas you up, we might as well start big," I said. "Besides, this can be our song."

She strode over to peer past my shoulder at the sauce simmering in the pot. "This can definitely not be our song." She hesitated for a moment. "Do we need a song?"

I lifted a shoulder. That same teenaged girl inside me was swooning, telling me that yes, we needed a song, but that it should be romantic. I handed the girl in my head a scrunchy and a hydro flask and told her to beat it. What was happening to me? "No, of course not." I stood, pushing the stool away, suddenly needing to feel a little more manly.

"Does it hurt your ankle to stand for too long?" April said, watching me stand in front of the stove.

"Everything hurts my ankle," I said honestly. "Except being in bed with you. Today it didn't hurt almost all day, and that's a first."

"You had some distractions," April said, smiling. "I can stir. Or ... ?"

"Make a salad?" I suggested at her implied question.

"Sure." April went to the refrigerator and found the ingredients easily enough. Soon, the gate buzzer sounded through the house, and I hurried off to let my brother and nieces in.

"Thanks for the invite," Cormac said, stepping in behind

two squealing girls dressed in tutus for no explicable reason. "I was going a little nuts with the whole weekend ahead of me, to be honest."

I laughed as the girls leapt around the tree, talking excitedly to one another in a language I hoped maybe they could understand. "No problem. Come in. Drink?"

"Yeah." I glanced over my shoulder to see my brother rubbing a hand up and then down his face, looking worn out and a little defeated, and my heart ached for him. I didn't know how to help, not really, but I knew I shouldn't leave Cormac alone. Moving here had been the right thing. My brother needed help. And support.

"Hey April," Cormac said, following me into the kitchen, where April stood dutifully at the stove, stirring the pot of sauce, her salad in a bowl on the counter.

She stepped away, coming to give Cormac a quick hug. "Hi," she said, and I noticed the way her eyes scanned his face, the worry that crept into her expression as she let him go and went back toward the stove. "How are you? The girls?"

Cormac laughed, but it was a tired and hopeless sound as he slouched into a chair and accepted the tumbler I pressed into his hand. "We are hanging in there," he said. "What are we drinking?" He lifted the glass, inspecting the caramel brown liquid inside.

"Bourbon," I said. "But it's not as good as HalfCat's."

"Oh, yeah? What'd you think?" Cormac asked before taking a sip.

I told my brother about our visit and the three of them

laughed at my recounting of Mr. FluffyNuts and the crazy rules of the counties over which the bar sat.

"Daddy!" A shriek erupted from the front of the house, sending all three of us to our feet and through the doorway to the parlor.

I stopped in the parlor, Cormac glancing around frantically at my side. We spotted Taylor standing outside the powder room door, looking worried. "What's going on?"

"Maddie's in there," Taylor said, pointing at the door. I tried to imagine what kind of shriek-worthy emergencies could happen in tiny bathrooms but came up short.

A muffled sobbing sound came from inside the bathroom. Cormac stepped closer as April and I hovered just beyond. It seemed to me like bathroom problems were probably dad issues. "Honey?" Cormac called through the door. "You okay?"

"No!" A shriek came back in reply. "I want Mommy!" This last part devolved into miserable crying.

Taylor stepped closer to her father, looking up at him, and his hand cupped the back of her neck protectively as he glanced over at me. Cormac's face was bereft, his eyes exhausted and his mouth drawn. "I know honey, we all miss her. Can I help with ... this?"

"No!" Maddie was nearly hysterical inside the bathroom now, and her hiccupping sobs could be heard clearly through the door.

"What happened just before she went in there?" Cormac asked Taylor, squatting low to look her in the eye.

Taylor's eyes went wide and her mouth opened to begin her denial of fault. "I didn't do anything."

"That's not what I asked," Cormac said patiently.

Maddie was wailing, her sobs nearly forming the word "Mommy," which was heartbreaking to hear. I gripped April's hand tightly as we exchanged a worried glance. My mind raced, trying to figure out what I should be doing, how I could help.

Taylor began explaining everything that had happened since they'd arrived at my house, and April and I ventured nearer the door. I knocked lightly. "Mads, honey, it's your uncle. Can I help?"

The sobbing halted for a second, and then began again more quietly. Taylor was still giving Cormac a blow by blow of the activities that had led up to this crisis. "And then I told her that purple looks nicer with yellow."

"Right," Cormac said, his voice thinning in impatience. "And she went in the bathroom?"

"No," Taylor said. "Then we had a skipping contest."

Maddie's crying had grown softer inside the bathroom, and a loud hiccup came through the door, followed by an inquisitive, "Ape-will?"

I felt April stiffen at his side in surprise. "Yes, Maddie? I'm here," April said, shaking her head lightly.

"Can you come in?" Maddie asked.

April turned wide eyes on me and I released her hand, nodding that she should go in. April cracked the door and asked, "Okay. What's up, honey?" and disappeared inside.

Cormac turned to stare at the closed door and then met my eyes. We exchanged a confused look as murmuring could be heard from inside the bathroom. I didn't know what to think—was I pushing April too far into my family by expecting her to help my niece in the bathroom? A few minutes later, there was a flush, the sink running, and then both girls emerged. Maddie held April's hand, and her little face was streaked with tears.

"Is everything okay?" Cormac asked, half to April, half to Maddie.

Maddie nodded, and April said, "Everything is fine. Just a bit of girl stuff is all."

Cormac's mouth dropped open slightly and he sighed. "I'm gonna just go finish that drink," he said, standing and heading back to the kitchen.

"That was phenomenal," I said to April as we followed him Cormac to the kitchen, little girls in tow. "What was going on?" I couldn't pull my eyes from her face, which was flushed and glowing. I was impressed, and maybe just a little bit in awe at the easy way she'd handled whatever had just happened. A fleeting thought flew through my mind—April would be an amazing mother. I pushed it down as soon as I thought it. Too soon. Way too soon.

"Later," April promised.

A few minutes later, we all sat around the table in the dining room, spaghetti steaming on our plates as the smells of garlic and warm bread wafted through the house. The girls ate happily and Cormac did too, quietly interspersing bites with sips of the red wine I had opened.

"So," I said, wishing the atmosphere was just a little more relaxed. My brother did not seem to be in the mood for conversation, but I felt like I owed April a nice time. "Plans for the weekend, girls?"

"Ballet practice," Taylor informed me. "And Daddy's taking us to the ice castle."

I glanced at Cormac. "They have an ice castle here?" I had visited an ice hotel in Sweden—it had been over the top, with the reception desk, the bar, the beds, all carved from ice.

Cormac lifted a shoulder. "That's how it's advertised. I guess we'll see."

Maddie beamed at April across the table. "Ape-will will come."

"I will?" April had clearly not been informed of this agenda item.

"Tomow-woh." Maddie stuffed a big piece of garlic bread into her mouth then, defying any further clarification.

I glanced at April, feeling an anticipation I almost wished I didn't and also feeling simultaneously jealous that Maddie could so simply say what she wanted. I wanted April to say yes too. I wanted to spend time with her—as much as she'd allow. I wanted to tell her how much better I felt when she was nearby, laughing and smiling and exercising her intense hatred of the holidays in a way that was almost comical. I wanted to reach my hand toward her, capture her soft cool skin in my own and never let go.

But I didn't do any of that. I just watched her, smiling encouragingly, and celebrated inside when she shrugged and asked, "What's an ice castle?"

The evening wound down, both girls ending up tucked in with blankets in front of *Frozen* in the small den off the parlor while April, Cormac, and I sat in front of the fire in the living room.

"What was going on there in the bathroom?" Cormac asked April, and I looked at her, equally curious.

She sighed, and her eyes flitted from one of us to the other. "She was upset because Taylor had told her something." April paused, and then dropped her eyes, and I was suddenly worried. April didn't look eager to share. But it was far too early for real girl problems, wasn't it?

Cormac rubbed a hand over his face and leaned forward, dropping his forearms on his knees. "What was it this time? Something that would lead to an aneurysm, no doubt."

April's eyes widened as they flew to Cormac and stayed on his face. "Yes," she said, her voice showing her surprise.

"This isn't the first time," he said wearily, and my heart clenched with sympathy.

"I guess Taylor told her that if you ... um, well, that if you go number one and number two at the same time ..."

"It'll cause an aneurysm and you'll die like Linda did," Cormac finished for her.

I felt myself deflate, suddenly feeling ashamed that my own happiness had been keeping me from noticing how my family was struggling.

April nodded and looked guilty, as if she'd invented this bit of ridiculousness herself. "I assured her that wasn't true," April said.

"Taylor's been searching for a reason, I guess. Something that caused the burst that killed her mother." Cormac leaned back again. "I'm hoping it's just a phase. Doesn't seem to matter how many times I tell her it wasn't a thing she did that caused it, that it isn't something that will happen to her."

"She's just trying to process it, I guess," I said. It made sense to me. I'd been trying to process my own injury—why it had been me, why it had happened at all.

"I just wish she'd stop terrifying Maddie in the process," Cormac said.

I sighed and leaned back, wishing there was something I could do to help my brother.

ENTER THE WIZARD
APRIL

It had been a long evening, one that had ended with me coaxing Maddie from the bathroom and then agreeing to go visit an ice castle—whatever that was—with Callan's family.

It was hard to say no to a tiny girl with wild blond curls and garlic bread stuffed into her mouth. And while I wasn't sure what an ice castle was, or if spending all my free time with Callan's adorable family was the right thing to do, I wasn't about to let Maddie down.

And there was something in the way Callan was looking at me too. The light shining in those dark magnetic eyes matched Maddie's in a way—hopeful, eager. Or was I just imagining it?

I realized I probably needed to take a step back and do some thinking. I'd ridden the wave of impulse most of my life—in college relationships that had always moved too fast and gone horribly wrong, usually because I thought something was happening that definitely wasn't, and then later in my career. Impulse felt good, but I knew it was not my friend, even if its tiny curly-headed sidekick was adorable.

Plus, the ice castle sounded interesting. "So do they actually carve a castle from ice?"

"Sounds like it, right?" Cormac said, and the glint in his eyes and the wry twist of his mouth told me that this castle might be slightly less grand and royal than my imaginings. But I knew Cormac wouldn't dash his daughters' hopes.

"It sounds incredible," I said, putting extra emphasis into my words as I had grinned at Maddie and Taylor.

Taylor had lowered her fork and given me a frank look. "Practice is at ten. We'll go to the ice castle afterwards. You guys can meet us at the studio." After this incredibly grown-up declaration of organized planning, Taylor had picked her fork up and continued eating, leaving Callan and I to exchange glances.

"Are you free tomorrow?" Callan had asked.

"You guys really don't have to—" Cormac started.

"I'm coming either way," Callan assured him.

Warring emotions had whirled in my chest. Here was a real family doing real family things—something I hadn't gotten once my father had decided to play Santa's Helper for the rest of my childhood somewhere far away from me. But it also wasn't my family. It was like a movie I was watching, and I knew that there would be an end to the movie, and that it could be a sad one that would make me cry. But just like with *Steel Magnolias,* I couldn't stop watching even though I knew how it would end. I nodded. "I'm free," I said to Callan, swallowing hard.

A smile crept slowly across his full lips, lifting just the corners at first and then revealing the shining white teeth, as his dimples appeared in the stubble at the sides of his mouth and the mesmerizing eyes glowed. And in that second, I knew something else had just happened. I'd said yes to more than a ballet rehearsal and a tour through a tent full of ice cubes. I'd said yes to Callan Whitewood. Yes to whatever was possible here, for whatever amount of time. And damn the consequences.

I had pushed away the voice warning me about impulsivity, reminding me about every bad decision I'd ever made.

Callan's gleaming eyes were impossible to resist, and I lifted my wine glass to the amazing family around the table before me. "Tell me more about this castle," I said, and I allowed myself to settle into the warmth and happiness I felt, even knowing it might be fleeting.

⁊

I returned to the hotel after dinner, after a long kiss that turned into an extended make-out session at the front door that might or might not have turned into something else on the new area rug just beneath the soaring twinkling Christmas tree in the parlor.

"I'll pick you up at the hotel at nine-thirty," Callan promised as he said goodnight, and I had agreed, every part of me smiling.

Now, back in the half-decorated room at the inn, reality threatened to set in. The impersonal setting of my room, coupled with the bare tree in the corner and my suitcase on the stand next to the closet, reminded me that this wasn't my real life. This wasn't my home, and these people—warm though they might be—were not my family.

But I pushed that doubt away, too swaddled in the lingering warmth of Callan Whitewood's embrace, his kiss, his ... everything, to let it affect me. I got into my pajamas, put on HGTV—I had to keep tabs on the competition, after all— and climbed onto my bed to call Lynn at home.

"Hey you!" Lynn picked up after the first couple rings.

"Hey," I said.

"It's been like a year since you've called. Your texts are so suspenseful! How's Broken Tree? Have you won over the network yet?" Lynn's voice made me miss home, empty though it was in many ways. But the ache of missing the familiar was overshadowed by the pulsing bubble of happiness growing inside me.

"Well, I don't know about that. It's Singletree, by the way. Though they changed the name officially for the month."

"To what?"

"Er, to Christmas Tree."

"You. Are. Kidding!" Lynn laughed. "You are living in a town named for the thing you despise with the fire of a thousand burning suns?"

"Yes." I settled back into the pillows on my bed, waiting for my vehemence about all things Christmas to set in. It didn't arrive. "But I actually think maybe this has been good. I don't mind Christmas stuff so much after this immersive exposure. The people here are really into the holidays."

"I guess that's why you're there," Lynn said, sounding pleased. "And the job is good? Things are staying on track?"

"They are, actually."

"You sound so surprised," Lynn laughed.

"My work life does not historically go smoothly."

"This is true."

"But yeah, we filmed the first three houses. We've got the week to chill while all the film is reviewed, and then next week will be make it or break it time. Two more houses, including the big one."

"And is that Mr. Grumpy super-hot soccer star?"

I laughed. "Right. Yes."

"He's cool with you filming now?" Lynn sounded surprised and I realized how much had happened in the last week that I still hadn't told her. I'd texted that we'd spent some time together, but that was it. Only Annabelle knew all the details.

"Yeah ..." I wasn't sure how to begin. "He's actually a really nice guy." The word "nice" made me cringe. Callan was so much more than nice, and the mention of him had parts of my body remembering it and suggesting things that didn't even make sense and were certainly not nice.

"Nice, huh?" Lynn's skeptical tone said she knew exactly where I was headed with this. "What's going on?"

"I've been seeing him a little bit."

"Right. With a clipboard in your hand and a bunch of cameras behind you. It's your job." Lynn emphasized the last word and the way she did it made any actual reminders of my tendency to screw up jobs totally unnecessary.

"Maybe a little more privately, actually." When Lynn didn't immediately answer, my mouth started moving at a rapid pace, and I machine gunned out the details of the past week, from Santa's sleigh to the HalfCat Distillery to dinner at Callan's house with Cormac and the girls.

"Oh shit," Lynn breathed when I finally paused for breath.

"Like ... 'oh shit, that's great and I'm really happy you're happy,' or ..."

"Oh shit, April." Lynn ignored her question. "This is not going to end well. You can see that, right?"

I could not see that. Not exactly. "I don't know," I said, my voice wavering. "I mean ..."

"What's the plan then? You come home and you guys have a long-distance thing that you keep totally secret from the only living relative you have besides your mom?" We both counted my father as dead since I hadn't seen him in years. He wasn't dead, actually, but the fact that he'd gone off and started a new family made him dead to me, even though he still insisted on sending me birthday cards.

"I hadn't really thought ahead that far," I said, the words sounding inadequate even to me.

"Rob will shit," Lynn said plainly. "And then you'll lose another job."

I sighed. My uncle would be angry, that was for sure. But part of me wondered if he would let it go if he realized this thing with Callan was real. Was it real? "But I think this might be something beyond just a fling," I suggested. "I really ... like him." The word 'like' was inadequate to capture my feelings, but all other options were too much just yet.

"You do, huh?" Lynn's voice lightened. "Are you sure it isn't just the sex? Or his fancy big house? Or the fact that he's Callan fucking Whitewood of the enormous underwear billboard?"

"I mean, it is the sex ... partly. He's just ..." My mind whirled and I closed my eyes. "It's like magic when we're together, like he knows exactly what to do to me. It's like he's some kind of wizard or something."

"He's a dick wizard?"

Dick wizard? Who even says that? I laughed, and when I got hold of myself again, said, "Yeah, he's some kind of dick wizard I guess. But he's sweet, Lynn. And he's got this vulnerable side I'm getting glimpses of here and there, like even though he's been this famous soccer star, he's kind of lonely. It sounds like he hasn't had anyone to talk to in a long time. And his brother and nieces are great too. They've really included me, made me feel welcome."

"It's going to be hard to leave," Lynn warned.

"I think I'm ready for you to stop playing devil's advocate and just be my friend."

"Yeah? Okay. I can do that. I just want you to be happy, April. But for selfish reasons I don't want to lose you to some crazy little Maryland town that changes its name for every holiday."

"I don't think they do that. It sounds like this is the first time—"

"Really not the point."

"Right."

"Okay, girl. I'm happy for you. Just be careful, okay? And for God's sake, don't let your uncle find out you're banging the help again!"

A snort-laugh escaped me. "The help?"

"The cast, whatever. It just sounded better like that. Dramatic. You're in TV. You get dramatic. The dick wizard."

"He's not even going to appear. Just his house. I'm not banging his house."

"How would that even work? I'm getting a visual on that I'm not liking a lot. Quick, talk about something else."

"Chinchillas," I said quickly.

"Do not bang a chinchilla." Lynn's voice was serious and I giggled. "They're tiny. I don't know how that would work exactly. Maybe with like a tiny dildo or something ... either way, you'd probably kill the poor thing, and—"

"Okay, thanks. I'm marking houses and chinchillas off my perv list."

"Yeah. Good idea."

"I miss you," I said.

"Me too. Keep me updated."

"I will. Love you."

"Love you too. Bye." Lynn hung up and I sat for a long time on my bed, thinking about Callan Whitewood (who I would now accidentally call "dick wizard" in my head for all of eternity), chinchillas, Christmas, and my uncle. Not necessarily in that order.

Spending the weekend with Callan and Cormac and two little girls who were enthusiastic about literally everything was like spending time in an alternate universe. I didn't talk to my uncle, and except for a brief meeting with the production team, I didn't really think about work.

Instead, for the first time in a long time, I just lived, taking in the world around me and actually enjoying it, draped though it was in red, and green, and candy-cane striped everything. The little girls' ballet rehearsal was an adorably chaotic event with music from *The Nutcracker* running through the background, and the "ice castle" was a tent filled with tables draped with white tablecloths and small ice sculptures on display.

"It's not quite a castle," I whispered at one point to Callan, who held my hand almost through the whole weekend, sending intermittent chills through my body as my traitorous mind chanted, "dick wizard, dick wizard."

"No," he said, and was about to offer more of his thoughts on the distinctly un-palacelike tent full of ice, when Taylor said in a low and reverent voice, "It's magical."

"Elwww-saaa," Maddie added, her eyes rounding at the cardboard cutout of Elsa from *Frozen* that stood in one corner.

The little girls were awed by the sculptures, so whoever planned the ice castle for the town clearly understood their target market well. I could appreciate that. Cormac, for his part, tried to be enthusiastic, but I could see the exhaustion in his eyes and I sensed that the kind of tiredness he suffered wasn't related to sleeplessness, though I was sure that was part of it. I wished I could help him more, but I wasn't sure exactly how to do it. I did my best to offer him smiles and understanding, knowing it wasn't enough.

Once the girls and their father had gone home, we went back to Callan's house again, and my week off stretched out before us, each day an unscheduled opportunity to spend time together. And that's what we did. I slowly brought things from the hotel to Callan's, without really realizing what was happening. But by Friday, I sat next to him at the breakfast table drinking coffee and checking email, and realized I hadn't spent a single night at the hotel since the week before.

A tiny finger of panic had threatened to rise in my throat now and then during the long peaceful week, but I ignored it. There was nothing to worry about, I told myself. I was living in the moment. And the moment was good.

"This is nice," Callan had said at multiple points. He'd said it at dinner as we sat on the couch with takeout and watched a Christmas movie marathon. He'd said it as we helped Annabelle unload the truck that brought the excess decorations from the inn to the outbuilding Callan had offered for storage. He'd said it as we walked the riverside, hand in hand, while the cold December wind whipped the surface of the water and my hair.

It *was* nice. It might have been the nicest week I had ever had—filled with companionship, warmth and a strange coziness that seemed to emanate from the twinkling tree and jolly stockings hanging at Callan's hearth. Seeing my name on one of the stockings had been a bit of a shock, but Callan explained that Maddie and Taylor had insisted upon it. And that was nice too.

It was more than nice, if I was honest. It was glorious. Callan's dark expressive eyes were almost always on my face, and he found reasons to touch me constantly. He whispered sweet things to me in intimate moments—things about my body, my hair, the way I smelled, my smile.

My heart was swelling with unfamiliar feelings related to Callan, and each day—each moment—that passed, grew the feelings. But the words that threatened to escape my lips seemed too big, too much for a man I'd known a short time, one whom I'd be leaving in another week.

As Callan buried himself inside me one night in his bedroom, the excitement of the sex ratcheted up several notches by the incredible day we'd spent shopping and seeing a movie, my ecstasy-soaked mind scrabbled for some coherent words. But when "dick wizard" escaped my lips and Callan stopped moving suddenly, I was pretty sure I had not found them.

"Did you just call me a dick wizard?" He moved his head away from my neck, still holding me pinned to the mattress, his mouth slightly open in surprise.

"No."

"You did. That's what you just said."

I thrust against him, hoping to distract him back into finishing what he'd started.

"Am I a dick wizard?" he asked, grinning now. "I like it."

"No, that's not what I said."

Callan chuckled and began moving again, much to my relief. But when we finished, he started laughing again.

"You gave me a nickname," he said. "And I like it."

"I did not," I insisted, hating that my stupid brain was still chanting the ridiculous phrase. "I said, 'sick lizard.'"

"You called me a sick lizard?" Callan sat up and crossed his arms in front of him.

"No. Not you, I was ... I was thinking about a lizard my friend has. It's very sick."

"Really?" Callan's tone made it clear he was not buying this.

"Yes?" I tried.

He grinned at me then and shook his head. "Okay. Fine." But as we snuggled together and drifted toward sleep, I was pretty sure I heard him whisper, "dick wizard."

PARK YOUR SLEIGH AT MY PLACE
CALLAN

The week April spent at my new house was potentially the happiest I could remember. My ankle had still hurt, of course, but something about having April nearby made the pain less poignant somehow. Or maybe it was that the magnitude of other feelings growing inside me made my perception of the pain less, somehow. When pain had been the only feeling I'd had, I focused on it. Now I had other feelings to consider—some of which I was frankly afraid of.

I'd known this girl a short time. This quirky, beautiful, honest and practical girl who was unlike anyone I'd ever known. As a pro soccer player, my life had been full of people who told me what they thought I wanted to hear and people who suggested the world should be exactly the way I wanted it just because I had some talent at driving a ball down a patch of grass. But April wasn't impressed by that. She seemed to focus on the present, on the moment—and that was good for me. God knew I'd spent enough time looking back at what I'd been, at what I'd lost.

And when she'd dubbed me the dick wizard ... well, I had felt a twinge inside my heart. It had been a feeling that lay next to amusement and charm, somewhere near to sentiment and nostalgia, but squarely in the realm of adoration. Maybe even something deeper, I realized. Only April would accidentally utter such a ridiculous moniker and then try to cover it up with something even more ludicrous. I loved the raspberry stain of embarrassment on her cheeks as she explained that her friend had an ailing lizard. She was beautiful. She was adorable.

I wanted her to be mine.

"You look amazing," I told her when she emerged from my bathroom, her hair in an elaborate knot at the back of her head and the long velvet sheath dress we found for her to wear to the ballet showcasing every curve I'd come to know by heart over the past week.

"Thank you," she said, her eyes running the length of my body and slowly coming back to my face, more heat in them than had been there when the door opened. "You look good too."

I had broken out my favorite suit for the occasion, the dark grey Italian made for me last year. The cloth was fine and fitted, and paired with a deep green tie, I felt confident. The look in April's eyes only buoyed my confidence more.

I held the door for her in front of my house, helping her into the truck as she pulled her long coat tighter around her.

"It's freezing!" she laughed, and the sparkle in her eyes as they met mine made my heart squeeze tightly inside my chest.

"I'm not used to the cold," I told her. "Next time I'll warm the car before I put you inside it."

I went around, and once inside the car, I blasted the heater, wishing I'd thought to heat it ahead. It was freezing, and the predictions were calling for snow this week. I knew April had to get back to work, and that when she finished, she'd be leaving, so I didn't feel guilty about wishing for a storm to dump feet on the area, making it impossible for anything to happen on schedule. I'd take whatever excuse I could get to keep her here now. To spend more time with her. To maybe find the courage to ask her to stay. Or at least to come back.

"Are you ready for *The Nutcracker*?" she asked me, a grin pulling her berry-glossed lips wide, and my mind jumping immediately to what those lips would look like wrapped around certain parts of my body.

"Your tone makes me think you're expecting something less than professional quality from this production," I said, forcing myself to think of things besides the fact that April called me "dick wizard" or how much I wanted to go on earning the name.

She lowered her brows and her hand squeezed my arm. "We did see the rehearsal," she reminded me.

"I liked the part where the little boy who is playing the mouse king ripped off a couple of the heads, screaming about how there should only be one head."

"Think he'll do that in the show?"

"We'll have to wait and find out." April had scooted as close as she could to me on the bench seat, leaning into my shoulder as I drove, her hand resting on my thigh. I would have made the drive last forever if I could, but it wasn't long before we were pulling up in front of the little theatre and had to get out or risk being late for the curtain.

Cormac was waiting for us in the lobby, looking put together in a dark suit and a red tie.

"Hey," Cormac said, greeting me with a clap on the back and a handshake. "You clean up pretty good when you try. Hello, April." He kissed April on the cheek as she smiled up at him.

"Are the girls excited?" she asked.

"Over the moon," he confirmed. "Especially since they're the only girls in the dressing room to receive a dozen long-stemmed red roses each." He gave me a wry smile.

"Isn't that appropriate?" I asked innocently as I felt April's eyes staring intently at the side of my face.

"I had to explain what 'break a leg' meant," Cormac said as I helped April off with her coat.

I grimaced. "And maybe," I said, limping slightly toward the coat check. "Maybe 'break a leg' is a little too on the nose at this point." I nodded at my own leg.

"I bet they are thrilled," April said, moving along with me. "I can't wait to see them."

"The roses were from both of us," I said, earning a huge smile from April. I turned our coats into the coat check, not really noticing the action as I took the tickets and stuffed them into my pocket. My mind was stuck on that huge smile, on the very fact of being here with April, feeling like a couple. I liked it. Hell, I loved it. She was like a life raft that had appeared from nowhere atop a broad empty sea where I'd already resolved to spend the last of my days floating until the eventual end came. Instead, here was April, and the hopeless shipwreck of my life had turned into an exotic cruise.

April had my hand as we found our seats, and after the welcome speech from the woman who Cormac explained was the director, the show began.

All in all, it was only an hour long, something I found myself becoming more grateful for as group after group of tiny dancers took the stage. When Taylor and Maddie appeared for the *Waltz of the Flowers*, I was surprised at the way my heart fluttered and pulsed inside me—like there was a chance it just couldn't hold much more. Taylor kept her face serious, moving her arms with the other girls and performing a very respectable rendition of the steps she'd learned and practiced. Maddie started out with the group, but then she seemed to notice the audience seated out in the dark expanse of the theater, which had been empty during their one dress rehearsal in the space. Her eyes rounded, and gradually she stopped moving, except to take a few steps closer to the edge of the stage and to shield her eyes from the stage lights and peer out into the dark. My heart stuttered— was she scared? I hoped she wasn't going to cry.

The audience chuckled and cooed appreciatively, but

Maddie seemed fixated and had forgotten entirely that she was supposed to be waltzing, turning and leaping with the other flowers.

"Daddy?" She called loudly, searching for him. "Daddy are you ow dere?"

I poked Cormac in the arm, grinning at him as I urged him to answer her.

Cormac got to his feet awkwardly, but then Maddie went on. "Did you bring Uncle Cawan and Auntie Ape-will? I can't see you!"

Reluctantly, I stood took my feet too, and April followed suit. We waved, feeling awkward and fully aware we were causing a disturbance in the audience as other parents grumbled around us.

"Is dat you? It's so dark."

"Yes, honey," Cormac called back. "Now go ahead and dance. We're watching."

Maddie dropped her hands and straightened, clearly realizing the dance had gone on without her, and then she turned and scuttled into the center of the group of girls. She managed to pick up at the spot they'd reached, just before the final steps of the dance.

We took our seats again, Cormac sighing and sinking low in his seat.

April reached across and gave his arm a squeeze. "They're so great," she whispered. And then she looked at me, and my too-full heart stretched even further to accommodate the realization that I'd already fallen. In just over two weeks, at a time when I was sure there wasn't a thing that could pull me back to the land of the living, here was April. I took her hand, twining my fingers through hers, and I sat through the rest of the show, almost wishing it would never end so I could just bask in the nearness of her and the happy realization that life did, in fact, move forward, even when you thought it couldn't.

The girls wanted everyone to go together for ice cream after the performance, so that is what happened, and I was glad to prolong the evening. And when we'd parted ways and April and I were alone in the dark cab of my truck, I turned to her.

"Come home with me?" I wanted to hold her close, to feel her breath against my neck, to slide my hands into the hair I loved. I wanted to tell her how I felt, or at least maybe hint around it, find out if maybe she felt the same thing. I thought she did. Her eyes seemed to say she did.

"I didn't pack a bag," she said, her voice low and regretful. "I can't do the walk of shame in this dress tomorrow, and I sent the clothes I'd had at your house out to be laundered."

I grinned at the mental image her walk of shame brought up. "No, I guess not," I said.

"But you could easily do it in your suit," she added.

I glanced at my own attire and realized she'd just given me an invitation. "Your place then?"

"If you don't mind," she said. Her voice dropped even lower and she stared at her hands as she added, "I don't want to say good night to you. Or goodbye, actually."

"I'd see you tomorrow either way." I said this, hoping

maybe she didn't just mean for tonight but unwilling to risk being wrong.

She didn't look up, but I saw her chest rise as she took a deep breath, steeling herself. "I mean at all. I don't know how I'm going to go home, knowing that you're here. That we're ..." she trailed off, and then raised her eyes to meet mine. "We're ... we're something, right? I'm not imagining things?"

I felt my skin heat as I realized I was not alone in my feelings, and I turned to face April in the close cab, ignoring the protest from my ankle as I pushed it into the floorboards so I could turn fully. "You're not imagining things."

She smiled wide for just a second, as if this confirmation was a relief to her too. She lifted a hand to the side of my face, letting it linger there a long moment before trailing it down and running her finger across my lips. Her touch left a trail of tingling skin, and I fought the urge to rocket myself into her. But as her hand dropped, so did the smile. "So what will happen? What will we do when I go?"

I smiled with a brightness I didn't feel. "They have these things called airplanes," I said.

April stuck her tongue out at me and poked me in the leg, but then let her hand stay there, palm flat to my thigh. "I'm going to take half your name away if you're going to be sarcastic."

"So I'll just be 'wizard?' I like it."

"You'll just be a dick."

I couldn't wait a second longer, and despite the protest in my ankle and the tightness of the fitted suit I wore, I leaned across and pulled April in hard for a kiss. I had to feel her softness in my arms, feel her lips against mine. Her arms went around my neck, and her side of the kiss was every bit as ardent and demanding as mine. When we pulled apart, each a little breathless, I said, "We'll figure it out. It'll be okay." I didn't have the confidence that colored my voice—I didn't like the idea of a cross-country relationship. But I had money. I could make it work. "We won't say goodbye."

"Okay," she said quietly, and I knew she wasn't sure she believed me either.

We drove back to the hotel, and April paused in the lobby to greet Annabelle, who was dressed like a nutcracker tonight, bright red circles pasted on her cheeks and a very tall soldier's hat on her head.

"Don't you two look lovely," Annabelle gushed, taking us in.

"We were at the ballet," I explained.

"Oooh, the Kennedy Center?" Annabelle clapped her hands together and looked wistful.

"Uh, no," April corrected. "Miss Rosie's School of Dance. They put on *The Nutcracker* at the high school theater."

"Oh," Annabelle said, but she didn't look any less excited about that. "Well, you two have a good night," she said.

"You too," we said, almost in unison, before heading for the elevator.

"Don't crack too many nuts up there!" Annabelle added, giggling. April and I exchanged a look and then burst into laughter as the elevator doors closed on the lobby.

"My room isn't exactly ... " April began, opening her door for me.

"I've seen it," I reminded her.

"Right, but it's just ... it's not very homey."

"And for a hotel room in the most over-decorated inn on earth, it's painfully un-Christmassy."

April shrugged, dropping her coat over the chair once we'd entered. "Yeah. Sorry."

I smiled at her, and pulled a garland from where she'd stuffed it behind the armchair. "I can help." I crossed the room and draped it over the headboard, and then flicked the switch on it to turn on the lights. "There you go, that's a start."

"Yeah, that won't keep me awake," she said, smiling.

"I wasn't planning on letting you get much sleep anyway," I said, and everything in my body came alive when April pressed herself into my arms in response.

"Come on wizard," she whispered. "Keep me awake."

I held her against me, reaching behind her to unzip the velvet dress that had been holding in her delicious curves all night. The dress accentuated her softness, and rubbing my hands from her waist over the gorgeous swell of her ass under the soft material had me harder than I could ever remember being. Now, with the dress pooled at her ankles and April in my arms wearing only some very small, very lacy underthings, I thought there was a chance I might pass out, since all the blood in my body had clearly migrated to my wizardly dick.

"God, you're beautiful," I said, my tone holding all the worship I felt for the woman in front of me. I stepped back to admire her, and when she kicked away the pool of her dress, wearing black lace and high red heels, my heart stopped for a moment. "Fucking perfect."

"You're not so bad, either," she said, her eyes meeting mine and holding my gaze as her hands came up to push the jacket from my shoulders. We held each other's eyes as she loosened my tie, finally sliding it from around my neck and tossing it to the chair to meet her coat. She stepped nearer still, going up on her toes to kiss me while her fingers worked down the buttons of my shirt and my hands slid along the expanse of soft silken skin on her back. She pulled my shirt-tails from my trousers and pushed my shirt off.

Except she hadn't remembered to remove the cufflinks. Now my hands were trapped in the hanging shirt, leaving me laughing as I held them up for her to see.

"Oh crap," she said, her glittering eyes full of humor. "I'm no good at the sexy disrobing, evidently."

I chuckled and fished for the cufflinks, pulling off the shirt and tossing it aside. "You're doing fine," I said, stepping close enough to press my erection into April's hip.

"Oh," she said, sucking in a sharp breath. "Well then." Her hands dropped low to unfasten my belt and press my trousers and briefs from my hips, her eyes widening in fascination as my eager cock sprang free, standing at attention. For a moment, she stared at it, and just when I was about to feel a bit uncomfortable, she grinned up at me and tilted her head to one side. "That's a pretty impressive staff, there, wizard."

"Think so?" My heart was pounding in my ears, I wanted her so badly. But part of what I loved was this—this irreverent and unexpected humor. April was many things, but she was never predictable.

"Can you perform any magical spells with this?" she asked, gripping me tightly in one hand, sending my balls tight up against my body, ready to explode. I took a deep breath, fighting for control.

"I'm glad you asked," I growled. I scooped her up then, and her hand released me, but its absence was replaced by the firm heft of her body against my chest. I deposited her on the bed, heels and all, and took a moment to let my eyes wander the length of her. "Abra cadabra," I said, moving to rest above her, my knees on either side of her thighs and my hands slipping beneath her. I deftly unclasped her bra and tossed it aside.

"That was impressive," she said in a breathy voice.

"Just wait," I chuckled, and a moment later, I'd slipped down between her legs, easing her panties to one side so I could perform several tricks I knew in the soft folds of her, my tongue and fingers working in unison until she was arching off the bed, her legs shaking on either side of me, one of those sexy-as-hell shoes digging into my back as she cried out my name.

Feeling her come, being here, as close as I could get to her without being inside her, with her scent and her skin and her taste flooding my senses, I was close to coming myself. I had to force my mind away a bit, to things that were slightly less arousing, so that I didn't humiliate himself on her bedspread.

"I want you," she breathed. "So, so much."

I could think of little else, and as I climbed up to press

kisses along the gorgeous soft swell of her belly, between her breasts and over her collarbone, my wizard's staff was howling at me to just get to the main event already. But I was intent on taking my time, even if it killed me.

We'd used a condom every time so far, and as I reached for my pants, where I'd stuck a few into my wallet in optimism that I might end up in exactly this spot, April said, "no."

I froze. She didn't want this? My attention went to my iron-hard dick. Oh god. I could stop now. Of course I could. But it wasn't going to be fun. I looked back up at her, meeting her eye. "You want me to stop?" I tried not to make my voice desperate.

"God, no," she said, her own voice a moan. "I just don't want a condom. I want to feel you. All of you."

Shit. I had to give my eager dick a hard squeeze to keep it from exploding at those words. "But ..."

"I'm on the pill, and I'm clean."

"I am too," I said, recalling the test I'd had to take after I'd learned about my ex's tendency to sleep with anything that had a wizardly staff.

"Then come back," she said, a smile in her voice that matched the one dancing in her eyes.

I didn't need to be asked twice. I slid back over her, my weight on my forearms as the end of my cock notched between her legs. "God, April. You're ..." I slid in just an inch, the tight wetness enveloping the sensitive tip of my dick and overwhelming my senses. "You're fucking perfect. You're ..." Another couple inches, and words were beginning to fail me. "God, so tight. So hot, so ..."

She returned something unintelligible, and then we abandoned words altogether, letting our bodies communicate everything we felt.

I worked to maintain a slow patient rhythm, but April's cries spurred me on until I was thrusting into her helplessly, flexing every muscle in my body as the sheer pleasure of feeling her wrapped around me, hot and tight and welcoming, took over every sense I possessed.

I came spectacularly, stars and then blackness washing through my vision at the end, and as I panted, trying not to crush her as I collapsed, I wondered absently if maybe I'd been screaming. The garland was draped over me, and I realized it must have fallen as I finished. "Was I yelling some kind of wizard chant at the end there?" I asked.

April's eyes held a strange look, but a happy smile hid in the corners of her mouth as she pushed the greenery from my head. "No," she said, her hand stroking my neck. "You did say some other stuff though."

I drew my head back. Oh shit. "What?" I wondered what I might have said in a purely unguarded moment that I didn't know about now.

"You said you loved me." Her voice was quiet, and there was a question in it.

I cringed inwardly. I would have liked to have had more control over that particular sentiment. But its spontaneity didn't make it less true. "I think I do," I said simply.

April kissed me softly. "I didn't know it was possible in such a short time," she said. "But I think I do too."

I wrapped her in my arms, burying my face in her soft

hair, a kind of happiness washing through me that I hadn't known was possible.

I slept that night in a deep dark cocoon of warmth and belonging, the kind of sleep that I'd previously thought only saints must be able to achieve. Free from worry, free from pain. And filled with a kind of whole satisfaction I had never experienced before.

SEX SWINGS ARE FESTIVE ... RIGHT?

APRIL

I awoke early, turning my head to see the comforting side of Callan's broad strong back beside me. I pressed myself into him, tucking my knees behind the hollow of his legs and absorbing the warmth of his skin with my chest as my arm wrapped over him. He grunted in pleasure, but didn't wake up fully, and after a few moments, his breathing was deep and steady again. But I couldn't sleep any more.

The previous night had been overwhelming in some ways, and when Callan had said he loved me, happiness had bloomed in me like a field coming to life after years of drought. But the release I felt at his words was chased by a rapid and fierce worry. I didn't know how a long-distance relationship would work, if it would work. It wasn't something I'd ever tried or wanted. And more than that, I didn't want to leave him. The more I thought about my life in Los Angeles, the more empty and hollow it felt. Lynn was there, and my mother, but aside from them, my life was an endless run of take-out, television, and loneliness. The town of Singletree had filled my days with warmth, humor, and friendship. How could I ever go back and feel like my life was what it was supposed to be, even if Callan was a part of it?

Suddenly the job I'd worried so much about losing was barely a blip on my radar. The job was what would require me to go back, the job I had been so concerned being with Callan might ruin was something I no longer felt like I even wanted.

I scooted quietly from the bed, pulling on a T-shirt and sweatpants, and popped open my laptop. Filming would resume the next day, assuming Uncle Rob didn't have any bad news to impart as a result of viewing the initial footage. I had only two more houses to do—a small cottage near the town square, and Callan's.

I scanned my email, seeing nothing too worrying until I found Uncle Rob's name in the list of waiting messages.

To: April Hall
From: Robert Hall
Re: Holiday Homes Wrap up

April:

You've done an excellent job. The footage so far is perfect. Nice work.

Please call me Sunday to discuss the showplace home. I have a few thoughts.

-Rob

The showplace home was Callan's. I shook my head, trying to imagine what Uncle Rob's 'thoughts' might entail.

I didn't get to think about it too long. Callan rolled over and propped his head on his hand, watching me with a smile on his sexy full lips. "Come back to bed, April," he suggested.

His bare chest, messy dark hair, and next-day stubble were enough to send me leaping back beneath the covers. And the low morning growl in his voice had me already tingling in anticipation of his touch.

The morning slipped away on breathy moans and warm hands, low chuckles and kisses that made my soul ache at how perfect they were.

Just before noon, Callan pulled his trousers back on as I packed a little bag. There was no point in wasting the time we had left being apart. I'd stay at his house for the last few days I had left in town.

As we rode out toward the big plantation house, thick white snowflakes began to drift down around us.

"God, could anything be more perfect?" Callan asked. He flashed me a smile that sent my heart soaring again.

"I don't think so," I said, finally letting myself believe in this. In us.

We spent the day lazily in front of the fire, with hot chocolate and books and movies, tucked together on the couch. As evening fell, Callan stretched and put down his kindle. "Is my house tomorrow?"

I shook my head. "You're last. I have the Wentworth cottage tomorrow. Shouldn't take long. It's tiny."

Callan nodded. "So Tuesday, then. And I should just make myself scarce?"

"You can be here if you want, to help kind of direct the guys around. But it's not like I don't know the house at this point."

Callan grinned at that.

"If you want to stay in the shadows or go see the girls, that'd be okay, too."

He nodded. "You know I'd much rather stay out of the spotlight."

I did know that.

"And they're not going to mention whose house it is, right?"

"Your cover is safe," I promised him. "They're interested in the house, not in you."

"Thanks a lot," Callan said, pretending to be offended.

"I'm pretty interested in you," I said. "If it's any consolation."

"It is, actually," he told me, sliding closer on the couch.

My phone chimed then, and I held up a finger to Callan, asking him to pause for just a moment. But when I checked the screen, it was a text from my uncle.

Shit! I was supposed to call him and had forgotten. "I'll just be a second," I told Callan, standing up and taking my phone to the parlor to talk while staring up at the magnificent tree.

"Hey Uncle Rob," I said when he answered my call. "Sorry I didn't call before. Got busy."

"No worries, April. You're doing a great job out there, so just keep it up."

"I'll try," I said, glowing a bit with the praise.

"So listen," he went on. "We've been talking a bit back here about a way to really make this last house a home run."

"Um. Okay." A chill went through me for no reason I could identify.

"It's the soccer star's place, right? Whitewood, from the Sharks?"

"Right," I said slowly, my stomach souring.

"Well, let's get that guy on camera then. I want him giving the tour. I've got a new contract coming from the lawyer tomorrow for him to sign."

"I don't think he'll go for that," I said, trying to sound businesslike. "He's very private and it took a lot to get him to even agree to let the cameras in."

"Work your magic then, April. The guy is a big deal, and the way he disappeared after that injury had all the tabloids churning. Combining the house with his sudden discovery in this small town—and having it on our network—that will be huge."

I needed to talk him out of this, figure out how to convince him it was a bad idea. My brain clicked and whirred, but nothing came to me. Still, I had to try. "No, I don't think—"

"Make it happen, April. Your job depends on it." With that friendly sign off, Rob hung up.

"Shit," I whispered, staring at my phone. There was no way Callan would agree. And now my uncle had put me in an impossible situation. I knew how much Callan valued his newfound privacy. How could I even ask him to sacrifice it just to save my job? "Shit," I said again, stuffing my phone into my pocket. What the hell was I going to do now?

I wandered back into the living room, guilt circling me, threatening to pounce on me, hold me down. I already knew what Callan would say. There was no point even asking him.

"Hey," he said as I drew closer to the couch where he still sat reading. "Everything okay?"

"Yeah," I said. "Work stuff."

"You hungry?" he asked, pushing off the throw to stand. He drew himself to his full height and then stretched, pushing his arms far over his head, causing his long-sleeved T-shirt to lift slightly at the waist. My eyes dropped to the tanned firm skin exposed there before sliding back up to his face.

"Yeah," I said.

"I'll make something. Do you like shrimp?"

I nodded, feeling like every word out of his mouth was designed to emphasize how perfect he was, how precious this thing I'd found with him was—how much I'd do to keep it.

The rest of the evening was like that—Callan being amazing, and me worrying that I was carrying the grenade that would blow everything we had into pieces. The question was, should I pull the pin?

The Wentworth Cottage was adorable. It might as well have been made out of gingerbread, or maybe featured in a fairy tale. It had little red and white awnings over the big front windows, a shingled roof that curved at the edges, and a white picket fence strung with a garland. The couple who lived there were equally adorable, and they greeted me and the camera crew eagerly at the front door.

Mr. Wentworth was an unassuming little man, balding with glasses and wearing a green cardigan sweater with a large candy cane stitched across the left side. "I wore my favorite holiday sweater for this," he said, taking my hand and smiling broadly.

To me, this indicated that this man had more than one hideous sweater to choose from for occasions like this one, and a small giggle escaped my lips. "It's perfect."

"The other ones were probably too raunchy for this crowd," Mrs. Wentworth chimed in, her grey helmet of curls not moving as she tittered behind her hand at her statement. Now my mind was turning over ideas, trying to figure out how a holiday sweater might be raunchy.

"This one is merely phallic," Mr. Wentworth pointed out, raising his hand to make sure I saw the long shaft of the candy cane.

"Right," I said, wishing I didn't blush quite so easily. Was this little old couple actually talking about how a candy cane looked like a penis? I had to be reading too much into things,

I decided. "Well, it's nice to see you again. Thanks for allowing us to film today."

I had met the Wentworths when I'd first arrived and had done my initial home visits, and all had seemed perfectly normal then—no references to penises or candy canes. I had been a little distracted then, of course, but I reassured myself knowing all was in order. "We'll do the filming just as we did the walkthrough before," I told them. "So feel free to stay close, or you can head off and ignore us until we're done."

"Want to run to the pantry for a quickie, Mabel?" Mr. Wentworth asked his wife, his face splitting into a lascivious grin.

"Frances, we have a house full of people." She swatted his shoulder.

"The risk of getting caught just makes you hot and you know it." He threw an arm over her shoulder, pulling her into his side, and then I swallowed my surprise as his hand dropped low and gave Mrs. Wentworth's breast a hearty squeeze. A loud sudden cough erupted over my shoulder, and I turned to see one of the cameramen doubled over. Clearly he'd heard and seen this, and was trying to get control of himself.

"Ah, okay then," I said, dropping my gaze down to my clipboard as I tried to avoid making any more statements that might give Mr. Wentworth a chance to say inappropriate things. Where was this coming from?

"We'll start in the living room by the tree," I said, mostly for the cameramen, who immediately swept past me to set up. I followed them, not wanting to get in the way, but continued reading aloud. "And then into the kitchen, followed by the sunroom at the back of the house, and finally the guest room."

"Um." A loud noise of concern came from Sean, one of the cameramen. "Was this here when you did your walkthrough?"

I looked up from my clipboard to see what Sean was looking at, just as the Wentworths trundled past me.

"The bolt is off the threads," Mr. Wentworth said. "And it's just plain stuck. I was up on the ladder all morning trying to get that down for you, but finally, I just plum gave up."

"I hung the garland on it though," Mrs. Wentworth said. "To make it blend in better to the theme."

I gazed at the contraption hanging in the center of the room, draped with a Christmassy garland. There was no way this had been here before. No level of distraction would have caused me to miss the leather and wood contraption swinging from the ceiling. The Wentworths were standing next to it, regarding it the way you might look at a cake that didn't turn out quite right, but which you would still be offering your guests.

"Okay," I said. I was here to solve problems. I might have no idea how to solve the issue with Callan and Uncle Rob, but this? I could handle this. "So, is this a ... never mind," I said quickly.

But it was too late.

"It's our sex swing," Mr. Wentworth said, without a lick of shame in his voice. "The exposed beams in here make it the perfect place to hang it. Plus, we like to look at the tree."

Oh for the love of Santa! I tried to keep my face neutral as my heart rate sped up. "Sean," I turned to the cameraman who was bright red with the effort of holding his breath so he didn't laugh. "Can you get that ladder so we might get up there and see if maybe one of you guys can loosen that stuck bolt?"

Sean cleared his throat loudly, tried to speak, and released a garbled sound before nodding and heading for the front door.

As I turned back to the sex swing, hanging merrily in the center of the living room, something on the tree caught my attention. And then something else. Oh god, how distracted had I been when I was here before? This was not happening ... I had enough problems. As my eyes traveled over the Christmas tree, I realized I should have inspected the actual tree decorations much more closely when I'd been here before. I lifted a hand to one of the hanging decorations and stepped closer. "Are these ...?"

"Nipple clamps," Mrs. Wentworth said, coming to my side. "Aren't they pretty?"

I could only nod. No, they were not pretty. They were creepy, and why were they on the tree? What exactly was happening here? I turned to look at the demure Mrs. Wentworth, who was quickly morphing from sweet little matronly lady into some kind of sexual diva in my mind. "Oh," I managed. "And this is ..."

"A cock ring," Mr. Wentworth said. "The missus spent hours spray painting those with glitter." He grinned at me as the second cameraman, James, sputtered in the corner of the room while I struggled not to laugh, or cry, or pass out.

"And here is," my hand moved toward another item hanging on the tree as my eyes widened and my breath caught.

"That's an anal plug, dear," Mrs. Wentworth said. "Surely you knew that," she laughed as if she'd just corrected me on the names of the reindeer, not on the fact that the gaudy red plastic plug hanging from the Christmas tree was meant to go up someone's actual butt.

"So your tree is themed," I said, feeling somewhat comatose suddenly. My thoughts scattered as I gazed around at the cozy cottage that had suddenly become some kind of octogenarian pleasure palace. It wouldn't matter if Callan did the show or not. I was going to get fired for not realizing the Wentworths were sex fiends.

"Yes," Mr. Wentworth said. "We thought it would be a good representation of who we are." He and his wife were holding hands, and their fingers were stroking one another somewhat eagerly. I took a step away, feeling oddly touched and repulsed all at once.

Just then, Sean returned with the ladder. "Let's see if we can get the sex swing out of the shot, shall we?" He asked merrily, evidently having regained control of himself outside.

"We might need to just ... adjust the décor on the tree," I said, hesitant to actually touch half the items dangling from the pine branches before me.

"Oh, do we have to?" Mrs. Wentworth pouted.

I turned to her, telling myself Mrs. Wentworth was just the nice old lady I'd met before, even if she did have a far more active sex life than ... well, than anyone. "We do, I'm afraid," I said. "The show is PG, and we try to avoid too much suggestion of ... well ... sex."

"It's not like we're going to actually have sex on camera," Mr. Wentworth said loudly. Then he looked over at the camera James was setting up and his face smoothed as an idea clearly popped into his head. "Unless—"

"No, of course not," I cut him off. "Do you have any other decorations for the tree? Maybe something a little more traditional?"

Mrs. Wentworth sighed. "In the back shed. There's a box out there. I think it's labeled 'boring holiday décor.'" I sincerely hoped that meant glass bubbles and reindeer. Boring sounded pretty good at that moment.

I nodded at James to go investigate as I began reluctantly plucking sex toys from the tree and making a small pile at my feet as the Wentworths murmured their disappointment.

Relief claimed me when the couple didn't put up a fight about changing their décor, and I began to feel a little bit more confident about my ability to do my job. Now I just needed to decide how to handle Callan's house. Would I do what my uncle expected? Or was there maybe a way I could give him something so spectacular he wouldn't care whether Callan was on camera or not? And what would happen when my uncle realized my level of involvement with Callan Whitewood? Could I keep it a secret at this point, even though I knew very well I was in love with him?

A full hour later than planned, the filming was finally underway, the Wentworths watching hand-in-hand as the crew progressed through their de-sexified house slowly.

By the time they'd finished for the day and I'd had a final pre-filming meeting with the crew back at the inn, I had decided what to do.

I composed an email to my uncle, hit 'send,' and closed my laptop, feeling like I had done the best I could in a difficult situation. But this was my job. I'd handled it like a professional. Everyone would just have to accept that this was work—it wasn't personal.

I was just preparing to text Callan, to let him know I was heading over and to ask if I should pick up some food, when Annabelle approached me in the lobby, a wary look on her pretty round face.

"Hi April," she said, her voice a couple notes too high. Her Mrs. Santa costume must have been too tight, I figured, knowing Annabelle would certainly sacrifice her own comfort in the name of holiday cheer.

"Annabelle! How are you?"

Annabelle held a box in her arms, and it looked heavy, but she hugged it tightly to her and dropped her eyes to it for a moment.

"Hey," I said when my friend remained silent. Annabelle seemed upset. Something was wrong. "What's going on? Is everything okay?"

A strangled sound erupted from Annabelle's mouth and she shook her head. "I'm so sorry," she said.

"What? Why are you sorry?" I had no idea what was happening, but a surge of concern welled up in me for my friend. Annabelle and I might not have known each other long, but I genuinely cared about her—and about all the other people I'd met in this strange little town.

"Mr. Whitewood, erm ... Callan, asked me to give this to you." She pressed the box gently toward me as my heart began to sink inside me.

The box was full of my belongings—the things I'd taken to Callan's and left there. Most of my clothes had been at Callan's house. Until they were put into this box and dropped off here. What had happened? Confusion and hurt made it hard to think. Why would he stuff my things into a box and drop them off without even seeing me? I quickly checked my phone, looking for an explanation, but there was nothing from him at all.

"What? What did he say?" I asked Annabelle.

"He was angry, April." Annabelle was crying softly, tears running down her cheeks. "He said he'd spoken to his lawyer."

"What?" My head spinning, I tried to make sense of this. "His lawyer?"

Annabelle was just nodding now, her eyes wide as if in anticipation of me falling to pieces suddenly. I thought she just might, once I figured out exactly what was happening.

His lawyer.

"Oh god," I said, realization dawning. "The new contract." My uncle had said that legal had already forwarded the new contract. Callan must've seen it already—seen the network's changed intention to feature him on the show along with his house. "Oh no." I dropped the box on a nearby table, knocking askew a tree made from peppermint candies, and rushed to the side of the lobby to get some privacy, my phone in my hand.

I dialed Callan's number, but he didn't pick up. When his voicemail played, I struggled to find the right words. "Callan, it's me. I was about to come over ... Annabelle gave me the box ... but, the contract, Callan, it's not what you think, it's—" I trailed off, unsure how to explain, and the long beep sounded, ending the recording.

I texted him:

April: Can we talk? There's been a misunderstanding. Don't worry about the contract.

I waited for a reply. As I began to worry it simply wasn't going to come, three dots danced at the side of my screen. After what felt like an eternity, a reply came:

Callan: I understand. You should have asked me. My house will not be on the show and neither will I. We are done here.

Pain shot through my chest. Done?

April: Can't I explain?

Callan's silence was the only answer, and though I waited another ten minutes, nothing more appeared on my screen. Finally, I pushed my phone into my pocket and walked back over to where Annabelle stood, wringing her hands.

"Did you speak to him?" Annabelle asked.

"He doesn't want to talk to me," I said, shock fading and turning to something much darker, much more painful. The silver lights twinkling all around us in the lobby, coupled with the oversized candy canes and army of nutcrackers had begun to feel as if they were closing in on me, leering at me, laughing at me. Even Annabelle seemed like she might actually be wearing that ridiculous costume just as a means of making fun of me.

Suddenly, the holiday felt exactly as it always had—worse. Red and green and all things merry would always remind me of heartbreak and devastation, and now I knew it would be that way for the rest of my life.

"I'm going to go upstairs, Annabelle," I said, picking up my box. "I'll talk to you tomorrow." Without waiting for an answer, I went to the elevator, shielding my eyes against the glow of faux candles lining the mantlepiece on the lobby wall and trying in vain to block out the sound of carols playing over the sound system throughout the inn.

20

SMASHING THE SNOW GLOBE
CALLAN

I should have known it was all too good to be true.

April.

Singletree.

This house.

My life.

My lawyer had called around noon to tell me to check my email, and then proceeded to walk me through a new contract from April's network, requiring direct participation in filming. The new contract stipulated that I be on camera no less than ten minutes in the edited and final footage, which meant participating in the entire tour of the house.

"Fuck them," I told my lawyer, my voice sounding low and foreign to me. It was a voice I hadn't used in a while, one that had grown from disappointment in the previous year when everyone I'd trusted had turned out to be in it for something other than me. Hell, my lawyer was probably among those I could include, but I paid him, so at least he was upfront about it.

But April ...

The only thing I could understand was that she had spent the time to get close to me, so that she could push this revised contract at me, figuring I'd been softened up enough not to argue.

Cormac and the girls came over for dinner—mostly because I forgot they were coming—and found me in front of the fire with a bottle of HalfCat bourbon on my lap. I'd given up on a glass several hours before.

"This again?" Cormac said, finding me there. The little girls had scampered over to greet me and had promptly turned tail and fled, heading for merrier parts of the house. Even they could see I was in no state for company. "What's going on?"

"Nothing."

"Where's April?"

"Who cares?"

Cormac sat down heavily, a sigh whooshing from his lips as he did so. "Better hand me that bottle." I did, and he drank greedily, grimacing as he finished and set the bottle aside.

I glanced at it, but my head was already pounding and I wasn't sure I could walk. I'd find out soon enough though, I'd have to piss eventually.

"Tell me what happened."

It was my turn to sigh. "Standard shit," I said, running a hand over my jaw. "She was using me. For the stupid show."

"The Christmas show," Cormac said, as if he needed to

state the obvious to get his brain centered on this conversation.

"Yeah."

"Explain."

I glared at him, but regretted it immediately. Cormac's face was drawn and gaunt—had he lost weight? He looked worse than I felt, and I knew he had his own burdens to carry. The high-pitched shrieks and laughter from the back of the house reminded me that my brother's problems might be slightly more significant than my own. "It's nothing. Just feeling sorry for myself, man." I tried to get up, but my ankle, and Cormac's hand on my wrist, stopped me.

"Don't walk away from me." His voice was steel, and I met my brother's eyes, surprised at the anger simmering there. "You'd finished with this, and I'd finally gotten to close the lid on this particular box of shit. I didn't have to worry about my little brother anymore and could go on just worrying about everything else. And now, here we are again, right back where we started. So you're going to tell me what the hell wrecked the best thing to happen to you in a long time."

I narrowed my eyes at him.

"April," Cormac clarified.

I knew what he'd meant, I just wasn't ready to agree that she'd been something good. From where I sat, she was maybe the worst thing that had ever happened to me. "I trusted her, man."

"Right."

"And the whole time, she was just trying to get close so she could advance her own career. Her network pushed over this new contract today—one day before the cameras are supposed to come in here and film all the Christmas shit I spent a fortune to put up."

Cormac's face softened slightly. "What was the new contract about?"

"They want me on camera." I stared into the fire, thinking about putting myself in front of the media again, imagining the ridiculous articles with my name in them, the way they'd spin my reclusive move to the middle of nowhere, call this show a desperate grab for the glory and fame I'd lost. Or worse, make me out to be the piteous has been they'd painted me as after Becky had done her tell-all interview, calling me a pathetic shell of myself. "They want me to give a tour of my home for the show."

"I see. And what did April say about it?"

"Nothing."

Cormac raised a brow at me and I turned away. "She didn't tell me they were going to send the new contract at all. I guess she just figured I'd sign it and everything would be fine."

"Did she know about it?" Cormac asked.

I thought back to the message she'd left. The one I'd deleted without hearing. But her texts had made it clear she knew about the contract. "Yeah, she knew."

"So what did she say?"

I stared at him. "I haven't spoken to her."

Cormac laughed, and the sound made my blood boil. "This is funny?" I shot to my feet and turned on my brother, nearly toppling back to the couch as the bourbon swished around in my bloodstream and my ankle screamed. Damn that HalfCat. I steadied myself with a hand on the round head of the snowman standing at the end of the couch. "This is exactly why I left the West Coast. Everyone close to me has an agenda, something they're trying to gain by knowing me, getting near."

Cormac continued chuckling, much to my irritation, and then took another long swig of the bourbon. "You're so fucking full of yourself," he said, wiping his mouth. "How far from the spotlight do you have to get to see that the world doesn't revolve around you?" He shook his head and stood up, looking toward the back rooms where the girls had gone suspiciously quiet. "We're gonna head out. I suggest you pull your head out of your ass and figure out a way to get back the first person you've met that actually didn't care who you were and might even have loved your sorry ass."

The anger burning in my blood had cooled, as my drunkenness and Cormac's words settled in.

"Girls!" Cormac called, and soon they were all scuttling back out the front door, leaving me alone again.

Just like I'd always been.

I found my phone an hour or two later, when I'd sobered up a bit and managed to force myself to eat something. There were no more messages from April, and I felt both satisfied to see that she'd taken my point seriously, and somewhat disappointed to find that she'd stepped away so easily. But maybe that just proved the point—she hadn't been in it for anything to do with me, with us. She was in it to advance her failing career, to save her own butt. And everything else? Had been an act.

7

The sound of buzzing woke me. At first I thought it was just a particularly poignant hangover symptom, but after a while, I realized it was the buzzer on the front gate. I stumbled to the front door to answer it, and April's voice came through the speaker.

"*Holiday Homes* here for filming, Mr. Whitewood." She sounded determined and confident, and my heart sank in response. I didn't want her to be confident about *Holiday Homes*. I wanted her to be confident about me, about what we'd been to each other. But then I remembered that there was no us. That had been a dream.

"Yeah, that's not happening," I said back.

"You signed a contract."

"Fuck the contract. And I didn't sign it. I'm not appearing on camera." Anger flared in my chest, making it easier to act like a self-important asshole. My brother's words echoed in my mind and I pushed them away.

"Callan, don't worry about appearing. But you did sign the previous contract, remember?" Her voice had softened, and I heard an edge of pleading there now.

I sighed. Despite my determination to be angry, I also wanted to see her, to hear her tell me she'd been using me to my face. "Fine." I punched the button to open the gate, and went back upstairs to run a comb through my hair and brush my teeth. The doorbell rang as I was pulling jeans on, and I took my time getting back down to open the door, my ankle and my heart protesting the whole way down the stairs.

After a deep steadying breath, I pulled open the door. April stood there, her gorgeous face pale, dark smudges beneath her eyes. The camera crew waited just behind her, and while I wanted to see them all as greedy vultures, ready to pounce and fight, all I saw was the woman I had fallen in love with, looking tired and upset, next to the guys she worked with.

"Hi," she said quietly, and then cleared her throat and glanced to one side, as if remembering we weren't alone. "Hi. Can we come in and set up?"

I took a deep breath and stepped back. "Come on in."

April's eyes scanned my face for a long second before she moved forward, and I could see the questions there.

I was at war with myself. I was angry—she hadn't been honest with me, right? But just seeing her face made it somewhat clear that maybe I'd jumped to conclusions a little bit. I'd been hurt before—by so many people who'd stuck close when they knew I had things to give them, when being close to me meant getting things for themselves, but who had fallen away like ants jumping from a sinking stick when they'd realized I was no longer on the way up. It had been painful, because I'd been too self-absorbed to consider who the people around me were before that. I'd been a star, and even I hadn't been able to see past the trappings of that for a long time.

And when I'd fallen—literally and figuratively, it became

apparent that the world I'd built was flimsy and fragile. And in the fallout, I hadn't been able to determine what was real from the construction I'd lived in for so long. I'd fractured any real relationships—like those with my teammates on the Sharks—in the process. And then I'd been alone.

Was I blindly slashing at the real connections in my life again in my anger?

The crew moved in behind her, and April stared down at a clipboard in her hand. "We'll start in the parlor where the big tree is, if that's all right." She looked up at me from beneath her dark lashes, shy around me now. Tentative.

Every cell in my body screamed at me when she looked at me that way. I wanted to simultaneously comfort her and fall on her, pounding her into the wall with my cock until she screamed my name. Instead, I nodded. "Sure."

I stood by as April directed the crew, and I ended up following them around the house as they filmed, wishing April would stop and talk to me, wishing I hadn't been so aggressively short via text the night before. As she directed shots, answering questions from the two guys with cameras, April barely looked at me, and she didn't speak to me at all.

She didn't ask me to be on camera. She didn't mention the new contract. She was professional, efficient, and so beautiful it made my bones ache beneath my skin with the want of touching her.

As they got close to the end, the cameramen trudging out into the light snow covering the lawn out back to shoot some of the yard and the river, I caught her wrist in my hand. "Hey," I said, realizing that when she left my house today it might be the last time I ever saw her if I didn't figure out a way to make things right.

April stared at the place where my fingers circled her arm, and then her eyes slid up to mine, lingering there for a long moment. "Please let me go," she said. And I sensed that she meant more than that I should release her hand.

"April," I said, still holding on. "We need to talk."

"I wanted to talk last night," she said quietly, turning her shoulder so the cameraman on the back lawn couldn't over-hear. "You wouldn't speak to me."

"I was angry. I—"

"I know," she said, finally pulling her wrist from my grasp. "I got that."

"April, I jumped to conclusions."

She gave me a look then, long and searching—a look that I thought might have taken inventory of my soul, my heart, everything I was—and then she turned away. "I can't do this," she said simply. And then she walked away from me, meeting with the nearest cameraman and pointing between her clip-board and the house. They moved around to the front of the house just as the sun was beginning its late-afternoon slide into Virginia on the other side of the river.

The lights hung on the big house flickered on with the gathering darkness, and the crew took a few more shots of the place, glowing merrily against the smattering of white covering the ground from the weekend snow. I stood outside with them, watching, shivering in the cold but not really feeling it anywhere except in my ankle, and my heart. My house looked beautiful. And happy. Like the kind of place a family might spend happy mornings by the fire, evenings on the back lawn, Christmases enjoying the glow and glitter of the lights and the warmth of being together.

I knew the place would look great on the show, but it would be much like the rest of my life had turned out to be— a false representation, a hollow shell.

April turned to me as the cameramen went back to the van, and her head nodded once. "We're all done," she said.

"Okay," I managed.

For a long moment we stood there, our eyes locked as we each lingered on the front drive of my house, and I thought maybe she'd drop her wall and we could talk, maybe we could try. But then she said, "Thank you for your cooperation. Goodbye." She turned on her heel, climbed into the van with the men, and moments later, she was gone.

I watched the van make its way down the narrow lane leading away from my house, and when it turned the corner out of sight, I realized I had succeeded. I'd accomplished my goal of driving everyone away and securing complete and total solitude.

It hurt more than my ankle as I turned and went back into my big empty house.

21

ANOTHER CRAPPY CHRISTMAS
APRIL

Filming Callan's house all day was potentially the hardest thing I had ever done. He'd been there, practically at my shoulder, the entire time, as we'd moved from one spot to another over the course of five long hours. He'd been right there the whole time.

When he'd touched me and asked if we could talk, I'd nearly broken down and said yes, and my heart was asking me now why I hadn't as I sat in the quiet of my room staring at Chip and Joanna on television but not really seeing anything.

I'd done the right thing—on all counts. So why did I feel so empty?

I was going to lose my job, there was no doubt about that. I'd ignored my uncle's demands and moved forward on the first contract as if we'd never spoken about Callan appearing on camera. I'd thought hard about it, and despite the way I was feeling about Callan right now, I didn't think he deserved the treatment my uncle had in mind. I wasn't going to be part of parading him out in front of the cameras so curious fans and gossipmongers could speculate about why he'd moved here, why he was alone, or how severe his limp still was. I knew him well enough to know he would hate all of that, and he certainly didn't deserve it, so I had decided not to even mention it to him.

Of course, my uncle's lawyers hadn't had the same thoughts. And evidently Callan had seen the contract even though I'd never intended to even tell him about it.

What hurt was that Callan assumed I'd been hatching some kind of plot all along, that my entire motivation was to get him on camera. I poured myself a small glass from the flask Annabelle had delivered to my room earlier with a plate of Christmas fudge. Moonshine and fudge didn't actually go well together, I learned. But sugar and alcohol were my vices, and tonight I needed them.

My heart twinged again, as my mind wandered back over Callan's reaction to the contract. He wasn't even going to talk to me about it, wasn't going to let me explain. After getting to know me better than most people in my life ever did, he still didn't see that I wouldn't have done that to him.

"What a selfish, arrogant jerk," I muttered, not really believing the words as they slid from my lips. I lay back on the pillows covering the head of my bed and tried to focus on Jo's latest shiplap project on television, but all I could think about was Callan.

And my future. I was absolutely out of a job. Again. And my uncle was going to be angry, too. Besides firing me, he might actually disinherit me and tell me I was officially out of the family. Not that we had much family. Rob, my mom and me. No wonder holidays sucked.

I had buried my phone in my purse, too focused on dousing my sorrows in alcohol and fudge when I'd first arrived back to think about calling anyone. But now, as my stomach protested my choice of evening meal and my loneliness threatened to overcome me, I dug it out.

I'd missed a call from Lynn, and two from Callan.

I called Lynn, feeling like my friend might be the only person left in the world who cared about me, who understood me. "Hey," I said miserably when Lynn picked up.

"Hey yourself," Lynn said cheerfully. "How are things? How's your soccer star?"

He was beautiful. He was angry. He wasn't the man I thought he was. He was gone. "He's an arrogant jerk. We're done."

"What? Why?"

I explained everything to Lynn as briefly as I could.

"And he tried to talk to you today when you were there?"

"Yeah, but it's too late, right?"

"Why?" Lynn asked. "Why is it too late?"

I sighed in exasperation. "Because he's already decided what kind of person I am. And if he thinks I'd do that to him —spend two weeks pretending to be in love with him just so I could get him to do the show—then he doesn't know me at all."

Lynn didn't say anything for a long minute. Then she said, "Don't get mad at me, okay?"

"For what?" I didn't think I had the capacity to generate yet another emotion today. I was spent.

"For telling you you're being an idiot."

I pressed my lips together, waiting to feel angry. I'd been right though, I didn't have the energy for anger—I only felt empty. "What?" I whispered.

"Do you love him?"

"I thought maybe I did."

"And your plan now is what? Come home, get a new job, forget all about him?"

It sounded awful. And impossible. "Yeah."

"April, it sounds like he wanted to talk about it. Don't you owe him that much?"

"He thinks I'm a manipulative bitch," I pointed out. "If he thinks I would do all that—go to that length just to set him up, there's no point."

"It was a misunderstanding. At least talk to him. Don't just leave. You'll be miserable forever if you don't at least talk it out."

I sank into the pillows again—Annabelle had added about thirteen extra while I had been out filming today, along with the alcohol and fudge, and a little card telling me she hoped everything was okay. "Maybe."

"Call him."

"I don't know if I can."

"Do it for me," Lynn said.

"For you?"

"If you come home, and you didn't even talk to him to find out if there might be a way to get past all this, you'll be a miserable pain in the ass for months. And I'll have to deal with you. So do it for me. Just talk to him. Just see if maybe there's really something there."

My heart twisted, writhing in pain or maybe pulsing in hope. Either way, I knew it would be next to impossible to talk to Callan, knowing he thought the worst of me already. I also knew I couldn't be anywhere near those deep dark eyes again without melting. It had been near impossible to keep my resolve while we'd filmed all day. Holding myself steady was part of why I was so exhausted now. I didn't answer, but I let out a long tired sigh.

"When's your flight home?"

"Tomorrow," I told her. "I got the red-eye."

"I hope you're not on it."

"That's not very nice," I said.

"I hope you find a reason to stay in Pine Tree."

"Christmas Tree. I mean, Singletree."

"Right," Lynn said.

I sighed, the breath coming from somewhere deep inside my soul where all the disappointments in my life swirled in a dark eddy that threatened sometimes to suck me down. "Good night."

"Good night," Lynn said.

And just like that, I was all alone again.

I woke in a haze, a pillow half-stuffed in my open mouth and about twelve others wedged uncomfortably into various body parts. The television still droned from across the room, where *House Hunters* was in the midst of a pre-holiday marathon. The light in the room was soft and diffuse, and it took me a few moments to realize I'd passed out after hanging up with Lynn, and that it was morning. I needed to get packed and clear out of Christmas Tree. I was on a red eye back to my real life tonight.

The thought made me feel sick.

Or perhaps that was the fudge and moonshine swirling in my stomach.

When I was able to move my limbs, I checked my phone for the time. Seven o'clock. I didn't technically need to be leaving until almost twelve hours later, and I'd gotten a late checkout. Not that I had anything to do except feel hollow and alone all day. It might make more sense to just head to the airport, I figured.

The crew should have already left—they were both on flights the previous night, having bought refundable tickets just in case something went wrong with filming. They both had families to get back to, and it was Christmastime, after all.

I stumbled to the bathroom and ran water into the tub, deciding I could put off actually accomplishing anything for at least another hour.

When I emerged, my skin pruned and my hair hanging in wet ribbons down my back, I felt slightly better, if not more hopeful. At least I wasn't hung over. Desolate, hopeless, and completely alone? Yes, but not hung over. So I had that going for me, at least.

I packed up my things, dried my hair and took a deep breath before leaving my room. I needed to say some good-byes—mostly one. And then, after a quick bite, I'd be on my way. No point lingering around here.

Downstairs, I found Annabelle at the front desk as usual, cheerfully handing keys to an older couple who must have been visiting someone for the holidays. They had that grandparental air, I thought—optimistic and proud.

"Hello," they said in unison, turning away from the desk to head to the elevator. "Merry Christmas."

"Right," I said, unable to manage anything much more appropriate.

Annabelle's wide blue eyes were sympathetic when I turned back to her. "Hey," she said softly.

"Hi. Thanks for all the stuff. The fudge, especially. And the moonshine."

Annabelle smiled. "I hoped it might help. I mean, I know it can't ... that's not to say ..." She shook her head, a blush rising in her cheeks.

"It's okay," I told her. "Callan hates me because he thinks I tried to manipulate him to take advantage of his fame for the show. I don't think there's help for that."

"Oh, I see," Annabelle said, folding her hands on the desk in front of her.

"It's hard to take you seriously with that ..." I waved at Annabelle's head, which was sporting a hat and fake hair combination meant to look like one of the Whos from Dr. Seuss's Whoville. The pigtails stuck straight out to the sides before angling sharply upward to the ceiling. She wore a strange prosthetic under her nose that made her whole face look a little bit rodent like, and I found it hard to look right at her.

"Sorry," Annabelle said, peeling the prosthetic off. "Better?"

"Yes," I said. "Anyway, I guess I'll be checking out this afternoon. I just wanted to let you know I probably don't need that late checkout."

"Oh, don't worry about that. You've got the room as long as you need. Just keep it. Just in case."

I shrugged. "Thank you. I think I'm going to go get something to eat over at Lottie's."

Annabelle nodded. "Of course." Her face was sympathetic and all the nodding she was doing was making her hair bounce dangerously. "Please don't leave without saying goodbye."

"I wouldn't!" I took Annabelle's hand on a whim, squeezing it firmly. I felt a rush of warmth for the other woman, and realized it was going to be hard to say goodbye to her. Harder than it should be, given how long I'd know her. But I hadn't made a lot of close connections in my life, and I'd found more in Singletree in the short time I'd been here than I had in Los Angeles in a lifetime.

That was something to think about. Something I would definitely not be thinking about, I told myself as I crossed the town square to Lottie Tanner's bakery and cafe. It would only make it harder to leave. I put that into a little locked chest along with any and all thoughts of hot ex-soccer stars. Locked up tight.

Sure, that would work.

"April!" Lottie called as I pushed through the door, fighting a stiff and very cold wind on the sidewalk outside. "You're still here! I'm so glad!"

"Why are you glad, Lott? She doesn't have her cameras with her. You and the chinches had your fifteen minutes. It's over." The ever-cheerful Helen sat at the counter in front of Lottie, sporting a red and green velour track suit and a Santa hat.

"Hello Mrs. Tanner, Mrs. Manchester," I said politely. "It's nice to see you again." I ignored Helen's eye roll at this pleasantry. I turned to Lottie. "I'm leaving this afternoon, but was hoping for some breakfast before I get on the road."

"Of course! Sit down anywhere. Don't mind Helen. She's going through withdrawal. Makes her mean."

I eyed the old woman skeptically and smiled back at Lottie. "Withdrawal?"

"Her granddaughter Tess says she spends too much time playing video games and made her commit to leaving the house every day."

"Sounds reasonable," I said, wary of the evil look Helen was giving me.

"I'm right here," the old woman said, crossing her arms over her chest. "I can hear you, you know."

"Sorry, dear," Lottie said. "But it's true. You've been very grumpy. Not at all in the holiday spirit."

"Well, I'll join you in that," I said to Helen, earning me a thumbs-up. I took off my coat and gloves as I turned to scan the small space, which was homey and comfortable, decorated with a few plush chairs near low tables, and a few more traditional restaurant tables with hard chairs. In one of these sat a familiar figure I hadn't noticed when I came in. I cringed, wondering how much he knew. "Hello, Cormac."

The man looked up from the laptop screen in front of him and gave me a warm smile. "Hey April, how are you?"

I didn't answer this, figuring there was no point. He surely knew what had happened between me and Callan, though the fact he didn't scowl or throw anything did reassure me.

"About as well as my brother then, huh?" He waved at the chair across from him, watching me with his head tilted as I hung up my coat and took the seat. "He's pretty upset, you know."

I didn't want to hear any more about how Callan felt betrayed, about how I'd used him. "I know. But he didn't bother to listen to my side of things. I'm upset too," I said, almost accusingly. "And I'm going to lose my job because of it."

Cormac's eyebrows went up, but he didn't comment on this. "He knows he screwed up." This was delivered quietly, as if Cormac was waiting to see how I would react before telling me more.

If it had been Callan sitting here, I figured, then maybe it'd be worth rehashing. But I didn't know if it was worth talking things over with his brother. "Well none of it matters now. I'm going home tonight, I'll find a new job, and this insanity will be behind us both."

"Right," Cormac said, sounding doubtful. "That sounds simple."

I squinted at him, partly annoyed at him because he was the one who'd suggested I get close to Callan in the first place. "Does everyone in this town feel like everything is their business all the time?"

"Pretty much," he said. "But my brother is my business. He needs to meet someone, settle down. I thought you might be the one."

"Um." I shifted uncomfortably in my seat, part of me wanting to open up to Cormac, and part of me a little put off that he was being so upfront about something that I felt should be private. "Clearly not."

He waved a hand, as if to dismiss that idea. "Misunderstanding."

"He won't even listen to me explain," I said, starting to feel angry now. Lottie came over with a coffee pot and a menu just then and leaned in with a smile.

"How are things with Callan?" she asked, a conspiratorial grin on her face.

"They've had a fight," Cormac told her.

Lottie's eyebrows shot up. "A fight? Oh no. What about?"

My head went back and forth between these two near-strangers as they discussed my most recent life disaster as if they were a part of my immediate family. This town was full of insufferable busybodies on top of the ludicrous devotion to the worst holiday on record. It would be refreshing to get back to Los Angeles where everyone just minded their own business.

Except.

Except it wouldn't. Being left alone wasn't actually what I wanted, not if I was being honest with myself.

An hour later, I had an empty plate in front of me and had told Lottie and Cormac the whole story. Even Helen had pulled her chair nearer, and she snorted in a somewhat sympathetic fashion now and then.

Lottie was about to say something when my phone rang, and I lifted it to see who was calling. Uncle Rob. I swallowed hard, fear and worry rising in my throat. This meant he'd probably seen the footage then, or at least been told I didn't comply with his request. I excused myself and went to the corner of the bakery to take the call.

"Hi Uncle Rob," I said.

"I'm disappointed, kiddo," he said. I was about to explain, but my uncle cut me off. "I was skeptical when I gave you the shot, honey, and I know now I should've listened to my gut. You're too soft for television, April. It's just ... well, it's not going to work out." He paused, but I was too busy trying not to cry to get a word in. I'd known it was coming, but it still hurt. "I wanted to help out," he went on. "You and your mom have had a rough road. And you're family, so ..."

I had just opened my mouth when he dove back in.

"But there's a point where business is business."

I waited, but it seemed that was the extent of Uncle Rob's 'you're fired' speech. "Okay," I said.

"Okay?"

"I expected this call. It's fine." As I said the words, my tears dissolving somewhere inside me, unshed, I was surprised to find that it actually was fine.

He paused, and I suspected that a man like Rob, who thrived on confrontation, was somewhat let down by this. "Oh, well. All right then. Merry Christmas, April."

"You too," I said, hanging up.

I turned back around, and nearly jumped backward into the plate glass window. Helen was standing just behind me, looking interested, her light blue eyes fixed on my face. "Fired, are you?"

"Yes."

"Television?" Helen asked, looking weirdly interested. "Production, right?"

"Yes," I said, wondering where this particular line of questioning was going.

"Well, no one listens to old ladies, I know that. But Ryan's got a new production company, and he's been struggling to find anyone with any experience here in Maryland. I could introduce you. For a price."

A little trickle of shock worked its way through my system. "Um, what?"

Helen sighed as if barely tolerating my lack of understanding. "My soon to be grandson in law, Ryan McDonnell? Maybe you've heard of him?"

"Ryan McDonnell?" I parroted. "The movie star?"

"Helen, that's a great idea!" Lottie had rushed to her friend's side and was grinning from ear to ear. "And then you don't have to leave at all, dear," she told me.

It was like the town was trying to adopt me or something. It wasn't an altogether unpleasant feeling, actually. "Um, sure, I mean ... I'd love to talk to him about it."

"Right." Helen whipped an iPhone from inside the pocket of her sweat suit and wandered away, barking into the phone.

"You should go ahead and cancel your flight, dear," Lottie told her.

I met Cormac's eyes over the older woman's head, and he smiled and shrugged. "Once you've been absorbed into Singletree, it's pretty hard to get out," he said. "That's how I ended up here."

Lottie went to his side and laid a hand on his shoulder. "And we're keeping you," she said. "Even if your brother is a moron."

"He's had a rough time, Lottie," Cormac said. "We all have."

Her face softened and she patted his shoulder. "I know, honey."

"Ryan's on his way!" Helen announced, seating herself next to Cormac's table again and giving me a meaningful look. "Now, about the price."

I felt like my world was spinning out of control. Hadn't I come in here to get a muffin? And now suddenly, I was supposed to cancel my flight and meet a movie star? "Oh, okay, well ..." I reached for my purse.

"I don't want your money," Helen barked. "But Juliet and Ryan won't hook me up with any of the California-grade weed you've got out there. I don't suppose you have any connections, do you?"

I actually felt my jaw drop open.

"Oh for fuck's sake, everyone's a prude," Helen said, sliding off the high stool and shuffling back to the counter. "I need another brownie, Lottie. None of them have had pot in them so far, but I'm willing to keep looking."

Cormac began packing up his computer, shuffling things into his messenger bag. "Well, I need to go get the girls," he said. Then he fixed me with a stern look. "You're staying then, right? At least you're not leaving today?"

My head was spinning. "I have no idea what I'm doing."

"Join the club," he said, pulling on his coat. "This is a good place to be lost though, I promise. Don't leave tonight, okay?"

I watched him leave, pulling his phone from his pocket as he went out the door and calling someone on the sidewalk as he walked away, head down against the wind. I had about fifteen minutes of relative silence during which I tried to figure out what to do, when the door opened again, and my day got even weirder.

"Hello," the movie star said, coming in the door and stamping his feet on the mat to get the snow off. "Hey Lottie, Gran." He fixed his famous icy blue eyes on me. "You're April?"

I nodded as Ryan McDonnell sat down in the seat Cormac had just vacated.

"Let's talk about production," he said, and I decided to just give myself over to the strangeness of Singletree.

22

WIZARDING DICKENS

CALLAN

I had to admit that I'd been ready to give up. I'd allowed myself to be a little bit defeatist, spending the day after April had filmed my house feeling sorry for myself and grumbling around my big empty house. But when Cormac called and told me she wasn't leaving town immediately, it seemed like maybe it was time to slap myself around a bit and get to work.

Cormac's words helped too.

"No one else is going to set up your life for you, bro. You'll have to actually do something."

It was true. For years, other people *had* pretty much set up my life. Soccer had come naturally to me, and when the scout had seen me play in high school, it really had felt like everything just happened after that. College, more scouts, my agent—they'd all arranged things so I really didn't need to think too much. I'd just had to do what I loved, and continue doing it well.

Until I couldn't.

But now? Now my brother was right. There were no more scouts, no agents coming to make me offers that were too good to be true. I'd have to take some responsibility. And though the realization was a little bit scary, it was also exciting.

And I was going to start with April. But I'd need a little help.

I was on the phone most of the day, and by that night, everything was in place. The only thing left to do was to see if I could get April to cooperate, and Annabelle promised she would help with that.

The call came earlier than I was expecting, and I was glad. "So she's in for the night?" I asked Annabelle, my heart rising into my throat.

"Yes. She said she has a lot to think about and after eating muffins all day at the bakery she didn't want dinner."

"Are you ready?" My heart was beating furiously, and I wiped my sweaty palms on my jeans.

"I think so," Annabelle said. "I had Andrew set up the television like you said. Hopefully this will work!"

"If everyone plays their parts, it will," I said. "Though I have no idea how April will react." I tried to imagine her face—the last time I'd seen her she'd been so closed, so cold. A spike of fear shot through me. What if this didn't work? What if I'd been reading it all wrong?

"Really?" Annabelle sounded skeptical of my doubt. "She's in love with you, Callan Whitewood. I'm sure of it."

Even hearing Annabelle say it made my heart rise with hope. "She's mad at me though."

"She won't be able to stay mad after this," Annabelle said.

"I hope not."

"I better go," Annabelle said. "I'll see you when you get here."

I was already dressed and all I needed were my car keys. I flicked on the Christmas lights, took one long last look at Christopher the tree, which would always remind me of April, and went out.

The drive to the Candlestick Inn had me feeling nervous and worried. The slick roads around town didn't help either. Winter had well and truly arrived, in the form of freezing temperatures and black ice. I wondered absently if we'd be having a real white Christmas, but I cleared my head of that thought. I couldn't think about Christmas yet—I was too busy working on today.

I parked and went inside, meeting Annabelle at the desk.

"Is this ridiculous?" I asked, suddenly doubting every bit of planning I'd done all day and wondering if it wouldn't be better just to go back home.

"No," she said, and the way she drew out the word told me she meant it. "No, this is perfect. She is in the Dickens Suite, after all."

"Maybe she'll just be angrier at me for bothering her." I was trying on the words, but they didn't feel true.

"Quit being a pansy. Do you have the recording?" Annabelle's blue eyes glittered with excitement, and I found a fondness for her growing inside me. Even if she was a little over-enthusiastic about the holidays. She waved me toward a table at the edge of the lobby next to a severe-looking nutcracker soldier, and after disentangling one of her alarmingly upright ponytails from the statue's rifle, she sat down across from me. "Andrew says once you're on the network, you'll be able to see all the devices you can cast to. Hers is 'Dickens.'"

"Okay," I said. "Yes, I see it here."

"Be ready to go," Annabelle warned. "As soon as you take control, whatever is playing on your phone will be on her screen."

"Man, I hope she isn't in the bathtub or anything."

"Oh!" Annabelle hopped up again and scooted back behind the desk, picking up the phone and making a call. She grinned and nodded as she spoke, and then gave me a thumbs up.

"What did you do?"

"I told her we'd had some frogs get into the plumbing and that the guy was here getting them out but that it was impor-tant no one takes a shower or a bath for a while."

I was pretty sure that was not a legitimate plumbing problem experienced by hotels. "She believed that?"

"She sounded a little skeptical, but said she wasn't plan-ning to take a bath or shower right now."

"Good." I flicked through my phone, setting up the video so I could easily hit play. I did not need to be thinking about April in the shower or bathtub at the moment and told my overeager wizarding staff as much. Internally, of course.

The clock struck seven, and I connected to April's television, hit play, and held my breath.

23

GHOST OF CHRISTMAS GLITTER
APRIL

I was sitting on the edge of my bed with my legal pad in my hands and the *House Hunters* marathon on television in front of me. It was time for a pro/con list, and I had every intention of working on it, but after the insanity in the bakery, I was a little drained. Still, when you were offered your dream job by Ryan McDonnell less than an hour after being fired from your not-dream job, you thought pretty seriously about moving across the country.

But that would have me moving into the town where Callan lived.

And given that he was a stubborn jerk, that could be bad.

I wished my heart would quit jumping around like an over-eager puppy, telling me it would be good instead. Of course Singletree wasn't only about Callan now, though he weighed heavily on my mind. But I also thought about Annabelle, Lottie and Helen, Cormac and the girls and all the other people I'd met and fallen in love with since I'd come here. Maybe I could live here without ever seeing Callan?

I was just about to begin the list when *House Hunters* went dead. And something else came on my screen. Some ONE else.

Callan.

"Hi April," he said, looking handsome and perfect as he sat in an armchair next to the soaring Christmas tree in his parlor. What the hell was happening? Why was Callan on my television? Was I having some kind of moonshine-inspired hallucination? I shook my head, but he was still there, eyes deep and dark as ever, boring into me. Could he see me?

"Um, hi?"

Callan's voice cut off my response, and I realized with some relief that he couldn't hear me. "You're probably wondering what I'm doing on your television. Especially because I think you're pretty angry with me right now."

"Yeah, I am," I said, though my voice lacked conviction. Mostly, I just wished I could rewind a couple days and live forever in the time I'd spent at his house, in his arms, in his warm soft bed.

"First," he said, that deep voice rich and smooth enough to make my ovaries stand to attention. "First, I owe you an apology. I should have given you a chance to explain the second contract instead of jumping to conclusions. Cormac told me you lost your job because of it. And I'm sorry. But we can talk about that later."

I couldn't believe what was happening. He'd hijacked my television to give me a half-assed apology?

"I'm here now to give you a warning. Kind of a warning. More of an announcement. Or an alert?" Callan seemed to be struggling for words. "I don't know what to call it. I'm just telling you something. To prepare you. So what is that called? An announcement, I guess. Dammit, I'm rambling. This isn't good at all." He dropped his gaze from the camera for a second and seemed to be thinking. He looked back up. "I'll just get on with it." He took a breath and leaned forward, his face serious.

I felt myself lean forward in response.

"Tonight you'll be visited by three ghosts," Callan said, and I couldn't help the snort-laugh that escaped my lips. Was this *A Christmas Carol*? Three ghosts? I looked around my suite. It was the Dickens Suite, after all.

"First," Callan said. "You'll see the ghost of Christmas past."

Callan's image flickered away and was replaced by footage of snow falling.

My heart was beating very rapidly, and I forced myself to take a few deep breaths, to calm down. What was he doing? And was he going to let me watch *House Hunters* or not? I put the pad and pencil aside on the bed and stood up, but the face that appeared on my screen next had me sitting back down. Hard.

"Hi honey." Someone I hadn't seen in years appeared on my screen, sitting in a folding chair in front of a window through which was a bright green lawn and a blue sky. His face carried more wrinkles than it had the last time I'd seen it —which had been more than twenty years ago now—and he was thinner than I remembered him. A churn started low in my gut as my father continued to speak. "It's a little early, I guess, but I wanted to wish you a merry Christmas."

"Bastard," I whispered through my teeth. I wanted to turn him off, to smash the television, to make him stop talking. How dare he tell me merry Christmas? He'd been the one to singlehandedly ensure I'd never have a merry Christmas again.

"Listen April. I know you're angry with me. I know you have been for years. Since that night ..." He had the grace to drop his eyes to his hands. He looked back up at me, and his eyes were shining, pleading. "Since the night I left," he said, voice stronger now despite the unshed tears standing in his eyes. "I wanted to come back for you so many times, I can't even tell you. Second-guessed myself a million times after I left. And the timing ... honey, I know the timing was awful." He shook his head.

I sat frozen on the edge of my bed, my hands in my lap. I was surprised to feel a drop of wetness land on my thumb. My father had left almost twenty years before, and he still had the power to make me cry. Why was Callan showing me this?

"The thing I need to say to you, April, is this. I don't ask your forgiveness; I know you can't give me that. I don't ask you for anything, but maybe an effort to understand. Things between your mother and I—well, they weren't good. They had never really been good, if you want the truth, but none of this was her fault. We'd been struggling, and it all came to a head that night. I don't know if you're old enough now that you can understand this, but ..." he dropped his eyes again, maybe struggling for words. "Relationships can be hard," he continued. "Sometimes they get complicated and so layered with hurt and resentment that you lose the thread. You lose the reason why you were together in the first place, and everything just feels like hurt and anger. And that's where your mother and I were. But we had you. And so we stayed together. For a long time."

I was crying for real now. This. This was the thing my mother wouldn't talk about. This was what no one had ever bothered to explain to me.

"I don't know for sure what your mother told you, honey. But you need to know that none of it was because of you. I didn't leave *you*. I left what felt like an impossible situation—and I know you won't believe me, but I did it *for* you. Because I didn't want you to see me become the angry, resentful man I would have been if I'd stayed."

He looked up again, one of the tears making a steady path down his cheek. "Not fighting harder for you—for a chance to talk to you, to see you regularly—that's been the single biggest regret of my life. And time passed, you know? And then it felt like you hated me so much, and I guess I assumed by then you were better off without me, that I should just let you move on."

He sighed and shook his head. "But honey, I never did. Maybe externally. And yes, I tried to give myself another chance, I tried to forgive myself for whatever part I had in that first terrible marriage. I decided to live in hope instead of regret. And I met Laura. But I never forgave myself for you, for the mess I made with you. And not a day goes by, April, that I don't think of you and pray for you and wish to know you, to be part of your life."

He stopped talking then, and just stared into the camera as tears ran unheeded down my cheeks, spattering on my hands and my jeans. My emotions were jumbled and confused, leaping over one another for a spot up front—hurt, anger, confusion, sorrow ... and love—that unwanted longing that had lived in the back of my heart for so many years, that wish that one day my daddy would come back, would tell me it wasn't my fault.

"I'd like to see you sometime, honey. If you'd ever maybe be okay with it. I know you're out in Maryland now, and I hope you're having a wonderful time. Callan seems like a really good guy." My father tilted his head, and a half smile lifted his lips. "It's hard to believe you're old enough to be dating grown men," he said. "But I guess I gave up the chance to have any opinions there."

A strangled noise escaped my lips and I dropped my head for a second. It was too hard to look at my father now, to hear the words he was finally saying, the words that smoothed the edges of the jagged rip that had been in my heart for so many years.

"I'm sorry, April. For leaving you, for not explaining things better when you were little, and for not being a part of your life since then. I would have been, but ... well, this isn't about me and your mother. It's about me and you. And for all the things I didn't do right there. I'm sorry." I looked back up to see another tear trailing down my father's cheek. "I'm proud of you, April. And I know maybe it doesn't feel like it, but please know that I'm always here for you."

The screen went blank, and I sagged. It was as if years of tension had been unlocked and had just left my body, flowing from my fingers and toes and leaving me drained and floppy as a rag doll.

For a long minute, the television remained blank, and I cried.

If there were going to be two more ghosts, I wasn't sure I'd survive them.

When I'd regained control of my breathing, I got to my feet, went to the counter, and poured myself a shot of moonshine, downing it fast and then putting both hands on the countertop and taking some steadying breaths.

I waited, on edge, but nothing happened. And frustratingly, *House Hunters* did not come back on.

As the clock on my mantle ticked and the hour wore on, I wondered if that had really happened at all. It had been such a strange day, maybe my exhausted mind had fabricated my father's appearance on my television. Maybe I was dreaming. I crossed the room to the window, lifting the sash and letting a wash of frigid air sweep into the room, carrying the scent of snow.

"Not dreaming," I said out loud, shivering. Part of me wondered if maybe there was a camera inside my room somewhere, but I quickly dismissed the notion. Callan had hijacked my television, maybe. He wouldn't bug my room.

I turned back toward the television after struggling to

shut the window and frowned at the snow falling on the screen.

"Get on with it," I grumbled, snatching a sweater from the chair back. As I did, the screen flickered again, and Callan reappeared.

"Hi," he said.

My battered heart beat hard at the sight of him, and despite my lingering anger with him, I wished I could find him, maybe press myself into his arms for a few minutes and tell him about my father. I still felt mad at Callan, but more than that, I felt a pull to him. In the past couple weeks, he'd become the person I talked to, the person I thought out loud with, the person I depended on. And that was a lot after years of depending only on myself.

I sat back down on the end of the bed, steeling myself for what might come next.

"I hope you're doing okay," he said. "In case you're wondering, there aren't any cameras or anything in your room, so it's not like I can see you." He leaned forward a bit toward the camera. "But god, April. I want to see you. I know it's only been a day or so, but you have no idea how much I miss you. You swept in here with your gorgeous hair and your television crew, and ... well, you shone a light into part of me that I guess had been dark for a really long time. And I screwed it all up. And I miss you."

I shivered, staring into the fathomless depths of his eyes on the screen. It was exceedingly hard to hold onto my anger.

"Get ready for the next visitor, okay? The ghost of

Christmas present." Callan flickered away, and a moment later, Lynn appeared on the screen.

"Hey girl!" she chirped. "Oh my god, this has been the most insane day. I can't believe Callan Whitewood called me ... to help him win you! What have our lives turned into? Seriously."

Lynn laughed, and my heart lightened with the sound of it, so familiar and reassuring. Lynn had been family to me since high school, and seeing her round pink cheeks and soft blond hair on the screen made me feel instantly better. "So I'm totally coming out there if you decide to stay, but I wouldn't have gotten there in time today. So you get me on camera instead—where I totally belong, by the way. Someday!"

Lynn had dreams of acting. Dreams she literally never pursued. At all. But I was used to hearing about them, so this nod to all things familiar made me feel even more at home with Lynn on my screen.

"Here's the thing. Apes, as much as I miss you here in LA, I think it's time to face facts. For one thing, you don't have a job. And this is not an especially affordable place to live. Unless you're thinking of taking that apartment you looked at after college over in Santa Monica. The one with the closet bar across the living room? Where the bathroom door didn't close because the toilet was too big? I mean, if that's what you want for your future—living in a literal closet and being able to poop while chatting with whoever's on the couch—then by all means. I mean ... who am I to stop you?

"But I'm thinking you need more than that, and I know

you deserve a lot more. And while I've never been to Snaggle Tree, Maryland, myself, it sounds like a pretty good place. A place with people who care about you. And April, it sounds like a place where there's a ridiculously hot guy who would do just about anything to make you happy.

"I miss you like hell, but, April? What do you have to come back to?"

Ouch. I cringed at the truth of it. Though my mother was still in Los Angeles, there wasn't much else there for me now besides Lynn. And I knew that Lynn would always be my best friend, no matter who lived where. That was just a fact.

"Think about it, okay?" Lynn added. And then she winked and did a little gun motion with her hand. And she was gone.

And I was alone in my room again, snow falling gently on my television screen, and my mind whirling in too many directions at once. Could I really stay here?

I'd sat with Ryan McDonnell for two hours that morning. And once I'd gotten past the shock and obvious nerves that came with the fact that he was completely famous and really handsome, I'd listened to what he had to say. He'd come to Maryland for a weekend, fallen in love, and never really gone back.

Come to think of it, there were a lot more parallels between our stories than I would have ever assumed I might find with a legitimate celebrity. We both came to Maryland from Los Angeles—somewhat under duress in both cases. We'd both assumed we would be heading right back home but had ended up staying longer than intended. And Ryan had found the love of his life here. That was what had made him stay.

What about me, I wondered. Had I found the love of my life?

I didn't know about that, but what Ryan offered was a solid job. And a promotion at that. He was looking for a production manager for the company he'd formed here in Maryland. I'd be producing film projects for him, but I'd also have a hand in helping select those projects. It wasn't reality television, and it wasn't some over-tinsled home show. It was feature-length film, something I'd always wanted but hadn't dared to hope for. Something I wasn't sure I could even do.

Hadn't I just failed spectacularly twice? Maybe I wasn't cut out for production at all. Maybe I should have been talking to Lottie about getting a job at the bakery instead.

I pulled the sweater tighter around me in the quiet closeness of my hotel room. A sense of anticipation brewed within me. I knew what was coming. Or at least, I knew there had to be a ghost of Christmas future to follow on the heels of those last two visits. But what would it be? Who would it be?

The snow continued to fall on my television screen as the hour stretched on, and I was beginning to have that strange feeling again that maybe I'd imagined it all. And in the silent waiting, my mind went to Callan.

Here was a man who'd come to Singletree to escape in many ways. He was hurt, wounded by disappointment and broken expectations, and within days of him arriving, I'd barreled in with cameras, threatening to expose him again to the very thing he'd been trying to escape. I couldn't blame him, maybe, for jumping to the worst conclusions when he'd gotten the second contract. It had been a big enough stretch for him to agree to the first. And I knew that he'd done it not because he cared a lot about his house being featured on *Holiday Homes,* and not even because he'd signed a contract, no matter how unwittingly. He'd done it for me.

Callan had been willing to put himself out of his comfort zone because I needed him to. Maybe I needed to step out of my own comfort zone a bit too.

As I had this thought, the sound of music filtered up from somewhere outside. As I strained to listen, the music grew louder, and I realized it wasn't only music—it was voices. A lot of them. And they were outside my window.

I stood and went over to put up the sash once again, and when I did, the cold air whooshed in on a chorus of "We Wish You a Merry Christmas." I peered out to see at least fifteen people bundled against the cold and standing beneath my window on the sidewalk below. Annabelle was there, along with Andrew the bell boy and a couple of the other guys I'd seen moving things around the hotel. Lottie and Helen were there, and so was Ryan McDonnell, his arm around a beautiful dark-haired woman who must have been his fiancée, Tess. I nearly choked when I recognized Juliet Manchester at Tess's side, along with a huge dark-haired man that must have been the bodyguard Ryan had mentioned, Jace. Wiley Blanchard from the distillery was there, and so were the Wentworths and six or seven other people I'd seen around town. It seemed like every single person I'd met since coming here had gathered outside to sing. I figured they'd move on any second, off to serenade another guest, but as soon as the song ended, they started up again with another familiar holiday tune.

I waved and smiled down at them, catching the eyes of Cormac and his darling daughters and getting an ecstatic wave from Maddie who broke from singing to yell, "Hi Ape-Will!"

Just as I started to wonder how long this might go on, there was a sharp knock at the door of my room, and I let out a little scream. I covered my mouth with my hand, waved down at the carolers, and took a deep breath. Whatever the ghost of Christmas future had to tell me, it was about to happen. I steeled myself and I turned, crossing to answer the door.

24

THE TROUBLE WITH ARMOIRES
CALLAN

*P*lanning the rest had been easy. I knew it was potentially risky to reach out to April's father, but once I'd spoken to Lynn, I knew I had to try. And when he'd been receptive, almost relieved, to tell me the story, I knew it was the right thing.

I wanted April to see a future she hadn't imagined before—one I didn't even see until just a day or two before. I wanted her to feel the magic around us in this place and know that there was a chance we could capture it and hold it forever if she was willing to try.

Standing outside the door to her room, hearing the distant notes of the carolers in the cold night beyond her windows, my heart hammered and a slick of sweat coated my palms. It wasn't just April's future I wanted to show her. It was my own as well.

I took a deep breath, wiped my hands down the thighs of

my jeans and knocked. "Now or never, Whitewood," I muttered beneath my breath.

When the door swung open, April stood inside, her beautiful face flushed and her eyes shining with tears. Her hair was down loose over her shoulders, and she wore a soft white sweater that my hands longed to touch. She was flushed and gorgeous, and for a long second, I forgot everything but her and how desperately I needed her in my life, at my side, holding my hand.

"Future?" Her voice was almost a whisper, and for a second her word confused me, spun my brain off track even more than it already was.

Future yes. God, that was what I wanted with her.

"Yes," I said, "I'm the ghost of Christmas future. Can I come in for a minute?"

She looked uncertain, but stepped back, making room for me to step in and shut the door. God, I wanted to touch her. She looked so innocent and young, standing there with her eyes wide, her chest heaving slightly. I wanted to lay my hand along her cheek and pull her to me, bury my face in her hair and tell her it would be all right, I'd never let her go again. But I hadn't earned that right yet.

"Did you want to sit down?" April asked me, and then she looked quizzically at the snow falling on her television screen. "Or, do we need the TV?"

I shook my head. "No, there's no multimedia presentation for this one. Just me."

"Okay," she said, and she waved me over to the armchairs, sinking into one and folding her hands across her knees.

I wasn't sure I could sit and say what I needed to say, but I took a steadying breath and sank into the cushioned seat, trying to remember where I needed to begin.

"April," I started, feeling already like nothing I could say would be adequate to explain myself. But I had to try. "I owe you an apology first of all."

She was shaking her head slowly, and she leaned forward suddenly, interrupting me. "I should have told you about the contract!"

I couldn't do this. I couldn't sit here three feet away from her. I needed to touch her, if she'd let me. I stood, and moved to where she sat, her glowing eyes following my every move. I sank to my knees before her, taking her hands in mine. "Don't interrupt, okay? I have a lot I need to say."

She sighed and nodded, letting me hold her soft hands in mine on her knees.

My ankle screamed in protest at the position on the floor, but I refused to pay attention to it tonight, almost feeling like I deserved the pain, and the sharp edge of it kept me alert, thinking straight. "When my lawyer called about that second contract, I jumped to conclusions. I assumed things about you, about your intentions, about your character—things that, if I'd given myself a little more time to think about them, I already knew weren't true. I'm sorry about that, and I'm sorry I didn't give you the chance to explain."

April nodded, but she kept her promise and didn't interrupt, her raspberry colored lips pressed together beneath wide eyes.

"It was only because in the past, with other people who

have been in my life, it wouldn't have been a leap to assume they intended the worst. They usually did. I came here, to Singletree, in part because I wanted to get away from everyone in that life. And I didn't trust anyone new as a result. Or more accurately, maybe, I didn't trust myself to be a good judge of people. I figured I'd come here, be an uncle to my nieces, be a support to my brother if I could, and die quietly and alone."

A visible shiver went through April as I said that, and a little blossom of hope opened up in my gut.

"And before I got my head on straight, there you were," I continued, remembering the way April had bustled into my house, bossy and beautiful. "And I didn't know it at the time, but you saved me."

"Saved you?" April asked, scooting forward in the chair and then sliding out of it, joining me on the floor so we were kneeling face to face, our hands linked in the middle.

"Yeah." My heart was galloping in my chest, both with April's proximity and with the next words I wanted to say. "The future I'd imagined for myself was going to be empty. I thought it was what I wanted, maybe what I needed to ensure no one could hurt me again, no one could use me. But you showed up, and suddenly I saw a different future. One with kisses in the back of Santa's sleigh, one with cats in ridiculous little wheelchairs and a town full of people so insane they change the name of the place to match the season." April was nodding slowly. "I saw mornings lazing around in bed with you tangled up in my arms and nights filled with the sounds you make when I touch you. And I saw my nieces dancing through my house smiling and laughing, even though they've been through hell, and my brother having a place to relax and hand over the reins for a while. I saw a family I'd never really imagined."

Tears were welling in April's eyes and as I took a breath, one spilled over the edge of her lashes, and I wiped it away with a thumb.

"I saw a house filled with love in a place I had never even considered before. A woman I want to spend my days and nights with, and a future filled with people I trust and cherish, and love so much it hurts." I stopped, worried maybe I'd gone too far.

The tears were flowing down April's face as she stared at me, and her bottom lip was quivering. It took every ounce of restraint I had not to kiss that full perfect lip.

Soft strains of "Silent Night" were coming in through the cracked window beyond where we knelt on the floor, and it felt as if everything in the world had frozen still, waiting for a response from April.

"Can I talk now?" April asked, and I laughed, thankful for the break in the tension.

"Yeah, sorry."

She sniffled and pulled a hand free to wipe her face. Then she cupped my jaw, leaned forward slightly, and pressed her lips to mine softly.

I forced myself to stay still, to kiss her back softly, but not to give into the wild urge to pull her into my arms and never let her go. The tentative kiss was a tease, but I pushed my desire down as far as I could. There were still things to be said. And goodbye was still a possibility, but God, I hoped she wouldn't say it.

April pulled back and released me, her hands returning to mine. She dropped my gaze and giggled. "Sorry, just needed to do that once." Then her eyes rose to mine and her face was serious. "I love the picture of the future you painted. I love that you think I could be a part of that. I grew up without a family—no cousins, no aunts, no big gatherings. So you know that's something I've always wanted."

I stiffened, feeling a "but" approaching.

"But I don't know how we could really do it. I mean, I have an apartment back in Los Angeles. Friends, my mom ... I have a really big armoire ..."

"An armoire?"

"Yeah, it's really hard to move."

Was she just finding excuses because she didn't want to tell me she didn't feel the same way? "Oh, well—"

"And the thing is ... I don't want to haul that thing all the way across the country just because some movie star offered me a job and a really hot guy needs extra people to help populate his holiday gatherings."

I squinted, tilting my head to the side. "You don't?"

"No," she said, smiling. "I mean, it's tempting, because he is really hot."

"He is," I agreed, my hope buoyed by the hint of a smile playing in the corner of April's mouth.

"But it's not enough. I mean, if the hot guy just needs bodies to seat around the holiday table ... I guess he could find anyone really." She looked meaningfully at me, and I frowned.

"April," I said, suddenly terrified she really was about to say no, but then I realized I'd left out one very important thing. "I'm in love with you. I think maybe I have been from the moment you walked into my house. The future I'm imagining is everything I want—but it only works if you're a part of it. Please stay. Please give us a chance." I squeezed her hands tightly and said the words once more, to be sure she heard them. "I love you, April."

My heart was in my throat and I was finding it hard to breathe as I watched her, her dark lashes lowering in an arc against her rosy cheek for a beat. And then she looked up, her eyes gleaming and a smile on her beautiful lips. "I love you too," she whispered.

My entire body zinged to life as if I'd been hit by lightning at the words and I gripped her hands tighter. "Say you'll stay."

"I mean, the armoire is pretty heavy."

"I'll go get it myself if you'll stay."

April nodded, and as I finally gave up my efforts at self-control and wrapped her in my arms, pressing my mouth firmly to hers, she managed to say, "I'll stay."

The kiss that followed was long, sweet, and equal parts demanding and frantic, and slow and languid. It started with both of us on our knees and ended with us on the floor, arms and legs wrapped around one another, both of us breathing heavily and me so close to coming in my pants that I had to roll away from her, taking some deep breaths on my back while focusing my mind on something decidedly non-sexual.

"Are you reconsidering your armoire offer?" April asked.

"No, I was thinking about Mr. FluffyNuts."

"Why?" April laughed.

"Because you've got me a little bit excited over here, and I don't want to humiliate myself by messing up my pants."

April burst into laughter, and she rolled closer to me, laying her head on my chest. "I'd think you would just use magic to calm yourself down. Being a dick wizard and all that."

It was my turn to laugh. And then I just held April against my chest, loving the easy feeling between us, and the soft curves of her pressed against me. As we lay on the floor, I realized we could still hear the carolers singing outside. I hadn't given them the signal to stop yet.

I moved, getting slowly to my feet and pulling April up with me, tucking her against my side with an arm around her. If I had my way, I'd never let her go again. We moved to the window and pushed it open farther, leaning through and waving down at the crowd of people with pink noses below.

"Oh, I forgot something," I said, pushing my hand into my pocket and retrieving the small package there. I handed it to April, watching her face light up at the sight of the small red box.

"What's this?" she asked, looking back up at me.

"If you open it, you'll find out," I said, nodding at the box.

She did, and when she lifted the little lid to find a gold heart gleaming with a diamond at its center, her face crumpled and she let out a strangled sob.

Oh god, I'd wanted to make her happy, not make her cry. "Oh, I um ..."

"It's perfect," she said, pulling the necklace from the box. "I love it. It's exactly like the one I got all those years ago ... I never knew what happened to it." She held it out to me and then turned, lifting her hair. After I fastened it around her neck and she turned back to me, I kissed her gently.

The crowd broke off in the midst of "Jingle Bells" and cheered when they saw us kissing.

"Thank you," I called down. "Thanks for all your help."

"Come down for some hot chocolate at the cafe?" Lottie Turner called up hopefully, and then turned to the crowd. "Everyone's welcome. Come have a drink!"

The crowd made a rolling noise of assent, punctuated with laughter and smiles, and they moved around the sidewalk toward the cafe across the square.

"I had kind of hoped to keep you up here for a while," I said, leaning down to bite the shell of April's ear.

She shivered against me and moaned. "We'll just go for a bit."

I nodded and helped her into her coat after closing the window. Downstairs, Annabelle broke into tears when she saw us and came running around the desk to pull us both into a hug.

"Come to the cafe for a drink?" I asked her.

Annabelle glanced around the empty lobby and then nodded, first putting up a sign that read: "Be right back."

25

FESTOONED FOR GOOD

APRIL

The town square gleamed and glowed as I crossed beneath the huge sparkling tree with Callan and Annabelle, and for the first time in my life since I'd been very young, Christmas felt a little bit like magic. I held Callan's arm, Annabelle's arm linked with mine on the other side, and a crowd of people moved into Lottie Tanner's bakery and cafe ahead of us—a crowd of people who felt more like family than anything I had experienced before.

It was a lot to process, I thought, because so much had happened in a very short amount of time. From the devastation of my last television implosion to the idea of moving across the country for my fantasy job and the man of my dreams. The words Callan had given me, along with the heart necklace, closed the open wound I'd been carrying for two decades, or at least went a long way toward healing it. I smiled up at him as he held open the door and wondered if I could possibly be happier. I didn't think so.

Maybe if Lynn and my mother were here, I thought, but as soon as I'd had a second to think this, I was swept up in the excited greetings of the townspeople who'd been caroling out in the cold beneath my window.

"Oh, look at this," Mrs. Wentworth beamed, stepping in near to see the little heart hanging around my neck. Her husband was at her side, nodding knowingly. "It's beautiful dear," the older woman said, and then she turned her gaze to Callan, letting her eyes travel slowly the length of his body, roving down and back up, hanging for just a moment longer than necessary right around his waistline. "And you've done very well for yourself here," she said, her voice deepening slightly.

"Indeed," her husband said. "You know," he added, giving me a lascivious grin, "sometimes it can be fun to switch things up, do a little sharing, if you know what I mean."

I did not know what he meant, but I had a feeling I would if I thought enough about it. Had we just been invited to swing? "Erm," I managed to say.

"That's very flattering," Callan said gallantly, and I wondered if he'd gotten Mr. Wentworth's full meaning. "But for now, we're happy just having each other." Yep, he had.

Mr. Wentworth nodded. "Of course, my boy. Of course you are. Well, you enjoy this spicy little tamale, and if you start to need another flavor, you know where to find us!"

"Sure thing," Callan said, tightening his grip on my arm.

"Oh my god," I laughed, my body warming as he met my eyes and grinned.

We got our coats off and went to sit down on a low couch

where Lottie was directing us to go. Cormac and the girls were in the chairs next to us, and the entire cafe was noisy and warm and full.

Before I had a moment to think about what I might like, a mug of steaming chocolate was pressed into my hand, and Lottie gave me a wink. "Hot chocolate," she said.

"Thank you, Lottie!"

Callan and I touched our mugs together before taking a sip, and our eyes locked for a long moment. I felt my stomach tighten as I stared into the deep coffee eyes I loved, and inside them I saw everything Callan had talked about—friends, family, future ... love.

Cormac leaned over the back of the couch and said, "The chocolate packs a punch." He stared down into his mug after taking a sip. Like everything else, the hot chocolate tasted like it had met the HalfCat. Then he looked up suddenly, and his gaze traveled between Maddie and Taylor, both drinking greedily from their own mugs. "You don't think she might have ..."

"I'm sure theirs was undoctored," Callan assured him. "But they might sleep extra well if not."

Annabelle came to sit on the arm of the couch. "That was really so romantic," she gushed. "It was very exciting to get to help a little bit."

"Thank you for that," I said. "Thank you for everything."

My friend smiled and squeezed my shoulder. "Of course," she said. "It's been amazing having you at the inn. I feel like I gained a friend."

"You did," I assured her.

"And you're staying in town?"

"I might need to go home for a little bit, just to tie up loose ends and talk to my mother in person," I told her. "But after that, yeah. I think I am."

Annabelle grinned and stood up to go mingle just as Maddie scooted closer to my knee, glancing up at me and then staring down at her shoes, suddenly shy.

"Hey you," I said, leaning forward to greet the little girl.

Maddie looked up at me then with a careful smile, chocolate covering her upper lip from one side to the other like a well-groomed mustache. "Hi Ape-will."

"Did you have fun singing?" I asked.

Maddie nodded, and then gave me another searching look. There was something she wanted to say, but hadn't found the courage to get out, I realized. As the tiny girl stood, one hand on my knee, her fingers absently exploring my denim-clad leg, Taylor stood and came to her side.

"Hi Taylor," I said.

Taylor glanced at her uncle, who was deep in conversation with her father, and her face relaxed a little bit as she leaned in to speak. "We are glad you're staying," she said quietly. "Uncle Callan needs you."

My heart warmed even further, threatening to melt altogether. "I'm glad to be staying," I said.

"But we wondered something," Taylor said, and Maddie's big eyes found her sister's face, expectant. "We wondered if now that you and Uncle Callan are going to be together, are you going to get married?"

I glanced at Callan. "Maybe someday," I said quietly. "I hope so."

"So you might have little kids of your own," Taylor said, nodding sagely.

"Well, I mean, not anytime soon," I said.

"Well," Taylor said slowly. "Do you think that until you have your own kids, that maybe you'll still want to see me and Maddie sometimes?"

That was it. My heart turned to complete mush. "Of course I will," I told them, putting down my mug and gathering both girls in my arms and pulling them onto my lap. "I will want to see you all the time," I continued. "Any time you want to see me!"

Maddie didn't say anything, but her little fingers wove into my thick sweater and after giving me one more long searching look with those huge blue eyes, she pressed her blond head into my shoulder. Taylor did the same thing on the other side, and moments later, my arms were full of warm, sleeping little girls.

"You've got friends for life," Cormac commented, nodding at his daughters. "Need me to rescue you?"

I smiled down at the sleeping girls, and then around at the friends gathered with me inside the cafe. From across the room, Helen Manchester gave me a little salute from her seat between Ryan McDonnell and Juliet Manchester. Lottie Tanner leaned against the counter of her shop, a tall girl with soft brown curls at her side—her daughters, Paige, and Amberlynn, I thought. I'd seen photos at Lottie's house. The cafe was filled with people and noise and so much love, I wished I could stay there, just like that, forever.

"I think I'm good," I told Cormac, hugging my twin burdens just a little tighter. My mind went back to Christmastime the year before, when I'd been busily ignoring everything related to Christmas, and spent the actual day with my mother at the movies, trying to pretend I didn't care. This was so much better. This was what this time of year should be. I thought of my mother and of Lynn, and wished they could be here. But there would be time to see them—and I thought I might convince my mother to come live here too. I could see my mom hanging out with Lottie and Helen, maybe finding a happier life for herself in this funny little town.

As I turned my gaze back to Callan's, meeting his eyes over Taylor's head, I felt a tear tracking down my cheek.

"Are you okay?" Callan asked, concerned.

I nodded, wishing I had more arms so I could pull him into me too. "I'm so much more than okay," I told him. "I didn't know it was possible to be so happy."

"You have a whole future filled with happy," Callan told her, wiping the tear away. "I promise."

I felt the promise of his words skitter through me like glitter sprinkling down from the ridiculous bow on the basket Annabelle had given me when I first arrived. And this time, I hoped the glitter would stick to everything because I never, ever wanted to be rid of it.

"I love you," I told Callan.

He kissed me softly, leaning over the sleeping girl in my arms. "I love you too," he said.

And just like that, I decided I loved Christmas too.

EPILOGUE
CALLAN

$\mathcal{O}$ne Year Later

I stood in the parlor near the soaring tree, watching April spin through the house like some kind of dervish, her red sheath dress hugging her curvy figure and making my trousers feel a few sizes too tight every time she passed. "You're making me dizzy," I told her as she sped by, stopping to fluff one of the shiny red pillows on the living room couch once more.

"I just want it all to be perfect," she said, finally stopping in front of me. Her cheeks were flushed, and her blue eyes glittered in the sparkling light from the tree.

"It is perfect," I assured her. "Besides, no one really cares if it's perfect. Christmas parties are about being together, not about the decorations."

April narrowed her gaze at me. "They are about decorations," she insisted. "Which is why I've spent the last two months decorating for this."

I rolled my eyes, but pulled her into my chest, my entire body still thrilled every time she was close enough to touch. "And they're about love," I whispered, tucking my head so I could nibble the shell of her ear, which sent her skin rippling with goose bumps every time.

Tonight, especially, was about love, I thought, only April didn't know it yet. When she'd moved permanently in January, she'd spent a couple weeks at the inn before I'd finally convinced her just to move in with me. "The house is too big for me alone anyway," I had insisted. "And then you'll always be around to help me remember the gate code when I forget my remote."

She'd agreed, and she'd convinced me to change the code to something I'd remember, and we had finally settled on 1225, a number I hadn't quite understood at first. "Christmas," April had said with a smile. "The day that brought us together."

In the year since I'd met her, April had gone from being the most anti-holiday person I'd ever met to embracing all things glittery and festive with such enthusiasm sometimes all I could do was sit back and sigh. Between April and my nieces, Singletree Manor had been decorated to within an inch of its life this year, and April had insisted on hosting a Christmas party to show it off.

"I do love you," April said, relaxing a bit in my arms and sliding her own arms around my neck. The doorbell rang just as she pressed her lips to mine, and I regretted setting the gate open tonight for the guests. At least if they'd had to buzz from the gate, I would have had time to kiss her.

We went to the door together, and pulled it open to find Samuel Bass and his two twin boys standing in front of us, looking starched and uncomfortable in red and green bow ties. Their mother dashed up behind them, carrying a wrapped gift. "Hello Coach Whitewood," the boys said in practiced unison.

Mrs. Bass beamed. "This is for you," she held out the gift to April. "Thank you so much for inviting us to your home. It's lovely."

"Come on in," I said, waving the family toward the living room. The boys relaxed visibly after delivering their rehearsed line, and within five minutes of entering, there were no bow ties in sight.

"The guys have been talking all week about the Christmas tournament you organized," Mr. Bass told me a few minutes later, standing near the fire with a beer in his hand.

The Bass family, and a lot of the other guests who were arriving steadily for the party, were new friends I had met as a result of agreeing to coach a travel soccer team. I'd become one of the leaders in the league, offering direction and helping to organize additional opportunities for the players —like the Christmas tournament.

"I'm excited about it too," I told Mr. Bass. "Your boys have a lot of talent. I'm really glad to have them on the team." The talented twins dashed by right then, chasing Taylor and Maddie through the crowded living room as the girls shrieked. April caught them at the door and I saw her bend down to tell them something and then point back toward the playroom, where movies and toys had been set up to keep the smaller guests occupied.

The house filled up rapidly, guests mingling all through the first floor as the lights glowed and Christmas music played. April and I were busy, hosting and helping our guests get everything they needed, but after a couple hours the party took on its own rhythm, and April found her way to my side.

I put an arm around her, loving the feel of her soft silky skin against my palm. "You look amazing tonight," I told her.

She grinned up at me, "So do you."

"Are you ready to get the game going?" I asked.

April had done a lot of online research about appropriate activities for holiday gatherings, since she had never really been to one as an adult. She'd decided that a party game was needed, and had settled on a game where guests opened gifts in order and could steal from one another. The gifts were all little things, and many of them were kid-appropriate, since April partially organized the game with Maddie and Taylor in mind.

"If everyone could find a seat," April called, turning down the music. "We'll play the game."

Maddie had gone through the crowd, offering everyone the chance to draw a number, which would determine who went first. April had drawn number one—I had set it up that way, and though she'd tried to give it back, Maddie had insisted she had to keep it. So when everyone was settled, April stood back up. "I drew number one, so I guess I'll go first, even though it feels pretty rude at our own party."

"Here you go," Helen Manchester picked up a big box

with a glittery green bow and shoved it toward April, nearly spilling her Manhattan in the process.

"Helen," Lottie scolded. "She gets to pick."

"No, she doesn't," Helen assured her friend. "She wants that one."

April glanced at me and I nodded, so she shrugged and took the big box. She pulled it onto her lap as she sat on an ottoman and pulled off the wrapping paper and ribbon, opening the box only to find another box inside. Maddie came over to help her as she unearthed box after wrapped box, accumulating a mountain of paper as she opened each one.

"This is the best present ever," Maddie lisped reverently as she helped open the gifts.

Finally, the box in April's hand was so small, she seemed to realize there could not be another inside it, and just as she was about to open it, Maddie took it from her and handed it to me.

"Hey," April protested.

Taylor stood and came over to pick up all the wrapping paper and stick it into a trash bag, clearing the area around April. And then I stepped in front of her, dropping to a knee with the box in my hand and my heart pounding madly. The girls and I had practiced this, and they'd done their parts perfectly. Now it was my turn.

"April," I said, as her hands flew to her face, which was turning pink. "You barreling into my life was the best thing that ever happened to me. You barged in here, bossy and demanding, and pulled me out of the darkest days I've ever known. You gave me a chance to find myself again, helped me discover a new life and were gracious enough to agree to be a part of it. Since you've been here, I have lived a better life than I ever knew was possible. I face each day with hope and excitement, mostly because I know it will be another day with you."

A tear was streaking down April's cheek and her hands had begun to shake.

I kept my eyes locked on April's as the crowd began to murmur around us, realizing what was happening.

"I'm hoping you might be willing to agree to spend some more time with me," I went on, lifting the small box and opening it to reveal a perfect solitaire diamond ring. "I'm hoping you'll be willing to stay forever. I'm hoping you might agree to marry me."

April was nodding, slowly at first and then madly, her dark hair sliding around her shoulders. "Yes," she whispered, and then she seemed to remember the crowd around them and her role as hostess. She stood up and nearly shouted, "I said yes!" so those in the back could hear.

I stood too, and slid the ring onto April's finger as her eyes locked on mine again.

"You've made me so happy," I said, leaning in to kiss her.

The gathered guests erupted in cheers and applause, and April whispered, "you can have forever."

I pulled her tightly against me again, my entire body warm and happy as the future glowed like the lights on the enormous tree in the parlor.

Forever sounded perfect. And with April at my side, every day of that forever would be just like Christmas.

<<<>>>

Sneak Peek: Second Chance Spring (Paige and Cormac's story!)

CHAPTER ONE: Paige

My Guilt is Organic

The late April rain was pouring down in buckets, sheeting my car and making it nearly impossible to see out the windshield. I squinted and leaned over the steering wheel like an old woman, shouting into the car's speakerphone. "I'm on my way, Mom, I promise. I'm sorry I'm late." I swallowed hard and said it before she had a chance: "Again."

"You be careful out there, young lady. That rain is torrential right now." My mother's voice filled the dark car, and though she sounded annoyed, I was still happy for the company. I hated driving in the pouring rain at night. There were no streetlights in this part of our small town, and the low clouds and rain didn't help with visibility. Mom went on, laying it on thick as only she could do. "Don't rush just because you're nearly an hour late for family dinner."

"Mom, you don't have to pile on the guilt. I come by it naturally."

"Good. I'd hate to think I raised you to believe it's perfectly acceptable to be an hour late to a family dinner."

I sighed as my hands gripped the wheel, both out of frustration and for better control. "Do you want me to rush or to be careful, Mom?" I guided my little car through a traffic circle and then signaled to turn into Mom's neighborhood.

"Be careful, for goodness sakes. And try to do it in a speedy fashion." Standard Lottie logic. "The pot pie's getting cold. Why do you have to work so late?"

"I told you to go ahead and eat without me!" Frustration sent my hand into my hair, pushing my bangs back off my face as I pulled to a stop at the curb in front of Mom's colonial cottage. "I'm here. I'll be at the door in a sec."

The door of the brick-fronted house opened not two seconds later, and Mom's rotund figure appeared in the glow from within, holding her phone to her ear as she peered out at the car through the water sheeting down.

I switched off the engine and sighed. Having Mom in my life was a blessing, and the woman loved me fiercely. But sometimes I wondered if it wouldn't be freeing to have Mom love me just a little less fiercely. Or maybe just as fiercely, but from a greater distance.

I pulled my keys from the ignition, grabbed my purse, and made a dash for the front door. Lottie stopped me just outside under the little overhang. "You're soaked! Remind me to give you an old umbrella I've got before you go tonight."

I shook the rain from my hair and arms and removed my shoes as I stepped inside. "I have an umbrella, Mom." It was on the passenger seat in my car. It just hadn't made sense to go to the trouble of opening it up for a fifteen-foot walk.

"Then remind me to teach you what those are used for. We must've skipped that when you were little."

"Good to see you, Mom." I pulled my mother into a hug, and felt her relax.

"You too, Paigey. Come in. Your sister's waiting." Mom stepped back and led the way to the dining room.

"Hey," Amberlynn waved from the table, where she sat with a half-full glass of red wine and an expression somewhere between relieved and irritated. "Took you long enough."

"You didn't have to wait," I said. I'd made that clear to my mother when I'd called from the clinic an hour ago to let her know I was going to be late. Right before I scarfed the fries left over from my lunch and chased it with a vanilla latte supplied by my ever-adored physician's assistant. Though Leslie's job in no way meant she was actually supposed to act like my actual assistant, the fact that we were best friends made her a great asset at work.

The clinic where I worked was usually calm and my hours weren't overwhelming at all, but now and then we had a crazy day. And those days always seemed to coincide with my mother's dinners.

"Sit down, for Heaven's sake. Let's eat. This pot pie is undoubtedly a gelatinous disaster inside a crust at this point." Mom put the pie down on the table, pursing her lips and shaking her head, making her spray-frozen bob brush her shoulders on each side.

"Well, when it sounds so appetizing," I said.

"Don't sit yet, Paige," Amberlynn said, her voice low.

"I thought you were starving."

"Just thought you would want some wine before the

inquisition begins." Amberlynn pointed to the kitchen just beyond the table.

"Oh please," Mom said as I ducked past her to pour myself a glass of wine.

"Mom? You want?" I raised the bottle and looked over my shoulder.

Mom sighed dramatically. "Well if we're all going to behave like lushes tonight, I guess I'd better. Are you planning to stay over then, Paigey?"

I returned to the table with the bottle. "Mom, one glass with food before I go home in two hours should be fine."

My mother raised an eyebrow, but put up no further argument, and I poured myself a glass much less generous than I would have without the presence of the judgy eyebrow.

"The pot pie is great, Mom," I said around my first bite. It was. And it was miles away from the usual protein shakes and cereal dinners I made for myself.

"Oh, you're just saying that." Mom waved a hand and pretended the compliment wasn't absolutely required at Sunday dinner.

"Of course she is, Mom. You'd be annoyed if one of us didn't say it." Amberlynn took another big bite, and through a full mouth added, "though she's completely right. This is amazing."

We talked about her cafe on the town square in downtown Singletree, which she had recently renamed and had a huge sign made for, and about Amberlynn's job at the high school. And then all eyes turned to me, and I gave as brief a summary of my work at the family clinic where I was a general practitioner as I could. It turned out that hearing about scads of kids with runny noses and coughs didn't make for great conversation, and as busy as I always was at work, very little changed in the small-town practice I ran.

"And did you treat any handsome men today, Paigey?" Mom looked ever hopeful as she brought up her favorite topic and Amberlynn grinned expectantly. Since my younger sister was engaged and my older sister had escaped to New York City, they were rarely the subject of Mom's matchmaking meddling at this point. But in my aging and clearly withering state as a divorcee at almost thirty-one, I was dead in the crosshairs.

"That would be a no." Not that I would have been excited about the idea of dating a patient, but at this point, if a good-looking single man happened to wander through the clinic doors, I wouldn't send him to the other family practice across town.

"You have to get over Adam," Mom said sadly, shaking her head and folding her small hands over her generous middle.

"Mom, stop that!" I half laughed, half snorted. "We are not grieving my marriage. I was married less than a year and the whole thing was clearly a mistake."

"The wedding was so beautiful," Mom said sadly.

"Turns out marriage is about a lot more than the actual ceremony," Amberlynn said through a mouthful of peas and carrots. "Don't think Adam got the memo."

This was not my favorite topic, but it was practically a requirement of Sunday dinner to rehash my short-lived marriage to my high-school boyfriend. The fact we'd stayed together as I'd gone off for college and medical school made Adam seem loyal and true. I should have known that no red-blooded eighteen-year-old male would agree to wait for eight years for regular sex. It turned out Adam wasn't waiting. He was waiting for me, don't get me wrong—he just hadn't realized that monogamy was an expectation of marriage. It was easy to cover his dalliances when we were both away at school, but it turned out to be tougher to do when we shared a house in a small town like Singletree, Maryland.

Adam was not a bad guy. But he was not husband material, and the entire experience had made me feel like I'd wasted the best years of my life with one man who didn't deserve me in the end. Now I was over thirty and still getting grilled about my prospects over Sunday dinners. I imagined these same dinners in the future—seeing myself as a sixty-five-year-old woman, getting interrogated by my ninety-year old mother.

I sighed, finishing the meal and pushing my plate away. "Let's not rehash all that tonight," I suggested hopefully.

Mom shook her head and finished her meal, sipping her wine. "Amberlynn, I'm just glad you and Wiley both understand the commitment you're making."

I squeezed my eyes shut to keep from rolling them. Wiley was a great guy, and I knew Amberlynn had found one of the good ones, but I didn't want to play the comparison game or hear about my sister's wedding plans—for the ninetieth time —tonight.

"He's great, Mom, and I think we'll be good. We've talked about everything. We should be fine. Happy, I hope."

I gave Amberlynn a reassuring smile. I didn't want to take one second away from her happy ending just because I didn't get one of my own, though it seemed like there was something behind her forceful assertion that they would be happy. "You guys will be fine," I said softly.

"So," my sister said, rising to clear the table. She smiled sweetly at Mom and then we both carried plates into the kitchen. "Did you tell Mom you're moving yet?"

I glared at her and looked back to make sure Mom hadn't heard.

"So that's a no, I guess."

"Not yet. It's not a sure thing." I set the dishes on the counter and opened the dishwasher, and my sister and I fell into our routine, her rinsing plates and handing them to me to put inside the racks. "I told them I'd need a few weeks to think about the offer."

Amberlynn nodded. We'd talked at length already about the job offer I'd gotten from a clinic in Baltimore. It would be a bigger practice in a bigger place—and would hopefully represent bigger opportunities for me. Both as a physician and as a woman who might like to meet someone besides the handful of single men still in the small Maryland town where I grew up. "I'll miss you if you go, sis."

I stopped moving for a minute and looked at my sister, brushing a strand of her long blond hair back over her shoulder as she rinsed dishes. "I'll miss you too."

We finished up and I kissed my mom and sister good night, and then drove home to my own quiet cottage. This was the life I'd built, and it was good. I had everything I needed. I had a family that loved me, a dog to greet me at the door when I came home. I was successful and healthy. So why didn't I feel happy?

CHAPTER TWO - CORMAC

Rocks are not Nutritionally Balanced

"Here's a snack. And here's a snack. And you can have this one, and this one." My older daughter, Taylor, had never met a rock she didn't like, and every single one of the tiny pieces of gravel that filled the Singletree Park playground evidently seemed a perfect snack for her three-year old sister Madison to her. She was filling up Maddie's upturned shirt with rock after rock. "You can eat these before dinner," she told her sister. Madison stared up at her big sister with adoring eyes filled with trust.

"Or maybe we just save them for later," I suggested, deciding I'd better intervene before Sunday night turned into a fun-filled night of emergency room visiting. "Rocks don't taste good and they're not easy on the teeth. Also, your body can't digest them." I reached down and helped Madison smooth the front of her shirt, letting all the little pebbles fall back to the ground.

Madison looked relieved.

"Taylor, it's your job to look out for your little sister," I said, squatting down to look into the deep serious eyes of my older daughter. They reminded me so much of her mother's eyes that I actually had to fight off the choke that rose in my throat every time she looked at me a certain way. "You know she can't eat rocks, but she might not know that."

A small crease appeared between Taylor's eyebrows—also

like her mother, and I swallowed hard. "I have to be the mommy now." The deep liquid pools of my daughter's beautiful eyes at once revealed the deep misery she felt over losing her mother, and the strong sense of responsibility she'd managed to take on at only seven.

"No, Sweetie. You have to be a little girl. Your job is to play and have fun, but you do have to look out for your little sister and help her get bigger like you." I tried to keep my voice upbeat.

"But she needs a mommy," Taylor said, and the crack in her voice matched the one deep in my heart. Despite the warmth of the sunny Sunday afternoon, despite the glorious sunshine, brilliant green trees and fresh-cut grass, I was having trouble remaining positive.

"She has everything she needs in her daddy and her big sister," I told my serious older daughter. "Now go up in the crow's nest and see if you spot any pirates. I thought I heard cannons a second ago." I turned to address Madison too, who'd been watching our conversation thoughtfully while testing a small rock with her teeth. I took it from her and shook my head. "We don't eat rocks," I said.

Madison grinned and leaned into me, tucking her small head beneath my chin and nearly bursting my wounded heart. She always had a knack for knowing when I needed a hug or a little snuggle. She pressed her tiny body into mine and I stood up, holding her in my arms.

"Are you going to go up with your sister and look for pirates?" I pointed to the highest point on the playground, which was a fantastic wooden structure made with wide planks and ropes to look like a castle or—to some kids—a ship. There were two towers, more slides than I could easily count, and plenty of things to play on in between. Was it wrong that I felt slightly jealous my home town had never had such a cool playground?

"Pi-wats." Maddie wiggled in my arms and I put her down, her feet already moving to carry her up to where her sister was using one of the big plastic telescopes mounted on top to search for pirates.

I watched Maddie climb, then sighed and sank back down onto the bench where I'd been sitting. For another twenty minutes, I watched the girls play and tried to feel grateful for the old-fashioned goodness my adopted home town embodied. Singletree was as safe a place as you could get, made up of wide streets with big old trees arching above and beaches lining the land where it met the Chesapeake. People were kind and generous, and it was the kind of place that had hayrides and corn mazes in fall, and a cherry blossom festival in the spring. It was the kind of place I'd always wished I had grown up.

It was the kind of place my wife had grown up.

And now she was gone.

Linda had actually grown up somewhere along the Gulf, but Singletree, Maryland was our adopted home. She'd found the place on a business trip—she was a travel writer and had been scouting quaint inns along the Chesapeake— and we'd moved not long after. I was an accountant and could work from just about anywhere, so I set up a home office in the house we bought, got a tiny office with a partner in town, and together we began our perfect family.

But perfect was a myth, and one I would never buy into again. Linda had died four years later, suddenly and unfathomably. And now I was a single father, living in the quintessential American small town where no one was ever alone. And I'd never been lonelier.

"Daddy, I told Maddie she can't fly, but she won't listen!"

I shot up, my blood going cold, bounding to the top of the play structure, where Madison was trying to wrestle her short legs over the side of the highest point, her small hands scrabbling on the sides of the structure.

"I can fly! Like a angel!"

I pulled Maddie from the side of the turret, crushing her to me as my heart raced. The talk of angels had started when Linda died. Maddie had been so young when she'd passed that she didn't really remember her mother, but Taylor had misty memories, and she'd decided to think of her as an angel now, sharing her vision with her sister and peppering me with questions about angels at every turn.

"Let's go home, guys." I descended the structure with Madison in my arms. She'd stopped struggling and had relaxed against my shoulder, and I envied her the exhausted sleep I knew would hit her as soon as she was in the wagon we'd towed from home.

Taylor refused to come down for five minutes as I wheedled while staring up at her, searching for the one thing that would keep me from having to march back up. I understood her emotions, a mix of frustration over not being the one who got carried and general seven-year old angst, but eventually the promise that she could make the noodles for dinner brought her down.

Together, the three of us started along the sidewalk for home, pausing to watch as a horse and carriage clip-clopped by on the street next to the park, carrying an Amish family within. There was something so reassuring about seeing them, tucked into their little carriage—it made me realize that not all things had to be done immediately, that it was okay to take our time.

"Can we get a horse?" Taylor asked as we resumed walking.

I laughed. "No, I don't think so."

Maddie, as predicted, had already fallen asleep, or so I thought. But as soon as Taylor ventured into the frequently visited topic of a dog, she bolted awake. "We get a dog!"

"Come on, Daddy. You said maybe before." Taylor turned her serious little face up to mine. With Taylor, you didn't say yes unless you meant yes, and "maybe" was practically a binding promise that one day a yes would come.

"I still say maybe."

Taylor huffed and dragged her feet the rest of the way home, but as I went through the exhausting work of feeding my daughters and putting them to bed, my mind turned over the idea. And when I sat alone on the couch in the living room, with a windy and wet storm rolling over the town, a glass of whiskey in my hand and a heavy sadness in my heart, I thought that maybe it would be nice to have a dog. For the girls, of course. But maybe for me, too.

Maybe a dog was the thing that was missing.

CHAPTER THREE - PAIGE

Sweat and Sugar

Now and then I got a Monday off when our new doctor worked, so I took my time waking up on a day I would normally have been rushing around. The blustery storm that had lasted all weekend had littered the streets with leaves and small branches, but it also felt like it had washed the world clean. I leashed up Bobo, my mutt, and then I locked my front door, tied my key onto my sneaker laces, and stood on my front walkway, swinging my arms and warming up my shoulders. Bobo sat expectantly at my side, looking up at me with chocolate eyes. He was used to this routine. Since he got to run at the end of it, I was pretty sure he thought waiting for the warm up was worth it. I took five more minutes to warm up my legs, watching the neighborhood move around me as I did so, smiling out at the steady rhythm of my hometown.

Baltimore would not be like this, I knew. If I accepted the spot at the bigger practice, I'd probably have to join an actual gym instead of running through the streets—and Bobo would become an apartment dog. I'd have to warm up and work out surrounded by other sweaty bodies, loud gym music and blaring televisions. But, I told myself, it was probably a small sacrifice to make if it meant moving up to a more serious work environment—an office where I'd treat more interesting symptoms than runny noses. I wasn't sure Bobo was going to agree with my logic. But in general, as long as he got belly rubs and the occasional treat, he was a pretty easy-going dog.

As I ran in place, warming up my hamstrings, I let my eyes fall on the house diagonally across the street from mine. The man who lived there was outside corralling his two little girls, trying to get them into the car without much luck. He lifted the tiny blond girl in his arms and put her into the backseat, leaning in to buckle up her car seat, while the older girl wandered around the side of the house.

The girl was calling something to her father and pointing to the backyard, but it was clear he hadn't heard, and by the time he stood back up, looking around for her, she'd disappeared.

"Taylor!" he called, and the panic and exhaustion in the voice that drifted through the clear air pulled at something inside my chest.

The little dark haired girl reappeared, and the man scooped her up. I couldn't hear his words, but heard the stern but relieved tone of his voice as he carried her toward the car.

I knew I was staring, and I might have done a few more quad stretches than were generally required before a run, but something about the scene fascinated me. I'd never gotten to know the little family that had moved in across the street six or seven years ago. I'd met the wife a few times when they'd first moved in. She'd come to a book club I used to belong to, and I had bumped into her at the grocery store once or twice. But after a while, I'd stopped seeing her out and about, and a couple years ago, I'd heard that the young woman had died suddenly, and my colleagues at the hospital said it was an aneurysm. Sudden and catastrophic.

The neighborhood had rallied, of course, taking

casseroles and muffins to the doorstep. And that had really been the only time I had spoken to the man, his eyes swimming with grief as I'd handed him a loaf of banana bread and a bag of chocolate chip cookies for the little girls.

I had felt sorry for them then—his sadness had been palpable and heavy, even there at the doorstep, and I'd wanted to reach out and touch him, do anything to help lift that heavy mantle of weariness from his shoulders. How difficult would it be, I marveled, to be left alone with two children so young to care for on your own? Not to mention the aching sadness of losing someone you love?

But over the years since then, he'd seemed to manage. He'd never asked anyone for help as far as I knew, and the little family mostly kept to themselves. I saw him at the park sometimes, wagon and snacks in tow as he watched the little girls scramble over the old wooden structure where I had played as a kid. I'd extended a workout there once because he'd been playing with them—not in that half-hearted way most parents seemed to do, one hand on their phones while they pretended to participate in their children's adventures. He'd actually clambered up to the top of the structure and was calling out cannon directions for his oldest while the littler girl excitedly pointed and jumped at his feet, helping him use the telescope. They'd been battling pirates, I had decided. And I'd been impressed by how much fun they seemed to be having, how wholeheartedly he seemed to be playing with his daughters.

Now the man was backing out and then disappearing down the neighborhood street in his blue sedan, and I remembered that I was supposed to be out for a run. Bobo hadn't forgotten, nosing me into action by leaving a big wet spot on my thigh.

"Okay, buddy," I told him.

I set off in the same direction my neighbor had gone, starting at a gentle trot and eventually working up to a leg-stretching, lung-challenging pace for as long as Bobo could handle it. It was more of a workout for him than me, since his legs were so short. He was not made for running, but he had a very positive attitude about the whole thing. I loved running through the quiet Monday morning streets, enjoyed the scent of fresh rain in the air, and the smell of something green and fecund mixed with the salt air of the Bay nearby. Bobo smiled up at me from my side.

Maybe it was because I was in the process of deciding whether to leave, but I found I was becoming nostalgic about the charms Singletree had to offer, and I told myself to stop letting it rattle around in my brain. My mother was nostalgic enough for the whole family.

I wrapped up my run in the town square, cooling down on the grass for a few minutes before tying Bobo to a heavy chair outside next to a water dish and stepping through the doors of my mother's cafe, now called The Muffin Tin.

"Paigey girl!" Mom called from the counter. "So good to see you survived."

I shook my head, "What are you talking about?"

"You didn't call or text after driving home last night. I was awake all night imagining you in an accident." My mother's face took on a dramatic wide-eyed look.

"Really, Mom?"

A wide smile broke out on her face. "No. You know I'm blessed with the sleep of the dead. But still, it'd be nice if you spared a thought for your aging mother now and then. I worry."

I went behind the counter and poured myself a cup of coffee, kissing Mom on the cheek. "I spare plenty of thoughts for you."

Mom smiled and waved a hand toward the cinnamon rolls and muffins beneath the counter. "Can I tempt you?"

"This is why I have to run," I said. "But no. Today is Monday. Another day to start my healthy eating plan. I'm going to be good."

"Fine. Let me know when you're done being good. I just finished a batch of your favorite pumpkin muffins."

I groaned, thinking about how soft and warm those muffins would be. "I'm staying strong, Mom." I took a seat at the long counter and fished a sheet of the abandoned town newspaper from the stool beside me. The news in Singletree was limited to school events, fundraisers, and a few burglaries now and then. It was the type of small town where it really did seem like nothing ever really happened. The front page carried an "upcoming events" box that called out the annual Cherry Blossom Festival in large block letters. "Are you planning the cakewalk again, Mom?"

"Who else would do it if I didn't?" Mom pretended to be annoyed, but I knew she lived for the Cherry Blossom Festival. And every other festival this crazy town put on.

"Someone would, I'm sure."

"You're helping too."

How could I tell my mother that if I took the job in Baltimore, I might not be around for Festival this year? "Of course I am."

"You know, Paigey," Mom began, and I could see the wheels turning in her matchmaking brain. "A nice young man was in here this morning that I haven't met before. Very handsome."

"And?"

"I got his card for you. He's an insurance adjuster. Just in town for a few days, but he seemed charmed by the place." Mom handed me a business card and then scooted off to help customers.

This was completely typical. My mother was determined to set me up with anything on two legs that seemed vaguely single. It was touching and humiliating all at the same time. When she came back my way, I said, "Okay, Mom."

"You're going to call him?" Mom clapped her hands in front of her.

"No, I'm not going to call a random stranger because my mother told him I'm single and desperate and in need of a companion. I was saying 'okay' to appease you."

"I don't feel very appeased when you put it like that."

"Sorry."

I read the rest of the small paper and finished my coffee, then bid my mother goodbye, woke my sleeping mutt, and strode slowly home to enjoy the remainder of my day off. I turned up the music in the living room and danced through the house with the vacuum cleaner, spent some time in my garden as Bobo looked on, and even managed to make my lunches for the rest of the week to take to work. Healthy eating, accomplished.

And despite the perfect day, the abundant sunshine, and the fact that I'd maintained enough willpower to avoid the pumpkin muffin even after my mother had put it on a plate under my nose, I felt strangely empty. I was certain it was just the simplicity of my small town life. Baltimore would change everything.

It had to.

*

That night I hadn't meant to become a pervy spying neighbor. And in my defense, I wasn't exactly trying to do any pervy spying. It just kind of happened.

I'd poured myself a glass of wine and was carrying it to the living room, passing by the big window in my dining room that looked out across the street, and there was a beacon of light shining from the house a couple doors down across the street. The hot neighbor with the little girls.

It wasn't a beacon, not really. It was more like a fascinating movie rolling out for anyone to see. He was there, in his garage, which was lit up inside with a golden glow, and he was in the middle of it, shirtless. My neighbor was beating the living hell out of a huge heavy bag suspended from the ceiling of the garage. A faint beat echoed across the street, and as I narrowed my eyes—which, weirdly, seemed to help me hear better—I could tell it was coming from over there.

The night was soft and dark everywhere else, but the light shining out of his garage made it impossible not to watch for a while.

He moved like a pro boxer, light on his feet, with his hands up in front of his face. And every time he hit the bag, it rocked, and the muscles all along his arms and across his back rippled with the exertion. The light from his garage caught the shine on his skin, the perspiration only serving to emphasize that muscled torso even more.

I stood there for a while, mesmerized. My own house was darkened, except for the room I was heading for, and I knew he wouldn't be able to see me if he glanced this way. And I used that as an excuse to watch, struggling not to salivate, as my neighbor worked out.

He. Was. Incredible.

And I wished I had never seen him working out because now I'd never get the image of those rippling muscles out of my mind. He was sturdy, strong and lean ... and he seemed like the perfect father.

And just like that, I had a serious crush on my neighbor. One I'd go ahead and keep ignoring, because it certainly wouldn't make any difference to my own plans either way.

Want to read the rest? Go grab it here!

SNEAK PEEK: SECOND CHANCE SPRING CHAPTER 1: MY GUILT IS ORGANIC

PAIGE

The late April rain was pouring down in buckets, sheeting my car and making it nearly impossible to see out the windshield. I squinted and leaned over the steering wheel like an old woman, shouting into the car's speakerphone. "I'm on my way, Mom, I promise. I'm sorry I'm late." I swallowed hard and said it before she had a chance: "Again."

"You be careful out there, young lady. That rain is torrential right now." My mother's voice filled the dark car, and though she sounded annoyed, I was still happy for the company. I hated driving in the pouring rain at night. There were no streetlights in this part of our small town, and the low clouds and rain didn't help with visibility. Mom went on, laying it on thick as only she could do. "Don't rush just because you're nearly an hour late for family dinner."

"Mom, you don't have to pile on the guilt. I come by it naturally."

"Good. I'd hate to think I raised you to believe it's perfectly acceptable to be an hour late to a family dinner."

I sighed as my hands gripped the wheel, both out of frustration and for better control. "Do you want me to rush or to be careful, Mom?" I guided my little car through a traffic circle and then signaled to turn into Mom's neighborhood.

"Be careful, for goodness sakes. And try to do it in a speedy fashion." Standard Lottie logic. "The pot pie's getting cold. Why do you have to work so late?"

"I told you to go ahead and eat without me!" Frustration sent my hand into my hair, pushing my bangs back off my face as I pulled to a stop at the curb in front of Mom's colonial cottage. "I'm here. I'll be at the door in a sec."

The door of the brick-fronted house opened not two seconds later, and Mom's rotund figure appeared in the glow from within, holding her phone to her ear as she peered out at the car through the water sheeting down.

I switched off the engine and sighed. Having Mom in my life was a blessing, and the woman loved me fiercely. But sometimes I wondered if it wouldn't be freeing to have Mom love me just a little less fiercely. Or maybe just as fiercely, but from a greater distance.

I pulled my keys from the ignition, grabbed my purse, and made a dash for the front door. Lottie stopped me just outside under the little overhang. "You're soaked! Remind me to give you an old umbrella I've got before you go tonight."

I shook the rain from my hair and arms and removed

my shoes as I stepped inside. "I have an umbrella, Mom." It was on the passenger seat in my car. It just hadn't made sense to go to the trouble of opening it up for a fifteen-foot walk.

"Then remind me to teach you what those are used for. We must've skipped that when you were little."

"Good to see you, Mom." I pulled my mother into a hug, and felt her relax.

"You too, Paigey. Come in. Your sister's waiting." Mom stepped back and led the way to the dining room.

"Hey," Amberlynn waved from the table, where she sat with a half-full glass of red wine and an expression somewhere between relieved and irritated. "Took you long enough."

"You didn't have to wait," I said. I'd made that clear to my mother when I'd called from the clinic an hour ago to let her know I was going to be late. Right before I scarfed the fries left over from my lunch and chased it with a vanilla latte supplied by my ever-adored physician's assistant. Though Leslie's job in no way meant she was actually supposed to act like my actual assistant, the fact that we were best friends made her a great asset at work.

The clinic where I worked was usually calm and my hours weren't overwhelming at all, but now and then we had a crazy day. And those days always seemed to coincide with my mother's dinners.

"Sit down, for Heaven's sake. Let's eat. This pot pie is undoubtedly a gelatinous disaster inside a crust at this point." Mom put the pie down on the table, pursing her lips and shaking her head, making her spray-frozen bob brush her shoulders on each side.

"Well, when it sounds so appetizing," I said.

"Don't sit yet, Paige," Amberlynn said, her voice low.

"I thought you were starving."

"Just thought you would want some wine before the inquisition begins." Amberlynn pointed to the kitchen just beyond the table.

"Oh please," Mom said as I ducked past her to pour myself a glass of wine.

"Mom? You want?" I raised the bottle and looked over my shoulder.

Mom sighed dramatically. "Well if we're all going to behave like lushes tonight, I guess I'd better. Are you planning to stay over then, Paigey?"

I returned to the table with the bottle. "Mom, one glass with food before I go home in two hours should be fine."

My mother raised an eyebrow, but put up no further argument, and I poured myself a glass much less generous than I would have without the presence of the judgy eyebrow.

"The pot pie is great, Mom," I said around my first bite. It was. And it was miles away from the usual protein shakes and cereal dinners I made for myself.

"Oh, you're just saying that." Mom waved a hand and pretended the compliment wasn't absolutely required at Sunday dinner.

"Of course she is, Mom. You'd be annoyed if one of us didn't say it." Amberlynn took another big bite, and through a full mouth added, "though she's completely right. This is amazing."

We talked about her cafe on the town square in downtown Singletree, which she had recently renamed and had a huge sign made for, and about Amberlynn's job at the high school. And then all eyes turned to me, and I gave as brief a summary of my work at the family clinic where I was a general practitioner as I could. It turned out that hearing about scads of kids with runny noses and coughs didn't make for great conversation, and as busy as I always was at work, very little changed in the small-town practice I ran.

"And did you treat any handsome men today, Paigey?" Mom looked ever hopeful as she brought up her favorite topic and Amberlynn grinned expectantly. Since my younger sister was engaged and my older sister had escaped to New York City, they were rarely the subject of Mom's matchmaking meddling at this point. But in my aging and clearly withering state as a divorcee at almost thirty-one, I was dead in the crosshairs.

"That would be a no." Not that I would have been excited about the idea of dating a patient, but at this point, if a good-looking single man happened to wander through the clinic doors, I wouldn't send him to the other family practice across town.

"You have to get over Adam," Mom said sadly, shaking her head and folding her small hands over her generous middle.

"Mom, stop that!" I half laughed, half snorted. "We are not grieving my marriage. I was married less than a year and the whole thing was clearly a mistake."

"The wedding was so beautiful," Mom said sadly.

"Turns out marriage is about a lot more than the actual ceremony," Amberlynn said through a mouthful of peas and carrots. "Don't think Adam got the memo."

This was not my favorite topic, but it was practically a requirement of Sunday dinner to rehash my short-lived marriage to my high-school boyfriend. The fact we'd stayed together as I'd gone off for college and medical school made Adam seem loyal and true. I should have known that no red-blooded eighteen-year-old male would agree to wait for eight years for regular sex. It turned out Adam wasn't waiting. He was waiting for me, don't get me wrong—he just hadn't realized that monogamy was an expectation of marriage. It was easy to cover his dalliances when we were both away at school, but it turned out to be tougher to do when we shared a house in a small town like Singletree, Maryland.

Adam was not a bad guy. But he was not husband material, and the entire experience had made me feel like I'd wasted the best years of my life with one man who didn't deserve me in the end. Now I was over thirty and still getting grilled about my prospects over Sunday dinners. I imagined these same dinners in the future—seeing myself as a sixty-five-year-old woman, getting interrogated by my ninety-year old mother.

I sighed, finishing the meal and pushing my plate away. "Let's not rehash all that tonight," I suggested hopefully.

Mom shook her head and finished her meal, sipping her wine. "Amberlynn, I'm just glad you and Wiley both understand the commitment you're making."

I squeezed my eyes shut to keep from rolling them. Wiley was a great guy, and I knew Amberlynn had found one of the good ones, but I didn't want to play the comparison game or hear about my sister's wedding plans—for the ninetieth time—tonight.

"He's great, Mom, and I think we'll be good. We've talked about everything. We should be fine. Happy, I hope."

I gave Amberlynn a reassuring smile. I didn't want to take one second away from her happy ending just because I didn't get one of my own, though it seemed like there was something behind her forceful assertion that they would be happy. "You guys will be fine," I said softly.

"So," my sister said, rising to clear the table. She smiled sweetly at Mom and then we both carried plates into the kitchen. "Did you tell Mom you're moving yet?"

I glared at her and looked back to make sure Mom hadn't heard.

"So that's a no, I guess."

"Not yet. It's not a sure thing." I set the dishes on the counter and opened the dishwasher, and my sister and I fell into our routine, her rinsing plates and handing them to me to put inside the racks. "I told them I'd need a few weeks to think about the offer."

Amberlynn nodded. We'd talked at length already about the job offer I'd gotten from a clinic in Baltimore. It would be a bigger practice in a bigger place—and would hopefully represent bigger opportunities for me. Both as a physician and as a woman who might like to meet someone besides the handful of single men still in the small Maryland town where I grew up. "I'll miss you if you go, sis."

I stopped moving for a minute and looked at my sister, brushing a strand of her long blond hair back over her shoulder as she rinsed dishes. "I'll miss you too."

We finished up and I kissed my mom and sister good night, and then drove home to my own quiet cottage. This was the life I'd built, and it was good. I had everything I needed. I had a family that loved me, a dog to greet me at the door when I came home. I was successful and healthy. So why didn't I feel happy?

SNEAK PEEK: SECOND CHANCE SPRING CHAPTER 2: ROCKS ARE NOT NUTRITIONALLY BALANCED

CORMAC

"Here's a snack. And here's a snack. And you can have this one, and this one." My older daughter, Taylor, had never met a rock she didn't like, and every single one of the tiny pieces of gravel that filled the Singletree Park playground evidently seemed a perfect snack for her three-year old sister Madison to her. She was filling up Maddie's upturned shirt with rock after rock. "You can eat these before dinner," she told her sister. Madison stared up at her big sister with adoring eyes filled with trust.

"Or maybe we just save them for later," I suggested, deciding I'd better intervene before Sunday night turned into a fun-filled night of emergency room visiting. "Rocks don't taste good and they're not easy on the teeth. Also, your body can't digest them." I reached down and helped Madison smooth the front of her shirt, letting all the little pebbles fall back to the ground.

Madison looked relieved.

"Taylor, it's your job to look out for your little sister," I said, squatting down to look into the deep serious eyes of my older daughter. They reminded me so much of her mother's eyes that I actually had to fight off the choke that rose in my throat every time she looked at me a certain way. "You know she can't eat rocks, but she might not know that."

A small crease appeared between Taylor's eyebrows—also like her mother, and I swallowed hard. "I have to be the mommy now." The deep liquid pools of my daughter's beautiful eyes at once revealed the deep misery she felt over losing her mother, and the strong sense of responsibility she'd managed to take on at only seven.

"No, Sweetie. You have to be a little girl. Your job is to play and have fun, but you do have to look out for your little sister and help her get bigger like you." I tried to keep my voice upbeat.

"But she needs a mommy," Taylor said, and the crack in her voice matched the one deep in my heart. Despite the warmth of the sunny Sunday afternoon, despite the glorious sunshine, brilliant green trees and fresh-cut grass, I was having trouble remaining positive.

"She has everything she needs in her daddy and her big sister," I told my serious older daughter. "Now go up in the crow's nest and see if you spot any pirates. I thought I heard cannons a second ago." I turned to address Madison too, who'd been watching our conversation thoughtfully while testing a small rock with her teeth. I took it from her and shook my head. "We don't eat rocks," I said.

Madison grinned and leaned into me, tucking her small head beneath my chin and nearly bursting my wounded heart. She always had a knack for knowing when I needed a hug or a little snuggle. She pressed her tiny body into mine and I stood up, holding her in my arms.

"Are you going to go up with your sister and look for pirates?" I pointed to the highest point on the playground, which was a fantastic wooden structure made with wide planks and ropes to look like a castle or—to some kids—a ship. There were two towers, more slides than I could easily count, and plenty of things to play on in between. Was it wrong that I felt slightly jealous my home town had never had such a cool playground?

"Pi-wats." Maddie wiggled in my arms and I put her down, her feet already moving to carry her up to where her sister was using one of the big plastic telescopes mounted on top to search for pirates.

I watched Maddie climb, then sighed and sank back down onto the bench where I'd been sitting. For another twenty minutes, I watched the girls play and tried to feel grateful for the old-fashioned goodness my adopted home town embodied. Singletree was as safe a place as you could get, made up of wide streets with big old trees arching above and beaches lining the land where it met the Chesapeake. People were kind and generous, and it was the kind of place that had hayrides and corn mazes in fall, and a cherry blossom festival in the spring. It was the kind of place I'd always wished I had grown up.

It was the kind of place my wife had grown up.

And now she was gone.

Linda had actually grown up somewhere along the Gulf, but Singletree, Maryland was our adopted home. She'd found the place on a business trip—she was a travel writer and had been scouting quaint inns along the Chesapeake— and we'd moved not long after. I was an accountant and could work from just about anywhere, so I set up a home office in the house we bought, got a tiny office with a partner in town, and together we began our perfect family.

But perfect was a myth, and one I would never buy into again. Linda had died four years later, suddenly and unfathomably. And now I was a single father, living in the quintessential American small town where no one was ever alone. And I'd never been lonelier.

"Daddy, I told Maddie she can't fly, but she won't listen!"

I shot up, my blood going cold, bounding to the top of the play structure, where Madison was trying to wrestle her short legs over the side of the highest point, her small hands scrabbling on the sides of the structure.

"I can fly! Like a angel!"

I pulled Maddie from the side of the turret, crushing her to me as my heart raced. The talk of angels had started when Linda died. Maddie had been so young when she'd passed that she didn't really remember her mother, but Taylor had misty memories, and she'd decided to think of her as an angel now, sharing her vision with her sister and peppering me with questions about angels at every turn.

"Let's go home, guys." I descended the structure with Madison in my arms. She'd stopped struggling and had relaxed against my shoulder, and I envied her the exhausted sleep I knew would hit her as soon as she was in the wagon we'd towed from home.

Taylor refused to come down for five minutes as I wheedled while staring up at her, searching for the one thing that would keep me from having to march back up. I understood her emotions, a mix of frustration over not being the one who got carried and general seven-year old angst, but eventually the promise that she could make the noodles for dinner brought her down.

Together, the three of us started along the sidewalk for home, pausing to watch as a horse and carriage clip-clopped by on the street next to the park, carrying an Amish family within. There was something so reassuring about seeing them, tucked into their little carriage—it made me realize that not all things had to be done immediately, that it was okay to take our time.

"Can we get a horse?" Taylor asked as we resumed walking.

I laughed. "No, I don't think so."

Maddie, as predicted, had already fallen asleep, or so I thought. But as soon as Taylor ventured into the frequently visited topic of a dog, she bolted awake. "We get a dog!"

"Come on, Daddy. You said maybe before." Taylor turned her serious little face up to mine. With Taylor, you didn't say yes unless you meant yes, and "maybe" was practically a binding promise that one day a yes would come.

"I still say maybe."

Taylor huffed and dragged her feet the rest of the way

home, but as I went through the exhausting work of feeding my daughters and putting them to bed, my mind turned over the idea. And when I sat alone on the couch in the living room, with a windy and wet storm rolling over the town, a glass of whiskey in my hand and a heavy sadness in my heart, I thought that maybe it would be nice to have a dog. For the girls, of course. But maybe for me, too.

Maybe a dog was the thing that was missing.

SNEAK PEEK: SECOND CHANCE SPRING, CHAPTER 3: SWEAT AND SUGAR

PAIGE

Now and then I got a Monday off when our new doctor worked, so I took my time waking up on a day I would normally have been rushing around. The blustery storm that had lasted all weekend had littered the streets with leaves and small branches, but it also felt like it had washed the world clean. I leashed up Bobo, my mutt, and then I locked my front door, tied my key onto my sneaker laces, and stood on my front walkway, swinging my arms and warming up my shoulders. Bobo sat expectantly at my side, looking up at me with chocolate eyes. He was used to this routine. Since he got to run at the end of it, I was pretty sure he thought waiting for the warm up was worth it. I took five more minutes to warm up my legs, watching the neighborhood move around me as I did so, smiling out at the steady rhythm of my hometown.

Baltimore would not be like this, I knew. If I accepted the

spot at the bigger practice, I'd probably have to join an actual gym instead of running through the streets—and Bobo would become an apartment dog. I'd have to warm up and work out surrounded by other sweaty bodies, loud gym music and blaring televisions. But, I told myself, it was probably a small sacrifice to make if it meant moving up to a more serious work environment—an office where I'd treat more interesting symptoms than runny noses. I wasn't sure Bobo was going to agree with my logic. But in general, as long as he got belly rubs and the occasional treat, he was a pretty easy-going dog.

As I ran in place, warming up my hamstrings, I let my eyes fall on the house diagonally across the street from mine. The man who lived there was outside corralling his two little girls, trying to get them into the car without much luck. He lifted the tiny blond girl in his arms and put her into the backseat, leaning in to buckle up her car seat, while the older girl wandered around the side of the house.

The girl was calling something to her father and pointing to the backyard, but it was clear he hadn't heard, and by the time he stood back up, looking around for her, she'd disappeared.

"Taylor!" he called, and the panic and exhaustion in the voice that drifted through the clear air pulled at something inside my chest.

The little dark haired girl reappeared, and the man scooped her up. I couldn't hear his words, but heard the stern but relieved tone of his voice as he carried her toward the car.

I knew I was staring, and I might have done a few more

quad stretches than were generally required before a run, but something about the scene fascinated me. I'd never gotten to know the little family that had moved in across the street six or seven years ago. I'd met the wife a few times when they'd first moved in. She'd come to a book club I used to belong to, and I had bumped into her at the grocery store once or twice. But after a while, I'd stopped seeing her out and about, and a couple years ago, I'd heard that the young woman had died suddenly, and my colleagues at the hospital said it was an aneurysm. Sudden and catastrophic.

The neighborhood had rallied, of course, taking casseroles and muffins to the doorstep. And that had really been the only time I had spoken to the man, his eyes swimming with grief as I'd handed him a loaf of banana bread and a bag of chocolate chip cookies for the little girls.

I had felt sorry for them then—his sadness had been palpable and heavy, even there at the doorstep, and I'd wanted to reach out and touch him, do anything to help lift that heavy mantle of weariness from his shoulders. How difficult would it be, I marveled, to be left alone with two children so young to care for on your own? Not to mention the aching sadness of losing someone you love?

But over the years since then, he'd seemed to manage. He'd never asked anyone for help as far as I knew, and the little family mostly kept to themselves. I saw him at the park sometimes, wagon and snacks in tow as he watched the little girls scramble over the old wooden structure where I had played as a kid. I'd extended a workout there once because he'd been playing with them—not in that half-hearted way most parents seemed to do, one hand on their phones while they pretended to participate in their children's adventures. He'd actually clambered up to the top of the structure and was calling out cannon directions for his oldest while the littler girl excitedly pointed and jumped at his feet, helping him use the telescope. They'd been battling pirates, I had decided. And I'd been impressed by how much fun they seemed to be having, how wholeheartedly he seemed to be playing with his daughters.

Now the man was backing out and then disappearing down the neighborhood street in his blue sedan, and I remembered that I was supposed to be out for a run. Bobo hadn't forgotten, nosing me into action by leaving a big wet spot on my thigh.

"Okay, buddy," I told him.

I set off in the same direction my neighbor had gone, starting at a gentle trot and eventually working up to a leg-stretching, lung-challenging pace for as long as Bobo could handle it. It was more of a workout for him than me, since his legs were so short. He was not made for running, but he had a very positive attitude about the whole thing. I loved running through the quiet Monday morning streets, enjoyed the scent of fresh rain in the air, and the smell of something green and fecund mixed with the salt air of the Bay nearby. Bobo smiled up at me from my side.

Maybe it was because I was in the process of deciding whether to leave, but I found I was becoming nostalgic about the charms Singletree had to offer, and I told myself to stop letting it rattle around in my brain. My mother was nostalgic enough for the whole family.

I wrapped up my run in the town square, cooling down on the grass for a few minutes before tying Bobo to a heavy chair outside next to a water dish and stepping through the doors of my mother's cafe, now called The Muffin Tin.

"Paigey girl!" Mom called from the counter. "So good to see you survived."

I shook my head, "What are you talking about?"

"You didn't call or text after driving home last night. I was awake all night imagining you in an accident." My mother's face took on a dramatic wide-eyed look.

"Really, Mom?"

A wide smile broke out on her face. "No. You know I'm blessed with the sleep of the dead. But still, it'd be nice if you spared a thought for your aging mother now and then. I worry."

I went behind the counter and poured myself a cup of coffee, kissing Mom on the cheek. "I spare plenty of thoughts for you."

Mom smiled and waved a hand toward the cinnamon rolls and muffins beneath the counter. "Can I tempt you?"

"This is why I have to run," I said. "But no. Today is Monday. Another day to start my healthy eating plan. I'm going to be good."

"Fine. Let me know when you're done being good. I just finished a batch of your favorite pumpkin muffins."

I groaned, thinking about how soft and warm those muffins would be. "I'm staying strong, Mom." I took a seat at the long counter and fished a sheet of the abandoned town newspaper from the stool beside me. The news in Singletree was limited to school events, fundraisers, and a few burglaries now and then. It was the type of small town where it really did seem like nothing ever really happened. The front page carried an "upcoming events" box that called out the annual Cherry Blossom Festival in large block letters. "Are you planning the cakewalk again, Mom?"

"Who else would do it if I didn't?" Mom pretended to be annoyed, but I knew she lived for the Cherry Blossom Festival. And every other festival this crazy town put on.

"Someone would, I'm sure."

"You're helping too."

How could I tell my mother that if I took the job in Baltimore, I might not be around for Festival this year? "Of course I am."

"You know, Paigey," Mom began, and I could see the wheels turning in her matchmaking brain. "A nice young man was in here this morning that I haven't met before. Very handsome."

"And?"

"I got his card for you. He's an insurance adjuster. Just in town for a few days, but he seemed charmed by the place." Mom handed me a business card and then scooted off to help customers.

This was completely typical. My mother was determined to set me up with anything on two legs that seemed vaguely single. It was touching and humiliating all at the same time. When she came back my way, I said, "Okay, Mom."

"You're going to call him?" Mom clapped her hands in front of her.

"No, I'm not going to call a random stranger because my mother told him I'm single and desperate and in need of a companion. I was saying 'okay' to appease you."

"I don't feel very appeased when you put it like that."

"Sorry."

I read the rest of the small paper and finished my coffee, then bid my mother goodbye, woke my sleeping mutt, and strode slowly home to enjoy the remainder of my day off. I turned up the music in the living room and danced through the house with the vacuum cleaner, spent some time in my garden as Bobo looked on, and even managed to make my lunches for the rest of the week to take to work. Healthy eating, accomplished.

And despite the perfect day, the abundant sunshine, and the fact that I'd maintained enough willpower to avoid the pumpkin muffin even after my mother had put it on a plate under my nose, I felt strangely empty. I was certain it was just the simplicity of my small town life. Baltimore would change everything.

It had to.

That night I hadn't meant to become a pervy spying neighbor. And in my defense, I wasn't exactly trying to do any pervy spying. It just kind of happened.

I'd poured myself a glass of wine and was carrying it to

the living room, passing by the big window in my dining room that looked out across the street, and there was a beacon of light shining from the house a couple doors down across the street. The hot neighbor with the little girls.

It wasn't a beacon, not really. It was more like a fascinating movie rolling out for anyone to see. He was there, in his garage, which was lit up inside with a golden glow, and he was in the middle of it, shirtless. My neighbor was beating the living hell out of a huge heavy bag suspended from the ceiling of the garage. A faint beat echoed across the street, and as I narrowed my eyes—which, weirdly, seemed to help me hear better—I could tell it was coming from over there.

The night was soft and dark everywhere else, but the light shining out of his garage made it impossible not to watch for a while.

He moved like a pro boxer, light on his feet, with his hands up in front of his face. And every time he hit the bag, it rocked, and the muscles all along his arms and across his back rippled with the exertion. The light from his garage caught the shine on his skin, the perspiration only serving to emphasize that muscled torso even more.

I stood there for a while, mesmerized. My own house was darkened, except for the room I was heading for, and I knew he wouldn't be able to see me if he glanced this way. And I used that as an excuse to watch, struggling not to salivate, as my neighbor worked out.

He. Was. Incredible.

And I wished I had never seen him working out because now I'd never get the image of those rippling muscles out of my mind. He was sturdy, strong and lean ... and he seemed like the perfect father.

And just like that, I had a serious crush on my neighbor. One I'd go ahead and keep ignoring, because it certainly wouldn't make any difference to my own plans either way.

Want to read more of Cormac and Paige's story? You can grab their book here!

ALSO BY DELANCEY STEWART

Want more? Get early releases, sneak peeks and freebies! Join my mailing list here or scan the QR code and get a free story!

The WILCOX WOMBATS Series:

Checking the Center

The Wedding Winger

Grumpy Goalie

Puck Proposal

The KASPER RIDGE Series:

Only a Summer

Only a Fling

Only a Crush

Only a Secret

Only a Touch

Only a Chance

The SINGLETREE Series:

Happily Ever His

Happily Ever Hers

Shaking the Sleigh

Second Chance Spring

Falling Into Forever

The DIGITAL DATING Series (with Marika Ray):

Texting with the Enemy

While You Were Texting

Save the Last Text

How to Lose a Girl in 10 Texts

The Text Before Christmas

The MR. MATCH Series:

Prequel: Scoring a Soulmate

Book One: Scoring the Keeper's Sister

Book Two: Scoring a Fake Fiancée

Book Three: Scoring a Prince

Book Four: Scoring with the Boss

Book Five: Scoring a Holiday Match

Mr. Match: The Boxed Set

The KINGS GROVE Series:

When We Let Go

Open Your Eyes

When We Fall

Open Your Heart

Christmas in Kings Grove

The STARR RANCH WINERY Series:

Chasing a Starr

THE GIRLFRIENDS OF GOTHAM Series:

Men and Martinis

Highballs in the Hamptons

Cosmos and Commitment

STANDALONES:

Let it Snow

Without Words

Without Promises

ACKNOWLEDGMENTS

A quick thank you to those who made this book — and so many others — possible.

Dawn Alexander, for always being the voice of sanity when I become hooked on a name, a word or an idea. She ensured that this book was not completely festooned with my favorite holiday word.

Melanie Harlow, for being a friend and colleague, for guiding and steering me, and for giving me the bad news when I need to hear it.

Kelly Greer, for being a friend and the best PA I never knew I was looking for! I honestly don't know how I ever did any of this without you.

Lisa LaPaglia, for being a friend, a reader, and able to pitch in at a moment's notice when I called.

And... the Fancies! I love you guys. Thank you for always being my happy home on the Intertubes.

(And if you're not part of my reader group on Facebook, Delancey's Fancies, come join us! You won't be sorry!)